# A LITTLE BROKEN

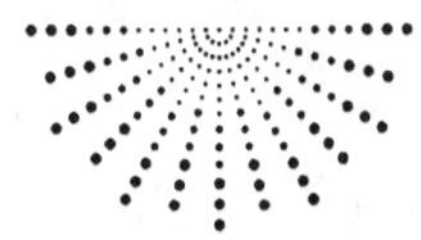

## KELSIE RAE

TWISTY PINES PUBLISHING, LLC

A Little Broken
Cover Art by Cover My Wagon Dragon Art
Editing by Wickedcoolflight Editing Services
Proofreading by Marjorie Lord
Published by Twisty Pines Publishing, LLC
March 2025 Edition
Published in the United States of America

# Family Connections

## Colt & Ashlyn
### (Don't Let Me Fall)
Jaxon
Griffin
Dylan

## Theo & Blakely
### (Don't Let Me Go)
Ophelia
Tatum

## Macklin & Kate
### (Don't Let Me Break)
Everett
Finley

## Henry & Mia
### (Don't Let Me Down)
Archer & Maverick (twins)
Rory

### Biological Siblings
Colt & Blakely
Theo & Macklin

# PROLOGUE

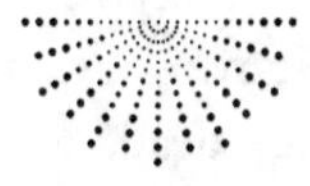

## TATUM

*Dear Archer,*

*Hi.*

*I screwed up. I've been hiding in my room too long. Now, my parents are forcing me to hang out with Ophelia and the rest of the girls.*

*Yeah. Like that'll pull me out of this.*

*I know they're just freaking out because I'm basically a hermit nowadays, but really? A hang out with Lia? Of all people? I still don't understand what you saw in her. She's kind of the worst, you know? No offense.*

I scratch the words out.

*Actually, I take it back. You can take offense to it, and so can she. The only person*

*Ophelia's ever cared about is herself, Archer.*
*Honestly, I thought you had better taste.*


My bottom lip wobbles, and a tear slides down my cheek as my pen hovers above the page. I always get to this part but can never write it. Not yet, anyway. The part where I admit my undying love for the guy. Okay, undying might be a bit of a stretch. Then again, he's dead, and I still love him, so the term is pretty fucking fitting now that I think about it. It doesn't make it any easier, though. Telling him the truth. That I love him. Love. Not loved. Because even though he's gone, these feelings are pretty fucking real. And they're only the tip of the iceberg. Admitting that his absence hurts. That it's killing me. That I feel like I'm drowning with no hope of breathing ever again. Not when the man with the power to give it to me, to help me breathe, is six feet under. That's the real doozy. The one I can't figure out how to express, no matter how many times I open this stupid journal and write a letter to a man who will never read it.

It also doesn't help that he was in love with my sister despite Ophelia choosing Archer's twin brother instead. The reminder makes my chest ache, and I squeeze the pen in my hand, determined to alleviate the pressure in my chest even if it kills me. I feel like an anaconda is wrapped around my chest, slowly squeezing the life out of me. Second by second. Minute by minute. Day by day. Month by month. What happens when I get to a year? When the anniversary of Archer's death finally hits? Will that be the day I stop hurting? Or will it be the day I stop breathing altogether, unable to fight the stubborn anaconda and its punishing hold?

A tear hits the paper, the splash making the ink spread and swirl. I drag the tip of the pen to the next line, desperate to wrap up the letter before I lose my nerve.

*Really thought you had better taste, Arch.*
*But it's good to know you weren't perfect.*
*Miss you.*
*-Tatum*

"TATE?" *KNOCK, KNOCK.* "TATE, YOU IN THERE?"

I close my journal and wipe my cheeks. "Yeah, Mom. I'm here." I let out a slow breath.

"Perfect! Your sister just pulled up."

*Of course, she did.*

I fight the urge to climb into bed and cover my head with a blanket for the rest of the week, no matter how impossible it feels.

*Come on, Tate.*

"Tate?" my mom calls. I can hear the concern in her voice. It's probably warranted, even if I wish it wasn't.

Sucking my lips into my mouth, I answer, "I'll be right out."

*Breathe.*

With another deep inhale, I check my makeup in the mirror, fixing the black smudge beneath my left eye before opening my bedroom door.

Spending so much time alone in my room for too long finally bit me in the ass. My parents arranged a girls' night with all their kids' friends, aka my real and pseudo-cousins, depending on the girl in question. As if company will make this pain go away.

*I wish.*

Yeah, my parents are hoping a little girl time will pull me out of my funk. That it'll fill the gaping hole in my chest, even if it's only for a night. And I can't even be mad at them for it. Because I know I'm spiraling. I know I'm drowning in an abyss of hatred and sadness and pain. If the roles were reversed, if I had to witness someone I love hurting like I am, I'd be anxious to fix it, too. To find a solution or a Band-Aid or...something. Apparently, desperate times call for desperate measures because they're here, and if I want to stop hearing my mom's concern tainting every single word she says to me, then I need to go.

My mom stands in the hallway, her messy red curls piled on top of her head as she scans me up and down.

"You look nice," she says, taking in my ripped jeans and black tank top.

Tucking my chin-length hair behind my ear, I force a smile. "Thanks."

"They're outside," she adds, stepping back to give me more space.

My body feels like concrete, but I force it to move, wrapping my mom in a stiff hug and heading into the blustery weather. It's not that I don't love my mom. I love her more than pretty much anything. My parents are awesome. Like, literally the best. But it doesn't mean they can fix what's broken inside me, no matter how much they want to. I know it, and I think they know it, too. Which makes all of this so much harder.

The girls are all piled in one car, making this a squishy adventure at best. Dylan is behind the wheel, and Finley rides shotgun. Rory, my not-blood-related cousin; Raine, my cousin's girlfriend; and Ophelia, my I-wish-we-weren't-blood-related older sister are in the back.

Ignoring her, I head to the opposite side of the car and squeeze in beside Rory without a word. We've never really been close, but there's something to be said about broken hearts. And when they're broken because of the same man? I don't know. Maybe we're more alike than I gave us credit. I might be in love with a dead man, but Rory lost her brother.

Not that it matters. I still have to survive this night with Ophelia, so the sooner we pull out of the driveway, the sooner we can get to the restaurant, fake a happy meal, and I can go home again.

*To what?*

I don't have anything.

I shove the thought aside.

Finley turns the volume up on the radio, and I rest my elbow on the edge of the passenger window, staring through the glass as my hometown whirs past.

When we stop at a light, a motorcycle pulls up beside us. It looks like a nice one. Black. Chrome. Leather. Shiny. Like it's been washed recently. The guy driving it sits back, balancing on the behemoth between his legs as he stretches his arms over his head. He must've been riding for a while.

When he catches me staring, my head snaps forward. Then, I peek again. His face is shielded thanks to the black helmet, but it's angled and faces me head-on. He's watching me.

Slowly, he draws a frown on his face shield, then points to me.

*You're sad.*

It's like I can read his thoughts.

Instead of confirming or denying his assumption, I lift my shoulder an inch and suck the inside of my cheek between my molars.

*Why are you sad, Tatum?*

*He's in a better place, Tatum.*

*Everything's going to be okay, Tatum.*

*You need to let him go, Tatum.*

With a slow nod, the stranger raises a fist into the air, moving it up and down a few inches.

*One.*

*Two.*

*Three.*

He flattens his palm.

My brows pull downward as I'm dragged back to the present and mouth, "What?"

The stranger tosses his hands in the air and repeats the motion.

*One.*

*Two.*

*Three.*

He holds two fingers up this time, making them relatively parallel to the asphalt.

Scissors.

He wants to play Rock, Paper, Scissors.

I roll my eyes, caught off guard but also grateful for the distraction. He lifts his chin, curling his hand into a fist for a third time. Giving in, I mirror his movements, dipping my closed hand a few inches down and up in rhythm with his.

*One.*

*Two.*

*Three.*

His hand stays fisted, choosing rock, and I flatten mine, creating paper.

Paper covers rock.

I win.

The biker tosses his hands into the air again and shakes his head in defeat. Giving me his full attention once more, he draws a smile in the air with his index finger. It's stupid and playful and corny, but my stomach flutters, my mouth lifting into a ghost of a smile before I can stop it. He wants me to smile. To stop being sad. If only it was that easy. And maybe if I knew who the stranger was, I'd argue with him. I'd point out how delusional his request really is. I can't choose to be happy when I feel like my world's been ripped apart. But I also can't deny how a stupid game of Rock, Paper, Scissors at a stoplight has lifted the suffocating pressure more than my countless sessions with my therapist or sob sessions with my parents. And that's…something.

Isn't it?

Satisfied with the minuscule bone I've thrown him in the form of a weak smile, the stranger bends over his bike, twists the handle, and flies down the road.

As I watch him disappear around the corner, the familiar weight I'm used to carrying settles back on my chest. But it was nice. The tiny reprieve. Even if it only lasted a minute.

At least it was a minute.

And maybe, with enough time, I'll be able to collect more.

Or maybe not.

# TATUM

A FEW YEARS LATER...

"Seriously, I cannot believe you did this," I muse.

"It's your birthday, and you're my best friend," Rory reminds me. "I literally had to do this."

She didn't, but I appreciate her thoughtfulness nonetheless.

I kind of hate my birthday. I kind of hate a lot of things, but I especially hate my birthday. It's another reminder that a year has passed and he's still gone. To be fair, a lot of things remind me of Archer Buchanan's absence. Specific dates. Holidays. Smells. Books. Honestly, my birthday is pretty low on the totem pole, all things considered. Doesn't make it easier, though.

Slipping out of the Uber, I hook my arm through my best friend's, who also happens to be Archer's younger sister, and peer up at the venue. Rough brick exterior with glowing windows peppered across the front. Music echoes through the air. The band must've already started playing. Tilting my head, I listen to the familiar beat while the scent of weed mixes with the beer and sweat clinging to the air. Not a great combination, but I won't complain. There are so many people here. They crowd the front of the building, creating a long line from the main entrance out to the dark road. This is insane. The energy really sells the place, though. Hell, it's electric. I bite the inside of my bottom lip to keep from grinning like a full-blown lunatic.

"See? I knew you'd love this," Rory adds.

"Who are we seeing?" I ask. "Because it kind of sounds like..." I pause, listening to the muffled, almost-familiar chorus filtering from the building.

"Like...your favorite band?" Rory finishes for me.

My jaw drops, and I stop midstep, twisting my best friend to face me fully. "Are you serious?"

"Maybe."

With a squeal, I grab Rory's biceps and jump up and down. "You have no idea how excited I am!"

"I thought you might be," she laughs.

"Are they headlining?" I hesitate. "What am I saying? Of course, they aren't headlining. Doomsday isn't big enough for that. If they were, I'd know about it. Who are they opening for?"

Looking down at the ground, she kicks a pebble with her sneakers. "Well, uh, IndieCent Vows, actually, but..."

My brows pull down, and she peeks up at me.

"Don't worry. I didn't call in any favors, if that's what you're thinking," she rushes out. "We can even slip out before Dodger and the guys take the stage if you're really worried about it. But it's your twenty-first birthday, Tate, and Doomsday is your favorite. I would've made this happen even if they were playing in a ditch across the world."

She's right. She would've. Rory's sweet like that. Thoughtful. Caring. Maybe even a little self-sacrificing to a fault, if I'm being totally honest. She's the opposite of me in every way, and I couldn't be more grateful. Honestly, I can barely stand my own presence most days. Having two of me in a friendship? Yeah, we'd kill each other.

Lips pursed, I push, "You promise you didn't call in any favors?"

"Promise. I even got the tickets on a shady site instead of calling Raine or Dodge to get them for free, so if my credit card info is stolen, it's all your fault."

With a laugh, I loop my arm through Rory's and walk us toward the entrance, grateful our whereabouts are still hidden from my family, thanks to a shady website and Rory's bravery. "Come on. It sounds like they're already playing."

"Yeah, because *someone* couldn't get her butt in gear at the hotel."

"When you said our activity started at seven, I thought you meant it in a it-starts-at-seven-but-the-cool-kids-show-up-at-nine kind of thing."

"No, I meant it in a get-your-butt-in-gear-because-we're-going-to-miss-your-favorite-band-if-we-aren't-on-time-but-I-don't-want-to-ruin-your-birthday-present-so-I'm-trying-to-play-it-cool kind of thing."

My mouth lifts. "You've ruined nothing. And thank you."

"You're welcome."

Let me be clear. I have nothing against IndieCent Vows. Actually, their music is pretty awesome, but the main singer, Dodger Anders, is the older brother of Raine Anders, and Raine Anders is best friends with my older sister, and well, let's just say, the connection is a little too close for comfort when I haven't had an actual conversation with my sister in who knows how long, and I'd like to keep it this way. It isn't personal, it's just... Oh, who am I kidding? Of course, it's personal. It's Ophelia. The one person who's shadow I'll never be able to step out of. Like a piece of hot coal, my phone burns a hole in my purse, acting as a reminder of the unanswered text Ophelia sent wishing me a happy birthday.

I shake off the mental intrusion as we open our purses for security, walk through the metal detector, and head toward the ushers scanning tickets.

After Rory shows the tickets to an old man with a bushy white mustache, he says, "ID please."

"ID?" Rory squeaks.

The bored expression vanishes from the usher's face, and he looks us up and down with newfound interest. "This is a twenty-one and older venue."

*Well, shit.*

Without a word, Rory stands there like a deer in the headlights, so I move closer.

"I'm sorry, it's what?" I answer for her.

"A twenty-one and older venue," he repeats. His eyes bounce from me to Rory, then back again. "Do you have IDs?"

"Oh. Uh. Yes, but, uh… One second." Red hits Rory's cheeks as she fumbles in her purse for her ID, her hands shaking more and more with every passing second. I don't blame her. The line is building behind us, and it doesn't matter how long she tries to stall, her ID still won't magically show an earlier birthdate than the one I know it sports. Even though it's my twenty-first birthday, Rory won't be eighteen for another two months.

"You know what? I need to pee," I announce. "We'll be right back." Reaching for Rory's fumbling fingers, I drag us away from the line and back toward the curb in front of the building.

"Tatum, I am so sorry," Rory squeaks. Tears fill her eyes, and she dabs at the corners, careful not to ruin her makeup. "I swear, I had no idea!"

"Rory, breathe." With a light laugh, I roll my eyes. Not because it's fun to watch my best friend cry, but because if she didn't shed a tear or two by the end of the night, I'd be convinced she'd had her body snatched by an alien or something. "Seriously, Rore. Breathe," I tell her.

"Yeah, but it's your birthday, and I was trying to surprise you, and—"

"Trust me. I'm very surprised."

"Don't be a smartass." Her bottom lip wobbles. "But like, since when are there twenty-one and older venues?"

I bite the inside of my cheek in hopes of keeping my smartassery at bay and gently reply, "Since...forever?"

Her eyelids fall closed, and a tear rolls down her cheek, slipping past her defenses. I'd tell her to stop crying, but Rory's Rory, and there's a reason the family calls her Squeaks. The girl's been a tear factory since birth. Puppy commercial? She cries. Old couple at a fast-food restaurant sharing French fries? Let me get her a tissue. Got a B on a test? Cue the waterworks, people.

Even though she hates that particular trait, I find it... endearing, almost. And reliable. I can always count on Rory Buchanan to *feel*. Meanwhile, people describe me as an ice queen most days. I'm not complaining. I'd rather keep my emotions in check than let them air out at the drop of a hat. But I digress. I should've expected this. Something messing up my birthday. The venue is for guests twenty-one and older. We're not allowed inside.

Of course, we aren't.

Grabbing her shoulders, I force her to face me. "Rory, I'm teasing. You're totally fine."

"No, I'm not," she squeaks. "I feel so stupid!"

"It could've happened to anyone."

Her bottom lip juts out even more, and she wipes at her cheeks. "I ruined your birthday."

"You didn't ruin anything," I argue. Determined to fix the situation just to stop my friend's tears from falling, I scan the venue in search of…I don't know. A solution, maybe? And then, it hits me.

I grin. "Come on. I think I have a plan."

Keeping myself in full-alert mode, I sneak around the edge of the massive building to a large metal door. If it's unlocked, we can sneak inside and no one will know. It'll be perfect.

"Tatum," Rory seethes behind me, realizing my intentions. "Tatum, this is a bad idea."

I keep my head down, scanning the small alleyway one more time. Reaching for the door handle, I confirm it's locked with a quick twist of my wrist. "Shit."

"Did you really think they'd leave it open?" Rory argues.

Peeking over my shoulder, I find Rory with her arms crossed and her head cocked in challenge.

*Who's the smartass now?*

Holding her gaze, I knock my knuckles against the thick steel.

She gasps. "You did not just knock."

"I think I did."

"What if someone answers?" she screeches while trying to keep her voice down as she glances over her shoulder toward the crowded front.

"Then someone answers." I turn back to the solid door and make a fist, preparing for another round of knocking when the door pulls open, and a blond guy appears with a cigarette dangling from his mouth.

*Well, shit.*

I jerk back, nearly running into a stunned Rory behind me. Not gonna lie. The guy's built like a god. Broad shoulders. Strong arms. A black shirt hugs his biceps, and light reflects off his warm, coffee-colored eyes and tan skin.

Did my tongue just grow three times its original size? I think—yup—it totally did. He's…well, he appears to be a surfer-boy with a side of bad decisions, and the tattoos etched onto his forearm are enough to make a girl like me fall to my knees and worship the bastard right here, right now. That is, if I didn't have my best friend three feet away from me, and I wasn't already on a mission to sneak into the place.

Catching the unlit cigarette in his hand, the stranger scans us up and down before his eyes cut to the front of the building, his brows pulled low in confusion. "What are you—"

"We're with the band," I rush out, snapping myself out of whatever daze his annoyingly gorgeous face put me in. But seriously. This guy is something else entirely.

"Uh, Tate?" Rory starts.

"I've got this," I promise her while holding the security guard's intimidating gaze. "Like I said, we're with the band, so…"

His brows lift. "The band."

"Yeah. We've actually been knocking for a solid fifteen minutes. I came out for a smoke, and the door locked behind us, and…" I paste on a syrupy sweet smile and hook my thumb toward the propped open door. "Do you mind?"

His eyes roll over my body again. "Which band?"

"Doomsday," I answer. "Obviously."

"Obviously." His mouth twitches, though I'm not sure why he's so amused by our conversation.

"Tate," Rory repeats from behind me.

Ignoring her, I say, "Are you security or something? Because we left our backstage passes inside, so…"

*Now or never, Tatum,* I silently remind myself. *Ask for forgiveness, not permission.*

"You'll have to excuse us," I continue. "We need to at least catch the second half of the set." Stepping forward, I start to scoot past him in an attempt to act like I own the place. Like

I belong. Like I most definitely am not trespassing in hopes of easing my friend's guilt over not reading the fine print when she's the queen of following the rules.

The guy doesn't budge. His big, rock-hard body blocks the entrance, barely leaving any space for me to move past him. The problem is, I'm in too far to turn back now, so where does this leave me?

*Keep going.*

I continue my quest to enter, but the stranger grips the edge of the door, blocking my entry while somehow keeping us chest-to-chest.

*All right, so he's not so easy to bulldoze. Good to know.*

My gaze flicks up to him. "Is there a problem, Mr. Security?"

"You under eighteen?"

"Do I look under eighteen?"

He checks me out again and scratches his jaw with his free hand. When his gaze reaches my face, he shrugs. "Looks can be…deceiving."

I roll my eyes. "No, I'm not under eighteen."

His brow quirks. "Under twenty-one?"

"As of today, not anymore," Rory chimes in from behind me. "It's her birthday."

Keeping his focus on me, he murmurs, "Your birthday, huh?"

"Twenty-one years young," I answer.

"Happy birthday."

His coffee eyes swallow me whole, and my stomach flips. "Why, thank you."

"How long have you been with Doomsday?"

Doomsday. Right.

Sucking my lips between my teeth, I hold his gaze and mentally play out my options. Clearly, he's onto us. But I think he might have a thing for me—or at the very least, he's curious. Which swings the situation in our favor. However, I'd prefer it if he didn't escort us to Doomsday's dressing room, since I most definitely have never met anyone from the band. But getting inside the building is key if we want to actually watch Doomsday play tonight, so…

"Cat got your tongue, Birthday Girl?" he challenges.

"You know, usually, the security team isn't quite this chatty," I point out. "But if you don't let us in, Cooper will be sorely disappointed by our absence, especially when he's already on stage. I'm sure you don't want that, do you?"

"Cooper does love his toys," he agrees, repeating Doomsday's lead singer's name. His attention falls to my mouth as he lets the edge of the door go and pushes it open a little more, giving me space to slip beneath his toned bicep and forearm. As I move past him, my nipples brush against his chest. My lips part on instinct.

Well, shit. It's like my body registers the friction before my brain has a chance to catch up and shut down. Or at the very least, hide my response. But nope. This stranger gets to witness it first-freaking-hand.

*Fantastic.*

"Now, if you'll excuse me…" I wave behind my lower back, silently encouraging Rory to get her butt in gear. Like the obedient girl she is, she plays along without hesitation. As soon as I'm inside, Rory darts through the door, her fingers twisting in front of her. The question is…where do we go from here?

"You sure you know where you're going?" the security guard asks as if he's reading my thoughts.

"Yup." I peek toward both ends of the hallway, debating which way to go. It's a fifty-fifty chance. Left or right.

*Come on, Tate. Pick one.*

Left, it is.

I take a step toward the drum beat, praying it leads to where we're supposed to go.

"That's where the audience is," Mr. Security offers.

I freeze and peek back at him.

"Don't you want to be backstage with your boy toy?" he asks.

Yeah, that's probably where a groupie would be, isn't it?

Keeping my expression on lockdown, I counter, "I thought I was *his* toy, not the other way around. You know, since you said Coop likes his toys and all."

"Call it a hunch, but I have a feeling you're good at keeping boys like Coop wrapped around your finger."

He isn't wrong. I'm a sucker for leading guys on without giving in. Okay, sometimes I give in but not always. It depends on where my head is and how close I am to the anniversary of Archer's death. Call me a fickle bitch, but it is what it is.

"Cooper will find me after the set," I lie. "He likes the chase."

With a smirk, he folds his arms across his chest. "Don't we all."

My lips purse. "Have a good night, Mr. Security." Giving him my back again, I grab Rory's hand and start leading us a little further down the hall when a two-hundred pound linebacker in a black shirt rounds the corner.

Another one? Seriously? It's like we're trying to break into the Pentagon or something.

When he sees us, his gaze narrows, making my heart thrum faster as I weigh my options. Okay, we can run, or we can…continue lying out our asses and potentially be arrested for trespassing. Not the best way to celebrate my birthday, but hey. At least it'll be memorable, right? And I sure as shit am not backing down now, since we've made it this far.

"Hey!" the behemoth calls. "What are you—"

"They're with the band," Mr. Security announces from behind me.

The linebacker's attention snaps to him. "You sure they're legal?"

"Checked their IDs and everything," Mr. Security confirms. Listening to him lie through his teeth to protect me is kind of...hot. Or maybe I just haven't been laid recently.

"Of course." The linebacker's head dips. "Would you like me to escort them to—"

"I've got it," Mr. Security tells him.

"Sure thing, Pax."

Pax.

So he has a name. Interesting.

Part of me wants to face Mr. Security again, simply to taste his name while analyzing whether or not I find it fitting, but I don't want to push my luck. Not tonight, anyway.

"They're waiting for you," the linebacker adds.

"Just like always, am I right, Herb?" Mr. Security tosses back at him.

I can feel Mr. Security's footsteps over the thrumming music a few walls away. I shouldn't be able to, but I do. Hell, maybe it's my imagination. But it doesn't change anything.

*Step. Step. Step.*

He's coming closer.

Before I can overthink it, I grab Rory's hand, then race along the corridor and past the linebacker. "Thank you!" I yell as our feet slap against the concrete floor. When we reach the arena, my heart is still racing. I slow to a walk and sneak us into the mosh pit near the front of the stage. All things considered, it's shockingly easy, especially compared to our efforts since I knocked on the metal side door.

Once we're past security, Rory announces, "You're insane."

I grin back at her. "You know you love me. And thank you for the tickets," I add, glancing at the now-empty stage, "even though we missed Doomsday. This is amazing."

"It's memorable, I'll give you that much," she grumbles.

She's not wrong.

And even if it was unintentional, sneaking into the concert and flirting with a cute security guard is giving me a high like no other. Basking in it, I listen to Rory chatter on about her plans this upcoming year and all the amazing things she's planning to do. I have no doubt she will. The girl has the power to do anything she wants in this world. She's smart. Beautiful. And has more connections than the Queen of England, thanks to her family's fortune.

I'm not sure how much time passes before I turn back to the stage just in time to watch IndieCent Vows take their places. Or at least, that's who I assume is up there. The only one I know is... There he is. Dodger Anders. We've never met. I've been cultivating distance from all things Lockwood Heights since long before Archer's death. But Rory, not so much. As long as no one brings up anything to do with Jaxon Thorne, she's an open book. This includes my family, her family, and all of their friends, including Dodger's parents.

I study the man standing in the middle of the stage. Curly, light brown hair cut close on the sides and longer on the top. Freshly-shaven face to show off his chiseled jaw. Strong biceps and veined forearms as he cradles the mic. And the voice of a fucking angel, though he isn't singing at the moment. Nope, he's making a smartass comment about their guitarist being MIA, when a man with sandy blond hair appears. His head is tilted down as he tinkers with his sleek black guitar. When he lifts his head and smiles at the crowd, my jaw drops.

Well, if it isn't Mr. fucking Security.

What are the odds?

Rory laughs beside me, clutching her stomach as her body threatens to topple over. Ripping my stare from the Adonis on stage, I glare at my best friend.

"You knew?" I screech.

"Of course, I knew! I tried to tell you when we were outside, but noooo," she drags out through bouts of laughter. "Someone had to be a know-it-all and fix things without my help, now, didn't you?"

Shaking my head, I turn back to the stage as Mr. Security's long fingers begin plucking at the strings.

*Damn.*

# PAXTON

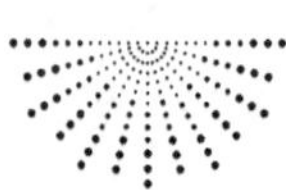

"Get your ass out here," a low voice grumbles through my earpiece. Surprisingly, it isn't Judge. It's Dodger. Not surprisingly, he's even more pissed than Judge would be. Okay, that's a lie. I've been on Judge's shit-list since I replaced his best friend as lead guitarist. Even so, it's not my fault Rudy died, now is it? But somehow, the weight of his ire always falls on my shoulders.

Urging me to get my ass in gear, Danny, one of our roadies, hands me my baby. An ebony Gibson Les Paul. She was my first purchase from my first paycheck, and fuck, if I've ever loved anything more. Over the years, I've collected at least a dozen guitars, hell, maybe two dozen, but this one? This one's my favorite. I slip the lime green strap over my head, all too aware of the time and how much of it I wasted.

Rolling my shoulders, I let out a slow breath, realizing I didn't get my smoke.

Fuck. Too late now.

It's a good thing the girl was cute. If only I'd run into her *after* I had my smoke. I tap the outside of my thigh, indecision warring through me. I need to be on stage. Scratch that.

I needed to be on stage ten minutes ago. Dodger is gonna kill me, and if he doesn't, Judge will.

I turn to Danny and give him a thumbs up. When he returns it with one of his own, confirming I'm good to go, I traipse onto the stage like I was fucking made for it.

I'll never get over this rush. The sounds. The lights. The energy.

"Aaaand, here he is. Everyone's favorite asshole," Dodger quips.

Laughter ensues from the audience as I move to the microphone set up in front of my spot on the right side of the platform. Adjusting it slightly, I reply, "Pretty sure the title belongs to you, Dodge."

Another wave of amusement rolls through the crowd, and Dodger shoots me the bird from the center of the stage while Judge—stoic as ever—watches me from the back, hidden behind his drum set as he twirls his drumsticks between his middle and pointer fingers.

*Yeah, yeah. I know I'm late.*

Then, like the peacekeeper he is, Tuke begins plucking at his bass guitar on Dodger's opposite side. The low, familiar melody is from one of our biggest hits. I'd like to say I wrote it, but if I did, I'd be lying out of my ass. Nah, writing music has never been my forte. Appreciating it, though? Yeah, that much I can do. As it pulses through the speakers, I lift my head toward the stage lights, basking in the familiarity.

And that's all it takes. The crowd. The sounds. The lights. It all disappears, leaving nothing but the energy I crave. Like a balm, it slips over my skin, and my fingers find the strings. I start strumming on the fourth measure like clockwork. Sweat already threatens to roll down my spine thanks to the stage lights, and I scan the crowd, feeding off their energy by the end of the first song.

A girl flashes me from the middle of the pit, her tits more

than a handful, and her big nipples peaked despite the temperature in the building. She squeals when she realizes I've seen her, her plump red lips mouthing, "I love you, Paxton!"

Of course, she does. Everyone here loves me. Well, the idea of me. Of the band. Of the persona IndieCent Vows has created for all its members. Yeah, it's easy to love a rockstar. The title alone is enough to make most girls fall to their knees.

Everyone but Birthday Girl.

How the hell didn't she recognize me? I haven't been able fly under the radar like that in…fuck, I don't even know how long.

"Marry me!" someone else yells from the mosh pit. A redhead with green eyes and black painted lips. I think it was her anyway. Realizing she has my attention, she grins and screams at the top of her lungs, repeating, "Marry me!"

*Yup. Called it.*

With a wink, I continue strumming the guitar when Birthday Girl comes into view a few rows toward the front. I almost fuck up the chord but recover at the last instant.

Well, would you look at that. Apparently, she made it.

Jaw unhinged, she stares up at me like I'm a goddamn magician. The lights cast shadows and highlight her heart-shaped face.

Yeah, my little Birthday Girl's pretty. Thick black hair. Pale skin. Smokey makeup. Like she's Snow White or some shit. It's her eyes that do it for me, though. Earlier, they looked…they look so fucking guarded, I couldn't help but want to sneak a peek at what she's hiding. Now, though? Now she looks like she's been knocked on her ass and she doesn't know what to do about it. Glad I'm not the only one. I'm not sure how she accomplished it, but the girl managed to do the impossible. When I opened the door to have a smoke before the set, she knocked me on my ass, too, and I haven't been knocked on my ass by a pretty girl since middle school.

Leaning away from the microphone so I don't interrupt Dodger's singing, I mouth, "Surprised?"

As if my attention shakes her from her thoughts, she cups her hands around her mouth and yells, "Security, my ass!" Or at least, it's what I think she says. It's too loud to actually hear her over the music playing in my earpiece and the buzz from the crowd. Even so, I can't help but grin. She actually bought that shit. Fuck. I love it.

Her head bobs with the music as I strum my guitar while Dodger breaks into the chorus. The audience feeds off it, belting out the lyrics like they're tattooed in their minds. I sneak another glance at...what did her friend call her? Tate. That's right. Everyone but Birthday Girl. Her pouty lips are motionless, even if she does look like she's enjoying the song.

*Huh.*

Apparently, she wasn't kidding about being here for Doomsday. The realization is a blow to the ego but only feeds my curiosity. And damn. If she's willing to sit through a set she's never heard, I'm determined to make it my best one yet.

After three more songs, she's jumping with the rest of the crowd, her best friend bellowing the lyrics beside her. Clearing my throat, I step closer to the mic. Dodger finishes whatever he's saying, then cocks his head at me, curious. What I'm doing. What I'm about to say. It isn't in the script, and hell if I know. I'm as clueless as he is.

And then it hits me.

My fingers wrap around the black microphone as I pull it toward my mouth.

"Now, we don't normally do this, but, uh,"—my attention

flicks back to the girl at the edge of the stage—"we have a birthday girl in the house."

"Woo-hoo!"

"All right!"

"Yay!"

All of the screams twist into a cacophony of elation as I continue. "And this birthday girl isn't celebrating just any birthday. It's her twenty-first. And we all know what that means, right? I think we need to do some shots."

"Shots! Shots! Shots!" the audience chants.

"What the fuck you doin, man?" Judge murmurs into my earpiece. I smirk back at him but don't bother answering. Instead, I crook my finger toward Tate in the crowd. "Herb, wanna escort our Birthday Girl and her friend onto the stage?"

"Are you serious?" Tate mouths from the floor. Or maybe she's yelling and it's too loud to hear her over the screaming fans. Not that it matters. "Hey, Danny," I add into the microphone, addressing the roadie backstage. "Wanna grab us some shots so we can celebrate in style?"

"Yessss!" The crowd goes wild, and I bask in the sound.

"Tate?" I prod, staring down at her like a king on his throne. "You gonna leave us hangin'?"

She doesn't look scared. Actually, she looks the opposite. Her teeth dig into the inside of her cheek as she bites back her smile when Herb appears beside her. It doesn't hurt that he knew who he was looking for from their little run-in earlier tonight.

Catching on, Tuke starts the first few notes of the famous birthday song on his bass, and I join in. Two notes later, Judge gives us a solid beat from the kick drum, and I start singing the lyrics. "Ha-ppy birth-day to you…"

With a jerky shake of her head, Tate grabs her best friend, walking up the stairs and onto the stage with her head held high while Baby scurries to keep up on her short legs. It's adorable, if not a little pathetic. The girl sticks out like a sore thumb. Or maybe it only feels that way when she's next to Tate. Yeah, Birthday Girl sure as shit knows how to steal the show. That much, I know.

By the time I finish the last few notes of *Happy Birthday,* Dodger is harmonizing from the center of the stage, and the crowd has their cell phone lights swaying back and forth. Tray in hand, Danny follows behind the girls. Eight shots with clear liquid sit lined up in two rows. Danny offers one for me to take. After I do, he shifts the tray to the girls. Baby waves it off before Tate grabs one of the small glasses. Then, Danny moves to the rest of the band.

"Twenty-one, huh?" I ask away from the mic.

Standing in front of me, she rocks back on her heels and keeps the shot glass pinched between her fingers. "Mm-hmm."

"So, is this your first shot?"

She clinks the edge of the glass against mine then brings the edge to her lips. "First legal one, sure."

Holding my attention hostage, she tosses the clear liquid back, and I do the same. As it slides down my throat, a trail of heat coats my esophagus, but I'm too distracted by the tip of Birthday Girl's tongue sliding across her bottom lip to care.

I've played this game a time or two. Pretty sure it comes with the territory when you're a rockstar. But never—and I mean never—have I had to fight the urge to grab someone and kiss them more than in this moment. Sweat beads along my brow and drips down my temple, the heat from the stage lights fucking scorching. Or maybe it's the look in her gaze leaving me burning as the world disappears around us.

"Happy birthday, Birthday Girl," I murmur.

"You know, Cooper's gonna be furious if you keep trying to take Doomsday's spot as my favorite band."

"Yeah, I think he'll live." I dip forward, my mouth hovering right above her ear, and whisper, "Liar."

Her mouth lifts into a smile, and since I'm so close, it causes my lips to brush against her cheek. The innocent touch shoots straight to my cock, acting like an inferno just like earlier when she slipped past me into the building. Instead of pulling away, I let my mouth skate across the edge of her jaw. "You're welcome, by the way."

Thumbing the edge of my guitar strap, she counters, "And what do I have to thank you for?"

"For letting you in the side door."

"It's cute you think I wouldn't have found another way if you hadn't answered."

"Cute, huh?" I return.

"We done fucking around?" Dodger calls. "I think our fans are ready for us to finish the set."

"Well, he's right about one thing," Tate murmurs. "You shouldn't keep your fans waiting." Her hand drops from my guitar strap. "Thanks for the shot."

Grabbing Tatum's wrist, I warn, "Don't disappear."

"And where would I go?"

"Not sure even you know the answer to that." I step even closer, dropping my voice low. "I know a runner when I see one."

"I thought you said you like the chase?" she volleys back.

The stage lights make her eyes fuckin' sparkle, but before I have a chance to answer, Dodger bellows into the mic the first lyrics of the next song in the set, and I let her go. Eyes gleaming with a challenge, Tate walks backward toward the edge of the stage. With every step, her gaze never leaves mine.

"Herb!" Dodger calls while Judge and Tuke carry the song all by themselves. "Guide these ladies backstage, yeah?"

Like smoke, Tate's amusement vanishes, and she glares at my bandmate.

"And make sure they stay there," he adds. "We gotta celebrate, yeah?"

*What the hell?*

Tate dodges Herb's attempted grasp but marches toward the curtains while Rory trails behind, casting a quick wave to Dodger before she disappears from sight. It only fuels my curiosity more. Do they…know each other?

Nah. Not possible.

*Is it?*

Twenty minutes later, the final notes ring through the air as Dodger belts out the last few lines of the song. They mingle with the crowd while everyone joins in, their phones lifted into the air like when we'd finished playing *Happy Birthday* to Tate. The familiar buzz ebbs through my veins, and I place my pick between my teeth, giving a few of the girls in the front row my signature smirk before grabbing the pick again and flicking it into the mosh pit. A few people dive for it, but a guy in his early thirties snatches it at the last second. Lifting it into the air, he screams at the top of his lungs while I laugh from the stage, drinking it all in. The sights. The sounds. The smells. Another epic night.

Once we're finished, we saunter toward the side of the stage when Dodger demands, "How do you know Squeaks and Tatum?"

I shake my head. "Squeaks?"

"Rory," he clarifies. "The *kid* you dragged on stage. How'd she get in here?"

I squeeze the back of my neck, feeling guilty, though I have no clue why. "I let them in."

"You *what*?" he snaps. "Pax, she's underage. Hell, she's not even eighteen!"

"Back up, Dodge. And I don't know them," I add. "They were trying to sneak in the side door, and I thought it was kind of funny, so I let them in. How do *you* know them?"

"They're family," he grunts.

My brows raise.

"From Lockwood Heights." He hesitates, scanning the back area. "Where are they?"

Good question.

Confused, I search the space, calling, "Danny? Herb?"

The roadie appears from the hall. "The girls were tired of watching from the side of the stage, so I set them up in one of the empty rooms and left Herb by the door to make sure no one bothers them."

"Good." Dodger's head bobs. "Let's do the encore, then we'll talk more."

3

## PAXTON

The guys were pulled away by our agent. Not me, though. No one cares what I do, so long as I'm where I'm supposed to be when they need me. Since I'm not a founding member of the band, I get a free pass from bullshit meetings, and tonight, I have no issue taking advantage of it.

As I slip down the hall, I find Herb standing in front of an open door. One hand is clasped over his wrist in front of him. An earpiece sits in his ear as he scans the premises for what's no doubt the thousandth time since Danny told him to keep an eye on my special…guests. Er, Dodger's special guests? Honestly, at this point, I'm not even sure, but I *am* curious.

When Herb's attention lands on me, I lift my chin in greeting. He steps aside, giving me access to the propped open door and the girls inside the room. Tate and Rory sit on one of the couches. The food from before the show has been cleared from the banquet table. Now, it holds different glass bottles, a bucket of ice, a bag of beef jerky, and a tray of pastries.

"At least they have good refreshments," Birthday Girl notes. She licks some cream from her thumb and picks up a second eclair from her plate. "Happy birthday to me, am I right?"

"You missed the encore," I announce.

Like a skittish deer, Baby snaps her mouth closed and turns to me with wide eyes. Meanwhile, Birthday Girl looks about as surprised as a doorknob.

Twisting on the green and white fabric couch, she sets her plate in her lap. "Funny. I didn't think security guards gave encores."

I give her a sheepish grin. "Hi, I'm Paxton, the lead guitarist for IndieCent Vows."

"Tatum," she returns. "Did you know your goon at the door is quite bossy?" She glances at the open door where the silhouette of our head of security stands in the doorway. Not gonna lie, the man's a brick wall with a military background and a no bullshit attitude the guys respect. Babysitting fans isn't usually in his repertoire, though.

Closing the last bit of distance between us, I sit on Birthday Girl's opposite side. "Herb's a good guy."

"Is Herb short for cayenne pepper or...?" Her nose wrinkles. "Because he is *spicy.*"

I bite back my mirth. "Glad he could give you a run for your money."

"Mmm, I wouldn't go that far," she quips. "Although, now that you mention it, I think you owe me."

"Oh, I do?"

"Mm-hmm," she hums. "The question is, what do I want? I guess I could always ask for an introduction, but that almost seems too easy, considering I spent the last hour under lock and key."

"To be fair, the door's wide open," I point out. "And from what I hear, you already know my bandmates."

"I meant Doomsday," she argues.

Figured as much.

"So you don't deny it," I return. "Knowing the band."

"We know Dodge." She shrugs. "And even then, I know *of* Dodge. His parents run in the same circles as Rory's, and Rory's parents run in the same circles as mine, and…"

"And Dodger's little sister is practically engaged to one of Tatum's older sister's best friends," Rory chimes in.

"Well, fuck." I grip the back of the couch but leave plenty of space between me and the girl on the next cushion. "Should I get a notepad so you can draw me a family tree? Or…"

"Wouldn't be the first time someone's asked for one," Tatum mutters. Her sarcasm is as thick as molasses. "We're all very close in Lockwood Heights."

"Seems so." My gaze narrows as I inspect her, searching for clues and analyzing my bullshit meter. It's quiet. Settling back into the couch, I say, "All right, I'll buy it. Can you explain why you know my bandmates but didn't recognize me when I opened the side door for a smoke?"

Rory snorts, then clears her throat and pulls her phone out in an attempt to look preoccupied when we all know she's shamelessly eavesdropping.

"Just because I know of Dodge doesn't mean I'm familiar with your band," Tatum reminds me.

I pull back and rub at my chest, pretending to be wounded by her admission, though honestly, I'm almost impressed. "Ouch."

"Pretty sure your ego can take the hit," Tatum muses. "You did good, by the way."

"Thanks. You, too."

With a laugh, she asks, "And what did I do?"

"Sat there and looked pretty."

"You think I'm pretty, huh?"

Mirth dances in her pretty hazel eyes and shoots straight to my groin like before. And fuck, if it isn't growing. The pull. The curiosity. The intrigue. Bending forward, I let my lips brush against the shell of her ear. It creates the same thick tension it did when we were on stage just like I'd hoped, and I feed off it, enjoying the push and pull more than she knows. "If I say yes, are you gonna let it go to your head?"

She dips away, peeking up at me through her thick, black lashes. "Maybe."

My chuckle ruffles the wisps of hair framing her face as I inch even closer. "You're a confident little thing."

"Why, thank you." She peeks up at me again, and I swear I could fucking drown in those pretty little eyes. "Now, I think the real question is…where's my introduction, Mr. Security?"

"Careful. If you keep calling me that, Judge or Dodge might overhear you."

"And if they do?" she asks.

"They'll set you straight. Speaking of which. In the next ten minutes, this room will be swarmed with fans who won backstage passes. Usually, the guys like some quiet time between the show and the meet and greet, but I already know they're gonna give me shit for pulling a fast one on stage. I might as well introduce them to the reason behind it, right?"

"As in…me?" she offers.

"Exactly."

Something flashes in her eyes, though it's too quick for me to analyze.

"Or," Tatum pushes herself to her feet and wipes her palms along her jeans. "You can sneak us out of here before we have to deal with any awkwardness, and you can introduce me to Doomsday like you promised."

"I never promised to introduce you," I remind her.

"Well, then it looks like I should be going."

"Tate, he won't say anything," Rory starts.

She shoots her friend a look. "Not now, Rore."

"He?" I interrupt. I shouldn't care. I don't even know this girl, but what's with all the smoke and mirrors? So she knows Dodge. Most women would be over the fuckin' moon to know a rockstar. Not Tate, though. The question is…why?

A strange, unspoken conversation transpires between the two as I watch, dumbfounded. Rory comes to some kind of conclusion, causing Tatum to look pissed.

"Because Dodger knows our families, Tate's afraid he'll tell them he saw us tonight which will open up an unnecessary can of worms," Rory explains.

"From what I've heard, you're not the only one with Lockwood Heights drama," I point out. "And who cares if they know you're here?"

Tatum scowls and folds her arms. "I may have told them I have the flu, which is why I couldn't come home for my birthday."

I nearly choke on my amusement but swallow it back. "Well, shit."

"Yeah, and I love my parents, so I'd prefer not to make them question their parenting skills or our relationship in general all because of a little white lie," Tatum answers.

When heavy footsteps echo from the hallway, Tatum pinches the bridge of her nose, adding a mumbled, "Fantastic," just in time for Dodger, Tuke, and Judge to walk in the room. Unsurprisingly, Judge looks dead inside, and Dodger looks…bossy as always. Meanwhile, Tuke's sucking down a joint like this is par for the course when it comes to touring.

He isn't wrong.

Looks like shit's about to get interesting.

4

# PAXTON

Clearing my throat, I announce, "Tuke, Judge. This is Tatum and Rory, or as I like to call them, Birthday Girl and Baby."

"You old enough to be here or are we gonna get the cops sniffing around for serving a minor alcohol on stage?" Judge demands.

Shit, I didn't think about that.

I pin Tatum with a stare and wait for her response, trying to gauge exactly how much shit I might be in if she lied to me in the alleyway.

"I'll be seventeen in June," she tells him, sober as a fucking nun before a smirk teases the edge of her lips. "Just kidding."

"Thanks for the fuckin' heart attack," Tuke grunts. "How old are you really?"

"It's my twenty-first birthday."

"And the baby?" Tuke prods. He turns to a red-faced teenager behind Tate.

"I-I didn't drink anything, I swear," Rory promises.

"Her name's Squeaks," Dodger corrects him. Not gonna lie. I'm surprised he lasted so long with keeping his big-ass

36

mouth shut. With his arms spread wide, he approaches and pulls her into a hug. "Hey, baby girl. How you been?"

"Good," she returns. "How are you?"

"Can't complain." Letting her go, Dodger scans her up and down again. "Been a while. Feels like you've grown an extra twenty inches."

I hold my breath to keep from laughing because the girl can't be over five feet tall, which would've made her a freaking toddler the last time he saw her.

"How's boarding school?" he prods.

Boarding school? Guess that explains the time between run-ins.

"Good," Rory answers. "I graduate this year."

"No shit?" Dodger grins. "That's amazing, Squeaks."

Beaming, she tucks her hands into her back pockets and rocks back on her heels. "Thanks. I'm so ready to move on, it's not even funny."

"I can imagine. Any plans after graduation?"

"I was just accepted to RHU, actually."

"No shit?" He smiles. "Judge's nephews were accepted there, too. Right, Judge?"

Judge's head lowers into a subtle nod, but he doesn't comment.

Dodge turns to Tatum and closes the distance, offering her his hand. "Not sure if we've ever been formally introduced. I'm Dodger, Raine's older brother. Heard a lot about you."

"Tatum." Grudgingly, Tatum takes Dodgers' tatted hand and shakes it once before letting it go and wiping her palm on the outside of her thigh.

"Ophelia's little sister, right?" He scans her up and down again. "You two look nothing alike."

"Thank god." Tatum grins and folds her arms.

Damn. Way to wear your emotions on your sleeve. Talk

about a one-eighty. I think I found the answer as to why she lied about being sick over her birthday. My interest multiplies. I mean, how can't it? Seems the girl has more bite than bark, which is saying something, considering this conversation. But the really crazy part? Dodge isn't up my ass about being late on stage tonight, which means this girl is officially my savior, and I owe her one. Big time.

"Speaking of family, I'd appreciate it if you didn't tell anyone we saw each other. I'm supposed to be at home with the flu, so…"

"Aren't you a little old to be lying to your family?" Tuke asks before stuffing a piece of jerky into his mouth.

"Aw, come on," she quips. "You're never too old to lie to your family. Right, Rory?"

With a fake smile, Rory presses her hands together in a prayer gesture. "Pretty please, Dodge?"

"You know your secret's safe with me." Head tilting, Dodger adds, "You guys should stay a while. We have drinks. Food. Whatever you want. Except no drugs."

He gives Tuke a pointed look, and Tuke grins around his mouthful of jerky. "Drugs are bad. Stay in school."

"Already graduated but great advice." Tatum clicks her tongue against the roof of her mouth and lifts a shoulder. "Unfortunately, we should get going, so…"

"You sure?" Dodger asks.

"Yeah, definitely. We'll call an Uber and be on our way. Rain check, though. For sure." The girl doesn't bother hiding her sarcasm as she gives him a thumbs up and takes a step toward the door.

Not gonna lie, it's hot as fuck. People don't stand up to Dodge, and they don't turn him down. They don't turn down anyone in the group. And it sure as shit isn't only 'cause we're famous, either.

"You sure you can get an Uber at this time of night?" he counters. "And after the concert? *And* in this part of town?"

The man isn't wrong.

Not only is the concert in the middle of nowhere, it's also late. Anyone willing to make the drive is likely already booked, which means the girls will be waiting at least thirty minutes until a ride becomes available.

"Pretty sure it isn't your problem," Tatum argues.

"You're right. It's your parents' problem, isn't it?" Dodger counters. "Should I call them now or…?"

Her gaze narrows. "I thought you said we could keep my parents out of this."

"And I thought you'd know why I have issues with young girls getting rides in the dark. Or have you forgotten what happened to my sister a few years back?" he challenges.

Aaaand, there it is.

The bane of my existence and one of the few mistakes Dodger has no issue holding over my head. You see, Dodger was supposed to give his sister a ride that night, but his bike wasn't working, so he asked me to pick Raine up instead. And I was going to. I just…wanted to get head from a groupie first. By the time I re-emerged from the back room where we were performing, Dodger was losing his mind about his little sister's stalker cornering her outside his family's tattoo shop. It was all my fault. All my fucking fault. And if Raine's boyfriend hadn't intervened, who knows what would've happened to her? The thought alone is enough to send a shiver down my spine, and I fold my arms, waiting for the feeling to dissipate despite knowing it never will. Not really.

The truly surprising part, though? Dodger isn't using my fuck-up to rub my nose in shit. He's using it to keep Birthday Girl from doing something stupid, and I can't help but want to applaud the bastard for it.

Refusing to back down, Tatum replies, "Pretty sure I don't have a scary ex–slash–stalker who's looking for an opening to kidnap me, so…"

*Damn.*

It's official. This girl must have balls of steel.

"I can give them a ride," I offer.

Everyone's attention slices to me.

"You have your bike," Dodger reminds me.

Shit. I didn't think about that.

"Uber, it is." Tatum takes another step toward the exit, looking less than displeased. "Come on, Rore."

"Tatum," Rory starts.

"Not gonna let an Uber driver take you girls home," Dodger says. "If you're gonna be this stubborn, I'll have Herb give you a ride back to your place after the meet and greet."

Well, shit. Seems my buddy's thought of everything.

*Your move, Tatum.*

Her lips gnash together. Well aware she's been cornered, she places her hand on her stomach, her brow dipping. "You know, I'm actually not feeling well, so…"

*Liar.*

And the fact she's using the same excuse she literally admitted to using with her parents? I cover my smirk with my hand, convinced the only thing that would make this interaction better is a bowl of popcorn.

"Why don't you catch a ride with Pax, and I'll hang out for the meet and greet?" Rory suggests from the couch. "Then Herb can give me a ride back to the hotel later?"

My eyes widen at the opportunity she's gifted me. When they lock with Rory's behind Tatum's back, she winks at me, proving she knows it, too.

Well, would you look at that?

*You might be my new favorite person, Baby.*

"What about the fans?" Dodger demands.

"You were late on stage," Tuke adds from the buffet, piling donuts and more beef jerky onto a plate like it's his last meal. "You know what that means." He stuffs an entire cream puff into his mouth, licking the powdered sugar off his thumb without bothering to hide his knowing grin.

*Asshole.*

Yeah, he knows the rules. We *all* know the rules. Whenever I'm late on stage, I'm the designated buffer during the meet and greets, since fans are known for using alcohol as liquid courage before meeting me and the rest of the band.

"Tell them I got food poisoning," I suggest.

Tuke laughs and collapses onto the couch with his plate of junk food.

"Food poisoning?" Judge challenges.

I shrug. "Yeah, why not?"

"Man, something's gotta be going around. Isn't that right, Tate?" Tuke asks.

Tatum nods. "It's a real shame, let me tell ya."

"I think you guys will survive without me," I say. "Now, if you'll excuse us." Grabbing Tatum's hand, I tug her down the hall before Judge or Dodge has a chance to second guess the decision.

By some miracle, she follows without complaint, matching my pace as we race toward the exit and slip past a few more security guards. Maybe she's even more desperate to get out of here than I initially pegged her for.

"Come on," I urge.

She doesn't say a word as we walk down the back hallway toward the same door I snuck her in earlier tonight. When I hold it open for her, she steps over the threshold, something swirling in her pretty eyes as she waits for me to guide her through the parking lot. The warm breeze ruffles her hair, giving me another whiff of her shampoo. Or maybe the scent is all Tatum. Not sure it matters. My mouth waters regardless.

Digging in my pocket, I find a cigarette and light it, letting the sweet nicotine fill my lungs to take the edge off the guilt I've been suffocating in since before the show. She peeks at the cigarette in my fingers. I offer it to her, but she only shakes her head and folds her arms.

When we reach my bike, I take one more drag, drop the cigarette, and put the bud out with the toe of my shoe before offering Tate my spare helmet.

She frowns. "You weren't kidding about the bike?"

"Is it a problem?"

Her lips thin.

"You got a thing against bikes, Birthday Girl?"

Her attention cuts to mine. "Only the men who own them."

"Damn." I press my hand to my heart like it just took a knife to it, then grab a piece of peppermint gum from one of the saddle bags. Crinkling the wrapper in my palm, I shove the gum into my mouth, adding, "Two strikes to the ego in one night."

"Again, I think you can handle it."

I snort. "You're probably right. The question is, can you handle being on the back of my bike?"

Her lips purse. "I'm debating."

"We could always go back inside."

She grabs the helmet from me and slips it on her head, her expression twisting with annoyance. Her fingers fumble with the strap beneath her chin, and I swat them away.

"Here." Slowly, I lift her chin. She follows my silent request, raising her head so I can see the strap underneath. When my fingers brush against her soft skin, her lips part, and my own lift with satisfaction, as I slide the buckle into place. "There. Much better."

I put my helmet on, swing my leg over the seat, and wait for Tatum to join me.

She doesn't.

Glancing at her, I tilt my head. "You coming or what?"

"Still debating."

"It's me or Dodge inside." I shrug. "Your choice."

Folding her arms, she points out, "You say it like you weren't trying to get out of there, too."

Damn, the girl got me.

"I was late," I tell her.

"For what?"

"For the set. Which is your fault, by the way," I add.

Arms folded, she pops out one hip. "So?"

"So, after one too many fuck ups, Dodger made a rule. If you're late on stage, you're in charge of handling the fans who've had too much to drink during the meet and greets."

"Yeah, because that sounds like it's such a chore for a guy like you," she counters.

My mouth lifts. "Depends on the fan. Where's your hotel?"

Pulling her phone out, she tells me the name, and I nod, familiar with the area. "Hop on."

With a sigh, she climbs on the back, her arms hanging limply at her sides as if she doesn't know what to do with them. I turn the ignition, and the bike rumbles to life beneath us. She fumbles for the handles beneath her ass, reminding me of an anxious baby bird or some shit.

Grateful she can't read the amusement on my face, I ask, "You ever been on a bike?"

"No?"

"Is that a question?"

She smacks my shoulder. "No, I've never been on a bike."

*Called it.*

"You're gonna wanna hold on," I tell her.

"I am holding on."

I rev the engine, and the bike jerks forward.

"Shit!" Tatum slams into my back, her arms wrapping around my waist.

"Now you're holding on," I quip.

"Smartass."

"Long way or short way to the hotel?"

"Short," she yells over the rumbling engine.

"Your wish is my command."

Turning onto the main highway, I start the short trip to her hotel. Minutes pass, and her muscles slowly loosen, the tension from when we first climbed on the bike morphing into an easy grip as we weave between cars.

"Woo-hoo!" she screams, though I doubt she knows I can hear her. I like it, though. The glimpse of the girl she seems to keep hidden when others are around. Or maybe it's just me she's hiding from. Nah, that's not true. Seeing her with the rest of the guys is all the confirmation I need. This girl's a vault, and I've always been a sucker for picking locks.

When we pull off the highway and stop at a light, she bends around me, yelling, "I changed my mind!"

I twist to look at her, my brows pinched in confusion.

"I want the long way," she clarifies. "If the offer's still on the table."

Glancing at the red light, I check left and right, confirming the road is empty before twisting my wrist and cutting through the intersection.

Her surprised squeal of laughter seeps from her chest and into my back, bringing a smile of my own as we dart across the dark road. Then, we're flying.

I've always loved my bike. Ever since the guys introduced me to motorcycles, I've been obsessed. The rumble of the engine between my thighs. The buzzing of the wind. The quiet in the chaos.

Tatum's thighs squeeze the seat, her knees pressing against my outer legs before her hands disappear from my waist and she spreads her arms wide. My panic lasts less than a beat until I look over my shoulder, finding her head tilted toward the pitch black sky. The shield covers her expression, but I don't need to see her face to know she's smiling. I'd bet my life savings it's a real one, too. Not the flirty facade she used on me to sneak into the venue earlier. Not the smartass one she wore as armor when she ran into Dodge and the rest of the band after the show. Nah. This one's for her. And for some reason I can't explain, my chest puffs up in pride. I put it there. That smile. Me.

Maybe I'm not a fuck up after all.

Scanning the winding road ahead of us, I slowly drift across the center line, treating the entire road as our playground because in a way, it is. It's only me and her and the night sky. The gentle breeze. The sprawling pavement. I sway us from left to right like it's a dance, and we're the only two people in the world who matter.

And maybe, for this moment, we are.

5

# TATUM

Okay, so maybe I have a thing for motorcycles. The thought sweeps through me grudgingly. It shouldn't. There's nothing wrong with motorcycles or the men who own them. Or at least, not in a literal sense. Even so, I can't get my sister's voice out of my head.

*"Us Taylor girls." My sister shakes her head and attempts to give me a reassuring smile. "Seems we're suckers for bikers."*

The memory flashes through my mind before I can stop it.

It was a few years ago. We were driving somewhere. Me, Rory, my sister, her friends. We were all piled into the car on our way to a girls' night I wanted nothing to do with. Some biker started an impromptu game of Rock, Paper, Scissors at the stoplight. By some miracle, he did the impossible. He managed to make me smile for the first time in what felt like forever.

I was so lonely back then. Okay, I'm still lonely, but I'm better at hiding it now. I'm also better at finding distractions. Just like the man in front of me. He's definitely a distraction, and a pretty one, too. If only he didn't have a bike. The less similarities I have with my good ol' sister, the better. And if she knew I was pressed up against some hunky badboy like Maverick Buchanan—the love of her life and Archer's twin brother—she'd probably laugh her ass off.

*"Us Taylor girls. Seems like we're suckers for bikers."*

*Gag.*

Wait.

I replay the memory again, the same way I've done a thousand times over the years, though I'd never admit it out loud. Raine was there, too. And even though I didn't recognize the biker, Raine did. She said it was…Pax. My attention slices to the back of the helmet in front of me.

There's no way.

Is there?

I scan Pax's broad shoulders and the curve of his spine beneath his T-shirt. Is it him? Could it be? That's ridiculous.

*Isn't it?*

Yeah, no, it's totally ridiculous, but also…I'm pretty sure Raine called the guy Pax.

Holy shit.

I thought about that day for years. Stupid, yes. But still. Funny how fate likes to fuck with me sometimes. What are the odds I'd be on the back of his bike a thousand miles from Lockwood Heights?

Fascinating.

Pax revs the engine, and I press my front to his back as he leans into the turn, driving us down a side road where a fast food restaurant waits. The neon light glows above us as we turn into the parking lot, and the scent of grease and salt hits my nostrils. When my stomach grumbles, Paxton's back rumbles against me.

He turns his bike off and lowers the kickstand to the black pavement. "I was gonna ask if you like burgers, but I'm gonna go with yes."

Refusing to confirm his assumption, I climb off the bike and start undoing the helmet strap beneath my chin. Pax bats my hands away like before, the same way he'd swat at a pesky fly. It shouldn't make me smile, but it does. I like how casual he is. How effortlessly sexy and caring he is, even though he hides it under the guise of annoyance or something. It's… also fascinating. His fingers are calloused. The gentle scratch shoots straight to my core while he slips the strap from the metal buckle and pulls my helmet off.

Eyes glued to me, his mouth quirks up, and I swear I can see the wheels turning in his brain, but he doesn't say a word.

It only makes me squirm more, and considering the fact that his calloused hands were just on me, it's saying something. "Is there a problem?" I ask.

"You look like you just had the best sex of your life."

My brows dip. "Excuse me?"

"The hair," he explains.

Reaching up, I smooth out my messy hair and tuck it behind my ear.

Paxton's smile stretches. "Sorry, Birthday Girl. Still sexy. Come on." He climbs off the bike and sets our helmets on the seat. "My treat."

"A burger and fries." I clutch at my chest. "My hero."

"Hey, if you're nice, I'll let you get a shake, too."

"*Let me*," I repeat with a scoff. "Clearly, you don't know me very well."

"Not yet." He reaches for the restaurant's door, holding it open for me. "But give me time."

*Yeah, not likely.*

Pax could be a Greek god—and honestly, he's competing pretty hard for the title--and I'd still never see him again after tonight. It isn't personal. It's a rule I have. And I might hate rules more than just about anything. But this one? This one, I promised to keep until my last breath after I found out Archer had already taken his.

*Don't think about him.*

There are two people in the restaurant and both are behind the counter. Their noses are glued to the young guy's phone.

"Come on, come on, come on," he mutters.

"Yes!" the girl squeals. "I told you Taylor's more than a pretty face."

"It was a lucky pass," the guy argues. "Thorne basically handed the puck to Taylor, and the only reason he's talented is because his dad used to play and—"

"Whatever, I don't want to hear your excuses. Just because my team is better than the Grizzlies doesn't mean you need to pout, Carlos."

I approach the counter and clear my throat.

Carlos shoves his phone into his apron. "Shit. Sorry. We were just watching the hockey game."

"I gathered," I reply blandly.

Not catching my drift, he asks, "You watch?"

I shake my head. "Not really."

"I didn't either," the girl chimes in. "Not until a few years ago when a bunch of hotties started playing. Seriously." She fans her face. "I don't know how hockey seems to attract the most gorgeous men ever, but I highly suggest you look up Griffin Thorne or Oliver Reeves or my personal favorite, Everett Taylor. They are the creme de la creme of the male population. I'm not even—" The worker's eyes land on Pax and she gulps. "Um. Uh. Can I take"—she clears her throat—"your order?"

Seems hockey players aren't the only creme de la creme of the male population.

Stealing a quick peek of the sexy as sin man behind me, I order a bacon cheeseburger with fries. Pax asks for the same, adding two shakes—one chocolate and one vanilla—before leading me to one of the empty booths. We're the only people here. Well, other than the workers who are back to drooling over my family on the ice. If I was smart, I'd probably be a little on edge about the whole thing. After all, I don't know Pax. Not really. But being impulsive and reckless is kind of my middle name, so I don't really care. Besides, if Dodger trusts him, then I do, too.

I'm not sure if they recognized him or thought he had a particularly pretty face. The workers. They're too distracted by the hockey game. They didn't ask for a name when we paid, either, handing us a receipt with a number on it instead.

I peek up at Paxton again. I don't know how I missed it in the alleyway. The confidence in the way he carries himself is unlike anything I've ever really seen. But it's so...effortless. Like it has nothing to do with his rockstar title and everything to do with the man himself.

Who is this guy?

Minutes later, our order number is called and Pax returns with a tray littered with food. He sets it down and starts divvying up our orders but hesitates when the only things left are the two shakes.

"Is there a problem?"

"Chocolate or vanilla?" he asks.

It feels like a loaded question, but I answer anyway. "Chocolate."

"Damn. Figured you for a vanilla girl."

My mouth twitches. "You have no idea."

He picks up the chocolate shake but doesn't set it in front of me. Instead, he brings it to his mouth and licks the top of the open cup with his tongue, gathering some creamy dessert with the tip before it disappears into his mouth, and holy shit, the imagery is enough to make me turn into a puddle or better yet, climb onto the table and spread my legs wide. I haven't been licked like that in who knows how long.

*Seriously, is it hot in here?*

If he knows what I'm thinking, he doesn't comment on it. Climbing into the booth, he sets the chocolate shake back on the tray, not claiming it for himself but not handing it over, either.

"See, but here's the thing," he continues, "I like chocolate, too."

"Then why'd you order vanilla?" I ask.

"Because I thought I'd be a gentleman and let you have dibs, but now that we're here..."

"Ah, so it's all a facade, is it? The whole gentleman bit."

He smirks shamelessly. "Maybe."

"Should we Rock, Paper, Scissors for it?" I lift my closed fist onto the table in preparation for our game. I shouldn't. There's no way he remembers our little interaction. Hell, it feels like a lifetime ago. But I can't help myself. I'm curious. If I managed to make even the smallest of impressions on him, when it's clear he made a pretty big one on me.

Staring at my hand resting on the table separating us, he notes, "A girl after my own heart."

"Seems that way."

He lifts his closed fist into the air. "On three?"

"Four," I decide. "Rock, paper, scissors, shoot."

Leaning forward, he rests his weight on his elbows and shows me his fist. "Game on, Birthday Girl."

He's sexy when he's competitive. Playful. Confident. And the smirk on this bad boy?

Damn.

Ignoring the tightness in my lower belly, I match his posture, leaving a few inches of space between our foreheads. "Ready?"

"Always."

"Rock. Paper. Scissors. Shoot," we say in unison.

I flatten my hand to paper, and he keeps his hand in a fist. Realizing he's lost, he groans. "Best two out of three?"

"And why would I agree to that?" I ask with a laugh. "I've already won."

He pushes the chocolate shake across the table. "Cut-throat. I like it."

With a grin, I pick the spoon up and take a big bite, letting the rich cocoa and sweet cream melt against my taste buds. Seriously. Chocolate's far superior.

"Way to dive right in," he quips. "Not even gonna eat your dinner first?"

"Not gonna let me revel in my victory?" I counter, dipping the red plastic spoon into the paper cup for another bite.

He watches as I lick the spoon, and something sparks in his eyes. "Seems like you're reveling in it just fine."

I laugh around my bite, then set the spoon back into the cup and reach for my burger. "To be fair, I'm pretty sure it isn't the first time I've beaten you at Rock, Paper, Scissors."

His brow quirks. "What?"

"I'm not some creepy stalker or something, if that's what you're worried about." I hesitate. "Honestly, I wouldn't have remembered, either, if it wasn't for Raine."

Just as confused as before, he unfolds the yellow wrapper around his cheeseburger but pauses instead of bringing it to his mouth. "Dodger's little sister?"

"Yup. A few years ago, we were in Lockwood Heights, and you pulled up on your motorcycle beside the car I was in and—"

"We played a game of Rock, Paper, Scissors," he realizes. Eyes glazed, he hesitates before letting out a low chuckle. "No shit. I remember that." Another laugh escapes him. "You won back then, too. Right?"

"Pretty sure I'm the reigning champion."

"Very sneaky, Birthday Girl." Taking a bite of his burger, he chews thoughtfully, his eyes never leaving me. After he swallows, he adds, "I lost on purpose that time, though."

"You can't lose Rock, Paper, Scissors on purpose."

"Can and did," he argues. "I had to do something to make you smile."

I look down at my untouched burger, lost in the memory. I was so pissed at my sister. Actually, I was pissed at everyone. For going out and having fun and moving on when I felt like I was being ripped apart, limb from limb. Tendon from bone. Skin from muscle. I was being flayed, and they were joking about…shit, I don't even remember anymore. Not that it matters. I was hurting, and I wanted everyone else to hurt, too.

Well, would you look at that. I did learn a thing or two from my therapist. Mom and Dad would be so proud.

"Kinda feel like I need to do something to make you smile today, too," Pax murmurs, somehow riding the line between making me feel like we're talking about the weather and something more.

Picking up my burger again, I say, "It was a bad day."

"I've had a few of those." He shrugs. "They fucking suck, am I right?"

A breath of laughter puffs from my lips, and I look down at my burger, nodding. "Yeah. Yeah, they do."

That's it. No digging. No why or what happened? Just a simple, yeah, me, too. They're the worst.

Honestly, I'm so caught off guard, I don't know what else to do but eat my burger. It's refreshing. Having someone willing to relate to you without all the added prying I've grown to loathe over the years. Sometimes, less is more, and very few people get it. That when you're mourning, you don't need a solution. You don't need a Band-Aid or a word of wisdom. You just need a *yeah, that fucking sucks.* Let me sit with you while we both wallow in self-pity and vent about how much fate hates us.

Don't get me wrong. I'm not stupid. I know living that way for too long can be detrimental in the big picture, but sometimes? Fuck the big picture. Even if it's only for a little while.

"So, what's it like?" I ask. "Being a rockstar?"

His shoulder lifts, and he smiles around his burger. "Can't complain."

Clearing my throat to keep my amusement in check, I murmur, "Of course not."

"Hey, there's nothing wrong with liking my job."

"Not at all," I agree. "What are your favorite perks?"

"Money, obviously. Makes life a hell of a lot easier. The private jets are cool. The women aren't a bad perk, either." He grins shamelessly. "Let's see, what else? It's pretty sweet being on stage and hearing the crowd chant your lyrics."

"Yeah, it looked like you were having quite the time up there earlier."

"Had to put on a good show for a new fan tonight."

"Is that what you were doing?"

He dips a fry in ketchup and tosses it into his mouth. "You tell me."

I could tell him I had fun. I could tell him he put on a hell of a show and gained a fan for life. I could tell him a lot of things, but I won't. Motioning to myself, I ask, "So am I a fan, or a perk?"

His eyes dance with mirth. "I dunno, are you a perk?"

My teeth dig into the inside of my bottom lip. Am I a perk? A groupie? It's what he's really asking. What I asked first before he turned the table on me. He wants to know if I'm planning to put out tonight. And if I'm being honest, the answer is *probably.*

It isn't only because he's hot. It isn't only because he whisked me away on his motorcycle and bought me dinner. It isn't only because it's my birthday and I'm a sucker for a solid hookup with no strings attached. It's because I hate what ifs and missed opportunities more than anything else in the world. Love me or hate me, but if I only get to live once, I have no problem making reckless decisions because there's nothing worse than living with regret. I should know. I've done it for years.

"No answer, Birthday Girl?" he prods.

"Depends on how the rest of the night goes," I reply, "but I think you already know that."

"Are you saying I have expectations about how tonight will go?"

"I'm saying you're a rockstar who's used to getting what he wants."

"And what do I want?"

*Me.*

With a shrug, I take another bite of my burger.

"All right, Miss Know-it-all, since you know me so well, throw me a bone. What's your favorite food?"

I lift my burger as if to say, Exhibit A. "Burgers."

He chuckles. "Really?"

"Sure."

"Okay. Favorite color?"

"Black."

His eyes fall to his black T-shirt, and he cocks his head. "Let me guess. Your favorite dessert is a chocolate shake?"

"Nailed it," I quip.

He reaches for his napkin, wipes his fingers, then leans back in the booth, his gaze never leaving mine. He probably thinks I'm being a bitch by refusing to play his game and tell him something about myself, but there's a reason I won't play. Because with a guy like him, I have a feeling one game could easily lead to two, and that's against the rules, er, rule, since I only have one.

"You're a pretty little liar. I'll give you that much," he murmurs.

"Who says I'm lying?"

"So you always happen to want what's right in front of you?"

I lift my shoulder again. "Maybe."

"Okay, favorite television show?" He lifts his finger. "Wait. You look more like a reader than a television show kind of girl. What's your favorite book?"

I keep my expression on lockdown, despite my internal flinch at how hard he hit the nail on the head. "Who says I'm a reader?"

"Closet reader," he clarifies, hitting the nail on the head way more than he has any right to.

I set my burger down and brush the crumbs from my fingers before lacing them in front of me. "And what gives you that impression?"

"You seem like you're someone who likes to keep things close to the chest."

"Yet here you are, prying like a seasoned expert."

His low chuckle makes my insides twist. "Or maybe just a kindred spirit. You gonna answer me?"

I could lie again. I could give him a bullshit answer. But something inside me clangs to give him the truth. As if the promise of never needing to see him again brings freedom with it. The freedom to be honest. To let my walls down, even if it's only for one night.

Wouldn't that be an interesting experience.

All right, Mr. Security. You've convinced me. I'll play. But only for tonight.

# 6

# TATUM

"*The Count of Monte Cristo*," I finally answer. "That's my favorite book."

Paxton's brows hitch. "No shit?"

"Is that a problem?"

He shakes his head. "Not at all. I've only seen the movie, though."

"Movie?" I grimace. "Come on, Pax. The book's better."

"The books are always better," he agrees. "I'll have to give *The Count of Monte Cristo* a read."

"You mean between rock concerts?" I tease.

"Guess so. Favorite food?"

"Lobster roll," I answer.

He nods his agreement. "Favorite color?"

"Blue. Like the ocean."

*And Archer's eyes.*

His head bobs again, this time slower. "Favorite dessert?"

"Chocolate shake. For real," I add. "What about you?"

"Anything home cooked, bright orange, and…also a solid chocolate shake, but I like mine with Butterfinger or Snickers chunks." He smirks. "Fuck, yeah."

"Favorite book?" I prod. "Wait, don't tell me. You're more of a TV show guy, am I right?"

"Right again, Birthday Girl. And I'm gonna go with... *Vampire Diaries.*"

I nearly choke on my bite of burger before wiping the edge of my mouth with the back of my hand. "Are you serious?"

"Tuke got me hooked. But it's only good if you're high—"

"And have a chocolate shake with Butterfinger or Snickers in it?"

"Exactly."

Tapping his shoe against my shin beneath the table, he adds, "So, other than a rockstar buying you dinner, do you have any other birthday wishes since I kidnapped you from your friend tonight?"

"Depends. Are we talking achievable or unachievable?"

"Achievable," he decides, watching as I pick up a fry from the tray separating us.

Not gonna lie. I'm starving. Rory picked me up straight from the airport, then we went to the hotel so I could change and freshen up before my birthday surprise, aka the concert, and we didn't have a chance to grab food beforehand. I haven't been back in town since I graduated high school from American Prep boarding school, but when Rory asked me to fly in for my birthday, I couldn't say no. As I chew, I weigh my options, grateful he didn't ask for the unachievable because that would've been...awkward. Probably shouldn't bring up my sister's dead ex-boyfriend on the first date, am I right? Then again, we've broached a few no-no's for first dates, but he hasn't pushed his luck, and honestly? It's kind of refreshing.

He's refreshing.

I swallow my bite and wipe the edge of my mouth with my thumb. "Well, let's take a look at how my birthday's been so far." The night replays in my mind. "Did a shot on stage."

"Check."

"Motorcycle ride."

"Check."

"Dinner with a rockstar."

"Check."

"Hmm." I take another bite, surprised by the buzzing beneath my skin as Pax stares at me from across the table. "I guess I could always let you cash in on those other perks you mentioned."

"Such as?"

"Me," I offer. "Although, in return, I expect a solid orgasm or two. Does that sound achievable to you?"

"Two?"

"What? Too vanilla?" I quip, glancing at the untouched shake on the edge of the table.

Intrigued, he shifts closer and drops his voice low. "And you saying I'm the one with expectations?"

"If we're gonna point fingers, you're the one who asked what else I want for my birthday since you kidnapped me and all." I kick him softly beneath the table. "So what do you say? Are you turning me down, Mr. Security?"

"I should," he counters dryly. "It might be good for you to be told no every once in a while."

"Who says I'm never told no?"

"Pretty faces like yours are used to getting what they want," he murmurs. "But you're right. After the whole kidnapping thing, I guess I can put out."

I laugh even harder. "So selfless."

"You have no idea." His elbows hit the table, and he shifts forward. "Are we talking dirty bathroom sex, or a little hand play beneath the table, *or* a quick trip to your hotel before Rory gets there?"

Well damn. I mean, I know I'm the one who suggested hooking up in the first place, but bathroom sex? Hand play under the table? Way to take things to a new level, Mr. Security. I don't know if I should be proud or a little scared. Not that he'll hurt me or something, but that he has no issue going head-to-head with a girl like me. I'm not used to being the one knocked off kilter. Usually, it's the other way around. I kind of like it, though. Being on the other side. The one volleying back instead of serving, so to speak.

His lips curve up on one side as he waits for my answer while refusing to back down or play off his suggestion like it's a joke.

Who is this guy?

"Is that a dare?" I challenge.

"Just a question."

"Mm-hmm. Call me crazy, but you don't seem like someone who asks…"—I lift my hand and do air quotes—"just a question."

"One game of Rock, Paper, Scissors, and you think you already have me pegged." He pops another fry into his mouth then shifts back in his seat again and crosses his arms over his chest, playing the bad boy rockstar part like he was made for it.

"Sorry, but pegging isn't my thing. Or at least, not on the first date," I add, letting him jump to whatever conclusion he wants by my not-so-thinly-veiled innuendo, er, in-his-end-o.

Snorting, he nearly chokes on his french fry before covering his mouth with the back of his hand and forcing the salty potato down his throat. Once he's safe from asphyxiation, he wipes his mouth with a napkin and reaches for the untouched shake, conceding, "All right, you win. I'll eat the vanilla."

I grin as he shoves an overfilled spoonful of ice cream

into his mouth to wash down what's left of the deadly french fry.

"How's it taste?" I tease.

"Like victory."

"Pretty sure you lost."

Smiling around the spoon, he glances at the front of the restaurant. "Did I?"

"Yup, pretty sure."

The two workers are busy flirting with each other, oblivious to our presence. They're probably counting down the minutes to the end of their shift when they can finally hook up, and why wouldn't they? It's Saturday night. They want to go home. And honestly, we should probably leave, too.

"Or maybe I'm in it for the long game." Standing, Pax rounds the edge of the booth and slides into my side.

"What are you doing?" I scoot a little further back so he has room on the cushion.

"Delivering one of your birthday presents."

As he corners me in the booth, a breathless laugh slips out of me. "Pax, I was kidding."

"About the pegging, sure." His hand hits my thigh. "Everything else? I guess I'm here to call your bluff."

Ooookay, shit just got real. And don't get me wrong. The idea of being finger-banged at an empty restaurant is a solid bean-flicking fantasy, but actually going through with it? I mean, I'm not crazy.

*Am I?*

My amusement withers like a flower in winter, though I'm anything but cold.

The air charges around us, and my eyes fall to his hand. I shift in my seat, staring at the contrast of his tan, weathered hands, compared to my milky thighs. "What bluff?" I breathe out.

"That you were kidding about wanting a solid orgasm or two." He slides his hand a little higher. "Tell me to stop."

My attention shoots to the workers, still oblivious. "You should know I won't fake it."

"I'd be disappointed if you did." He slips his hand further up my thigh, making my body tremble with interest. "You wet for me, Birthday Girl?"

I keep my eyes on his and spread my legs a little further apart. "Why don't you find out?"

Heat flickers in his coffee-colored eyes, turning them even darker. Hotter. Brighter. "Fuck, I want to kiss you."

I swallow, the blaze from his body seeping into mine as my opposite shoulder presses into the wall. "Then why don't you?"

"Because if I kiss you, I have a feeling I'll want to fuck you." His mouth hovers an inch above mine, and his fingers trace the outline of my underwear. He's playing with me. Teasing me. Toying with me. And holy shit, is it working. I feel like I'm on fire. Like every subtle brush of his fingers is stoking the flames inside of me, leaving me hot and bothered and more on edge than I have any right to be when he's barely touched me.

"And even though you clearly like it down and dirty," he whispers, "I think you deserve a bed so I can worship you fully."

"Who says I need worshipping?"

His chuckle is low and throaty, causing my core to tighten. "Anyone who ever tries to convince you otherwise, send them to me."

Body aching, I whisper, "And what will you do?"

"Let them watch as I worship you."

Fuck. The image alone is enough to make me come, but I force the feeling back, watching his chest expand on an unsteady breath. At least I'm not the only one affected right now. So, why isn't he doing anything about it?

"Let them watch you worship me, huh?" I breathe out. "That's pretty big talk for a man who isn't fingering me."

"I guess watching you ride my hand will have to do." He presses the tip against my entrance, the scrap of lace acting as the only barrier between us. My hips lift on instinct, longing for more pressure. Eyes hooded, he growls, "You're soaked."

"Am I?"

I scoot back a little more, and open my legs further, silently begging him to put me out of my misery. As if he can sense how on edge I already am, he drags his knuckles along my slit, then pushes my thong aside. The cool air makes me gasp, and he tilts his head, moving in for a kiss. Finally. I lift my head to meet him halfway, but instead of closing the last bit of distance, he pushes his forefinger into me. My lips part.

"Fuck." The word is nothing but air, but he hears it nonetheless, and I fight the urge to let my eyes roll back in my head as another wave of pleasure crashes through me. It's stronger than before. Sharper. And I swear if he stops, I'll knee him in the balls.

He hooks his finger inside me, slowly pulls it out, and pushes into me again, rasping, "Do you think they know what we're doing?"

My eyes cut to the workers. They're gathered around one of their phones, laughing at whatever's on the screen.

"Do you think they're pretending to be preoccupied so I'll keep going?" Pax adds a second finger, stretching me before pulling out and pressing his wet fingertips to my clit.

"Fuck," I repeat.

"I wonder if they have cameras. If they're watching you through an app on their phone."

My eyelids flutter, and I grip his wrist between my thighs, slowly rolling my hips against him.

"If they do, I'll have to track down the footage."

"Why?" I breathe out.

"Because I've never seen anything sexier than the way you look right now." He dips even closer. "Do you have any idea how hard I am? My cock is fucking throbbing. I'd give anything to pull it out and squeeze the tip, pretending it's this tight pussy."

He thumbs my clit again, and my heart races faster. I never knew I was a sucker for a guy with a dirty mouth, but this? This is doing it for me. It's clear Paxton knows exactly what he's doing. With his hand. His words. The slight rasp of his voice. It's too much, yet not enough. I need more.

"Fuck, I wanna kiss you." His gaze falls to my lips.

"You know, I think you mentioned that already."

He smiles but doesn't let up. "Wanna fuck this pretty mouth with my tongue as I'm buried inside you. Wanna feel this tight pussy squeezing my cock the same way it's squeezing my fingers. So fucking greedy, Birthday Girl. So fucking greedy."

Massaging my inner walls, he drags his fingers back and forth, in and out, while I try to slow my breathing. To steady it. To act like we're talking about the weather instead of filthy words I'll never forget, even if I wanted to. But I can't help it. I'm close. Really fucking close. I bury my head in the crook of Paxton's neck and shift my hips against him, trying to be subtle no matter how much the rhythm drives me insane. We're going to get caught. We're going to get caught, and I can't even find the fucks to give because all that matters is how close I am to coming and how freaking talented Paxton is with his fingers. So much so, I can only imagine what it would be like with his mouth or cock. An image of him licking the shake resurfaces, and I dig my teeth into his neck, falling apart. It's like he's pulling a thread and all I can do is unravel.

Shattering at the imagery, I orgasm, and he cups my sensitive flesh, giving me time to come back down to earth as my clit pulses and my thighs tremble beneath the table. As my breathing steadies, I open my eyes, finding his gaze glued to me. It shouldn't make me squirm. Shouldn't make me feel like I'm naked in front of a hundred people. But it does.

My eyes shoot to the workers, and I suck my lips between my teeth, praying they can't see the guilty as hell expression I know is growing on my face. Because let's be real, even the best liar in the world can't pretend like what just happened didn't actually…happen.

Oh my hell. I was just finger banged in public, and it might very well have been the best orgasm of my life.

What now?

Slowly, Pax pulls his hand out from under my skirt and lifts it above the table, licking his forefinger and middle finger as his eyes hold mine. "Well, would you look at that. I found a new favorite dessert." He smirks. "Told you I was in for the long game. Shall we?"

He's right. We've been here long enough. All things considered, it's probably best if I get out of here as soon as possible before my brain catches up with my libido and I have to come to terms with the fact that a stranger had his fingers in my va-jay-jay in the middle of a fast food restaurant on my birthday. Oh. My Hell. Even stringing those words together in my brain feels so wrong it's not even funny.

Ignoring the heat in my cheeks, I smooth out my skirt. "Uh, yup. Yup, that's a great idea."

The table's littered with what's left of our meal, and I start to clean up, anxious to get the hell out of here when he swats at my hand. "Stay."

"Stay?"

"Yes. Stay," he repeats. "I'll take care of this, Birthday Girl."

"Pretty sure you've already taken care of enough," I counter.

He crowds me against the table. "Trust me. I'm only getting started." Then he moves away and begins collecting our garbage.

If I wasn't still reeling from what just happened—or how hot his not-so-thinly-veiled comment makes me–there's no way I'd let him order me around. But I'm too stunned to argue as he picks up after us. I shouldn't notice the way his corded forearms are dusted with hair, or how his fingers are still damp with remnants of what we just did as he reaches for the empty cup of fries we devoured, but I do. My attention snaps back to his, and I gather whatever wits are still in my frazzled brain. "I think I know how to clean up a little mess."

"Yeah, but do you know how to let someone else clean it up for you?"

With a scoff, I settle back into the booth while he continues picking up every piece of garbage.

The veins along the back of his hands toy with me every time he reaches for something else, and I clear my throat. "Who knew you were such a gentleman?"

"Don't let the tattoos fool you." He bends toward me, his body stretching right in front of me as he grabs the last cup. It's my chocolate shake. Or what's left of it. Holding my gaze, he steals a bite and licks the spoon, dragging his tongue along the back of it as if he knows it was this exact imagery that pushed me over the edge moments before. Hell, you'd think it has a direct connection to my lady bits. And honestly? With the way they're still pulsing, it might.

"Wouldn't dream of it."

# 7

# PAXTON

I think I broke her. Not literally. Hell, I barely touched her. But she's quiet. And from what little I've gathered about the woman, I have a hunch she's rarely quiet. Did I push her too far? We haven't even kissed, but I finger-fucked her in the middle of a restaurant. It was empty, and she asked me to, but still.

The parking lot is empty as we walk toward my bike.

"Thanks for the, uh, the burger," Tatum murmurs. It's dark. There's a chill in the air. Digging in my pouch, I pull out a leather jacket and offer it. With a shy smile, she unfolds her arms and turns around, letting me dress her. Lifting her shoulder, she presses her nose to the thick material and breathes in deep.

"You good?" I ask.

"Smells like you."

I nod. "Is that a problem?"

With a slow shake of her head, she gives me her full attention. "You are many things, Pax. Stinky isn't one of them."

I chuckle and pull her into me. "You good with what happened inside?"

"Is this you being concerned about me?"

"About whether or not I pushed you too far?" I challenge. "Yeah. Yeah, that's what I'm concerned about."

"Well, you can breathe easy, Mr. Security. I wanted it. I liked it. And I don't regret it in the least." She rubs her lips together, peeking up at me through her thick dark lashes. "But you'll have to cut me some slack for making me feel like I have Jell-O for legs. That was, uh, you have very talented fingers."

"You know, I think I've been told that a time or two."

She groans and smacks my chest. "Blah, don't remind me."

Gripping her ass the way I wanted to in the restaurant, I tug her into me again, and she melts like butter. Probably still riding the high from her orgasm, but I'm not complaining. My cock's so eager to blow its load, any touch will do.

"I've had fun tonight," I admit.

"That doesn't surprise me. You seem like you're a fan of handfuls."

Another rumble of amusement claws its way up my throat. "Is that what you are? A handful?"

"Mm-hmm."

Reaching down, I grip the edge of her hip and squeeze her round ass. "Normally, I'm not so easy to read."

"Give me a little more credit," she quips. "Maybe I'm just really good at reading people."

I believe it. Those hazel eyes don't seem like they miss much.

Curious, I ask, "And what am I thinking now?"

Her gaze narrows as she smooths out the fabric over my chest. "You're hoping I'll invite you to my hotel so we can finish what you started."

"What *I* started?" I laugh. "You're the one who told me what you wanted for your birthday."

"And you were more than happy to oblige," she quips. "In a public restaurant."

"Gotta make your birthday a memorable one. After all, it's your twenty-first. Although, now that I think about it, I'm pretty sure I owe you at least one more *gift* for the evening."

She beams back at me, though I don't miss the edge of sass accompanying it. "You do, don't you? And maybe, if you're lucky, I'll return the favor."

"How generous of you. But it's your birthday, not mine."

Her brow lifts. "Unselfish *and* good with your hands?"

"You should see what my mouth can do."

Her smile widens. "You should see what *my* mouth can do."

My cock jerks in my jeans, and I move toward her, pinning Tatum to my bike as she stares up at me with a coy smile I'd give anything to taste. "Careful," I warn. "I'm already rock hard."

"Are you saying you don't want my mouth, Paxton?" She nibbles her bottom lip and peeks up at me through her thick, dark lashes.

My cock flexes again. It's addictive. The look in her eyes. The sass. The push and the pull I've felt more with her than anyone I've ever been around, and we just met. She's a fucking tease, but I like it. I like it a lot more than I should, and I fight the urge to grind against her right here, right now. "I feel like this is a test."

Her mouth curves just the slightest. "Maybe."

Unable to help myself, I steal a kiss, dragging my tongue along the seam of her lips as my hands find her waist. I push myself against her, letting her feel exactly what she does to me, my erection pressing against her stomach. After a sharp inhale, she tilts her head and opens her mouth wider. Chocolate's on her breath from her birthday shake. It only makes me crave her more. I dip my tongue into her mouth, committing her taste to memory. When I pull back, she sucks in a quick breath, her gaze nothing but fucking lava.

"Kiss me again," she orders. But I can still hear it. The breathiness. The plea. She thinks she's in charge, but she's as weak for me as I am for her. Putting us out of our misery, I bridge the gap between us, and she slips her fingers through the hair at the nape of my neck, tugging gently. The slight pain shoots straight to my groin, and I fight back my groan. Fuck, this girl is something else. Arching her back, she presses her body against mine. Her curves mold to me, and I like it. A lot.

"Gonna tell me to get on my knees yet?" she breathes out.

"Nah, but I am gonna tell you to open them."

"We're in public," she reminds me.

"Didn't stop us before."

She shakes her head, fighting back her amusement. "You know, you're way too famous to be this careless."

She's right. I am too famous to be pulling shit like this. Maybe it's because it's the middle of the night. Maybe it's because I'm supposed to be at the meet and greet instead of outside a burger joint pressed against a girl I've just met. Maybe it's because Judge's family pays for the best PR firm in the US—not because the band can't afford it, but because his family is anal about everything, but most importantly, public perception—who've already proven they know how to cover the band's tracks whenever necessary. And maybe it's because the girl in front of me isn't looking at me like she wants to fuck a rockstar simply to claim she did. Nah, she's looking at me like tonight is a secret. One meant for only me and her.

"Do you want to invite me to your place?" I ask.

"You mean the hotel room I'm sharing with Rory?" She pats my chest. "No thank you. But I'm sure you'll think of something, Mr. Security." Reaching for the helmet on the seat, she slides it on and tilts her head back. Grabbing her throat, I bring her toward me, squeezing softly before redoing the buckle. It's like a twisted game of deja vu. Only this time, I know what she tastes like. The reminder makes it almost impossible to keep my hands to myself, though somehow, I manage. Once her helmet is in place, I slide mine on and climb onto the bike. She joins me without a word, wrapping her arms around my waist without any prodding from me.

I don't ask if she wants me to take the long or short way this time. Pretty sure my cock will split through my zipper if I prolong this any more than I already have. When we stop at a light, Tatum's hands around my waist dip lower. Her fingers brush against me through my jeans, and I drop my head forward, trying to maintain some semblance of control. She squeezes me, not even bothering for subtlety, and it only turns me on more.

"Careful," I warn.

She strokes me again, and I swear I see stars.

Running my tongue between my upper teeth and lip, I pull out my phone.

ME

Get me a room at The Grande.

DANNY

For tonight?

ME

Yeah. Don't tell anyone else.

DANNY

Give me five. I'll put it under the usual name.

ME

Thanks.

Then I shove my phone back into my pocket, the light turns green, and we're off.

~

Tatum doesn't ask if I got a room. She doesn't ask why I got one, either. Nah, the girl's smarter than that, and she knows exactly what she's doing to me. How she has me wrapped around her little finger, the same way she was wrapped around mine at the restaurant. Despite being a rockstar, I don't normally do this. Invite a girl on stage. Buy her dinner. Ask her about herself. Book a hotel room. I'm more of a where's-an-empty-closet kind of guy. It's a little messed up, but it is what it is. So, this? This is throwing me off, but I'm too interested to back down now. Not unless she tells me to.

Tatum's standing by the elevator. Her long black hair a tousled mess from the helmet and the ride over here. She's still wearing my jacket. It's left open and reaches past the hem of her skirt. The sleeves go well past her fingertips, falling in loose folds by her bent elbows as she chews on the edge of her thumb. Gorgeous. *Nervous.* And gorgeous.

"Will that be all?" the receptionist asks.

I turn back to the front desk, finish checking in, and take the key to my room before leading us to the penthouse. It's quiet. Usually, my nights are filled with after parties, random faces, and alcohol. This is…different.

"I need to call Rory," Tatum murmurs. "Make sure she got to the hotel safely." She pulls out her phone, her hips swaying with every step before she opens the sliding glass door and closes it behind her.

She didn't ask permission. Not that she needed to, but still. Most girls I've been with would've said, "Are you okay if I call Rory?" as if my opinion—or my time—matters.

Tatum? Tatum doesn't give a flying fuck, and it's a hot as hell.

Resting her elbows on the balcony railing, she brings the phone to her ear, though I can't hear what's said thanks to the tall glass door separating us. Her long legs tease me from beneath her skirt, her silhouette acting like gasoline as the moon shines in front of her, highlighting her curves.

Fucking gorgeous.

When she hangs up a minute later, I grab a cigarette from my pocket and stride toward her on the balcony. The city lights are far below, though I'm too distracted by the girl beside me to care. I balance the cigarette between my lips and flick the lighter, my body craving the nicotine almost as much as it craves the woman beside me. As it flares to life, Tatum stares at the orange flame, her lips pursing when I take a deep drag.

There's that look again. I wondered if I'd imagined it when we left the concert, but here it is. Front and center.

"There a problem?" I ask.

"You smoke."

"You already knew that." I rest my elbows on the railing but keep my neck craned toward her. "And if my memory serves me right, I thought you said you snuck out to have a smoke before the show."

"And I thought you were less gullible than that," she counters.

"Ah, so not a smoker. Just a liar." I tap my temple. "I'll keep it in mind."

She sighs, her grip clenching on the wrought iron. "You should put it out."

"Why? 'Cause it'll kill me?" I ask, sucking in another plume of smoke, then blowing it out. "Only the good die young, Birthday Girl."

Something flashes in her pretty eyes, though it's gone in

an instant. Reaching up, she plucks the cigarette from my mouth, brings it behind her back, and presses her chest to me.

"Someone's feisty," I note.

"I don't like the taste of smoke."

"You didn't seem to mind at the restaurant."

"That was after gum *and* food," she points out. "Now, are you going to make me ask for a kiss or are you smarter than that?"

The girl doesn't have to tell me twice. My mouth lifts, and I pull her into me, kissing her neck. When the bud slips from her fingers and falls to the ground, I snuff it out with my shoe while my hands trail down her spine.

There it is again. Her unapologetic, hit-you-over-the-head-with-it remark. I like it. How she isn't afraid to speak her mind or tell me what she wants. It's rare. Most girls think if they voice what they want, they're dulling the fantasy or some shit, but they're wrong. And let's be honest. Most guys are idiots. If they aren't explicitly told what to do, they won't do it. If I had to guess, Tatum's learned firsthand, and instead of bitching about it, she became more blunt. It's a major turn-on.

As I trail my lips along her skin, Tatum turns her head, stealing a kiss. It's almost…hesitant. Nothing like before.

My brows dip, and I pull away. "You good?"

"Mm-hmm." She laces her hands around my neck, tugs me closer before I can question her, and opens her mouth, sucking on my tongue the same way I imagine she would my cock. The imagery is enough to make my head spin. I squeeze her ass, letting her feel me against her.

"Mm-hmm," she repeats, humming against me as if to say, "Yes. This is why I'm here." To hook up and get off. Not to look at the stars or learn anything about each other except what drives the other person wild. And she's right. I'm almost ashamed I needed the reminder.

I reach for the backs of her thighs and pick her up, ready to worship every inch of her after an entire night of foreplay. Once her legs circle my waist, I carry her inside, lay her on one of the leather couches, and pin her in place. With forearms on both sides of her head, I kiss her harder, grinding myself against her pussy as she mewls softly. The sound is like gasoline on an already blazing inferno, and it takes everything inside me to keep from ripping her clothes off and rutting into her like a wild animal. Ignoring my throbbing cock, I slide down her body, reach for her skirt, unbutton the top, and tug it down her legs and off her feet before doing the same to her thong. Spreading her pussy, I kiss her folds softly, blowing air on her clit until she squirms beneath me. Fuck, I love this. Watching what I do to her. How she reacts to me. The tiny whimpers. The quivering mess. Her leg muscles tighten as if she's thinking of closing them, but I dig my fingers into the soft flesh, keeping her spread wide for me.

I like her like this. At my mercy. Dripping. Begging. And so fucking ready for whatever I'm willing to give her.

Diving in for another kiss, I lap at her pussy, swirling the tip of my tongue against her opening and pressing the flat of it against her pulsing clit. Another gasp escapes her as her hands find my hair, twisting the strands into her fist until my scalp twinges as she pushes me against her center.

I think she likes it.

With a smirk, I look up before thrusting my tongue inside of her, and fuck, what I wouldn't give for it to be my aching cock. She's pretty like this. Desperate and needy. Her fingers claw at my scalp, threatening to yank every strand of hair from my head as I fuck her with my tongue, but the unhinged desperation only makes me greedier. To see how far I can push her. How quickly I can make her fall apart.

Her hips gyrate in tiny circles, meeting me move for move as I continue my assault. When I trust she won't move, I let go of her leg and glide my hand along the inside of her thigh. She feels like silk. Soft. Delicate. *Perfect.* Reaching her slit, I slide my forefinger inside, appreciating how wet she is as I move my mouth back to her clit. Sucking on her, I pump my finger in and out until her muscles clamp around my ears and her back arches off the couch. Spasming. And then... liquid.

She melts, her body oozing into the cushions as I kiss my way up her body, savoring every fucking inch. Gently, I drag my fingers along her hairline, pushing her hair away from her face. The girl's gorgeous. She's always gorgeous, but this face? This post-orgasmic, glassy-eyed, soft-smiled expression makes me want to puff out my chest and pound against it in pride. I put this there. Me.

With a soft kiss, I murmur, "Happy birthday."

She sighs, letting her eyes close. "I changed my mind."

"What?"

"I want three."

"Three?"

"Three orgasms," she clarifies before blinking away her post-orgasmic haze. "I want a third one."

"So greedy," I muse.

She shakes her head. "I believe you mean so *generous.*"

"Is that right?"

"Mm-hmm."

"And who's being generous?" I challenge, tossing her own word back at her. "You or me?"

"Me, obviously." She grins. "You're welcome for letting you touch me, by the way."

My fingers drag along her skin, committing every curve, every silky inch, to memory. "You are a prize."

"I thought I was a fan," she argues dryly. "And a perk."

"And a groupie?" I offer, well-aware she's seconds from smacking me. I can't help it, though. She's cute when she's fired up.

"You're pushing your luck, Mr. Security. Now about that third orgasm…"

I laugh and kiss her nose. "And how would you like it?"

"Well, let's see." She nibbles her bottom lip. "I've had your hand and your mouth. The only thing missing from the trifecta is the thing between your legs."

"You saying you want my cock, Birthday Girl?"

"Do you have a condom?"

My mouth quirks. "I'm a rockstar."

"Yeah, I'm aware this isn't your first rodeo, but thanks for the reminder." She rolls her eyes.

"What? It doesn't turn you on?"

"You being a famous rockstar who's had your dick in who knows how many holes?" She scoffs. "Hardly."

"Yet here you are," I point out. "Spread out beneath me, your taste still on my tongue and requesting a third orgasm."

Her eyes drop to my mouth as if my words alone are enough to get her there again before she meets my gaze once more. "Give me a little more credit. Maybe your charming personality got you here."

"Is that right?"

"Mm-hmm. That and your body." She drags her fingers beneath my shirt and along my spine, spreading a trail of goosebumps across my skin as she continues, "Although, if you want to stay here, you need to promise me something."

"What?"

I dive in for another kiss, but she presses her hand to my chest, stopping me. "One night only," she whispers.

I pull back, surprised by the sheer stubbornness in her pretty gaze. "Isn't that my line?"

"I mean it," she pushes. "At the show, you said you like the chase." She licks her lips. "Promise you won't chase me."

"Tate—"

"Promise me."

A stone lands in my gut. She wants me to promise I won't chase her after this? I stare at her, confusion and intrigue coursing through me. She really is serious. She only wants one night. One time. One memory to take with her as she goes about the rest of her life. And, it's not like I want more, but…damn.

She's confident. I'll give her that much. I've never had a girl draw a line in the sand like this. Like it really is meaningless. Like the only reason I'm here is to get her off. And even though I've been in her shoes more times than I can count in this profession—only wanting one thing from the girls I pick up after a show—it doesn't soften the hit to my ego.

So this is what it feels like. To be on the other side. To be the one pushed away. Fuck, I don't think I like it.

Refusing to let it go, I challenge, "What? You afraid I'll get attached or something?"

"Promise me, Pax." It's a whisper. A plea. And fuck, if it doesn't mess with my head.

"I promise." Unzipping my jeans, I shift them down and slip on a condom. Once it's in place, I grab her thigh, hooking it over my hip until my cock is pressed against her slit. "Ready?"

"Do you always ask your conquests that question?"

"Do you always chat this much when fucking?"

"Well, since we aren't technically fucking yet—"

Her jaw drops as I thrust into her, practically ripping the girl in two. And maybe I would've if I hadn't primed her earlier. Twice. Her core squeezes around me, practically weeping.

"Again," she begs.

I pull out of her, then shove myself back inside, and she gasps. "Just like that. Slow and hard."

Doing as I'm told, I repeat the movement, but this time she jerks her hips into the air and meets me halfway. Fuck, I'm so deep, part of me wonders where she ends and I begin. Her center squeezes around me with every thrust. I swear I'm about to black out as she tugs me into her and kisses me, hooking her legs around my waist.

"Careful," I growl. "If you keep squeezing me like that, I'm gonna come."

Her walls constrict around me again, and her breath brushes against my lips. "If you keep hitting that spot, then I'm gonna come."

My fingers dig into her thigh, and she arches her back even more, squeezing her eyes shut and clawing at my shoulder blades beneath my shirt as if she's determined to drag me down with her.

"Just." *Thrust.* "Like." *Thrust.* Her nails find my scalp and scrape against it as she falls apart beneath me, her body tensing then melting like before. "Pax," she moans.

I tumble after her, my cock spurting inside her tight little body until my arms give out and I collapse on top of her. It's like she's sucked every last piece of me, leaving me bone dry, exhausted, and so damn satiated, I'm pretty sure I can officially die a happy man.

My breath is unsteady as I try to slow my racing pulse, but I feel like I just finished a marathon.

*Now where's my gold medal? Oh, wait...*

With a smile, I kiss the crown of Tatum's head. "Stay."

Her lips brush against my Adam's apple, then she settles back into the cushions. "Promise me something. Something else," she clarifies, referring to her non-negotiable one-time-only clause before I entered her.

"How come you're the only one who's allowed to make requests?" I challenge. My fingertips drag along her sides as I savor her silky skin beneath me. "Stay with me tonight."

"Quit smoking."

I lift my head and look down at her. "What?"

"Promise me you'll quit smoking."

My eyes widen.

I've had women ask me a lot of shit, but no one's ever asked me to quit smoking. If anything, they ask for a hit after I light up, and I usually give it to them.

A sheen of indecision glazes her pretty eyes as she forces herself to look at me. It cuts straight through me, nearly knocking me on my ass despite the fact that she's very much still pinned beneath me on the couch.

"You're right about the good dying young, Pax," she whispers. "And I know you don't know me. I know I have no say in what you do with your life. I know you're an untouchable rockstar, but…you should quit." She sniffs and licks her lips again, her focus dropping to my chin, like she can't even look at me anymore, and fuck if it doesn't hurt. And even though I can literally feel her pulling away, part of me wonders if this is the first time I've really seen the gorgeous girl named Tatum since meeting her tonight. Dropping her tone even softer, she adds, "You should quit for yourself. For your fans. For the people who love you. Okay?"

Pushing her hair away from her face, I lean forward and kiss the tip of her nose in hopes of dissipating the little dark cloud that popped up out of nowhere. "Stay with me, and I will."

She shakes her head. "That's not fair."

"Why not?"

Her soft body stiffens, and she pulls away, pushing her

head even further into the couch cushions behind her. "Because we promised one night."

"So?"

"So, if I stay, this…whatever this is, will bleed into two, and I'm sorry, but I can't let that happen."

Disappointment surges through me, but I hold my ground. "Why not?"

Something clouds her pretty gaze before she states the obvious. "Because you're a rockstar."

"So?" I repeat.

"So, you're a rockstar and I'm… Pax, I'm no one." She slips out from beneath me and reaches for her clothes. "I'm not even a groupie. I'm just…some girl you hooked up with after a concert one time. Add me to the list, am I right?"

The accusation cuts, but I shove the feeling aside. "So, because I've done this before, you refuse to stay the night?"

She slips her shirt over her head. "I refuse to stay the night because I'm not interested in…anything else."

"Well, fuck." I force a laugh and squeeze the back of my neck as she shifts her skirt into place. "Talk about a blow to the ego."

She smirks. "I think you'll survive."

"Don't be so sure," I mutter, sliding the condom off, tying a small knot at the end, and tossing it in the trash. "Can I at least have your number?"

"No."

I jerk back, trying not to be offended, though it isn't exactly easy. Not when she seems so distant and unaffected. "Why not?" I ask.

"Because we already agreed to one night only and you're not allowed to chase me."

"Then don't run," I suggest.

Unamused, she drops her head back toward the ceiling. "Pax…"

"Give me a chance," I push. I don't know why. I've never been interested in more than a night, but this one? This one felt different. She felt different. I can't be the only one who felt…something. Can I? "Give me a chance," I repeat, more resolute than before.

"No."

"Why?"

With a sigh, she rolls her head forward, her eyes glazed with indecision. "Because I'm…"

I wait for her to finish, but when I'm only met with silence, I argue, "Don't tell me you're not interested, Birthday Girl. I had you moaning my name less than five minutes ago."

Her mouth lifts an inch. "You're good in bed, Pax. That doesn't mean you've earned my number."

"What about before?" I demand. "What about the restaurant? I'm not saying I want to marry you, but I'm also not stupid. You had fun tonight. We *both* had fun tonight, and if you're gonna play hard to get, I have no problem asking Dodge—"

"You can't do that," she rushes out. Her indifferent facade cracks, giving me a front-row seat to her panicked expression. Hell, she doesn't even look panicked, she looks…downright terrified.

My Adam's apple bobs in my throat as I study her carefully. She's hiding something from me. I just can't figure out what it is. "Why won't you give me your number?" I ask.

"Because I'm…because I'm already with someone."

"With someone," I repeat, feeling less than convinced. This girl spews more bullshit than a lactose intolerant person after a pound of cheesecake and a bottle of Ex-Lax to wash it down. But the panic? The terror? It's real.

*What are you hiding?*

"Yes, with someone." She scowls at me, clearly picking up

on my suspicion and unafraid of backing down. "I'm engaged."

My muscles seize, and I swear my vision cuts to black before I blink it away. But here she is. Standing in the middle of the hotel room. Looking thoroughly gorgeous in a just-fucked kind of way. Her hair a mess. Her lips swollen from my mouth. How did tonight turn upside down so quickly?

She lets her confession hang in the air. Lets it fuck with my head. Lets it taint the high of our night together, leaving me empty and confused and…fuck, is she really serious? "What did you say?" I breathe out, convincing myself I misheard her.

"I said, I'm engaged," she repeats. "That's why you can't see me again. Why you can't ask Dodger for my number. Because if you do, my fiancé will find out and—"

I surge to my feet. "Who is he?"

She flinches. "What?"

"Who is he? What's his name?"

She's gotta be lying. No one cheats on their fiance like that. Like we just did. No one spends the night connecting with someone—sharing pieces of themselves with someone —only to walk away without a backward glance. It's bullshit. It has to be.

"I— You—" She shifts away, reminding me of a cornered alley cat. "You have no right to ask me that."

"Cat got your tongue, Birthday Girl?" I demand. My cock is still hanging out for the world to see, but I don't give a shit. Not right now. I'm too fucking pissed. "What's. His. Name?"

"Archer," she blurts out. "His name's Archer, all right?" Regret and shame flash across her pretty face, proving I've hit a nerve. And for the first time since we finished having sex, I'm afraid she's telling the truth.

*Fuck, is she telling the truth?*

"Now, will you please just…let it go?" she whispers.

"Let it go," I repeat, convinced I must've rolled off the couch mid-orgasm and hit my head or something. But I didn't. No. Instead, I'm standing six inches from the girl who cheated on her fiance with me. A girl who I actually felt a connection with. And fuck, it hurts and only pisses me off more. Pinching the bridge of my nose, I ask, "What was this?"

She stays quiet, her lips forming a small 'o' as she breathes out whatever's left of her indecision and straightens her spine. "This was my last...hurrah before being tied down," she clarifies. "And who wouldn't want to take advantage of a night with a rockstar, you know?"

"So I'm just a rich dick to you."

"I mean, look at it this way. You got a fun night with a groupie, and I got a memorable birthday present from a rockstar. Sounds like a win-win to me, am I right?"

Red taints my vision. "You lied."

"I guess I did, didn't I?" She twists the gold ring around her middle finger and lifts a shoulder, appearing about as affected by our conversation as she would watching paint dry. "Even more reason to not track me down after I walk out the door."

I stare down at her, disgusted. Pretty sure she's never felt like more of a stranger than in this moment. "Who. Are. You?" I demand.

She flinches at the animosity in my voice before lowering her chin in a soft nod. "Have a good night, Pax."

Then, she walks away.

# 8

# TATUM

Dear Archer,

Hi.

I wipe at my tear-stained cheeks and scratch out the word before writing beside it. God, I'm a mess, and I don't even know why. Okay, scratch that. I might have an idea, but the possibility is something I refuse to acknowledge. It's just a bad day. That's all. Tomorrow will be better. Or maybe it won't. It's not like it matters anyway, right?

I shake my head and force myself to focus on the page in front of me no matter how impossible it feels.

*I miss you. I know it's stupid. I know you won't reply. You can't. You're dead. But my therapist told me to write to you. He said I should get some things off my chest. That I should tell you everything I wanted to say before you died.*

*I told him it was a waste of time, and in a way, I guess it still is. But it's been years, Arch. Years since you left. Since your life was ripped from you. And it's weird. Because it feels like it was yesterday. Like you were just here. Just a text away. That I'll see you at brunch...or at least I would if I still went to them.*

I shake my head and scribble out the sentence and start again.

*Then, I think of all the pain I've been drowning in since your death, and...it twists the time, making it drag out into...fucking eternity. Hell, it feels like it's been so long that I don't even know how to live without it. The pain. The constant ache. The reminder that you're gone and everyone else is still here. Living. It's why I hate brunch. Why I hate Mav and Ophelia and Lockwood Heights in general. Because you're supposed to be here, Arch. But you aren't. You aren't here. Does that make sense?*

A pathetic laugh escapes me as I wipe beneath my nose and continue writing.

*What am I saying? Of course, it doesn't*

*make sense. I'm writing to a dead person. None of this makes sense. All I know is I'm tired. So damn tired, Arch. I don't know what else to do. How can I let someone go when they were never mine to begin with?*

My pen hovers above the page.

*How can I let someone go when they were never mine to begin with?*

I suck my bottom lip into my mouth and bite down. Hard.

I can't.

*I've tried. Trust me, I've tried, Arch. But even now, I miss you. You used to tell me I could come to you for anything. I'm not sure if you would even remember telling me that if you were still here, but you did. And honestly, I miss that, too. Knowing I had someone. Someone who saw me.*

*Now? Now, I'm afraid I'm as much of a ghost as you are. But maybe it's how it's supposed to be.*

*Love,*

*-Tatum*

9

## TATUM

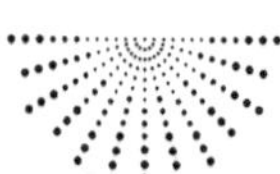

A FEW YEARS LATER...

Staring at my packed bag on the edge of the bed, I gnaw on my lower lip and press call.

It rings twice before a familiar voice answers, bringing a smile to my face.

"Hello?"

"Rore!" I keep my voice especially syrupy sweet in hopes of buttering her up a bit. "I miss you! How are you?"

"I'm good. How're the travels?"

Picking at the edge of the threadbare comforter, I lie, "Good."

"You sure about that?"

My nose wrinkles. "Okay, I guess I could be a little better."

"Uh-oh. What happened?"

"Nothing?"

"Tate…"

I bite the edge of my thumb and look up at the popcorn ceiling. I've been here for what, two? Three weeks? Damn, has it been a month already? Crazy how time moves differently when you're traveling.

"Tate?" Rory prods. "You there?"

"Yeah, I'm here." I close my eyes in an attempt to focus. "I was, uh, I was wondering if I could come out and see you?"

"See me, huh? What? Have you run out of money again on all your travels?"

"Ouch." I peek out the small window, so I can soak up my last sunrise in Cabo. "And no. Technically, I have a hundred dollars to my name, but thanks for the vote of confidence."

"I knew it!" Rory laughs.

"You know, I could always resort to picking up random dudes and bed hopping for the foreseeable future instead of visiting."

"Yeah, why not bring home a few STDs with your souvenirs?" she teases.

Refusing to let her shame me about my sex life, I toss back, "Hey, STDs, souvenirs, *and* a solid orgasm or two, since we both know—"

"Faking it is for pussies," she finishes for me. "Yes, I'm aware of your standards."

"Well, at least you've learned *something* from me."

"Uh-huh. I've learned your taste in men is deplorable."

With a smirk, I bring my knees to my chest on the bed and rest my back against the wall. "Bad boys do it better. What can I say?"

"Until they ask for more than one night."

My nose wrinkles. "Blah. I know. It's annoying. And they say we're the needy sex. But at least I'm having fun. How's that v-card treating you, anyway?"

"You're super funny," she grumbles.

"Thanks, I get it from my mom."

She snorts. "You know, you could always give one of your one-night stands a real chance."

"And cheat on my best friend?" I quip. "You know you're the only one for me."

"Yeah, yeah. I know you love me. It's too bad we're straight, am I right?"

"Yes," I groan, resting my forehead against my bent knees. "Life would be so much easier if we were attracted to women."

"Amen," she agrees. "So, does this mean you're finally giving in and coming to stay long-term, or is this only another *visit* until you earn enough money to leave me again?"

"Depends. Is your brother going to crash our party *again*?" I counter.

It was a few months ago. I was staying at Rory's apartment when Maverick showed up with Lia in tow. Talk about an oh-shit moment. I barely made it through the pleasantries before packing a bag and buying the first bus ticket I could find to get me out of there. Even if my sister hadn't tagged along with Mav, I still would've left, though. It's nothing personal. But looking at someone who shares the face of a person who died has a way of messing with your head, you know? Okay, maybe it is a little personal. Maverick is Archer's identical twin. They looked so much alike, only a handful of people could tell them apart. It's one of Lia's favorite things to brag about. That she could always tell them apart.

I could, too, you know.

And even if they don't look like exact replicas of each other, the in your face—pun intended—reminder isn't exactly an easy pill to swallow.

The history between Archer, Mav, and Ophelia is murky at best. Don't get me wrong. Mav is a good guy despite stabbing his brother in the back before taking his heart. Literally. Mav had HCM—a rare heart disease—but he kept the diagnosis to himself, wreaking all kinds of havoc in my sister's life. After Mav broke up with Ophelia, Archer rode in on his white horse, and she started dating him. Classy of her, I know. When I caught my older sister hooking up with Mav behind Archer's back, she swore she'd broken up with Arch first, but that didn't make it any better. She hurt the one person in this world who didn't deserve it, and what did Archer do? He forgave them, proving just how perfect he is. Was. Soon after, Archer passed away in a car accident. He was an organ donor, and Mav got his heart, shattering mine in the process.

Our families call it a miracle. Maybe it is, but I can't help but hold a grudge against fate for fucking him over like that. Archer was…he was as close to perfect as a person can be. Thoughtful. Caring. Kind. Charismatic. Genuine. He was amazing.

And even though Mav has spent years trying to be the best person he can be in hopes of…I don't know? Making things right with the world? It still doesn't ease the ache. The reminder that he's here when Archer isn't. That without Archer, he wouldn't be here at all. And Archer would.

But even then, even if fate dealt a different hand, Archer still wouldn't be mine. He'd be Ophelia's, or at the very least still obsessed with her. And if that isn't a punch to the boob, I don't know what is.

"Pretty sure Mav and Ophelia wouldn't fit in my new place even if they wanted to visit," Rory continues. "They're in Uganda for the next three months."

Her voice cuts through my thoughts. I shift my cell to my other ear, attempting to focus on our conversation instead of getting lost in the past. In the plaguing what ifs that never seem to rest despite the years they've haunted me. "That's, uh, good for them," I answer.

"Thought you'd like that." Rory chuckles. "But like I said, there won't be any surprise pop-ins. Which means, you should think about staying a while this time. As long as you're good with close quarters."

The last time we spoke, Rory mentioned she might be moving again, though I didn't know she actually went through with it. "Sick of the neighbors above, huh?"

"You have no idea," she mutters. "Besides, this place might be tiny, but it's only a mile from the beach, a five-minute walk from my classes, and the people beneath me own the place and are so freaking cute. They always leave the yummiest treats by my door. Seriously, you'll love them."

"I'm sure I will," I mutter. "Speaking of loving people and vice versa…"

"Yes?" She drags out the word.

Ignoring the skepticism in her voice, I announce, "After looking up flights, I may or may not have found a potential job in Harden Heights and put you on another resume."

"Tatum," she groans. "Every time you do that, I have to lie."

I gasp. "Excuse me! Who says you need to lie?"

"So, you'd like me to tell your potential employers how you have a penchant for sleeping in, missing shifts, and quitting at the drop of a hat anytime the going gets rough?"

My jaw drops. I'm surprised at how quick she had that locked and loaded. "Ouch."

"I'm just saying…"

"That I have a penchant for sleeping in, missing shifts, and quitting at the drop of a hat anytime the going gets rough?" I finish for her.

She doesn't deny it, and honestly, I'm impressed. Before I took her under my wing, she didn't have a backbone. Now, I can barely get anything past her.

Shoving my pride aside, I beg, "I swear I'll be good this time. The perfect employee, I promise."

"Uh-huh. Sure."

"Rore, I'm serious!"

"And what kind of job is it?" she asks.

"A cleaning service," I offer. "It's actually perfect for me. I can make my own schedule, the mansions are empty almost a hundred percent of the time so I don't have to see or talk to anyone and potentially piss them off, and I can listen to audiobooks or music while I clean. Oh, and did I mention the money is not only decent, but I can pick up as many houses as I want, which means I won't spiral. See? It's a win-win-win."

"Sure it is," she mumbles.

"Come on, Rore. I gotta find something to pass the time while you're at school."

"Promise me you won't get fired," she grumbles.

"Promise."

"And you'll put in a two weeks' notice like a thoughtful human being before you pick up and leave again."

I lift my hand despite Rory not being able to see me and reply, "Scout's honor."

She sighs. "When did you give them my name?"

"Right before I called," I quip. "And after I bought my plane ticket. Any chance you can pick me up at the airport in a few hours?"

"If I say no, do you have the money for an Uber?"

"I think we both know the answer to that."

Another sigh echoes through the speaker, and I know I've won her over.

"You owe me," she mutters.

"Add another tally to the count," I tease. "I'll text you the details. You're the best!"

I can hear the smile in her voice as she replies, "I know."

And she really is.

~

WHEN RORY MENTIONED SHE DOWNSIZED, SHE WASN'T kidding. The place is tiny. There isn't a couch. Or an actual bedroom. It's a studio apartment with barely enough room for one person, let alone two. Add in Rory's shadow, her demon German Shepherd, Hades, and the apartment is basically a can of sardines. Even so, Rory went the full nine yards in preparation for my visit. Twin beds are pressed against the walls on opposite sides of the room, and a television hangs on the end furthest from the front. It's framed by a door leading to the bathroom, and a small, half-empty closet I have no doubt should be—and would be—full if I hadn't called Rory, asking for a place to stay. Her clothes are lined up from pink to blue, creating a tiny rainbow with black and white fabric on both sides. Just like always. She hides it well. Most of the time, anyway. Her Obsessive Compulsive Disorder. Most people throw the diagnosis around like confetti. Writing off their preference for cleanliness as a silly quirk, when OCD is so much more. It's crippling. Consuming. And hits in the most random ways at the most random times.

"And here it is," Rory announces, squatting down to undo the leash from Hades' collar.

His tail whips my thigh, and I yelp in surprise as he dashes toward Rory's bed, jumping onto the fluffy blue blanket covering the bottom half of the mattress.

"Sorry," Rory says. "We're still working on Hades' manners."

"He's four," I remind her. "Pretty sure that ship has sailed."

"Hey, give him a little more credit!"

"You're right. At least he didn't try to bite my face off when I climbed into your car at the airport," I tease.

She sticks her tongue out at me but doesn't bother arguing. Rory's family has owned German Shepherds ever since her dad gifted her mom a puppy when they were dating. The rest is history. And even though I've always been one of their favorite people, Hades doesn't like anyone—and I mean *anyone*—but Rory. Now, it doesn't mean he attacks everyone who comes near her, despite my smartassery. Rory's family spent thousands of dollars on training when her OCD became too much after moving away. But he has no problem making his feelings about you very clear, and I've yet to meet anyone other than Rory that he's willing to warm up to. As Rory hangs up Hades' leash on the hook next to the front door, I take in the olive green cabinets and wood block countertops that separate the kitchen from the rest of the living space. Yup. This place is absolutely adorable. From the blue and white striped linens on the beds to the fluffy white rug covering the maple colored floors.

Gorgeous.

Facing me, Rory asks, "So, what do you think?"

"I think you're too good to me. Tell me you at least asked for help from…someone to swap whatever bed you had in here to two twins."

She grimaces. "Am I that transparent?"

"Yes. Yes, you are." Moving closer, I toss my arms around her shoulders and pull her into a hug. "And you're also the best. Thank you for putting up with me. I promise to start chipping in for rent as soon as I get my first paycheck."

She returns my hug, then lets me go. "I'll always put up with you. And don't worry about rent. I got it."

"Rory…"

"Seriously. Don't stress."

"I don't deserve you," I reply with a smile.

She grins back at me. "I know."

"So what's the nightlife like around here nowadays?" I ask.

"Depends on the time of year. There's a new place called The Pelican, though. I've been a few times. I think you'll like it, but we'll have to go tomorrow or something."

"Why not tonight?" I ask.

"School, then work."

I groan. "Blah, you're so boring."

"I believe the term you're searching for is responsible."

I cough into my fist, "Boring."

"Says the girl who would be homeless and jobless without me." She cups the back of her ear and tilts her head. "It's fine. I'll wait."

I roll my eyes. "Okay, I take it back. You're not boring. You're amazing and responsible and I don't know what I'd do without you."

Her mouth lifts, and she drops her hand to her side. "Much better."

"Smartass," I laugh. "But seriously. Thank you for letting me stay and for being willing to show me the bird place, even if it's not tonight."

"The Pelican," she sings.

"The bird place," I sing back. I rock back on my heels, scanning the apartment one more time. Yup. I'm going to like it here. "You mind if I use the shower while you're gone?"

"Have at it. Just be sure to—"

"Wash all the soap residue from the shampoo and conditioner before setting them back on the shelf and close the lid." I tap my temple. "You forget I know you, too."

Lips pursed, she gives Hades a scratch behind his ears. "Play nice, Hades. I know Tatum seems like she needs a bite in the ass every now and then, but let's give someone else that job, okay?" He licks her palm in response then rests his head on his blanket. Satisfied, Rory turns on her heel and snags her keys from the counter. "And on that note, I'll be back by nine."

"Love you," I call.

"Love you!"

# 10

# TATUM

I hate the quiet. I'm not sure who decided it's supposed to be peaceful, but I'm pretty sure my brain feels like it has a cheese grater pressed against it. Hell, even Hades is silent. Aren't dogs supposed to snore? I toss a piece of cereal at him to keep things interesting, but he only gives me the stink eye before shifting on the bed until his back is facing me.

"Rude," I mutter.

Reaching for my phone, I turn on a shuffle playlist, then set it down on the kitchen table.

I'm bored.

Usually, when I'm bored, I show up on a friend's doorstep or buy a plane ticket to a different country, but since I start a new job on Monday and I'm already staying at a friend's house, my options are…limited. Twiddling my thumbs, I scroll my social media when an IndieCent Vows song begins.

After my twenty-first birthday, I caved. Diving down the rabbit hole and basically memorizing every song written by the renowned band. I'm still not sure why. It's not like I thought it would help lessen my mild crush on their lead guitarist after the night we spent together or erase the memories I desperately wanted to wipe from my mind.

Okay, that's a lie.

I actually really like the memory...up until I lied out of my ass to the poor guy. To be fair, it wasn't the plan. To tell him I was engaged. But then he asked me to stay, and I actually wanted to, and...he probably hates me now. Hell, that's if he remembers me at all. It was one night. One stupid, meaningless night. Even so, I'm not too stubborn to admit that I think about it. About him. Where he is and what he's up to. How his life turned out. If he settled down. If he calls anyone else Birthday Girl.

Pax is...the strangest, most unique person I've ever slept with. How he rides the line between sexy rockstar and boy-next-door is something I'll never fully grasp, but he did it then, and based on these photos, I'm going to say he's still riding it like a champ. Speaking of riding, I wonder if he's seeing anyone. I dig my thumbnail into the edge of my middle finger, resisting the urge to search his dating history even when I know it's a terrible idea.

Before I can talk myself out of it, I open a new web browser and type in his name. Paxton Six. I doubt it's his real name, and if I felt like stalking the web long enough, I'm pretty positive I could find out what it is, but obsessing too much over a guy I want nothing to do with feels like bad juju, and I have enough of that as it is, thank you very much.

After typing his name into the search bar, I hit enter. Photo after photo appears in an instant. His hair's longer than it used to be. Shaggier. Guess he's leaning into the rock-star vibe now that IndieCent Vows isn't some up-and-coming indie band. Nope. They've made their splash and are holding strong. Smart man. The shaggier look suits him. My hand itches to reach out and touch it, but I stop myself. I pause on an image angled up from the edge of the stage. It's giving the perspective of a fan as he looks down at his guitar. His fingers are curled as they cradle the neck of the instrument while his other hand appears to be plucking the strings. I squeeze my legs together at the reminder of those hands and what they did to me before scanning the rest of the image. His skin glistens with sweat in the stage lights, highlighting his strong torso, broad shoulders, and the cords along his forearms.

Yup.

It's been around four years, and he's only grown hotter.

A low ache hits behind my sternum. I close the laptop, caught by surprise at how quickly it hit. The ache. Sucking my lips between my teeth, my attention catches on the edge of the worn notebook I've carried for years. I'm not stupid enough to let what's inside create a digital footprint that can be tracked or hacked or…seen by anyone but me. And even then, it's rare that I actually crack its pages open and reread the words I know are written inside. Yet, I can't let it go. Can't burn it or bury it. It's been around the world. Seen more countries than most people. It's funny. After Archer died, my parents forced me to see a therapist, hoping he could convince me to let the pain out. To let it go. As if writing my feelings would be easier than speaking them. And maybe it was. Maybe it still is. It's not like I haven't made a new entry or two over the past year, even if I'd never admit it out loud. Maybe today is one of those days. When I should purge the sadness instead of drowning in it.

Twisting a small gold ring around my finger, I chew the edge of my lip, then reach for the worn, black notebook.

I still remember when my mom brought home a six pack of them in rainbow colors. Black, blue, yellow, red, green, and purple-dyed leather. I gravitated to the inky cover immediately. It only deepened the divot between my mom's perfectly-shaped brows. She didn't say anything about it, though. Only turned her frown upside down as soon as she realized she'd been caught red-handed. Being worried about me. Some things never change.

With a sigh, I slip the notebook back in my laptop case and grab my phone instead. I dial my mom's number, bringing my cell to my ear.

As it rings, I nibble the edge of my black nail, ignoring the regret as it swirls through me. If I hang up, she'll only call back.

The call connects.

I exhale and rest my elbow on the table.

"Hey, babe," my mom starts.

"Tater Tot!" my dad chimes in.

I roll my eyes and shift on the chair. "Am I on speaker?"

"You really think I'd let your mom steal all the fun?" my dad asks. "I think the real question is, why in the world are you calling her and not me?"

"Figured you'd be at the chiropractor for your bad back, old man," I quip.

My mom's laughter tinkles through the speakers, but it isn't enough to drown out my dad's grumbled, "I'm not that old."

"You are, but it's okay. I still love ya," my mom counters. "So to what do we owe the pleasure, Tate?" she adds, addressing me. "It isn't even Sunday."

I smile in spite of myself. When I left Lockwood Heights years ago, my parents made me promise to call at least once a week after I ignored one too many phone calls. If I didn't reach out by Sunday, my phone would be in a constant state of vibration for the entire next week as punishment, along with a few dozen threats to call the police and track me down if I didn't respond to their texts. Don't get me wrong. I actually appreciated knowing they were thinking of me, even when I spent years pushing them away. Now, I find the weekly check-ins are the perfect way to recap everything that's happened over the last seven days. However, it's only Friday, so I'm early, and it hasn't gone unnoticed.

"We miss you!" my dad adds.

"Miss you, too. Just figured I'd check in and say hi."

"Well, hi," my mom replies before mentioning the name of a one-night-stand I had a month ago after I mistakenly brought him up to them. "How's the mysterious Roberto?"

"Roberto is no more."

"You killed him?" my dad chimes in, like we're discussing the weather instead of potential manslaughter.

I laugh. "No, but it's good to hear you think I'm capable of killing someone."

"We think you're capable of anything, Tater Tot," he reminds me.

"Not sure if I should be flattered or offended, but, uh, thank you?"

"You're welcome," my mom sing-songs.

"So, why no more Roberto?" my dad asks.

I stretch my legs out from beneath the table and cross one ankle over the other. "Because Roberto was a one-night-stand, which I've already told you about a billion times."

"I mean, I don't think you've told us a *billion* times," my mom argues.

"Yeah, only like ten," my dad agrees. "It's still fun to say his name, though. RIP, Roberto."

I pinch the bridge of my nose and hold in my amusement. "RIP, Roberto."

"So, where are you now?" my mom chimes in. "I was checking your location earlier today and it said you were flying over Texas?"

"I landed in Harden Heights earlier today."

"Aw, are you staying with Squeaks?" my mom asks.

"Yup," I reply. "I asked if I could crash with her for a little while, and she said yes, so, here I am."

"I love that. How's our Squeaks doing, anyway?" my dad questions.

"She's good," I answer.

"Seeing anyone?" my dad prods.

"Dad."

"You know her parents are gonna ask if we dug for dirt. She's almost as elusive as you are."

I smirk. "Yeah, but you're not even going to try to be subtle about it?"

"I think we all know your parents aren't known for being subtle, babe," my mom counters.

She's not wrong.

"So that's where I get it from," I say.

"Exactly," my dad confirms. "Don't say we never gave you anything."

I roll my eyes. "So generous."

"Always," he replies. "How's the new place?"

"Boring." I glance around the empty apartment and sigh. "Rory's at work, and Hades is ignoring me, so…"

"So that's why you called," my dad surmises. "Because you're bored and need entertainment."

With a grin, I drag my fingers along the edge of the table and reply, "Exactly."

"Well, honestly, I'm surprised we made the list. We're kind of boring over here, too. You could always call your sister, though. She's in Uganda—"

"I heard," I interrupt.

"Yeah? Well, she misses you. Asked if we could give her your new address so she can send a postcard?" my dad prods. "Says she texted you, but you didn't answer."

Guilt lines my insides as I look down at a knot in the wood table and trace it with my finger. "I've…been busy."

"Mm-hmm," my mom hums. "Well, just know she's thinking about you."

"Mm-hmm," I hum, mimicking her. "Well, I should probably get back to cleaning the house."

"Cleaning the house?" my mom laughs. "Come on, Tatum. Surely you can come up with a better lie."

"Okay, you really want to know what I'm going to do for the next two hours?" I ask.

"Hit us with it," my dad replies.

"I'm going to scroll social media and brain rot. Both of which are more interesting than this conversation. I was trying not to hurt your feelings by saying I needed to be doing something productive, but…" My dad's bark of amusement teases a smile from me as I shift my phone to my opposite ear. "I'll call you guys on Sunday, okay?"

"Deal," they say in unison. "Love you, baby!"

"Love you, too."

# 11

# TATUM

Okay, it's official. Rich people are way too trusting. Or maybe it's my boss who's lost her marbles. Who sends an address, gate code, and the location of a hide-a-key in an email labeled important info? My employer, that's who. Or maybe I think too much like a shady person, and I'm the problem. Who knows? Regardless, I'm late. Pressing a little harder on the gas, I try to stay focused on the winding road, though my eyes keep straying to the houses lining either side. Mustard yellow, lavender gray, hydrangea blue, sage green, and creamy white colonial style houses. Each is gated with stretching green lawns leading to the front of picture-perfect homes and expertly manicured flower beds that look straight out of an agriculture magazine.

Absolutely—and annoyingly—gorgeous.

When I reach the address, I roll down the driver's window and type the gate code into the keypad.

The wrought iron gate jerks to life, opening and letting me enter the pristine fortress as the ocean air filters through the open driver's side window and into the cab of Rory's car.

Thank goodness she's able to walk to and from her classes without needing a vehicle. Seriously, I owe her one. Or you know, a thousand. Salt clings to the air, and I breathe in deep, grateful my best friend decided to settle down somewhere so freaking beautiful.

Once I pull into the driveway, I cut the engine and grab a cleaning bin from the backseat loaded with all the supplies listed in my employer's email. Heading to the side of the yard, I search for the not-so-well-disguised rock beneath a hydrangea. I pick it up and flip it over. The hide-a-key is inside like the email said it would be. Satisfied, I walk up the stone steps to the front door and insert the key. It works. My lips part as I take in the tall ceiling, winding wood stairs, and floor-to-ceiling windows giving the perfect view of the back-yard, which happens to be the freaking ocean.

"Holy shit."

Don't get me wrong. My dad played NHL hockey. We're definitely comfortable financially, and I was exposed to plenty of fancy shindigs, experienced a plethora of extrava-gant vacations, and had some pretty epic birthday parties. Not to mention the fact that my parents' best friends included other professional hockey players. And the Buchanans. Who are the Buchanans, you might ask? They're Rory's parents, who are freaking bajillionaires. So, yeah. I'm used to expensive shit. But this? This is something else entirely. Maybe it's the view. Maybe something in the air is going to my head. Maybe it's because the ambiance isn't tainted by being located in Lockwood Heights so I can actu-ally appreciate it instead of resenting it. Honestly, I don't really care about the reasons. All I know is I am officially speechless.

"That's it. I'm moving in," I announce to the empty house when my phone rings.

Setting the bin of cleaning supplies on the marble floor, I

pat my pockets and pull out my cell, finding my best friend's gorgeous face staring back at me from the screen.

"Hey, Rore," I answer.

"Hey! How's the place?"

"Uh, freaking beautiful?" I offer. "I've already decided I'm moving in."

"Already, huh?" she quips.

"It's not like you couldn't use the extra space." I head up the stairs but stop at the landing. There's a perfect view of the waves lazily rolling in through the floor-to-ceiling windows. "So, is the sky bluer here? Is the sand whiter or something?"

"What are you talking about?" Rory asks with a laugh.

"I'm just saying, the colors I'm seeing from this view are so picturesque, I might actually vomit."

"Just as long as you clean it up," she replies.

With a scoff, I continue my journey to the second floor. There's another couch, television, and bookshelf in the middle of the space, along with a handful of doors leading to various rooms. I peek inside the first one.

"So? How is it?" Rory prods.

"Massive bed. Massive window. Massive fluffy rug. Massive closet. Massive bathroom." I tick off everything I see like it's my grocery list, though I'm more than impressed. "Wanna bet when the owner's home, there's a massive ego in here, too?"

She snorts. "Nice."

Closing the bedroom door, I move to the next one and give the knob a twist.

"Well, damn," I mutter. "Someone likes staying in shape."

"They have a gym?" Rory asks.

"Yup."

There are free weights, a squat rack, a punching bag, a treadmill, a yoga mat. You name it, it's there. Along the walls are tall, wide windows, giving a perfect view of the ocean like the one by the stairs. I close the door, continuing my perusal. Giving Rory a play-by-play, I find another bathroom, a laundry room, and two more bedrooms. Yup, it's the whole shebang. When I reach the last door, I realize it's cracked. Curious, I push it open. "Holy shit, there's a music room."

"A music room?" she asks.

"Yup, a full-blown music room." I flick the lights on, and my jaw drops. Half a dozen guitars in a rainbow of colors sit mounted along the wall. On the opposite side is a set of drums and framed posters of different bands from the eighties, nineties, and two thousands, along with a bookshelf of records. I squint and move toward them, realizing they're signed. The posters.

"Rore, you should see this," I murmur.

"What is it?"

"There are records, posters, guitars, a drumset." I move to the custom bookshelf and start flipping through the albums. Half of the options I don't recognize, which is saying something because I'm a sucker for underground bands. The other half vary from Broken Vows to The Who to Rage Against the Machine to...my mouth lifts when my attention catches on Doomsday's logo. "This is insane."

"Aw, I'm so jealous," Rory gushes. "It sounds amazing."

"It really is, but I gotta go. I'll catch up with you later, okay?"

"Sure thing. See ya!"

"See ya, Rore."

Taking the Doomsday vinyl from its case, I start the record player and wait for the familiar notes I had on repeat for years. I still haven't seen them play live. I almost bought tickets last year but decided against it. I still don't know why. Or maybe I do. Maybe it's because, whether or not I'd ever admit it out loud, Doomsday reminds me of Pax, and Pax reminds me of…a lot of things I'd rather not think about. Seconds later, the song starts, and I roll up my sleeves. Time for work.

By the time the house is clean, I'm convinced the owner is my soulmate. Man or woman, twenty or eighty, I don't discriminate. This person gets me. There's a sauna, and a gym, and a library, and a gaming room, and a hot tub over-looking the ocean.

*Siiiigh.* If only I was rich.

Sweat drips down my back, and my body aches. But it's a good ache. A productive ache. Like after a good workout. When you know you've pushed yourself but also accomplished something. And with how freaking awesome every inch of this mansion looks? Well, I can't help but beam up at it when the garage door opens and the familiar click-click of heels echoes from the hall.

My body freezes, my fight or flight response going haywire in an instant. My boss said no one would be here. Hell, it was one of the biggest perks when I applied. So, what am I supposed to do now?

An older woman with blonde hair pulled into a slicked-back bun stops short when she sees me.

"Hello."

"Hi?" I offer.

"I assume you're the maid?"

"Yes, hi," I repeat. "My name's Tatum."

"Nice to meet you. I'm Mindy." Her attention barely drifts over me before she pulls her cell phone out. "Are you finished?"

"Uh, yup." I grab the bucket from the floor and toss the last rag into it. "I assume you're the owner?"

"This is one of my client's residences."

"Oh." I hesitate. "Okay. Well, uh, if they would like me to make any changes or…do anything different during my next cleaning, tell them to reach out to my boss and she can pass the info along. Or, if they'd prefer, I can give them my direct number and—"

"That won't be necessary, but thank you."

"Got it." I grab my purse and rifle through it, finding Rory's keys. "I guess that's…that." I nod. "Have a great day."

"You, too." She looks up from her phone. "Oh, and one more thing."

"Yes?"

"Will you make sure the gate closes behind you when you come in? My client might enjoy the limelight, but having the paparazzi on his private property might put a damper on his day, you know what I mean?"

Enjoys the limelight? Who is the guy?

I stick a pin in the owner's identity and pick up the bucket and rags. "Got it."

"Thanks again, Tatum," she adds.

"No problem."

After tossing my supplies into the back of Rory's car, I turn the ignition on and back down the driveway when my phone rings.

"Hey," I answer. "Perfect timing. I just finished."

"Yay, me, too," Rory replies. "What do you want to do tonight?"

"I'm not sure. Are you going to be too busy to hang out with me like you were this entire week or…?"

"Hey, it's not my fault you decided to pop in and turn my life upside down at the drop of a hat, missy."

"Touché," I cave as I pull onto the main road. The sun is setting. Different shades of purple and orange paint the sky as a plume of smoke catches my attention.

"What's that?" I ask.

"What's what?"

"It looks like there's a bonfire at the beach."

"Oh. Yeah, some of the locals throw parties on the beach when the weather's nice. Once it gets cold, The Pelican's the place to be, but during the warmer months, it's usually a toss up between the beach and the bar," Rory explains.

"So, are we going?"

"You're not exhausted?"

"Of course, I'm exhausted." I laugh. "But when has that ever stopped me from going to a party?"

I swear I can hear Rory's eyes roll through my cell, and she replies, "One day, you're going to find a guy who convinces you to slow down and breathe."

"It's cute how you think that's true," I tease.

"A girl can hope."

"So, is that a yes? You'll go with me?" I prod.

Rory pauses.

"Please?" I beg. "Or we can dye our hair green..."

"What are you talking about?"

"When I was cleaning, I found an unopened bottle of green dye at the house and—"

"That's stealing!"

"It was in the trash!"

"You rifled through their trash?" she screeches.

"It was on the top, and I already said it was *unopened*," I emphasize. "Take a chill pill, girlfriend."

"You have problems."

"We both have problems," I remind her. "It's why we're best friends. Now, where was I?" I flip the blinker on. "Right. Sexy bonfire or green hair party?"

"Well, since you drive a hard bargain and all..."

I bite back my amusement. "Is that a yes to the green hair?"

"Tatum," she warns.

"So, it's a yes to the bonfire?"

Her pause brings a Cheshire grin to my face, proving I have her exactly where I want her.

"Fiiiine," she drags out, "but you know the rules."

"You get to shower first, and we need to be ready at the same time because if you sit down, you'll fall asleep, and then I can kiss my wingwoman goodnight."

"Exactly."

"Deal." My smile softens. "I'll see you in a few."

# 12

# TATUM

Man, I love a good party. The adrenaline. The wandering eyes. The buzz of anticipation. It's even better when I don't know a single freaking soul other than the girl beside me. I'm not sure why I've always preferred it this way. Getting lost in a sea of strangers compared to being surrounded by people who know every single thing about me. I don't know. I guess it makes things more interesting and gives me a chance to show them whatever side of me I want. Control. That's what it is. What I crave. What I need. Especially considering where my head's been lately.

Thanks to the sun disappearing beneath the horizon a couple hours ago, it's a little chilly. Rory folds her arms, rubbing her hands up and down her bare skin as she stares at the bonfire a hundred yards from us. She's probably second-guessing why she agreed to come with me but is too good of a friend to back out since we're here now. Rory's always been a wallflower. I used to be like her. Before my world fell apart. Before I stopped caring about anything at all…including what others thought.

"Come on." I loop my arm through hers.

Jutting out her bottom lip, she follows my lead. "You know, I could be in bed right now with Hades."

"You could," I agree as the sand squishes beneath my feet. Yeah, I ditched my shoes at the car as soon as I saw the silky white sand. "But then you'd be dreaming of hanging out with me instead of actually hanging out with me, so…"

She scoffs but keeps her pace steady with mine. "Yeah, because that's what I dream of."

"That, and the infamous Jaxon Thorne," I tease.

Another scoff escapes her, though it sounds more forced than before. "Whatever."

Leading us to a cooler, I open the lid. The options range from fancy IPAs to Diet Coke to hard lemonades. I grab a beer and a hard lemonade, shaking the ice off before handing the fruity drink to my best friend.

"Why, thank you." She untwists the cap and takes a small sip, probably anxious for the liquid courage as she scans the beach brimming with people.

Staring at her, I ask, "How have you survived college without me?"

"Easy." She smirks. "I stay inside and get straight As."

"Hey, I got straight As, too."

"Only after you realized your parents were going to cut you off and put a stop to your studying abroad if you kept failing the online classes on purpose."

She's not wrong.

I spent a lot of years punishing them for…what, exactly? I don't even know anymore. Heartbreak, I guess. And that life isn't all rainbows and butterflies, like I grew up believing. The thought makes me…sad. And a little bitter. Just like the beer in my grasp. I pop the top off of the bottle, bring it to my lips, swallow a few big gulps of bitter—*called it*—liquid, and wipe my mouth with the back of my hand.

Hundreds of people are scattered across the sand, clustered in groups of two to twenty. Some are dancing. Some are talking. Their ages vary, too. That guy can't be more than twenty-one, and that one? He's probably thirty-five. The girls' ages range the same way, most of them sidling up to others in the same age group. At least I won't have to neuter any men for hitting on someone who could be their daughter —or worse, *granddaughter*. I mean, to each their own, but also, yuck.

Let's see…that guy is too old. That one's too hairy. That one looks five drinks past bombed. And those guys…

I pause. There's a group of guys on the opposite side of the fire. They're cute. Like, drop dead gorgeous with a side of bad boy cute. Actually, cute's probably the wrong word choice. Sexy as sin? Yeah, those are much more fitting, if their looks are anything to go by. Tilting my head toward the group, I murmur, "They look like a fun distraction."

Rory follows my line of sight, then grabs my arm, forcing my full attention. "Nope. Don't do it."

"Whoa, there." I slip my arm from her grasp. "Why not?"

"Because they're younger than you."

"So?"

"And they go to my school?"

"So?" I repeat.

"And are really bad news?"

"Bad news, huh?" My eyes dance with mirth. "Pretty sure they're right up my alley, then."

"I'm serious, Tate," she orders. "Jagger, Ford, Hawke, and…" She rises onto her tiptoes and peers around. "I don't know where Roman is." She shakes her head. "Not that it matters. They're kind of known for being shady assholes, and I'm begging you to keep a wide berth."

My mouth quirks. "*Kind of* shady assholes?"

"Yes, okay?" She smacks my arm. "They also have the

entire student body at RHU wrapped around their fingers. Hell, they're basically the kings of Harden Heights entirely, and I'm not just saying that."

"I thought you were trying to turn me *off* of them, not wave a red flag in their direction like I'm a bull," I tease.

"This isn't a dare or a bet or anything else. It's a plea. Pick someone else. Anyone else. There are plenty of attractive guys here, and we both know you can take your pick from any of them, but those guys? I just...I want you to be safe."

"Safe," I repeat.

"Yes. *Safe*. Besides, they're brothers, and we both know you have a thing against brothers, remember?"

She isn't wrong.

"Fine," I grumble. "But only because you asked me nicely."

She rolls her eyes but brings the drink to her lips, muttering, "Thank you," around the brim before taking a sip.

When my gaze lands on a cutie with a cowboy hat, I smile and turn back to Rory. "Do you see the cowboys at twelve o'clock?"

Her attention slides to the men then back to me. "Yes?"

"The one on the left was staring at you."

She rolls her eyes again. "No, he wasn't—"

"Yes, he was," I push. "You should talk to him."

"Uh, no thank you."

"Why not?"

"Because he wasn't looking at me. He was looking at you."

"Uh, no he wasn't. His friend was looking at me. The other one? With the tan hat? He was looking at *you*."

She sneaks another peek, then stares at the sand beneath her feet. "Whatever."

"Got caught, huh?" I laugh. "Let me introduce you."

"I think I'm good."

"And I think exposure therapy's a good thing."

Her glare cuts to me. "You shouldn't even know what exposure therapy is, let alone how to use it against me."

"Then you shouldn't have told me what it is or how to use it against you," I quip. "Come on. If you do this, I'll even promise to do the dishes for a week."

"Yeah, but you do them wrong."

"Exposure therapy," I sing.

She groans. "Tate."

"Rory, he's only a boy."

"Yeah, but boys hate me."

I laugh even harder but stop my pursuit of cowboy to face my best friend again. "Boys do not hate you. Boys actually love you—or at least, they'd like to, long and hard, I might add—if only you'd let them."

"Tate…" It's a plea.

We've played this game before. Where I push her to do things outside of her comfort zone while she internally curses me for it. It's always a roll of the dice, and tonight isn't any different. There are times when she thanks me after, albeit grudgingly. And then, there are times when I'm pretty sure she wishes she never knew me or gave me a front-row seat to her insecurities and how fucked she is. It's okay, though. Because she knows it's what makes us kindred spirits. Both of us are fucked. Why? Because both of us fell for the wrong person, and there's nothing we can do about it, let alone let go of them when we both know they'll never love us back.

Picking at the label on my beer bottle, I suggest, "Just pretend." My tone is softer than before but even more weighted. More somber. Because we both know it's what I've been doing my entire life. Pretending.

Something hits her gaze as Rory stares at me, barreling right past my defenses. She forces herself to nod and wipes her hands against her denim skirt. "Lead the way, Tate."

I walk us toward the half-circle of guys. When we reach them, I say, "Why, hello."

The first cowboy smirks as he shamelessly checks me out. "Hello."

"Have you met my friend, Rory?"

His attention flicks to my best friend. "Hello, Rory."

She takes another sip of her drink and cradles the glass bottle to her chest. "H-hello."

"Name's Andrew," he replies. "You from around here?"

# 13

# PAXTON

"Fuck, man. Are you...are you Paxton Six?" the stranger questions.

Well, shit. So much for having a night off. I figured I might be able to get away with flying under the radar since it's dark and there are at least a hundred people on the beach, along with copious alcohol, but I guess it isn't my lucky night.

I should be used to it by now. being recognized everywhere I go. Usually I relish it. The reminder of how far I've come from where I started. But then there are nights like tonight. When I honestly don't give a shit anymore, and all I want to do is enjoy a beer in public without someone trying to kiss my ass or interview me like they work for a gossip magazine.

I barely cast a glance at the stranger, choosing to take in the moonlight reflecting off the dark water instead. I haven't been to one of the bonfires in forever. Jagger, Ford, and Hawke have been throwing them for years. They learned from their uncle, though Judge would never admit it. It's either a bonfire, or a fight night, or poker, or a drag race.

Whatever the hell they feel like doing. The town eats it up like a groupie would cocaine. I get it, though. In a small town like Harden Heights, anywhere the guys go is the place to be.

"You are Paxton, right? From IndieCent Vows?" the stranger asks. He sways in my periphery, proving he's had one too many beers for the night.

I clear my throat and lift my chin in greeting. "Yeah, that's me."

"Hey, I'm a big fan. Huge."

"Thanks." I lift my beer in a silent cheers motion and take a sip, turning back to the water.

"Sure thing. You from around here? How's it feel to be back? Are the rumors true? You know, the ones about Indie-Cent Vows being over and shit?"

I bring the beer to my lips again but hesitate before taking a sip.

Is it over? Honestly, I have no fucking clue. I knew Judge's family would want him back at one point or another. Knew they could pull the plug at any second, and we'd be through. But knowing time's up? That they need him enough to screw up my future, along with the rest of the band all because his nephews aren't pulling their weight or some shit? It doesn't feel real.

But the most fucked up part of all is that I'm not sure how I feel about it. Traveling the world is incredible but exhausting. Maybe it'll be nice to slow down for a little while. And maybe I'm being too easy on the rest of the band by buying their bullshit, glass is half-full perspective on everything. But being here again? I dunno. The wound might not be fresh, but it's still there. Still here. On these beaches. At these parties. Bringing me right back to the fucked-up kid with his head up his ass and one too many wrong decisions.

"Not gonna tell me, huh?" The stranger laughs. "Come on, man. I heard you're the one with the big mouth."

"If you're looking for the big mouth, you'll have to talk to Tuke." Pinching the bottle neck between my fingers, I take another swig when I catch a familiar face hidden in the shadows. Well, would you look at that? Roman Stone. The face of one of my many wrong decisions. Roman is my best friend's little brother and Judge's nephews' closest friend despite growing up on the opposite side of town. He's also the guy who has connections to everything in this town, and I mean everything. I scan him up and down, realizing he's grown at least two feet since the last time I saw him. Although, now that I think about it, it's not like I've made it a habit of swinging by home since I escaped a decade ago. Add in my mom's suicide and Roman's big brother's arrest, and I considered The Drift a no-fly zone. Honestly, I'm surprised Roman's still here at all. Figured he would've bolted given the chance, just like I did. Then again, considering the shit he's supposedly up to with Judge's nephews, it seems he's found good use for his connections on the wrong side of the tracks. I wonder if it'll bite him in the ass like it did with Rafe. I lift my chin in greeting. "Well if it isn't Rafe's shadow."

"Not since he got locked up," Roman returns dryly.

Striding toward me, he offers his hand and pulls me into a hug, slapping his opposite hand against my back. "How you been, Pax?"

"Been good, man," I return. "What's new?"

"The usual." He lets me go, then turns his focus on my new friend. "But since when does this town ask questions they shouldn't be asking?"

The stranger lifts his hand in defense. "I was only askin'—"

"Yeah, I know what you were asking," Roman mutters. "Go get yourself a beer and leave my man alone, all right?"

"Sure thing."

As the stranger trudges off, I give Roman the side-eye. "Seems you do have some say in shit."

"Yeah, pretty sure Judge's brother pulled the cord a little hastily."

I lift my hands in defense. "Hey, I don't know anything about it."

"You're saying Judge hasn't filled you in?"

"He likes to keep family business…family business," I offer.

"Yeah, well, even if he was good at keeping his mouth shut, considering your past, I'm sure you've still pieced together the reason he's here."

I shrug. "I may have picked up on a thing or two."

"Figured as much," Roman grumbles. "Not sure how they don't see the irony in trying to shut down what they started in the first place, though."

"So, you admit to organizing shady shit on the weekends?" I counter.

He smirks. "No comment."

"Yeah, that's what I thought." I laugh. "So maybe Judge's brother *was* onto something by calling him to come and whip your asses back into shape."

Roman's broad shoulders raise into a shrug before he tucks his hands in his front pockets. He's probably trying to look innocent, but I know him better than to buy into the act.

"Just because we know how to have a good time and make some good money while we're at it doesn't mean we're out of control," he mutters.

"It does to men like Titas," I clarify, mentioning Judge's brother. Roman doesn't argue, well aware it'll only be a waste of breath. "And your brother," I add. I could drop it. I should drop it. But I can't help myself. Not when I know Rafe would want me to say something. To push the subject, even if it isn't my place. "From what I hear, you've been following in his footsteps pretty damn close lately."

His eyes thin. "That's what you hear, huh?"

I lift a shoulder but don't comment, taking another sip of my beer.

"Have you seen him yet?" Roman asks.

"Not yet. Been writing him, though."

"Good," Roman says. "He misses you."

Sobering, my attention falls to the sand beneath my feet. "Yeah, man. Miss him, too."

*Every damn day.*

"How long are you in town?" Roman asks.

"Not sure," I admit.

"You want in on anything while you're here?"

I've thought about it. Fuck, I've thought about it a lot. However, pissing off my bandmates hasn't been on my to-do list, but twiddling my thumbs has left me bored and restless. Too restless.

"Judge will kill me," I point out.

"What else are you gonna do while you're in town?"

I scratch the scruff along my jaw, considering my options even though we both know there aren't many. Not really. This college town might look sleepy on the surface, but underneath? Well, let's just say looks can be deceiving. And without the band to distract me? There's only so much a guy like me can do.

Well aware it might bite me in the ass, my curiosity gets the best of me, and I ask, "What's next on the agenda?"

"Agenda," he chuckles. "Way to make it sound official and shit."

"Pretty sure you boys know how to run this town smoother than most Fortune 500 companies."

"Fuck yeah, we do," he agrees. "Like a well-oiled machine."

"Sounds about right." I laugh.

"We got a poker tournament next week."

Another low laugh escapes me. "Pass. I'd prefer to keep my money."

"Probably smart." Roman gives me a cocky grin and scratches his jaw, glancing at the bonfire a hundred yards away before turning back to me. "There's a fight comin'."

My hands squeeze into fists on reflex, but I force them to relax. "A fight, huh?"

He nods. "You still brawl?"

"Nothing official. Not since leaving."

*And your brother's arrest,* I silently add. It doesn't need to be said aloud. Roman knows the truth as well as I do.

"Bet you could make a decent amount if we push it right."

"And get my ass kicked in the process?" I joke.

"Nah, I remember watching you when I was a kid. That fight doesn't go away. It's in here." He taps his sternum. "And here." His finger moves to his temple.

He's right. It is. The trick is learning how to turn it off, not make it disappear altogether.

"Besides," he continues, "You said nothing official. I assume you still spar?"

"Here and there," I admit. "Depends on downtime."

He grins. "See, I knew it was still in there."

And that's the problem, isn't it? You can take the man out of the fight, but you can't take the fight out of the man.

My blood turns hot as memories flood through me. *Fight! Fight! Fight!* I can still hear the chanting. Feel the energy. Fuck, it feels like a lifetime ago. Sleepless nights. Running on caffeine, hate, and adrenaline. I would've brawled with anyone—and did—just to feel something. Fighting and fucking. Fucking and fighting. It was all I had. All I wanted. I might not've always been the best, but I never quit, and I sure as shit knew how to give as good as I got. Anything for a distraction. Anything to stay away from home and my spiraling mom.

"When is it?" I ask.

"Not for a couple months."

"Months?"

"We're trying to lay low," he mutters, but I don't miss the glint in his dark eyes.

*Lay low, my ass.*

Nah, they're waiting for Judge to grow bored and leave them to their own devices again. So am I. The sooner I can get back on the road, back on stage and away from the ghosts in this town, the better. Although, it'd be easier if they weren't up to so much shady shit.

"When you say lay low, you mean other than the poker nights, drag races, and, did I hear you're into sports gambling, too?" I quip.

"Thought you said you haven't heard anything," Roman counters.

I throw my head back and laugh. "All right, you caught me."

"Figured." His low chuckle joins mine. "So, are you interested? I can get you a good match."

He looks so much like Rafe, they could be twins. Same build. Same eyes. It's like I'm staring at Rafe's ghost, and it messes with my head.

Sobering, I turn away from him and answer, "I'll, uh, I'll think about it."

"Yeah, man. Sure thing."

I glance at the blazing fire a little further up the beach, ready for another drink when I see her.

*Well, I'll be damned.*

My gaze narrows as I observe the silhouette of a girl I've only met once. A girl I shouldn't even remember, considering my line of work. But I guess I'm a sucker for a familiar face.

She's talking to someone. Someone I've never seen before. A guy with a cowboy hat and brown boots.

"I'm gonna grab another beer. Do you want anything?" I ask Roman.

He shakes his head. "Nah, I'm good."

"We'll catch up later," I promise, jogging toward the girl who looks like she's about to puke.

What are the odds?

1 4

PAXTON

My heart races as I jog toward one of the few people I convinced myself I'd never see again. I'd tell myself I'm hallucinating, that I had too much to drink, but there's no way one beer would make me see a ghost. Not like this. And not this ghost, either. If I was smart, I'd get the hell out of here, but I can't help myself.

When I get near, I overhear her say, "Uh-huh. Yup. It's really nice weather this time of year. I should probably get going."

"Come on. The night's still young, you know?" the guy argues.

"I know, but I'm kind of tired, and—"

"Hey, Baby," I interrupt.

Baby's eyes dart to me and widen in surprise. "Uh, what are you…are you…?" She shakes her head. "Uh, hey?"

"Hey," I repeat, turning to the stranger. "I'm Pax. Nice to meet you."

"Nice to meet you, too." He frowns. "You know, you kind of look familiar…"

"Always had one of those faces," I agree. "Mind if I steal Baby for a sec?"

"Baby?"

"He's my boyfriend," Baby rushes out. "Nice talking to you, though." Threading her arm around my bicep, she smiles up at me, then drags me a dozen feet away from the poor bastard.

"Boyfriend, huh?" I quip.

"Sorry." She peeks up at me again, her face scrunching. "My friend likes to play my wingwoman even when I tell her I'm not interested in awkward, stilted conversations about the weather, but she's a terrible listener, so here we are."

"You know, you could always talk about other things," I suggest. "Like your favorite band."

She laughs. "I guess you make a good point. Speaking of favorite bands, what, uh, what are you doing here, and no offense, but how in the world did you remember me?"

Remember her? The entire night is tattooed into my memory despite my best efforts to drown it with alcohol and weed.

Biting back my scoff, I challenge, "You really think I'd forget my favorite baby face?"

She rolls her eyes. "My name's Rory."

*Trust me, I remember.*

I got a fucking earful after I met up with the band all those years ago. Well, Dodger, at least. Judge and Tuke don't seem like they give two shits about who I sleep with unless it messes with the band. But Dodge? Yeah, he had the obligatory, you hurt her, I kill you speech locked and loaded. Not sure why he cared, but it didn't matter anyway. Tatum's the one who fucked with me, not the other way around. I told Dodger I was nothing but a complete gentleman and dropped her back at her hotel after buying her dinner—as a friend. I'm still not sure why I covered for her. Why I didn't ask Dodger to warn Tatum's fiance that she's a cheating bitch, but I couldn't help myself.

*What the hell's wrong with me?*

"Nice to see you again, *Rory*," I emphasize. "Speaking of your *friend*..." My gaze flicks over the bonfire and the sea of people along the beach. It's like some fucked up game of deja vu. But I guess it's what happens when I've caught myself searching the crowd during a show, looking for a familiar face I swore I never wanted to see again. "Is Tate here?"

"Ah, so you remember *Tate's* name," she muses. "Interesting."

My mouth lifts. "I remembered yours, too." I look down to catch her analyzing me. Seems her shyness likes to take a backseat as long as she isn't the center of the conversation. "How've you been?"

"Fine?" She hesitates. "Sorry, I'm just...kind of in awe. What are you...what are you doing here? Is Dodge here? Is the band playing here, and I didn't know?"

"The band's taking..." My voice trails off when I spot her across the sea of people. Her hair's longer than before. Her legs look longer, too, if that's even possible. Tatum fucking Taylor. I wonder if that's still her last name or if she took her husband's? The thought alone makes my stomach sour. Throwing her head back, Tatum laughs at whatever the asshole next to her says, then steals the beer from his grasp and takes a drink. The long column of her throat teases me all the way from over here, and I squeeze the bottle in my hand.

"The band's taking..." Rory's words hang in the air, and I clear my throat.

"Taking a break," I finish, lifting my chin toward Tatum across the space. "That her husband?"

As she follows my gaze, her forehead wrinkles in confusion. "Husband?"

"Archer, right?"

Her lips part, and her skin pales as she tears her attention from Tatum to stare up at me. "Y-you know about Archer?"

"That him?" I ask.

Her head shakes back and forth, but you'd think she's seen a ghost. It only leaves me more on edge.

*Are you in on the lie, Baby?*

By the look on her face as soon as I said Tatum's husband's name, I'm gonna go with yes. Maybe she's covered for Tatum's infidelity more times than she can count and doesn't know what to say now that someone's called her out for it. Or maybe I'm missing something.

Trying to keep my frustration in check, I ask, "Who's she talking to?"

The worry lines around her eyes soften as she follows my gaze again and shrugs. "No idea."

"You don't know?" I ask.

"I didn't hear his name. He's"—she waves her hand toward the guy she was talking to when I approached—"what's his name's friend."

"So, fucking anyone with a dick behind her husband's back is a habit of hers, huh?" I turn back to Tatum, hating how she's only grown prettier. And my memory of her? Fuck, it doesn't even hold a candle to how gorgeous she is. My blood rushes south, and I throttle my beer bottle even more, hating my physical response.

Reaching for my arm, Rory twists me toward her. "What are you talking about?"

"What do you mean, what am I talking about?"

"I mean, you're not making any sense. No offense," she rushes out.

*Of course not.*

I bite back my scoff and try to focus on what really matters. "Rory, is Tate still married or not?" I demand.

Her brows dip in confusion. "Tate?"

"Yeah."

With a look making me feel like I've grown a second head, she shakes her head. "Tate was never married."

Feeling like a broken record, I shove my confusion aside and ask, "She's not married?"

The girl must have the patience of a saint as she gives me a kind smile and touches my forearm gently. "Tate is most definitely *not* married."

"So, she's single?"

"Yes?" It comes out as a question, and she laughs. "Tate's always single."

I repeat the words in my head, analyzing them for any hidden meaning, but I come up empty. She's single. She isn't married. Isn't even dating anyone. Was never dating anyone, by the sound of things. So, what the hell?

Jaw tight, I look down at Rory again and cock my head. "Always, huh?"

"Yup." She shrugs. "Just like the men she hooks up with, so I guess it's a win-win for everyone."

A win-win for everyone.

Everyone but me, since she lied to my face.

*What. The actual. Fuck?*

"And here I thought I was special," I mutter. The world feels like it's spinning as I glance at Tatum again. Her skin glows from the bonfire, making her look...untouchable, almost. Dressed in black. The sliver of skin peeking from between her low cut jeans and crop top. "She was never engaged, was she," I murmur.

It isn't a question, and honestly, I don't even mean to say it aloud, but it slips out anyway. She was never engaged.

Never. Fucking. Engaged.

"What are you talking about?" Rory asks.

I grit my teeth to keep from spilling anything else. "Nothing."

Seriously, I'm going to strangle the girl. I spent years—*years*—struggling over whether or not I made the right decision to keep my nose out of Tatum's marriage, knowing I was the guy who fucked over a stranger by sleeping with a girl I thought was single.

She lied to me. Right to my fucking face. And I bought it? I can't believe I actually bought it. The girl lied at the arena, too, and I brushed it off. But twice? Fuck that shit. I'm an idiot.

"You gonna talk to her?" Rory asks. The gentleness in her voice is almost enough to soften the red I'm seeing. Almost.

It's a good question. Should I? Could I? Without strangling her or smacking her ass?

"Haven't decided yet," I admit. "You gonna tell her you saw me if I don't?" I drag my attention away from Tatum again, right on time to see Rory's lips purse.

"Haven't decided yet," she returns.

My mouth twitches, and I pull her into a half-assed hug. "Good seeing you, Baby."

"You, too." She squeezes me back, then lets me go. "Hey, Pax?"

"Yeah?"

Her lips bunch on one side, like she's lost in a silent debate before coming to some kind of conclusion. "Did you..." She pauses. "Did you sneak out, or did she?"

"Does it matter?"

She hesitates, studying me as the firelight dances in her eyes. "Yeah. Yeah, I think it does."

"She left me," I answer.

*Told me she was engaged, then left me,* I silently clarify. The question is, why?

With a slow nod, Rory's gaze cuts to her best friend

laughing at something the other cowboy—who is not her husband—said. And I can't help but wonder what she's thinking. Why she cares. If Tatum pushes her away the same way she does me. Not that we're even in the same ballpark. Rory's her best friend, and I'm…I'm a guy she fucked once before lying straight to my face.

"Are you sticking around?" Rory asks.

I scratch the scruff along my jaw, unable to tear my focus from the cowboy's hand pressed against Tatum's lower back. She's just a girl. She's always been just a girl. I've had more than I could ever want, and I've never felt jealous. Probably because if I snapped my finger, they'd come running. But Tatum? Something tells me it would take a lot more effort than a simple snap of my fingers to have her again. That is, if I wanted her again in the first place. Which I don't. Although, some answers would be nice.

*Why did you lie?*

She wasn't playing hard to get. She wasn't playing a game at all. She wanted nothing to do with me, despite the mind-blowing sex we had.

*Why?*

Guess there's no time like the present to find out.

"I'll see you around, Rore." I slip past her, heading toward her friend, well aware if I don't, I'll regret it.

*You ready to chat, Birthday Girl? 'Cause I'm coming for you, and our conversation is long overdue.*

15

## PAXTON

The heat from the fire is like fuel. It spreads through me, feeding my resentment and confusion as I grab another beer from one of the coolers, pop the top off, and close the last bit of distance. She hasn't noticed me yet. She's too distracted by the man in front of her. It only pisses me off more.

"I know, right?" Tatum's laugh is as rich as I remember. Hell, it's richer. Throatier. Sexier. She touches the cowboy's bicep and grins up at him when her attention catches on me.

I lift my beer in a silent cheers, and she does a double take, her jaw dropping.

*Surprised, Birthday Girl?*

As soon as our gazes connect, she recovers and twists around, giving me her back as if it isn't too late to fly under the radar and pretend I'm not standing two feet to her left.

*Yeah. Not fucking likely.*

The fire dances around her silhouette, and the view shoots straight to my cock, reminding me of what's underneath. What I thoroughly explored all those nights ago. The visceral reaction only feeds my frustration.

133

I've thought about that night more times than I can count. Second guessing whether or not I made the right decision to carry her secret with me or if I was fucking over an innocent man who isn't even real. And here she is, pretending I don't exist.

Well, if this isn't a blow to the ego, I don't know what is.

Fuck, you'd think I pissed in her drink or some shit.

"Hey, Birthday Girl," I announce.

Her body tenses as she turns to face me, locking her arm with the cowboy next to her. "Oh. Hi, Pax. This is my…"— she gulps—"husband."

"H-husband?" the guy balks.

I scan the guy up and down, then let out a low laugh. "Seems you're as surprised as I am." I turn to Tate. "No offense, but I think you can do better, Tate. At least find a guy who knows how to cover for you when you're lying out of your ass, especially when it's a habit of yours."

Anger flares in her pretty gaze. "Who says I'm lying?"

*Your best friend*, I want to answer, but I bite my tongue. Stepping forward, I ignore her question, letting my attention roll over every inch of the woman. "You look good."

"Thank you." Her gaze flicks over me, though it's less blatant and a hell of a lot less curious. Like she's analyzing a math problem or some shit. "You do, too. Seems the rockstar life has treated you well."

"It has," I confirm. "What are you doin' here?"

"Visiting. Yup. Me and Carter love to travel."

"Been here two nights," Carter chimes in, his southern accent thick as hell.

"Carter, huh? What happened to Archer?" I cock my head. "Are you a black widow or something, Tate? Kill your husbands after fucking them over?"

Something flashes in her eyes, but it's gone too quickly

for me to analyze. She crosses her arms and lifts her chin in defiance. "Seems you're as funny as I remember, and while it's been a real treat catching up, our flight leaves in the morning, so…we should probably get back to the hotel."

"Really?" Carter's eyes pop with excitement like a kid on Christmas morning. "There ain't nothin' that would make me happier, darlin'."

She forces a smile and peeks at me. "Good to see you again, Pax. If you ever come to…Georgia, let me know." Her shoulder lifts. "Or don't."

"I'm from Texas, darlin'," Carter says.

I tip my head back and laugh. Seriously, where'd she find this guy?

"Yeah, but we're moving to Georgia," Tate clarifies through gritted teeth, too stubborn to give up the bullshit, though I'm not surprised. Once a liar, always a liar. "Remember, Carter?"

"Ah, hell. You're right. I thought you meant next week, not in a few months, once we get done unpackin', and everythin'."

"Great cover," I interject and clear my throat. "You mind if I steal your girl for a minute, cowboy?"

"I, well, I—" Beads of sweat cling to his forehead as he looks at Tatum like he's caught between a rock and hard place. He's probably weighing the pros and cons of backing down, curious if she's worth the effort of potentially having his ass kicked. Don't get me wrong. The guy looks like he's used to tossing around bails of hay. But me? I look like I was raised on the wrong side of the tracks, and desperate men are capable of anything. Right now? I'm desperate and pissed off that I bought her bullshit all those years ago.

Sensing his indecision, Tatum throws her boy toy a bone, grumbling, "I'll be fine, Carter. You can go."

"Sure thing. I'll, uh, I'll be right over here." He hooks his thumb over his shoulder toward a table set up with hotdog and s'mores supplies, then beelines it away from us.

Funny. If the roles were reversed, there's not a chance in hell I'd let her out of my sight. Honestly, even with the roles where they are, I still don't want to let her out of my sight. Not until she apologizes for lying to me and tells me her fucking reasoning behind it.

"He seems…" I hook my thumbs in the loops of my jeans and rock forward, bringing us chest to chest. "Like the furthest thing from a rockstar you can get."

Drawing a small zigzag in the sand with her bare toes, she stares at the ground and mutters, "Maybe my taste has changed."

"Apparently," I scoff. "Since your first husband was named Archer, right?"

With a glare cutting straight to my fucking bones, she warns, "Don't say that name."

I pull back, surprised by the animosity when she has no right to be pissed. Not at me. And not for this. Even so, I'm not completely heartless and with the look in those pretty hazel eyes? I'd have to be to not back off.

Lifting my hands in surrender, I mutter, "All right. Archer equals touchy subject. Noted." I lower my hands, scrutinizing her. Maybe she is telling the truth because it's clear this guy isn't made up like I initially assumed. Or maybe I'm wrong. Again. Why is this girl so damn hard to read? She lied to me. Multiple fucking times, and I'm tired of letting her get away with it all because she has a pretty face. I crowd her even more, commanding her full attention. "Doesn't mean I'm stupid enough to fall for the same lie twice."

She gives up on her little sand project and folds her arms. "You know, you almost had me fooled."

"How so?"

"I told you not to chase me."

I step toward her. She retreats, mirroring my movements as we slowly move away from the bonfire toward the base of the rocky cliffs not too far away. "This was an innocent run-in. Though, I'm pretty sure the last time you looked at me, the daggers were missing."

"Last time, I'd just had a couple solid orgasms."

"I'm happy to give you a few more, if you're interested."

"Aaaand, there he is." She scowls up at me. "As selfless as the last time we talked."

"Always." We move past a few more stragglers, but I doubt she notices. She's too focused on me. This conversation. And whether or not I'll let it go. Her lies. Her body. The mind-fuck she's put me through for *years*.

Not a chance.

"Why'd you lie to me, Tatum?"

Eyes round and innocent, she murmurs, "Who said I lied?"

"You really gonna play this game?" I grab her wrist and she screeches to a halt. Ignoring the heat licking at my palm from a simple touch, I bring her left hand between us, demanding, "Where's the ring?"

Not even bothering to look at her naked ring finger, she answers, "In my hotel room."

*Bullshit.*

I tug her into me, my need to be right battling with my need to kiss her just to see if she tastes as sweet as I remember. As sweet as I've reimagined more times than I can count, though I'd never admit it aloud. Moving even closer, I growl, "Not ready to surrender, Birthday Girl?"

"There's nothing to surrender to." Her hand presses against my chest, stopping my pursuit. "And even if there was, I'm not interested."

"Again with the lies," I tsk. "If you weren't interested, you would've left with your *husband*," I seethe through gritted teeth. "Funny how you've never talked about him on your social media."

Her gaze narrows. "Have you been keeping tabs on me?"

*Yes.*

This is also something that happens more than I'd like to admit, if I'm being honest with myself, let alone to the girl in front of me. But if I let her in on my little secret, she'll probably slap me before running in the opposite direction. Finally standing in front of her after all these years, the idea of her slipping away a second time is more than I can stomach. It's not like I love her or some shit, but it's clear we aren't through. Not yet. Not when she's been fucking with my mind for so long, only to confirm what a small part of me always knew. She's not married. She was never married.

"Seems I'm not the only liar," she seethes.

The fire in her gaze damn near burns me up on the spot, and I fight my smile. "You can put the claws away, Birthday Girl." I let her arm go. "I didn't go back on my promise."

"Yet, here you are."

"Here I am." I spread my arms wide.

She takes another step back before realizing the black rock wall is behind her and she has nowhere to run. Not anymore.

With a smirk, I add, "Now, what am I going to do with you?"

"Nothing."

"Nothing?" I challenge. "You sure that's what you want?"

Her tongue darts out between her lips, and she takes a deep breath. It causes her breasts to brush against my chest. The lack of light only shrinks the space between us, highlighting her shallow breathing and my heart thrumming in my ears.

My cock hardens in my jeans, but I ignore it, tilting my head. "Why are you acting like you hate me?"

She presses her hand to my chest, and my heart pounds even harder. "Because I wasn't supposed to see you again."

I shake my head, feeling like a caged beast. My muscles vibrate with so much adrenaline that if it doesn't expel soon, I might lose my fucking mind. Doesn't she get it? I haven't needed to see her to think about her. To wonder. To be curious.

My throat is dry, but I swallow past the thick cotton and tower over her. "Tell me to leave." My words hang in the air as she stares at my chest, refusing to look up at me. To give me a glimpse at what she's thinking, well aware if I'm given the opportunity, I'll read her like a fucking book.

"Leave," she whispers.

My shoes touch her bare toes as I shift closer, growling, "Say it like you mean it."

"Pax."

I grab her chin, forcing her to look at me. "Tell me why you lied."

"Because I knew if I didn't, you would track me down."

"I do like the chase," I agree.

"Exactly."

"And what's wrong with the chase, Birthday Girl?"

Again, her lips gnash together as she bites her tongue, refusing to let me in. To let me see exactly what she thinks so I can't form a rebuttal and she can continue living in the land of delusion.

"You liked me, Tatum," I push, giving in to the pull of her body as I press mine against hers. Like I knew it would, her body molds against mine, fitting me perfectly. "You liked talking to me," I rasp. "You liked being on the back of my bike. You liked what I did to your body."

"Stop talking." She wraps her arms around my neck, her fingers threading through my hair and tugging sharply. "Stop." She gulps. "Talking." Then her mouth is on mine. Biting. Licking. Sucking. Her fingernails dig into the nape of my neck. I groan into her mouth, the sharp sting shooting straight to my cock. And fuck me. The memory of our night together doesn't even hold a candle to this.

I grip her crop top in my hands, fighting the urge to rip it off her no matter how much I want to as she lifts her chin to give me better access to her throat. I dive in, scraping my teeth against her sensitive flesh. "If I didn't hate you for lying to me, I could fuck you right now."

With a breathy gasp, she whispers, "Who says you can't fuck someone you hate?"

I look behind me, taking in the distance between us, the bonfire, and the nearest person who could see us, let alone hear us.

"Promise you'll stay quiet," I order.

She nods and reaches for my cock, squeezing the tip through my pants before dropping to her knees.

The movement nearly knocks me on my ass. "What are you doing?" I demand.

"Making sure I stay quiet." With a quick zip of my jeans, my cock springs free, and she palms my shaft. No hesitation. No second thoughts. Bringing it to her lips, she swallows it completely until it hits the back of her throat. I slap my hand against the black rock to keep balanced.

*Fuck.*

We didn't do this last time. Didn't get this far. Didn't have enough time to explore each other and all the ways we could make each other fall apart. The idea alone has me begging to throw her on her back and spread her legs wide so I can taste her while she sucks me off. Part of me wants to. The other part? I want to savor this. The feel of her mouth on me. The tiny mewls hitting my erection and shooting straight to my balls. The feel of her hands cupping my sac, rolling me in her palm and tugging softly until I swear I might black out.

My chest swells with every dip of her head and sweep of her tongue. It isn't sweet or slow. It's punishing. Twisting my stomach into a tight knot of greed and lust. I hold her head on me, pumping in and out of her sweet lips as tears roll down her face. I want to hate her. I want to worship her. I want to make her see what she does to me. Want to make her regret it the same way I do. That she has all the power. Every fucking ounce of it. And instead of wielding it the way I wish she would, she's done nothing but torture me. Wreck me. Make me wanna smack her ass and come down her throat to prove I can. And I might if she doesn't let up.

Dragging my thumb along the edge of her mouth, I warn, "If you don't stop, I'm gonna come."

She swirls her tongue around the mushroom head, her eyes glued to my face and branding the image into my brain for the rest of my measly existence. I've had good head before. More times than I can count, thanks to one too many afterparties. But this? After all the years she's crossed my mind, knowing I could never have her again? This is something else entirely.

"You swallow me so good, Birthday Girl," I rasp, running my thumb along cheek. "So fucking good."

Her head bobs back and forth with a new level of fervor, as if my words—my praise—turns her on. It drives me further insane.

"Good girl. Just like that."

Squeezing the base of my dick, she massages me with her hand and her mouth as she hollows her cheeks.

"Fuck, Tate. Fuck!" My cock spurts inside of her, and she swallows it, licking every drop of cum while I unload in her mouth. My thoughts blur into a haze, the world around me disappearing until all that's left is me and her and how good this fucking feels.

Knees weak, I lean forward, letting the black rock hold my weight and dig into my palm. My mind reels, and I try to piece together how we got here. I approached her for answers. For the fucking truth. And now, here we are.

*What the hell just happened?*

My softening dick slips past her lips as I rasp, "That wasn't what I had in mind."

"Maybe that's why I did it." Her tongue darts out, and she licks the corner of her mouth. "Good to see you, Pax."

I offer my hand to help her stand, but she doesn't take it. Pushing to her feet, she folds at the waist, brushing the sand from her knees like she just finished building a sandcastle instead of giving me the best head I've ever had. And just like that, my frustration, my pent-up annoyance, flares back to life, leaving me dumbfounded and off-balance.

As she starts to move around me, I block her escape, demanding, "Give me your number."

"No."

"Give me your number."

Her attention flicks to me, finally gracing me with a look of indifference. "Why should I?"

"Because no matter how many times you deny it, I know you've thought of me, too."

With a slow blink, she looks down and adjusts her shirt. "I haven't—"

"You have," I growl. "And when you go home tonight and touch yourself, you'll think of me. But here's the thing, Birthday Girl." I move closer, forcing my hands to stay at my sides when all I want to do is tug her into me. "None of those orgasms will compare to what I'm going to do to you the next time I get my hands on you."

"Who says I'll let you get your hands on me again?" She peeks up at me another time, those thick, dark lashes reminding me of exactly what we did two minutes ago. My dick twitches.

"Tatum—"

"You don't know me, Pax. And trust me, pursuing me will only be a waste of time."

I stay quiet, pressing my lips into a thin line as I consider the woman in front of me. The air around us charges with every passing second while I attempt to piece together her motive for pushing me away. For lying. For being so damn stubborn when it's clear she's interested in me, too. Is she like this with everyone? And if she is, how the hell has she survived because looking at her makes me want to smack her ass. She's so damn guarded. Even now, with her head held high and nothing but acid on her tongue and the taste of my cum, I can't help but wonder... "Who hurt you, Birthday Girl?" I ask.

With the slightest flinch, hell it's so small I almost miss it, she ignores my question, raising her chin another inch. "It looks like my job here is done, so if you'll excuse me—"

"Give me a chance," I order.

"Why? So you can waste your time?" she challenges. "I hate to disappoint you, but I don't sleep with the same guy twice."

Her confession makes me pause, and I replay every sexual encounter we've had. My hands, my mouth, my cock. They've each taken a turn in her tight little pussy but only once. Never twice. Including tonight. Fuck, I offered to bend her over and make her come if she promised to be quiet, but I couldn't. Not without Tatum giving in and breaking her rule. So she did the only thing she could. The only thing we hadn't done before.

"It's why you gave me your mouth," I realize.

"Exactly." She shrugs. "One and done, Pax. It's all I'm looking for."

All she's looking for? She's driving me insane, yet she has the discipline to just…walk away after experiencing chemistry like this? Determined, I tell her, "Then let me take you out and return the favor."

"Take me out?"

"On a date," I say. "A real one. With lobster rolls, the ocean, and my mouth."

Her eyes flash in the moonlight, proving I've affected her by showing my hand and how much our conversation meant to me. Maybe I fucked myself over by showing it too soon, but this girl. Fuck, this girl. She's been messing with my head for so long, now that she's here, I don't know what to do with myself.

Arms folded, she rocks back on her heels, watching me.

"Give me your number," I repeat.

"And if I do?"

"I'll call you."

"I don't live here. I'm only visiting—"

"With your husband," I quip. "Yeah, I'm aware."

Rolling her eyes, she tosses her hair over her shoulder and admits, "Okay, I'm serious about the leaving part, though."

Maybe she is, maybe she isn't. But it doesn't matter either way as long as I can get in touch with her. As long as I can track her down and see her again because she might fight this, but there's something about her. Something calling to me. Something pushing me to keep going. Keep fighting. Keep climbing past those barriers even if it kills me. I move forward. "Give me your number, Birthday Girl."

With a huff, she mutters, "You really won't quit, will you?"

"Not a chance." Reaching up, I brush her hair away from her face, pinching the ends softly before letting it go.

"Fine," she whispers, though her eyes stay glued to my chest. "555-942-9932."

I nod, committing the numbers to memory. "When do you leave?"

"I, uh, soon. Just…call me or whatever, but I have to go."

I watch her feet dig into the sand as she jogs away.

"See you soon, Birthday Girl."

# TATUM

ometimes I surprise myself with how stupid I can be. Did I seriously just give Paxton a blow job at the bonfire after he called me out for lying all those years ago? Why, yes. Yes, I did. But the worst part? I had to force myself to brush my teeth, knowing it would erase his taste. Which is a problem on so many levels. One, cum does not taste great. Who wants it lingering in their mouth for hours on end, let alone waking up to it in the morning? And two, why does the idea of erasing said taste all because it's Paxton's make me feel like I'll never have a chocolate shake ever again?

Seriously, I am so messed up in the head.

After ditching Pax, I faked a stomach ache, and Rory drove us home without complaint, though I know she isn't stupid. Far from it. The girl's a genius who never misses anything. And if I had to guess, that probably includes my absence at the bonfire. The ride is relatively quiet, and once we're home, I wash my face, brush my teeth, and change into my pajamas before climbing into bed.

After Rory takes Hades outside to do his business, she

flicks the light off and takes her turn in the bathroom. Part of me wishes she would hurry up so I wouldn't be alone with my thoughts. Twisting the edge of the pillow case, I fight the urge to find my notebook and write an essay of what a terrible person I am and how sorry I am for lying. For missing Archer. And for not being able to erase Paxton's comment about lobster rolls and the ocean. He remembered. Who remembers something like that?

The quiet squeak from the bathroom door opening cuts through my thoughts as Rory pads to her twin bed and nudges Hades to scoot over. When he does, she slips beneath the covers, asking, "How was Cowboy?"

I pause.

*How was my fake husband?*

Well, let's see. Where to start? He's not the brightest crayon in the box, that's for sure. He also lost brownie points for letting me leave with Paxton without a fight. Not that I wanted a fight, but a little backup would've been nice. He was cute, though. Or at least, that was my first impression until Pax showed up out of nowhere. Now I can barely conjure up an image of what he looked like, only the way moonlight cast shadows on Paxton's face as he stared down at me while I gave him my mouth. What is he doing here, anyway? I should probably look up IndieCent Vows' schedule, so I can figure out how to lay low until they move on. Because if he finds out I lied to him again, he might literally kill me.

Okay, literally is probably a little strong, but I digress.

"Tate?" Rory prods.

*Cowboy. Right.*

"Cowboy?" I shift on the bed and shove my pillow a little further under my head. "He was fine, I guess."

"Are you going to see him again?"

"He's a tourist, so…probably."

She laughs. "And if he was a local?"

A breath of amusement escapes me, well aware we both know the answer. "I'd keep my distance."

"Why?" The sheets rustle in the dark room as Rory rolls toward me in her bed and Hades grunts in protest. "Because the idea of running into one of your one-night stands after you've sent them packing is uncomfortable?"

A sardonic grin stretches across my face despite the acid in her words. She has no idea how right she is. I stare at the ceiling, still reeling from the fact that I literally just experienced this very thing earlier tonight. "You know me too well."

"I do," she agrees. "It's also why I love you."

"Because you know me too well?" I ask with a laugh.

"Because you let me in long enough to get to know you," she clarifies. "Which I've learned over the years is kind of a miracle."

She's right. It is.

"I saw Pax at the bonfire," she continues, like her words didn't just knock me on my ass. Or at least, they would've if I wasn't already lying down.

My body stiffens, and I dig my fingernails into my palms, fighting the urge to lose my shit because if Rory saw Pax, I can't pretend my encounter with him was a figment of my imagination. "What?"

"Pax," she repeats. "As in...the schmexy guitarist. I saw him tonight."

I stick a pin in teasing her about her inability to say sexy and focus on the bomb she's dropped on me and what it might mean in the big picture. "You saw Pax?"

"Yup. Did *you* see him?" she asks.

Well, shit. I could lie. Tell her I didn't see him. Or I could spill the tea on everything that transpired. She wouldn't judge me. Not too harshly, anyway. But for some reason, neither option feels right. Like, if I lie, I'm a bad friend, but if I admit I saw him, I'll blurt out everything that happened, and she'll ask why I'm so adamant about keeping space between us when it's clear he's interested in more, and I'll have to go quiet, and she'll be reminded of how screwed up my brain is thanks to her older brother's death, and—

"Tate?" she prods.

"Uh, yeah." I gulp. "Yeah, I saw him. Only for a minute, though."

"What'd he say?"

"Just…hi," I offer vaguely, well aware that keeping the truth from her is *way* against the best friend agreement. "Did you…did you see him before or after I saw him?"

"Before, I think," she decides. "He seemed kind of pissed when he saw you with Cowboy."

Okay, definitely before. That's good. Really good. I think?

"Got it." I lick my lips, grateful she ran into him before the blowjob instead of after because that wouldn't be embarrassing at all. "Did he, uh, did he tell you why he's here?" I ask.

"Nope."

"Any idea how long he's staying?"

"No idea."

"Are IndieCent Vows playing or something?" I prod.

"No idea," she repeats.

With a huff, I roll toward her. "And what do you know?"

It's too dark to see her, but it doesn't soften the amusement in her voice as she answers, "I know he couldn't take his eyes off you while I was talking with him."

My heart thrums faster, and I fist the sheets in my palms. Her observation shouldn't affect me. Shouldn't make my stomach flip-flop or my heart flutter like a lovesick hummingbird. *Get with the program, body.* You don't care about Pax or his potential interest in you. You don't care about him at all. *You don't care about anything.* The thought is like a whisper, winding its way through me and leaving me… raw.

"Maybe you missed it because you were a little distracted," Rory offers.

By Cowboy. Right.

Why do I keep forgetting about him, again?

"Exactly," I argue. "Cowboy's cute."

"And Pax isn't drop-dead gorgeous?" she counters. "He's even schmexy when he's pissed. You should've seen his face when he realized you were at the party. It's like he was walking a love/hate tightrope or something."

I scoff. "He doesn't love me."

"But hate's on the table?" she counters. "I thought your little evening together ended…amicably."

"Amicably." I snort. "I mean, we screwed each other's brains out, so yeah. I'd say it was amicable."

*Or at least, it was until I told him I was engaged,* I silently add.

"Oh, shut up. You know what I mean," Rory pushes. "From what little you've told me, you guys had a pretty mind-blowing night together. Then you run into him years later and he looks at you like you stepped on his birthday cake."

"Rory!" My nose wrinkles. "That's a little harsh."

"You know what I mean. And then you disappear with the guy? What happened?"

"Disappear?"

"I saw you walk away with him," she points out. "Yeah, I didn't miss how you left that part out, by the way."

"Are you saying you were testing me, and I failed?"

"Yup," she answers, unashamed of her mind game performance.

"I think I'm rubbing off on you too much," I grumble.

"Probably," she agrees. "Now, spill. What happened?"

Fiddling with my gold ring, I replay my encounter with Pax. Both of them. I'm not some innocent little virgin. I've spent time with guys. Some good experiences. A lot of bad ones. But my night with Pax always stood out. Haunting me. Comforting me. He was…he was really sweet. And the sex? Yeah, it was incredible. But there was a reason I left afterward, and it's best I remember it.

"He wanted to…talk," I lie. "So, I went with him to find some privacy, then told him I'm only visiting and not interested and that's that. I'm not interested."

"Who isn't interested in a face like his, though?" she argues.

"Me," I decide. "We both know I don't backslide, Rore."

*Except I totally backslid.*

"Or, you know, you could give him a chance, see how it goes and play it by ear," she offers. "That is, if you're not *married* anymore." She emphasizes married while giving me a look that screams, *I'm not mad. I'm disappointed* with a sprinkle of *What the hell, Tate?*

To be fair, I've earned it. Her silent reprimand. Hell, I deserve a lot worse for keeping this from her.

I grimace, refusing to cower no matter how much I want to. Even so, it doesn't stop the guilt from swelling inside of me because yeah. When she says it out loud, it sounds a hell of a lot worse than I initially intended it to be.

"He told you, huh?" I mumble.

"Uh, yeah. The question is, why did you lie to him in the first place? And married to Archer? Seriously?"

My shame topples over me as soon her brother's name slips out of her. "Okay, that part was messed up," I concede.

"You think?" she snaps. "Start talking, Tate."

Chewing on the edge of my thumb, I sigh and give in, my conscience getting the best of me. "Look, it's not a big deal."

"Mm-hmm," she hums, looking less than convinced. Feeling her frustration, Hades lifts his head, looks at me, and lets out a low growl.

Ignoring him, I push forward, explaining, "After we hooked up, I may or may not have told him I was engaged so he wouldn't ask Dodger for my number."

"Tatum," she scolds.

"I didn't know how else to convince him to not pursue me."

She laughs. "Someone's cocky."

"You don't get it," I argue. "You weren't there."

"What's there to get?"

"We had a…connection," I mutter. "And for better or worse, I knew if I didn't draw a line in the sand, he'd cross it, okay? So I…I did what needed to be done. I drew a line in the sand."

"A fake line."

"Yeah, but it worked."

"It also paints you as a cheater."

"I've been painted worse," I remind her, but it doesn't take away the sting of the truth I've long since buried. That night? That night I *did* feel like a cheater. Because that night I connected with someone on an emotional level, not only a physical one. And that felt like more of a betrayal to Archer's memory than any of my other encounters with the opposite sex, and it's why I knew I needed to draw the line. Why I knew I needed to disappear. Even if it doesn't make sense. Even if I sound like a crazy person. I needed the distance to alleviate my guilt for connecting with someone other than a guy who's already in the ground. It's why my little run-in with Pax felt more weighted than even my best friend can imagine, let alone understand.

"You should come clean," Rory decides. "He seems like a really nice guy, Tate."

"Well, yeah. He's a charismatic sweetheart." *Until he finds out you lied to him.* "And a *rockstar*," I emphasize in an attempt to focus on the facts instead of my own guilt. "Even if I was stupid enough to do a one-eighty on my relationship stance —which I'm not—you really think opening the door for a rockstar is a smart idea?" I scoff. "Yeah, no thank you."

"Come on. It's been years," she pushes. "Maybe you should give him a real chance."

Yeah, that ship has sailed. He already knows the truth, even if I didn't full-on admit it tonight. Add in the fake number, and I might as well buy a shirt labeling me Paxton's mortal enemy if his reaction to my first lie is anything to go by.

"Just because he's a nice guy when he isn't pissy about me lying to him doesn't change anything," I tell her. "Honestly, it's kind of a tally in the wrong column, if you ask me."

The moonlight filters through the window, painting Rory as she props her head on her hand, clearly invested in our conversation as she plays with Hades' fur. "What? Nice guys are bad?"

"Nice guys are dangerous," I clarify. "You should know."

I don't throw her childhood crush in her face often, and I'm not trying to right now, either. But if anyone knows what it's like to fall for a nice guy only to wind up rejected by him, it's Rory. And me. But I digress. Yeah, Jaxon Thorne is the epitome of nice guy. He's sweet. Thoughtful. Dependable. He's perfectly unattainable and Rory's greatest regret. Once upon a time, they were best friends despite their massive age difference. She thought she could tell him anything. And it was true. She could. Everything but her feelings for the guy.

"I know," Rory finally mutters. "It's just...I don't know. Not every situation has to be like me and Jax or you and Arch. Like I said, Pax couldn't take his eyes off you."

"It doesn't mean anything, Squeaks," I say, trying to soften the blow. "I know your untouched, ripe-for-the-picking heart wishes it did, but…it doesn't. He's just a guy." The lie leaves a bitter taste in my mouth, but I swallow it back.

"Maybe you're right," Rory concedes. "You probably are, but…I don't know. Is it so wrong for me to want you to be happy?"

Caught between being offended and amused, I chuckle softly, arguing, "Hey, I'm happy."

"You know what I mean."

Propping my head in my hand the same way she is, I challenge, "Do I?"

"I'm just saying, we both know we're fucked when it comes to the opposite sex and our views of relationships."

"Fool us once, shame on us, fool us twice?"

"Not a chance," she finishes for me. Her words are heavy with melancholy, only adding to the weight of regret sitting on my chest since long before my run-in with Paxton tonight.

Anxious to end this conversation as quickly as possible, I face the opposite wall and close my eyes. "Goodnight, Squeaks."

"Can I ask you something?" she adds.

"Yeah?" I sigh.

"Do you ever…do you ever wonder who has it easier?" she whispers. Her words swirl into the black abyss separating us, leaving me more exposed than I'd like.

Knowing I'll regret it, I roll onto my side and face her again. "What do you mean?"

"Archer's gone."

The familiar pang in my chest sharpens, but I force my breathing to stay steady.

"And he…he never knew how you felt, and you have to live the rest of your life wondering what if, while knowing you'll never get the answer," she continues. "Meanwhile, Jax is…Jax is very much alive, and I did shoot my shot, and yes, he had every right to pump the brakes, but it's been years now, and even though I know how stupid it was to tell him how I felt, he never reached out. Never…tried to make amends or…or even tell me why I wasn't enough."

It's bullshit. She's more than enough. Hell, Rory Buchanan is incredible. She literally ticks every box on every guy's perfect girl list. Probably because she's a fan of lists in general, and the idea of not completing said list to its fullest is considered a travesty in the girl's eyes, but still. You can't change your age. And ten years is a hell of a lot of them to look past.

Trying to lighten the mood, I say, "I mean, technically, you blocked his number and vowed to never see him again, so I'm not sure how he could contact you to make amends, but…" Her quiet sniffle is louder than a foghorn in the silent room while also making me feel like shit for being so blunt. "Shit. I'm sorry, Rore."

"I think we both know why I vowed to never see him again, Tate." She pauses. "Do you want to know the really stupid part? Even though I have no reason to be hung up on him, and honestly, I'm not anymore, I still can't get myself to like, open up." Her quiet voice cracks. "To anyone. And how ridiculous is that, you know? It was a stupid, meaningless crush, and I still can't let it go? I know I'm pretty. I know there are plenty of fish in the sea, but the idea of being vulnerable enough to open the door with one of them feels about as freaking pleasant as rolling around on shards of glass."

I grimace. "Ouch."

"Exactly. And then there's you, and don't take this the wrong way," she warns, "but you've basically decided to cope with your lack of emotional intimacy by jumping into bed with any hot guy who says he's interested."

I jerk back. "I repeat, ouch."

"You know I'm right," she argues. "And honestly? You do you, but—"

"Thank you, and I will."

Ignoring said interruption, she repeats, "*But.* Seeing a guy who looked at you tonight the way I would kill to have a guy look at me, and yet you want nothing to do with him feels… empty, almost."

My body tenses at her observation.

*Well, shit.*

If Rory was anyone else in this moment, I'd probably chuck my pillow at them. But Rory is Rory. My confidante. My one and only. My sister from another mister. She's the only one who's managed to slip past my defenses since her brother's death, and even though I like to give her shit for being little miss rainbows and butterflies, I almost envy her. The way she's able to find a positive spin on most situations despite the matching shit-sandwiches we were given by fate. Even if I'm the one who claims the invincible title more often than not, she's always been stronger than me, and I think we both know it.

Tucking my hair behind my ear, I carefully point out, "I've been empty for a long time, Squeaks. You know this."

"Maybe we both are."

She sounds so…broken. So lost. It kills me.

"Nah. Don't lump yourself in with me." I climb out of bed and pad across the cool floor. Grateful Hades is on Rory's opposite side, I slide in beside her, pulling her against me the same way I wish my older sister would. "You're amazing, Rore. And one day, you're going to find a guy who's worthy of you. I promise."

She sniffles and burrows closer. "I think you will, too, you know."

"Always the hopeless romantic," I quip.

Another sniffle cuts through the quiet room. "Someone's gotta cheer for us, right?"

My heart cracks. The two hopeless underdogs. We're a real screwed-up duo, that's for sure.

"I'll always cheer for you," I announce, giving her one more squeeze. "Now, you need to let me get some sleep, since apparently, I'm not allowed to call in sick or I'll wind up on your shit list."

"And don't you forget it."

# PAXTON

L ifting my hand, I rap my knuckles against the heavy oak door and wait. Footsteps echo on the opposite side before Dodger appears and nods his head in greeting. "Hey, man. Come on in."

He opens the door the rest of the way, holding it for me as I step over the threshold and into the foyer. It's nice. Screams money, too. Vaulted ceiling. Spiral staircase. Tall windows like the place I've been staying. It's a family home, or so I've heard. Been passed down for generations. I tuck my hands into my front pockets and scan what I can see of the large house since it's my first time being at Judge's. Dodger's basement has the studio, so there's never a need to meet at Judge's when we're all in town, or at least it's what they tell me. Personally, I think it's because Titas, Judge's brother, is too much of a tight-ass to let someone from The Drift into his personal space, but what do I know? Yeah, this isn't Judge's place, even if his name is next to his brother's on the deed. It solely belongs to Titas Harden through and through, like everything else in this town.

As I walk through the foyer, Dodger closes the door

behind us, motioning to an office on the right. Black marble. Chrome accents. Monochromatic artwork. The place feels as cold as Judge's heart.

*Not surprised.*

Leaning against the glass desk in the middle of the room, Dodger asks, "So, what's up?"

I look around the foyer, finding it empty except for us. "Where's Tuke?"

"Last I checked, still in the Cayman islands, smoking enough pot for all of us."

"Sounds like Tuke," I laugh. "And Judge?"

Dodger peers around me. "He's—"

Judge walks into the room as if on cue. He looks as put together as always, but after sharing a bus and more late nights on tour than I can count, it's easy to see past the facade. Bags under his eyes. His shirt untucked. That's it. Two minor details, but it's enough. The guy's being drug through the wringer.

"Take a seat, Pax," Dodger suggests.

I sit on the black leather couch along the side of the wall beneath the window overlooking the quiet winding road while Judge takes his place behind the desk and Dodge leans against the edge of it.

Eyeing both of them, I note, "This feels…official."

"You said you wanted to talk shop," Dodger reminds me. "Figured this was the best place for it."

He's not wrong. Since IndieCent Vows' hiatus announcement, the paparazzi have been dying to be the first to find the why behind our decision. Then again, so have I.

"How are you liking the new place?" Dodger asks.

"It's all right." I hesitate. "Different."

"Than the tour bus or The Drift?" Judge chimes in.

"Both," I answer with a dry laugh. Pretty sure our tour bus

could've fit in the new kitchen, and The Drift? It's something else entirely.

Twisting in his office chair toward the window, Judge takes in the main road outside. "You'll get used to it."

I doubt it, but I don't bother arguing.

"So how are the nephews?" I ask.

"Pains in my ass, like always," Judge grunts.

"Any reason why your brother couldn't be the one to whip them into shape instead of shitting on our tour?"

"We wanted a break anyway," Dodger says, as if he needs to remind me that I've been feeling burnt out for years. Although, if I'm being honest, sitting on my ass in a mansion on the beach isn't exactly all it's cracked up to be, either.

I nod slowly. "It doesn't explain why Titas couldn't come here himself."

Crossing one ankle over the other with his hands in his pockets like we're talking about the weather or some shit, Dodger defends, "He's busy."

Sure, he is.

Instead of pushing a moot point, I cut to the chase, asking, "Can you at least tell me if the band is finished or not? I'm going out of my mind here."

"Then maybe you need to find a hobby," Dodger suggests dryly.

I smirk back at him. "I could always ask Judge's nephews if they have any suggestions."

The amused curve of Dodger's mouth falls. "Not funny."

My smirk grows. "Too soon?"

With a twitch beneath his right eye, Judge rests his elbows on the desk separating us, and I prepare myself for a brotherly lecture. Because that's what he is. That's what they both are. Brothers. Touring the world for years together will do that to you. Place a familial spin on a business relationship while giving everyone in the makeshift family front-row seats to the good, the bad, and the ugly. Usually, it's not a problem. Usually, we're making fun of each other or sharing inside jokes. Then there are times like this. When everyone's on edge, and the lines most people would respect with colleagues is long gone, leaving a shit-ton of room for overstepping bounds.

"Look, I know you don't want to hear this, but it's the same shit as before," Judge informs me. "The band is important, yes. But you've already made plenty of money, and family comes first."

I bite my tongue to keep from pointing out that when it comes to Judge's family, money and familial ties are a blurred line at best.

"Any idea when you'll have an update or a plan or…something?" I prod.

Judge sighs. "Not at this moment, no."

"And what do you know?"

His eyes narrow, proving I hit a nerve, though I'm too annoyed to give a shit. "I know you have more than enough money to be spending your time doing whatever you want instead of wasting ours by calling a meeting we've explicitly told you we're not ready to have," Judge replies.

Asshole.

My fingers dig into the arm of the leather couch. "You know, I ran into Roman the other day."

"And?" Dodger asks.

"And we talked," I offer.

"About what?" Judge pushes.

"About the fact that both of us are far from The Drift nowadays."

"Anything else?" Dodger prods.

I could tell him no. I could lie and not mention Roman's invitation to fight. But even though my bandmates don't always deserve it, I know where my loyalties lie. "Asked if I could still fight," I add.

Dodge exchanges a curious look with Judge, proving the information holds the weight I assumed it would.

"Did he, now?" Dodger mutters.

"Yeah." I scratch my temple. "The question is, why would he do that?"

"Don't play stupid," Dodger demands. "We all know we're here because they've been dabbling in some shady shit."

Stretching my legs out in front of me, I say, "Exactly. And if I can piece together why we're here, Roman can, too." My attention cuts to Judge. "And so can your nephews."

Like a vault, Judge gives nothing away as he agrees, "I'm sure they can."

"So why be subtle?" I ask.

"Because they're slippery little fuckers," he admits grudgingly. "And even if they don't want to acknowledge it when it's inconvenient for them, those boys carry the family name. They're expected to uphold a set of standards most don't understand. Especially Roman. If they did, we wouldn't be here. We'd be on tour, and there would be no need for you to find a new hobby, so if you feel like reminding Roman of this, be my guest."

Well, would you look at that? Seems the guy can string together more than two sentences after all. I hold his stare from across the office, fighting the urge to be an asshole, when it's clear he wants to claim the title after a speech like that.

"Why does it matter what your nephews do outside of school?" I ask. "Yeah, they're doing some illegal shit on the side, but having their shady uncle come and tell them to stop is a little pot-calling-the-kettle-black, don't you think?"

"Careful," Dodger warns.

"You know I'm right. And you forget I was raised here," I

add. "Judge is the one who started all the bullshit underground activities before his nephews were even in middle school. Can you blame them for following in his footsteps?"

"I'm aware of the part I played," Judge grumbles. "Why else do you think I'm here?"

"Then shut it down, and we'll be on our way," I suggest.

"It's not so simple." Judge scrubs his hand over his face. "Those boys might think they have a handle on shit, but their activities are starting to draw the wrong kind of attention."

"Which is why we need to dissuade the boys from running this city into the ground," Dodge argues, speaking for his best friend.

"And how do you plan to do that?" I demand.

Pinching the bridge of his nose, a dejected Dodge mutters, "Good question."

Judge only stares at me, his jaw ticcing.

It isn't the first time I've been on the receiving end of Judge's intensity. With nearly black, soulless eyes, a shaved head, and enough muscles to battle an ox, he's a scary motherfucker on his good days. When his blood is already simmering beneath the surface of his olive skin, and his sole focus is directed at you? He's downright terrifying.

"What is it?" I snap.

He leans back in his chair, and cocks his head. "You want something to do?"

"Other than sit on my ass and wait for the next tour, if there is one at all?" I scoff. "Yeah. Yeah, I guess you could say I could use a distraction."

"Stay on the paparazzi's radar."

I pull back, surprised. "You hate the paparazzi."

"Which is why I'm suggesting you stay on their radar. Not me."

"And how would this help us get back on tour?" I push.

"One. Mindy says any publicity is good publicity," Dodger

says, mentioning the band's publicist. "We need IndieCent Vows to stay relevant even if we're taking a break."

"It doesn't hurt that the more the public is focused on you, the less they'll be focused on my nephews," Judge adds without bothering to hide his annoyance.

He makes a good point on both counts. And if I agree, at least I'll have something to do. I'm going stir crazy here, and it's only been a couple weeks. The possibility of being holed up in one of Judge's family mansions while Judge and Dodger put out a few familial fires over who knows how long feels like torture.

"To what end?" I ask.

Judge sighs. "Until my brother decides his sons are in the clear."

"So we need Titas' approval?" I challenge.

"If you want to go on tour again, yes," Judge answers numbly.

The hilarity of the situation withers like spoiled fruit.

*Is he serious right now?*

I'm annoyed we're playing this game. Annoyed *I'm* playing this game, considering my lack of connection to the infamous and shady as fuck Titas Harden. Why the hell should he have any say in what I—or any of my bandmates— do in the first place? Attempting to keep my annoyance in check, I rest my elbows on my knees and state the obvious. "Your brother's a dick."

"Trust me, he knows," Dodger says under his breath.

"He's also the reason IndieCent Vows is what it is," Judge adds, albeit grudgingly. Twisting his chair toward the window again, he steeples his fingers in front of him, even more steely than usual.

"So what do you say?" Dodger offers. "Help us out. Keep the paparazzi's attention. Have fun. Fuck girls. Get into fights. All your favorite things."

"Sounds like a great plan. There's only one problem." Running my tongue along my upper teeth, I keep my frustration in check, reminding him, "You know I left that life behind."

"Then revisit it," Dodger offers. "Because right now, we don't have anything else." He motions toward the hallway. "Come on. I'll walk you out." He guides me toward the entrance, but the sound of our footsteps against the marble tile doesn't even begin to put a dent in my racing thoughts.

When we reach the front door, I say, "Can I ask you something?"

He nods.

"Why does this matter?"

He hesitates, peering over his shoulder to confirm we're alone in the foyer before giving me his full attention. "A lot of weight comes with a name, Pax. I know you don't get that 'cause…" His lips press together. "Look at it this way. At least it's one thing you don't have to worry about. But Judge? There's more at play here than it seems. We'll talk later, yeah?"

"Yeah, sure thing." I turn toward the front but hesitate. "Let me know if you need anything else, all right?"

"Yeah, no worries."

# 18

# TATUM

I'm late. I mean, technically, I make my own schedule, but sleeping in wasn't on my agenda this morning, and it's been one thing after another. As I pull up to the gate of my last house for the evening, I notice a car parked not far down the road. Someone's leaning against the driver's side door. Squinting, I realize they're holding a camera with a massive lens pointed directly at the house.

What the hell? If this isn't fishy behavior, I don't know what is. Maybe the owner of the house is famous or something? Or maybe not? Honestly, I don't even know.

When the creeper catches me staring, I punch in the gate code and wait for it to open. Once it does, I pull through but stay parked on the opposite side, refusing to move on the off-chance the creeper tries to ride my bumper and follow me onto the private property.

Thankfully, the gate closes without any issue, and I pull up the long driveway, parking in front. It's still strange. Having access to a random person's house. A potentially famous random person. Yup. People are way too trusting. My body aches from the previous two houses I finished cleaning today, but at least Rory can't give me shit for dropping the ball at work. And to be honest, I'm grateful for the distraction. But I could really use a nap.

One more house.

I saved my favorite for last. The baby blue colonial with the music room.

Once I'm inside, I set the cleaning supplies on the kitchen counter, head straight to the music room, and grab a Doomsday record from the collection. After setting it on the turntable, I position the needle and click play. It blares through the speakers as I get to work scrubbing, mopping, and dusting every inch of the mansion until it's practically sparkling.

Blowing the tendrils of hair from my face, I assess my work and smile when my attention catches on a worn book with a familiar cover. It's lying on the window seat overlooking the ocean. Curious, I move closer, recognizing the title. It's *The Count of Monte Cristo*. And not just any copy. It's the same edition I was reading when Archer died. The memory hits out of nowhere, fast as lightning and just as sharp.

I peek into the empty hallway, then check the time on my phone. I don't know why. It's not like anyone is ever home when I'm cleaning. Honestly, I would be convinced ghosts lived in all of the houses I clean if I didn't notice the fingerprints on the faucets or the unkempt sheets. Still, the book calls to me. Sitting in my favorite spot in the house. Begging to be opened. I haven't read *The Count of Monte Cristo* in months. I try to read it every year. Not because I'm necessarily in love with the story—it's a tragedy—but because it reminds me of him. Archer. I was in the middle of reading it for the first time when I saw him for the last time.

*"Hey, Tate."*

*My cheeks heat as I look up from the pages, finding the one and only Archer Buchanan staring at me.*

*"Oh. Hi."*

*"How's the book?"*

*I shrug and turn back to the pages. The words blur together, but the idea of holding Archer's ocean blue gaze is more than I can bear. Not without melting into a puddle on the spot. "It's fine."*

*The couch dips as he sits beside me. "It's one of my favorites."*

Breathe, Tate. Breathe.

*I sneak a peek at him. "Oh?"*

*"Yeah." He chuckles. "Although, I gotta say, Dante's quite the grudge holder."*

*I look down at the open pages again. "He is, isn't he?"*

*"Do you think he should pick Mercedes over his need for revenge?"*

*Nibbling my bottom lip, I consider his question and steal another peek at the boy beside me. "I mean, because of his best friend, he was locked up for years. He has every right to be pissed."*

*"True," Archer concedes. "I dunno, though. Part of me wonders if living out the rest of his life with Mercedes would've been worth letting his grudge go." He smiles. "But I* am *a sucker for a pretty face, so...maybe I'm part of the problem?"*

*I laugh. "You're never part of the problem."*

*"So confident," he teases.*

*I look back at my book, unable to hold his gaze for another second. "Hardly."*

*"You should be," he pushes. "You're a catch, Tatum Taylor. There will be plenty of guys lining up to take you out, and I'm sure they'll be more than willing to let go of their grudges if it lets them have a chance with you." Dropping his voice low, he adds, "Once you get to college."*

The memory makes my eyes burn, but I blink the feeling away. I shouldn't—I know I shouldn't—but the reading nook overlooking the ocean calls to me. I slip my shoes off, curl up on the cushion, and open the book.

~

"HEY! YOU HERE?" SOMEONE YELLS.

I jerk up in response and rub at my eyes. I have no idea what time it is, but the sun's set, painting the room in different shades of gray.

Holy shit, it's late. Like, really late, considering I sat down around 5 pm. I fucked up.

I reach down and grab the heel of my left shoe, trying to shove my foot into it as quickly as possible. The sound of footsteps echoes from the stairs, acting like gasoline on my already frazzled brain. My pulse gallops, and I reach for the second shoe.

"Yo? Where are you?" the same masculine voice calls. He's closer now. Right outside the door. A shadow moves along the crack, and my throat swells.

I'm so screwed.

Shoving my heel into my sneaker, I stand as the door's hinges squeak softly. Then, there he is. The owner of the house. Who just caught his house cleaner literally asleep on the job.

*Please don't fire me.*

I smooth my shirt out, peeking up at the stranger. "Hi."

With a small smirk, he rests his shoulder against the doorjamb, assessing me. "Hello."

A shiver races down my spine as I take in the man's strong jaw and long throat. The top two buttons on his white dress shirt are undone, giving me a perfect view of his dark skin. With black curly hair and chocolate brown eyes, a heavy dose of arrogance wafts off him. Why wouldn't it? The man's drop-dead gorgeous and clearly filthy rich if his home is anything to go by.

"And you are?" he prods.

"I, uh, I'm the maid," I announce. "Tatum."

"Roman." His long legs eat up the distance as he strides toward me, offering his hand. When I take it, he adds, "Nice to meet you, Tatum the maid."

"You, too." I gulp and slowly slip my hand from his grasp. "I should…get going."

"You from around here?" he prods.

"Yes and no."

"I haven't seen you before." He drops his voice an octave lower, though I have no idea how it's even possible, turning his already silky voice into velvet. "And I know everyone in this town."

My gaze flicks up to him. Holy shit, this guy's tall. Clearing my throat, I ask, "Do you want me to leave the hide-a-key on the kitchen counter or would you like me to lock up?"

Rocking back on his heels, he tucks his hands into the front pockets of his charcoal slacks. "You're leaving?"

"I'm, uh, I'm finished for the day, so, yes. Yes, I'm leaving. Have a great evening…"

*Shit, what was his name?*

"Roman," he repeats.

"Have a great evening, Roman," I murmur, moving around him.

He follows my movements with his eyes while the same smirk from before tugs at his lips. "See you around, Tatum the maid."

# 19

# PAXTON

The sun is gone, having dipped below the horizon while I was at Judge's. I consider stopping by my old gym to see if I can sign up for some training but decide against it. For now. Even if I *am* desperate to clear my head. My headlights cut through the darkness as I drive home. Noticing the lights slipping through the curtains, I frown. The maid must've forgotten to turn them off when she left. I pull up the winding path leading to the garage, but my brows pull down. There's a car out front. Sleek. Black. Toyota Supra with a straight six engine.

Only one guy I know owns this car.

*What is Roman doing here?*

I park in the garage, climb out of my car, and head inside. Tossing my keys onto the kitchen counter, I catch Roman by the unlit fireplace. "Hey, man."

"Hey. I like the place. It's nice."

"It belongs to Judge's family," I explain. "What are you doing here?"

"Checking in." With his feet propped on the coffee table,

he thumbs through a worn copy of one of my books. It's *The Count of Monte Cristo*.

"Where'd you get that?" I demand, surprising us both with my possessiveness over a book. It's probably because I just saw Tatum, and the wound is still fresh, but it's not like I actually care.

*Right?*

Roman closes the book, drops his feet to the floor, and sets it on the coffee table. "Your maid was reading it."

My brows dip. "What?"

"I said, your maid was reading it. Up in your music room," he clarifies.

"What was my maid doing reading on the job?"

Cupping the back of his head, he leans back on the leather couch. "No idea. She's cute, though. Pretty sure I woke her up from a nap." He chuckles softly. "You might wanna check the tape to see if she touched anything else."

Frustration flares inside of me, but I try to keep it in check, scratching my temple with my forefinger. "She was… sleeping?"

"Like a hot, black-haired Goldilocks," he confirms.

*What the hell?*

I unlock my phone and pull up the footage from earlier today, scrolling through the past few hours until a clear shot comes into view. When I see her, my stomach bottoms out, and I rest my ass against the kitchen counter to keep from falling.

There she is. Tatum Taylor. Curled up on the window seat in my music room like a fucking ghost.

"See?" Roman prods from the couch. "Cute, right?"

My attention shifts to him as I try piecing together why the bane of my existence was in my house earlier today. "What'd she say to you?"

"Only that she was the maid."

The maid?

*Visiting, my ass.*

I'm gonna kill her.

"Does she know this isn't your place?" I ask.

"No idea. It was my first time meeting her. Why?"

I consider my options and what I should or shouldn't divulge. Roman might be the closest thing I have to family, but even then, things with Tate have never been black and white. After the bonfire? They're grayer than ever.

"There a problem, Pax?" he questions.

*Yeah. Yeah, there is.*

My teeth grind, and I answer, "I know her."

"Well, yeah. She's your cleaning—"

"I mean from outside of her profession."

A divot forms between his brows. "So?"

So, the little brat lied to me. Twice. No, three times. Four? Fuck, at this point, I've lost count.

I'm an idiot. She lives here. Works here. And she honestly thought I'd let her get away with lying to my face after giving me a blow job and a fake number? Yeah, don't think I haven't already tried contacting her after our little rendezvous on the beach.

Not a chance.

Rubbing my jaw, I tuck my phone back in my pocket, stride toward him, sit on the opposite couch, and rest my elbows on my knees. "I'm gonna need you to do me a favor."

"I got you," he offers without any hesitation. "What do you need?"

"If you see her, call me. And I mean immediately. Do not let her out of your sight. We clear?"

"Sure thing."

"Thanks, man. I owe you."

"Two times," he clarifies.

My brows pull. "What do you mean?"

"Aren't you gonna ask why I'm here?"

Suspicion winds its way up my spine, and I ask, "Why are you here?"

Setting his feet back on the coffee table, Roman hooks one ankle over the other, getting comfortable. "Jagger wants to see you fight."

My eyes widen, but I stay quiet. Not gonna lie. When I last talked with Roman, I figured it was a moot conversation, especially considering my connection to Judge. There's no way Jagger, Hawke, or Ford would want me anywhere near their extracurricular activities.

"What's the catch, Rome?" I demand.

"No catch."

"Don't lie to me," I warn.

"I'm not lying. Hell, I'm not even officially extending the offer...*yet*."

"So, you might have an opening, but you're not sure?"

"Depends on how well you show up in front of Jagger." He shrugs. "My word only goes so far, and it's been a few years since I've seen you brawl."

Me and him both.

Officially, anyway.

Flexing my hands, I try to keep the influx of adrenaline from taking over my system at the opportunity Roman's presenting me. What it means for my future in the band, and what it means for now. The rush from a good fight is something else. It's addictive and more enticing than I care to admit. The only thing comparable is when I'm on stage, playing for thousands of people, and since that isn't an option at the moment, the idea of opening the door for fighting to give me my fix is tempting. Maybe a little too tempting.

The thought niggles at the back of my mind as I turn back

to Roman sitting on my couch. "I'm not interested in anything official. I only want to let off some steam."

"So let it off." He shrugs. "Come meet the guys. See what you think. See what they think. No commitment."

No commitment. It shouldn't surprise me that they want to see what I can do before they even consider giving me an opening. Not that I want one in the first place. The nephews are particular about who they invite to participate in their… activities. Whether they can keep their mouths shut. Whether or not they can bring in more bets. Whether or not they know how to put on a good show. Whether or not they can be trusted.

"What do you say?" Roman prods.

It's a good question. One I should genuinely consider after my conversation earlier with what's left of the band. When Roman mentioned a fight coming up at the bonfire, I wasn't sure he'd be able to convince the nephews to let me in, assuming I was too close to the source of their family friction to be trusted. Or, maybe they're more aware of IndieCent Vows' inner workings—and the lopsided power dynamics—to know better.

"Does Judge know?" I ask.

"It won't kill him," he replies, proving he's smarter than Judge gives him—or anyone else, for that matter—credit.

My mouth flickers with amusement. "That's a diplomatic answer."

"I learned from the best. So, are you in or not?"

"And it's no commitment?" I push.

"Already said it wasn't."

"Then, why waste Jagger's time?"

"Pretty sure Jagger will take any opportunity he can get to beat the shit out of someone." He chuckles. "Even if it's for free and without an audience."

Apparently, it's something we have in common.

Rolling my shoulders, I consider Roman's proposition along with the band's current situation. "Sure," I decide. "Why not?"

"All right, I'll let the guys know." He rubs his hands together and stands.

"Don't tell anyone," I warn. "Even if Jagger decides to give me a spot, I'm not guaranteeing I'll take it."

"You change your mind?"

"I'm on the fence," I return. "The band's PR doesn't like covering up my shit as much as they like covering up Dodger's and Judge's, and I'm not stupid enough to believe you won't exploit the fact that I'm a rockstar to drum up bets. It's too lucrative."

"Hell yeah, it is," he agrees without an ounce of shame. "But all right, man. We'll play it by ear. Make sure everyone's on the same page before we start putting out any feelers."

"Thanks, man."

"Anytime. I'll send you the address," he adds with a pointed look.

"I'll be there."

# 20

# TATUM

Sometimes, I kind of want to smack my best friend because no matter how much I try to ignore it, I can't stop thinking about what she said, especially after stumbling upon *The Count of Monte Cristo* at Roman's house earlier. Like seriously. What the hell? It's like I'm being haunted from beyond the grave.

*"Don't take this the wrong way," Rory warns, "but you've basi-cally decided to cope with your lack of emotional intimacy by jumping into bed with any hot guy who says he's interested, but seeing a guy who looked at you tonight the way I would kill to have a guy look at me, and yet you want nothing to do with him feels... empty, almost."*

*"I've been empty for a long time, Squeaks. You know this."*

I haven't talked with Rory about Archer and Jaxon in...I don't even know how long. But every time we do, it always takes a while to...I don't know. Recover, I guess. To put each boy back in their proverbial box instead of drowning in the past like I have been since the bonfire.

Determined to close said box even faster than usual, I've stayed away from my laptop—and the worn black notebook I know is hidden inside—all week. Throwing myself into cleaning, I scrub the marble floors until my hands are raw and my muscles ache. I still haven't been back to Roman's house yet. But I haven't gotten a call from my boss, either, proving he's yet to out me. I'm honestly more grateful than I'd like to admit. I kind of like cleaning. The monotony of it all. Everything except the quiet, which is where my trusty headphones come in.

I still haven't aired out all the nitty gritty details from my run-in with Pax at the bonfire to Rory. Or at least, not the blowjob part. She wouldn't judge. I know her better than that. No, I think she'd be worried. Or excited. Or both. Because even though I look like a loose cannon who's flailing around most of the time, I'm very much in control of every aspect of my life, including my perceived bad decisions and one-night stands. It's what makes the bonfire—and all things Pax—so terrifying. At the bonfire, I was *not* in control. Honestly, I'm impressed I managed to change the last digit of my phone number when I rattled off the numbers to Pax instead of relenting and giving him access to me when it's the last thing I need.

I've been waiting for my thoughts to mellow out. For the bonfire, and my conversation with Rory, and finding *The Count of Monte Cristo*, and my fuck up at work to drift away and leave me numb. But instead, I've felt like a livewire. Like the tiniest things—a memory, a smell, a simple thought—is enough to engulf me for hours, and I'm afraid it's driving me insane. Literally. Between my interaction with Pax and the reminder of Archer, I'm ready for a cold glass of…anything I can get my hands on.

Smoothing out my skintight red dress that leaves nothing to the imagination, I rub my lips together and smile at Rory through the bathroom mirror's reflection.

It's finally Friday, and the idea of finding someone to

distract me from everything else in my life is more appealing than almost anything. However, when I suggested a night out to Rory, she gave me a big, fat no. Not cool, but it also isn't the first time. Even so, I'm not ready to give up on her yet.

Fluffing my hair, I ask, "You sure you don't want to come?"

"Only for you to ditch me once Cowboy decides to take you home?" She gives me a thumbs up. "I think I'm good. Thanks, though."

"Technically, we don't know if Cowboy is going to be there," I point out. "It's not like I was able to solidify our plans before Pax interrupted." *And I gave him a blowjob*, I silently add, vowing to take that tiny little tidbit to my grave.

The last time we hooked up, I didn't sleep with anyone for six months. Six. Months. That's how much he affected me, and I refuse to give him that much power this time around. Yup. I'm ending the seven-day dry spell tonight, come hell or high water.

"Trust me, as long as Cowboy is still in town, he'll show," Rory argues. "You're like a pretty orange carrot being dangled, and he's a very hungry horse."

"Farm reference," I note. "Classy."

She rolls her eyes. "Go on. I need to take Hades for a walk, anyway. Have fun, but be safe, will you?"

"Always." I blow her a quick kiss and head to the main floor. There are perks to living across the street from a bar, and this is one of them.

Hello, no need for a designated driver.

A white pelican silhouette is engraved on the heavy wood door. It looks weathered and worn and artsy and surprisingly enticing. As I pull it open and step inside the bar, the smell of whiskey and cedar envelops me, bringing with it a hominess I can't help but appreciate. The lights are low, and classic rock plays on the speakers while images of lighthouses and ships battling huge waves hang on the walls. I'm kind of in love with it.

"How can I help you?" the bartender asks.

Keeping the hem of my dress *just* high enough for some sorry sucker to buy the rest of my drinks for the night without making myself look like I'm guaranteed to go home with them, I slide onto a barstool and order, "Jack and diet, please."

"Coming right up."

As he gets to work making my drink, I take in the patrons scattered around the bar. Yeah, there are definitely some solid options for tonight if Cowboy decides to no-show. Good. Maybe dressing up won't be a wasted effort after all. As the bartender sets a glass in front of me, heat hits my back, and I look over my shoulder before my head snaps forward.

Shit.

It's the man from earlier this week. The one who caught me asleep in his house.

Double shit.

I reach for my glass and bring it to my lips, praying he doesn't notice me.

"Hello, again," the man greets me.

So much for him not noticing me.

*Breathe.*

Peeking over my shoulder again, I murmur, "Hello, Roman."

"Ah, so she remembers my name."

"How could I forget? You're the guy who has the power to fire me, right?"

With a confidence I can't help but admire, he motions to the empty seat beside me. "You waiting for someone?"

I could say yes. I should say yes. But the idea of potentially rubbing him the wrong way when I already embarrassed myself in front of him feels about as appealing as…I don't know. Something awful. Besides, he is cute, and I could use a distraction since Cowboy's currently missing in action.

Despite my better judgment, I kick out the barstool beside mine. "It's all yours."

Three drinks later, Cowboy's still absent, and I'm on the dance floor with Roman. His hands are on my waist as he pulls me closer, letting me feel every inch of his very hard, very toned body.

Yup. This guy might be my boss, but considering the fact he caught me taking a nap at his place, I have a feeling a solid hookup might convince him to keep his lips zipped. He also looks like someone who knows what he's doing and is up for a one-night-stand which is perfect since I need one as soon as possible if I have any hope of dulling the memory of last week with Pax. "You should come back to my place," he says, proving we're on the same page even if I'm not ready to give in fully.

With a Cheshire grin, I murmur, "A bit presumptuous, don't you think?"

He leans closer, burrowing his head against my throat while letting me feel his smile against my skin.

"I prefer confident."

"You think I'm this easy?"

"I think you came to this bar looking for a distraction." He lifts his head, giving me a front-row seat to his grin. "All I'm saying is I'm happy to oblige, if you'd like me to. No strings attached."

"You're my boss."

"I'm your boss's friend," he clarifies.

My brows dip. "What?"

"That's not my house."

Confused, I shake my head. "You didn't tell me—"

"You didn't give me the chance." His gaze drops to my

lips. "And then I thought it was cute watching you squirm. But I promise I'm a complete gentleman." He bends closer and drops his voice low. "A complete gentleman who has no issue sneaking a pretty girl into his friend's house to use his jacuzzi for the night. What do you say?"

I should say no. I should go home and sleep off my buzz. But if I do, will I dream of Pax or Archer? Neither choice makes me feel any better. Actually, both kind of make me feel like shit, so…

Toying with my gold ring, I ask, "You good to drive?"

"Had one beer."

"Lead the way."

HIS CAR IS NICE. LIKE, REALLY NICE. BLACK. CHROME. Leather. It smells like money. A lot of money. Not in a pretentious way. It's more like the man knows how to appreciate the finer things in life, and I almost admire it. The soft, dark leather caresses the backs of my thighs as he drives us back to his friend's house.

I can't believe I'm doing this. I shouldn't be here.

*It's one night. It'll quiet the static.*

Holding onto the thought, I sink further into the passenger seat, succumbing to what's left of the alcohol in my veins.

After inputting the code, the wrought iron gate moves to life without even the softest of squeaks, and Roman peels up the drive. Once we exit the car, a tiny voice of reason echoes in the back of my brain, somehow managing to slip past the slight fog of alcohol. If Roman's friend finds me here and somehow connects me to being his maid, will he be mad? Is it like, a conflict of interest or something? I really don't want to be fired.

Folding my arms, I run my hands along my bare skin and stay back, hesitant to walk inside.

"There a problem?" Roman asks over his shoulder as he inserts the key into the lock.

Nibbling the inside of my cheek, I reply, "You sure your friend won't mind us being here?"

"I promise he'd like nothing more."

The amusement in his voice sparks my curiosity, but I'm too anxious to analyze it.

"Maybe we should…walk around the side to go for a dip in the hot tub," I suggest. "You know, instead of going inside. It feels weird."

"You don't want to borrow one of the spare swimsuits?"

"Do I need one?" I tease.

He tilts his head, his eyes rolling over me. "God, I hope not."

I laugh. "And you say you're a gentleman."

His low, throaty chuckle joins mine. It's a reminder of exactly how charismatic this man is as he lifts his hands into the air. "I promise I'll keep my hands to myself. Shall we?" He glances at the house again, then turns to me and presses his hand to my spine, guiding me around back. Crickets cut through the sound of the ocean as we make our way around the side of the house until the balcony comes into view. The hot tub's cover is already off as steam twists into the night air, looking far more enticing than I've ever seen it, which is saying something.

Did he plan to bring someone here tonight?

Probably.

It should bother me, and maybe it would if I wasn't so desperate to erase last weekend, but it only spurs me on. At least he knows how to have a proper one-night-stand with no strings attached. Unlike someone else I know.

*Don't think about him.*

Pulling my hair over one shoulder, I give Roman an innocent look. Catching the hint, he moves closer, unzipping the dress and exposing my back.

Just like always, an image of Archer flashes through my mind. Not just like always, an image Pax follows it. I shove both pictures aside, along with the familiar guilt accompanying them, and let the dress fall to my feet. In nothing but my white thong and matching bra, I dip my toe into the water. Heat licks up my skin, leaving goosebumps in its wake, and I sigh in appreciation before slipping the rest of the way in. It feels good. The burn. Reminding me I'm alive. I'm here.

Even though he isn't.

As I paste a smile on my face, Roman approaches me. The man's built like a linebacker. Broad shoulders, rippling muscles, and the promise of bad decisions. The sight is almost enough to dull Rory's words in the back of my mind.

*"Don't take this the wrong way,"* Rory warns, *"but you've basically decided to cope with your lack of emotional intimacy by jumping into bed with any hot guy who says he's interested."*

Well, would you look at that. She's right again.

Oblivious to my mental ping-pong game, Roman climbs into the hot tub and places his arms along the back, appearing every bit like the king of the underworld should.

I look back at the dark house. Or at least, it should be dark. One of the windows is lit. The music room, I think. I could've sworn I turned it off.

*Didn't I?*

I dip a little further beneath the water's surface, attempting to hide in the shadows.

"Is your friend home?" I ask.

"Does it matter?" Roman challenges. "It's only me and you out here."

Me and him.

Also, not an answer, but I need my brain to stop freaking out more than my next breath, so I let it go.

*Just do it, Tate. Get him out of your head.*

*Get* both *of them out of your head.*

Forcing my body to relax, I shift closer to Roman as the hot water bubbles around us. "So, are you going to kiss me or what?"

"I promised I'd keep my hands to myself," he reminds me. His attention falls to my mouth. "Though you are making it difficult." His eyes flick to something behind him. "It's a shame you're taken."

My brows furrow. "What?"

Lights turn on, and I squeeze my eyes shut in an attempt to ease the sting from the contrast. Blinking slowly, I let my eyes adjust before finding a very attractive, very unreadable Paxton.

*What the hell?*

Arms crossed, he stares at us.

Okay, this is bad. This is really bad. But also, what the hell?

*What. The. Hell?*

21

## TATUM

Nausea swirls in my stomach, my mouth open like a gaping fish as I attempt to piece together exactly what's happening and why the one man I don't want to see is currently watching me—half-naked--in a hot tub with a guy who picked me up at a bar.

"Wait— I didn't— What are you doing here?" I ramble. Seriously? Am I hallucinating or—

"Pretty sure I could ask you the same question." Paxton looks at Roman. "You can go. Thanks."

"Thanks?" I murmur under my breath. Something definitely isn't adding up, but I'm too blindsided to piece anything together. The sooner I get out of here, the better, and since Roman's my ride, it seems I need to get my ass in gear and follow him before he leaves me in the dust.

*Gentleman, my ass.*

I press my hands to the edge of the hot tub, preparing to climb out, when Paxton's calm voice cuts through the silence. "Not you, Birthday Girl."

I scoff and continue my retreat.

"Not if you want to keep your job," he adds.

My muscles freeze.

Shit.

This is his house. He's the friend Roman mentioned. Which means, I'm his maid, and he's my boss.

*Shitty, shit, shit, shit.*

"Nice meeting you, Tatum," Roman says as he leaves me alone with the one man I really shouldn't be left with.

Mind still reeling, I stare at my hands pressed against the hot tub. I'm shaking. And I really hope he doesn't notice.

*Lie. Lie. Lie.*

What kind of lie could I say right now to get me out of this?

*Think, think, think, Tate. Think!*

My eyes stay glued to my hands pressed against the edge of the hot tub, my body warring with itself as if the options of fight, flight, or fawn are about as complex as calculus. I need to get out of here. But if I do, will I lose my job? And who's to say Pax really has any say in my employment anyway? He could be lying, he could be—

Something soft hits the ground behind me. It's followed by a wave of hot water hitting my back, and I turn around, deciding it's better to face the asshole head on. There he is. Paxton Six. A very naked Paxton Six. His clothes are gone. Scratch that. They're a small heap of fabric on the patio.

My gaze shoots back to Pax. "W-what are you—"

"I'm enjoying my hot tub," he answers. "I think the real question is, what are *you* doing here?"

He doesn't look pissed, but he doesn't look too happy, either. He looks…distant, despite being two feet away from me. I wish I knew him better. So I could read him easier. So I could know if he's going to call the cops on me for trespassing, or get me fired, or…something.

"I…" I gulp. "I'm…also enjoying your hot tub?"

His mouth twitches as his eyes fall to my chest. "I can see that."

Folding my arms over my boobs barely covered by my wet, lacy bra, I drop back into the water, using it to camouflage me. "Okay, look. I'm sorry I trespassed. I didn't know…"

"Didn't know this place belonged to me?" He doesn't wait for my response. "You know, this is twice now that I've caught you trying to trespass. Is it a habit of yours or…?"

"I'd say no, but you wouldn't believe me, anyway." I force a smile despite the panic growing in my gut. "Although, if we're going to discuss technicalities, your friend invited me, so…"

"He did, didn't he?" Pax chuckles. "I would've done it myself, but it seems I misheard your number the other night."

I start to stand again. "I should get going—"

He grasps my hand. "Stay."

I look down at his calloused fingers encompassing my wrist. His grip isn't firm by any means. I'm sure he'd let me go if I moved away from him. But I can't convince my body to listen. To move. Instead, I simply…stare.

"Why?" I lick my lips. "Why do you want me to stay?"

"Because you were obviously here to get laid—"

"Pretty sure that ship sailed the moment you scared my date away."

"It doesn't have to," he returns, matter-of-factly.

My gaze flicks to his, and I realize he isn't trying to seduce me. He's trying to poke the bear. To make me feel guilty for hooking up with him. For playing him like a fiddle. For showing up in his jacuzzi with the intention of doing the same thing with his friend. The irony isn't lost on me, considering Pax is the one who set this whole thing up in the first place. I challenge, "You think any cock will do?"

"I think we had fun the first time…until you told me you were engaged."

I roll my eyes, annoyed, though I can't decide if it's because of Pax's comment, the fact that I was manipulated into being here, or if it's because a simple, innocent touch by the bastard is making goosebumps break out along my skin despite the hot water I'm currently standing in—both figuratively and literally.

"You're never gonna let that go, are you?" I seethe.

Removing his hand from my wrist, he grips the back of the hot tub with his arms spread wide. "Then there was the bonfire, where you sucked me off before giving me a fake number. That was a really good time. For me at least. Have you used the memory to touch yourself, yet?"

I scoff. "Don't flatter yourself."

*Yes.*

"Tell me, are you even really my maid or did you break into my house just to fuck with my head again?"

I laugh, despite myself. "You know, for once, I wish you were onto something because that would've been priceless, but no."

"You sure?" he questions.

I shrug, and my bra strap slips off my shoulder, making the cup gape for the barest of seconds. I yank it back into place. "Call it a happy coincidence."

He gives me a slow nod, dragging his gaze from my left boob to my face again. "You know, I'd say I believe you, but considering your track record…"

My hand fists beneath the steamy surface as I fight the urge to slap the bastard. He really is infuriating. But what's worse is his nonchalance about the whole thing. How does he do it? He's clearly not afraid to call me out on my bullshit, but he's also acting like he isn't pissed about any of it. Which is…confusing.

He isn't the first person I've lied to. But, other than family, he is the first to stick around instead of giving me the middle finger and disappearing from my life entirely.

So, why did he go through the effort to bring me here?

Unable to stifle my curiosity, I dip my body back into the water, sit, and inspect the man across from me. And he lets me. Without a need to fill the silence or shy away from my blatant perusal of every inch of his skin. Hell, he basks in it. The silence. The charged air. The interest I have no doubt is rolling off me as I look at him. "Did you bribe Roman to bring me here?" I ask.

The water ripples around him as he shrugs, looking far sexier than he has any right to, considering the circumstances. "Didn't need to."

"Why?"

"He's a friend who…" Pax scratches the scruff of his jaw, his movement causing a tiny ripple across the surface. "Likes to watch things explode."

"And us showing up on your patio was going to cause an explosion?"

He stays quiet, his jaw flexing as his eyes fall to my cleavage.

"You still want me," I realize. "That's why you convinced Roman to bring me here. It's why you're offering your cock since any will do. Am I right?"

His gaze cuts to mine. "I want to know why you keep lying to me."

"It's cute that you want to be the exception."

"It's cute that you think I'm *not* the exception," he tosses back at me. "Why were you nervous when Roman unzipped your dress?"

I flinch away, caught off guard by the subject change and how easily he read me. "I wasn't nervous."

"Guilty then," he clarifies.

"Why would I feel guilty?"

His brows raise. "You tell me."

My mouth presses into a hard line, and I shake my head, annoyed with how easily this man seems to get under my skin.

The truth is, I've always hated it. The guilt I carry from every fucking touch. Like I'm betraying Archer or even Paxton or…myself. There's nothing wrong with hooking up with strangers. But when your heart belongs to someone else —someone who's in the fucking grave and never wanted it in the first place—it's a different kind of ache. One that makes me feel…pathetic.

"This has been fun," I announce. "Watching you try to manipulate me into getting what you want, but I'm going to go."

"I didn't say you could leave—"

"And I didn't ask permission," I quip. "You don't own me."

"Don't I?" He smirks. "Because I'm pretty sure I'm your boss, and from the digging I had Roman do, I know you don't live off your parents' money—"

"You had Roman look into me?"

I can't decide if I'm more pissed or impressed, although if I ever see Roman again, he's getting a swift knee to the balls for dragging me here under false pretenses, that's for sure.

"I would've gone to the source," he adds, "but since I don't have your number…"

*Smartass.*

Moving closer, I almost brush my lips against his, but stop at the last second. "No amount of money will ever be enough to own me." I pull back. "Now, if you'll excuse me." The ground is cool beneath my feet as I step out of the hot tub, my satisfaction at gaining the upper hand pulsing through me. He can say and think whatever he wants about me, but the truth is, he has no idea who I am, and I have every intention of keeping it that way, even if he is my boss.

Paxton stands, gifting me with the perfect view of his rippling abs as the water trails down them. "Your ride's gone," he says, as if I need the reminder.

"Duh."

The ocean air kisses my wet skin, and I head toward my clothes on the back patio while Paxton stares at my ass. I can feel it. The way he's simmering like the water. Hot and bothered. Frustrated. It only makes me sway my hips more. Because even though he might've temporarily gained the upper hand by getting me here, with a gentle roll of my hips, I'm taking it back, and it's addictive as hell. Folding at the waist, I pick my clothes up, then face him again, letting him have his fill of my half-naked body as if I'm dangling a carrot in front of a horse like Rory joked earlier.

*Look all you want, buddy, but this will never be yours. Not again.*

"That's very kind of you to point out my lack of a ride," I reply, "but I'm sure I'll figure something out. Hell, maybe I'll hitchhike. After all, any cock will do, and I haven't been laid yet." I flip him off over my shoulder. "Goodnight, Pax."

"Call me boss," he corrects me.

I snort and keep on walking. "You're lucky I didn't call you an asshole, *asshole*."

As I round the corner of his house, I try not to lose my nerve while considering my options. Because yes, I could most definitely hitchhike, but actually going through with it while being half-naked feels like a bad idea. Scratch that. It doesn't feel like it, it *is* a bad idea. Period. So where does it leave me? Confirming I'm out of sight from the hot tub, I struggle into my dress. The red silk sticks to my damp body like a second skin, making it almost impossible to get the material over my hips, let alone cover my torso. I really should've dried off before putting this on, but here we are. Adjusting the fabric across my chest, I look down, realizing the red is already bleeding onto my lacy white bra.

*Fantastic.*

Now, if I can only figure out how to zip this thing up…

"Tatum, wait up," a masculine voice calls. Pax rounds the corner of the house, his heavy cock hanging between his legs as he stumbles toward me. I kind of figured he would've gotten dressed before chasing after me—if he wanted to chase after me at all—but I'm not complaining about the view.

"Let me give you a ride home," he offers.

A ride? He honestly thinks I'd let him give me a ride home after all of this? The thought alone is laughable, but I keep my amusement in check, announcing, "Aaaand here it is." I tear my attention from his bottom half and pop out my hip. "Proof you really don't know me at all."

Prying his attention from my body the same way I'd been eyeing his, he meets my gaze. "I know I pushed you too far. I get it. But I can't let you hitchhike home. Especially not looking like *this*."

His eyes fall to my mostly naked body, and I shouldn't be flattered. I'm not. Okay, I kind of am, but only because it's nice to be appreciated. Even so, I'm still in this position because of him. His manipulation tactic. His bullheadedness. His pride.

"You know, what? You are totally right." I give him my back and peek over my shoulder. "Mind zipping me up?"

Confusion shines in his toasty gaze, but he gives me a slow nod and moves closer. His fingers skate across my bare skin right above my ass before he grasps the zipper and tugs it along my spine. When his hot breath hits the back of my neck, I catch myself holding my own, and I force the oxygen from my lungs.

*Stay strong, Tatum!*

"Perfect," I quip. "Now, if you'll excuse me."

I take a step toward the driveway, but he reaches for my arm, stalling me. "Tate—"

"I'm not half-naked anymore," I point out. "So, you can let me go."

"Tatum." It's a curse, though he's not the first to find that particular inflection when saying my name. It only feeds my resolve as he scrubs his hand over his face, looking defeated. "Do you *want* to get kidnapped and murdered?"

"If it gets me away from you? Sure," I reply wryly.

"Just—grr!" He groans, and it's clear I've pushed him past his limit as he looks up at the navy sky hanging above us. "If you won't let me give you a ride, at least take my keys."

"What?"

"Here." He lifts his hand, showing a set of car keys. "They were in my pocket by the hot tub. Take them."

*Is he serious?*

"I'm not taking your car," I argue.

"Do I need to throw you over my shoulder like a toddler?" he grumbles under his breath.

"Do I really need to threaten your balls again?" I toss back at him.

"You win, Birthday Girl." He sighs. "You win, but I still need you safe, and since you've already made it clear you won't let me drive you home, take my car."

"And how will you get it back?" I challenge.

"You can keep it for all I care."

I scoff. "Whatever."

"Take the keys, Tatum," he begs. "I'll figure out logistics later. Please?"

*Tatum. Please.*

Two words I'm not sure I've ever heard him say. Before I can let myself overthink anything, I grab the fob from his hand, ignoring the brush of his fingers against mine as I steel my shoulders in an attempt to appear unaffected, but damn, is it hard. Forcing my expression to remain indifferent, I murmur, "Goodnight, *boss*."

"See you at work, Birthday Girl."

The softness in his voice catches me off guard and only frustrates me more.

*Son of a bitch.*

I couldn't sleep last night. Too stubborn to jerk off and give Tate the satisfaction of wanting her, while also being too amped up after our encounter to get any actual rest. After she left, I texted Roman, asking for him to do some sleuthing and figure out where Tatum lives. He sent me her address within five minutes, offering to pick me up and take me there.

I shower slowly, letting the cold water run down my body as I search for some fucking self-control. After drying off, I dress in some workout clothes, grab a banana from the kitchen, and head outside in time to see Roman pulling into the driveway.

As I open the passenger door, Roman greets me. "Hey, man."

"Hey." I climb inside and shut the door behind me.

"How'd it go?" he asks.

It's a good question. One I've asked myself a hundred times since the tail lights of my car shrunk in the distance as she drove it home. I thought I had the upper hand, but she proved me wrong. Fuck, did she prove me wrong. I still can't figure it out. How she does this to me. Why she affects me. Why I can't stop thinking about her, even when she rejects me over and over again before giving me a taste. A fucking morsel of interest. I know she wants me. I know she's as curious about me as I am her. So why does she keep pushing me away?

"No answer, huh?" Roman prods.

I give him the side-eye, debating how much I should say or if it's smarter to keep shit close to the chest. Then again, it's not like it would hurt. Getting some advice or something. Fuck, I don't even know what I need anymore.

"She's a pain in the ass," I mutter.

"A hot pain in the ass." He whistles. "Fuck, man. Do you have any idea how hard it was for me to keep my hands to myself last night?"

Jealousy sparks like a hot ember, but I ignore it, buckling my seatbelt. "Start driving," I order.

"All right." He lifts his hand in defense, then grips the steering wheel and turns down my driveway. "I can see why you feel like she's worth the effort, though."

My lips press into a thin line. "Glad one of us can."

With a laugh, he pulls onto the main road, flipping the bird to a paparazzi parked out front as we zoom past them. "Dude, I don't know how you put up with that shit."

"Comes with the territory of being a rockstar," I remind him.

He gives me an unconvinced look. "At least tell me the payout's worth it."

Staring out at the side mirror, I scratch my jaw as the paparazzi's car fades behind us. Even without the rights to any of IndieCent Vows songs, I've made more money playing the guitar than I could've dreamed of making when I was living in The Drift. And yeah, there are definite drawbacks to the fame, but overall? I'm a lucky bastard, and I won't deny it.

"Yeah, man. The payout's worth it. Although, from what I hear, you've figured out a way to handle the best of both worlds."

His mouth lifts. "Guess you could say that."

Then, he pushes the pedal to the metal, and we fly down the road toward Tatum's.

MY HEAD SWINGS TO THE SIDE, AND I SPIT BLOOD ONTO THE mat, ignoring the ringing in my ears. After Roman dropped me off at my car, I followed him to Jagger's for our sparring match.

Fuck, it feels good. The surge of adrenaline I've been craving since stepping off the stage a few months ago hits like a drug, taking the edge off the throbbing of my mouth after Jagger's one-two jab. To be fair, it isn't entirely my fault. Yeah, I'm a little rusty, but Jagger's a beast. He's fast, agile, and when he connects, he hits like a Mack truck.

"I told you to go easy on him," Roman calls from the edge of the mat. He dragged in a few folding chairs for him and Jagger's brothers, like watching me have my ass handed to me warranted front-row seats.

"If he wants in, he's gotta be able to take a hit," Jagger counters. "Just because he's a rockstar doesn't give him a free ride."

Free ride, my ass. I haven't gotten a free ride for anything in my life.

I take a swing, connecting with Jagger's jaw, knocking him off guard, but only for a second. Lifting his arms, he protects himself from my second blow, laughing when my fist meets the back of his forearms. "Not bad, Pax."

Chest heaving, I pause my jabs and stare at him, waiting to see if he's still on the attack.

Slowly, he lowers his hands and cocks his head, assessing me. "How come I don't remember you?"

"He's from The Drift," Hawke announces from beside Roman and Ford.

Surprisingly, the gang's all here. Jagger, Hawke, Ford. Even Roman decided to stick around. Guess they're curious to see if the rockstar's worth their time. And even though I know this is only an audition for a position I have no desire to take permanently, I'm grateful for the distraction. For the rush I can only get from three things. Playing in front of an audience. Good sex. And a solid brawl. Since IndieCent Vows is on hiatus, and Tatum's acting like a thorn in my side, this is the first fix I've had since the bonfire. And fuck, I've needed it more than I care to admit.

"We know people from The Drift," Hawke defends.

"For example, *you*," Ford jokes, referring to Roman.

"I'm also older than you," I add.

"And his last name isn't Six," Roman adds dryly.

The words syphon off my newly-found adrenaline, and I scowl, flexing my hands.

"That's right." Jagger scrubs the edge of his jaw with his taped knuckles. "Paxton…Turner, is it?"

I give him a short nod.

"You know, I think you're lucky," Hawke adds. "Wish our dad would've bailed like yours did."

The words hit like a lash, though I keep my expression indifferent. He has no fucking clue. What it was like. To have a man you looked up to. Respected. Hell, he bought me my first guitar. Gave it to me on Christmas despite my mom insisting we couldn't afford it. Only for him to leave without a word. Vanish into thin air, leaving nothing but a broken woman and a confused little boy to mourn him.

Ford's chuckle cuts through the memories, and he asks, "How'd you wind up playing with our uncle, anyway?"

Rolling my shoulders to stay loose, I answer, "Right place at the right time."

"Just like your run-in with Roman, am I right?" Hawke offers.

Jagger's expression stays locked down as he continues staring at me. It reminds me of his uncle. The way he leads his brothers. The way he's suspicious of everything and everyone. Even me. A stranger. A stranger with connections to his uncle, but a stranger nonetheless. Coming to some kind of conclusion, his mouth lifts on one side as he crosses his arms. "How long are you staying in town?"

I shrug. "Apparently, it depends on your father."

Ford chuckles. "Yeah, Daddy Dearest likes to keep Judge on a tight leash."

"Doesn't change the fact that they're trying to figure out how to shut us down," Hawke adds. "The question is, are you here to help them?"

His expression turns cold, and it catches me off guard. How easily he cannibalized his easy-going facade before showing me his true colors, and exactly how little he misses. Like a fucking hawk. And that's all it takes. I get it now. The reason why they're kings of their school and Harden Heights in general despite their age. They might've been born with a silver spoon in their mouths, but these brothers are far from soft. If I don't play my cards right, I have a feeling they'll have no problem chewing me up and spitting me out. The question is, what do they expect me to say?

"I think you're forgetting you are the one who invited me here," I point out. "Not the other way around. But sure, I'll bite. Clearly, you don't follow your uncle's band very much. Don't worry, I'll catch you up. Me? I'm the fuck up. Always have been, always will be, and since Judge was called in to keep your shit under wraps, you should know my involvement is the last thing he wants."

"Why?" Ford prods.

"Because it'll only do the opposite. Which is why I'm gonna have to pass."

"Pass?" Ford scoffs. "We haven't offered you anything yet."

"Yeah, but you're going to," I decide. "It's why you invited me here."

"He's right," Hawke announces, clearly impressed how I pieced together their plan despite the few pieces I was given in the first place.

"Listen, I've already been down this road. So, thanks. And I, uh, I had fun today." I glance at Jagger, finding his gaze still glued to me. "If you ever wanna brawl again, I'm in. But an official fight night?" I shake my head. "Like I said, I gotta pass."

Jagger stays quiet, his attention never wavering and far more unnerving than it has any right to be.

"Roman?" he calls.

With a slow nod, Roman steps onto the mat and approaches me. "Listen Pax, there's a lot of money—"

"I don't give a shit about the money."

"Neither do we." Hawke shrugs. "But it's an opportunity—"

"I don't give a shit about the opportunity, either," I return.

"Come on, man," Roman says. "We need you."

"Bullshit," I start.

"Do it for Rafe."

Feeling sucker punched, I jerk back and replay his comment, but a buzzing hits my ears, convincing me I misheard him. "What did you say?"

"I said, do it for Rafe," Roman repeats. Cooly. Calmly. Like he didn't just throw my best friend's name in my face. "We both know my brother would've done anything for you."

"Except stop pushing drugs despite me telling him it was

gonna bite him in the ass," I spit. "And would you look at that." My upper lip curls. "It did."

Unaffected, Roman argues, "Without him, you would've never picked up the guitar again. You wouldn't be where you are today. You wouldn't have this life. You wouldn't have anything without him."

My lungs stall as I stare back at him, and I swear it's like looking into his brother's eyes.

In a fucked up way, he's right. Without Rafe's arrest, I would've continued spiraling. Would've continued fighting and fucking and doing drugs until it killed me or put me behind bars. Seeing your best friend hauled away in hand-cuffs will do it to a guy. Shake you straight. But it doesn't take the guilt away. The reminder that maybe if I'd pushed Rafe harder, if I hadn't dropped it, he would've chosen a different path. He would still be free. And I'll carry the guilt of it for the rest of my life.

"Fuck you, Roman," I murmur. But there isn't any malice in it. How can there be? He's as much of a victim of his older brother's decisions as I am. Nah. My words are laced with defeat, and Roman knows it as well as I do.

Something flickers in his cool, dark gaze, but it disappears in an instant. "Someone pulled out," he explains. "Someone pulled out, and it would save us a big headache if you stepped in. One night. That's all."

"And if it blows up in your face?" I challenge. "It's not like I'm gonna be recognized or some shit, right?"

Leaning closer to Hawke, Ford mutters, "I think he's missing the point."

"Me, too," Hawke replies.

Meanwhile Jagger's eyes stay trained on me, but he doesn't say a word, and it's starting to piss me off.

"Who wouldn't want to see a rockstar brawl under-ground?" Roman explains. "The crowd. The opponents. The people throwing down bets. It'll be one of the biggest fights to date."

"Until your little fighting ring is exposed for the world to see," I argue.

Silence echoes throughout the room as each of the boys exchange guarded looks. Everyone except Jagger. Because this is a two-edged sword, and despite their arrogance, there's a reason they keep everything on the down-low. They don't exactly want the spotlight on them, either. Not if they can help it.

"We can handle it," Ford announces.

"Of course you can," I mutter. "You don't think there's an issue connecting me to what you guys have going on underneath the table? You said so yourself, everyone's going to recognize me—"

"And we said we'd handle it," Ford repeats.

I shake my head. "If I agree to this, it'll piss your dad and uncle off even more."

"Let us take care of Daddy Dearest and Uncle Judge," Hawke growls.

"Okay, so you've considered every angle," I assume. "And you'll take care of it." I nod slowly. "Sounds like you've thought of everything."

"You're making this bigger than it needs to be," Ford returns. "Half the fun of fight night—actually, every event we put on—is the fact that no one talks about it. Hell, no one even knows when it's happening or where it'll be until a few hours beforehand. There are no cameras. No evidence. No trace of anything. You might be a rockstar, Paxton Six, but we're fuckin' royalty around here. And if we want, you'll be nothing but a ghost doing your best friend's little brother a favor."

My fists tighten at my sides, and I fight the urge to smack the asshole upside the head. This is what Judge is worried about. This is why he's here. They're cocky motherfuckers who feel untouchable. And maybe they are…for now. But it's bound to catch up to them, and when it does? Who knows what could happen.

"Let me get this straight," I grit out. "You're *not* blackmailing me or trying to guilt trip me or—"

"Rafe's mistakes are his own," Jagger announces. "And that's final. You owe us nothing, and we all know you can walk out that door of your own free will. This is nothing but a proposition."

Ford settles back in his chair, looking less than pleased with his brother's contribution to the conversation. Meanwhile, Hawke stares at Roman, and Roman stares at me, his expression unreadable, and fuck if it doesn't remind me of Rafe's. But the worst part? Roman's right. Rafe would be all over something like this. A way to rake in a shit-ton of cash for a single, measly fight? Fuck, yeah. And how many times have I willingly fought before this? More than I can count. So, what's wrong with handing Rafe's little brother an opportunity to do the same?

One night. It's one night.

"Fine," I mutter. "Go for it. Exploit the shit out of me. But if you wind up in a cell next to your brother, it's on you, and I'm not hiding this shit from Judge, either. We clear?"

Roman nods. "Yeah, man. We're clear."

"And we're not going to jail," Ford adds, hooking his hands behind his head. "Stop being dramatic."

"Whatever you say, Ford." I pick at the tape along my knuckles, ready to get the hell out of here, when Jagger stops me.

"Hey, Pax?"

"What?" I seethe.

"You ever wanna brawl again, I'm game."

# TATUM

Headphones cover my ears as I grab the hide-a-key from its place and slip it into the front door lock. There's no need. It's unlocked. Which isn't very promising. Why would it be unlocked? Unless... My lips bunch on one side, and I twist the handle, pushing the door open while trying not to look like I'm about two seconds from having a heart attack...or killing someone.

It's been a week since our little hot tub rendezvous. Ever since, I've heard nothing but crickets and have never been happier. I've even managed to keep from searching a certain someone's social media, which is a little bit of a miracle, though I'd never admit it out loud.

Keeping my head down, I glance around the foyer, then deeper into the kitchen. It's empty. Maybe Pax forgot to lock up before he left? It's not like he doesn't already have a shit-ton of security. I lift the headphones off and let the black band hang around the back of my neck, listening for...something. I'm greeted with silence. Sweet, sweet silence. A relieved sigh slips out of me as I head up the stairs when the jarring clang of weights mingles with low grunts from the exercise room.

*Shit.*

Indecision courses through me, but I tiptoe toward the sound and reach for the door knob but hesitate. What if it's an intruder? What if it's Pax? Does it even matter? Honestly, I don't even know. Neither option leaves me with any warm fuzzies. I pause and press my ear to the door. The same sound of metal on metal ceases, replaced with a rhythmic thud, thud mingled with low grunts. The punching bag. Whoever's in there is using the punching bag. That has to be it. And, am I crazy, or is the heavy, stilted breathing…familiar, almost?

*"Careful,"* Pax growls. *"If you keep squeezing me like that I'm gonna come."*

*My walls tighten around him, my breath brushing against his parted lips. "If you keep hitting that spot, then I'm gonna come."*

Yup, I'd recognize that sound anywhere.

Definitely not a stranger.

I let my hand hover over the brass knob for a moment, wipe my palm against my jeans, and turn on my heel, striding toward the master bedroom without a backward glance. Why torture myself with a hot and sweaty Pax who's still pissy at me for giving him the wrong number?

Okay, pissy's probably a strong word. He wasn't mad per se. More amused than anything else, but still. I'd rather *not* replay the night, thank you very much.

The real question is, why is Pax here when he's literally never been here? To be fair, I don't have a lot of experience to go off of. I've only cleaned this place two or three times. But it's always been empty. Up until Roman. And today. Maybe he forgot I was coming. Maybe it's a coincidence he's still here. Maybe—

"You're late," a low voice calls.

I peek over my shoulder, finding a shirtless, sexy as ever Pax leaning against the bedroom doorjamb with his arms folded. Sweat clings to his sandy blonde hair as he cocks his head, staring at me. Yup. The image is just as droolworthy as I imagined it would be. And even though I kind of hate him, my knees still go weak at the view. Seriously, this man is… he's something else. When I recognize the bruises marring his right side and along his jaw, my brows knit. Where did those come from? Not that it matters. Besides, it's none of my business.

But also, I'm pretty sure they weren't there during the hot tub encounter. Were they?

*It doesn't matter*, I remind myself.

Sucking my lips between my teeth, I force myself to look him in the eye. "Am I late?"

"Your boss said you'd be here by nine."

"I thought you're my boss," I toss back at him.

Mirth toys at the edge of his mouth. "How's the bra?"

*Bra?*

Caught off guard, I look down at my chest. "Excuse me?"

"The white one," he clarifies. "From the hot tub."

My eyes thin. "You remember, huh?"

His gaze trails over me, making me feel more exposed than the half-naked man himself. "How could I forget?"

Refusing to play his game, I lift my chin a little higher. "Why do you ask?"

"Well, after leaving me with the view of your ass." He pushes off from the doorjamb and saunters closer. "You asked me to zip up your dress."

"And?"

"And, if memory serves me right, red silk and white lace don't exactly mix well when wet."

He's not wrong. My bra's ruined. And it was my best one, too. Now it's all blotchy and gross and…it's all his fault.

As he approaches, I try not to smack the guy as I glare up at him. "Seems like you know an awful lot about laundry for a guy who has a maid."

"Hey, I don't make you do my laundry...yet." He smirks. "Although, now that I think about it—"

"Are you going to let me work or are you going to keep yapping at me all day?"

"You're right. If I gave you access to my clothes, you'd probably dye them all out of spite." He bends closer, towering over me. Hell, he's so close, I can practically taste the arrogance wafting off him, and even though I should find it disgusting, it's annoyingly...hot as hell. My attention drifts to his mouth, and I swear he's going to kiss me before he side-steps me, spins around, and walks backward toward a chair near the window. "And now that I think about it, I should probably stay so I can keep an eye on you so you won't sabotage anything else."

"Are you serious right now?" I huff. "Pretty sure if I wanted to destroy your stuff, I'd do it off the clock."

He lowers himself into the cushioned chair as if it's a throne.

"What are you doing?" I demand.

"Sitting."

"Pax," I warn. "You're not supposed to be home."

"Is there a problem with me being here? In my own house? My own room?"

He wants me to say yes. Wants me to admit that his close proximity makes me uncomfortable, and not in a creepy stalker way, but in an I know what it feels like to have you inside of me kind of way. The reminder only makes my mouth drier.

Leaning back, he laces his hands behind his head as he relaxes, giving me the perfect view of his bulging biceps and rippling abs. "Do I...distract you?" he prods.

My attention drops to his lips again before I roll my eyes and give him my back. "I'll start in the bathroom."

With an angry flick of my finger, I turn the bathroom light on. It's connected to his suite and is as masculinely beautiful as its owner. Stupid Paxton. And his stupid face. And his stupid muscles, and his stupid hair, and his stupid comment about my laundry and his laundry, and—

I stare at the shampoo bottle through the shower glass.

I shouldn't. I really shouldn't. This is a very bad idea. A really, truly bad idea that could most definitely get me fired if Pax decided to lose his sense of humor which I don't exactly deserve anymore after everything we've been through, but...

I twist my ring on my middle finger.

Yup. This is happening.

Before I can talk myself out of it, I make my way back through the bedroom, ignoring Paxton's, "Where are you going?" question as I skip down the stairs and out to Rory's car. Now, where is that thing? I search the backseat, blindly reaching under the front seat until my fingers touch something small and cylindrical. There it is. The unopened green dye I found in the garbage a couple weeks ago at a different client's house. I figured it might be a fun alternative to cutting bangs the next time I was spiraling, but screwing with Pax feels like an even better alternative. Bottle in hand, I go back inside, keeping my fist closed around the tube's label so Pax can't see it in case he decides to go all nosy detective on me. I wouldn't put it past him.

"Where'd you go?" Paxton prods from the same chair as before.

"Had to get some stain remover for the shit spots on the toilet," I announce. "Which is really gross, by the way."

The man blanches. "I don't have shit stains—"

"No use denying it, boss. The proof is in the pudding, er, shit stain." I give him a cheeky grin and reach for the edge of the door. "Now, if you'll excuse me." With a click, I shut the bathroom door, then toss my keys onto the counter. If I'm doing this, I need to be quick. Opening the glass shower, I step inside and grab the shampoo bottle. I could always back down. Put the lid back on the shampoo and pretend this devious thought never sparked in the first place. Or, I could let it take hold and possibly get fired. But what a way to go. With a Cheshire grin, I pour the green dye into the bottle, give it a shake, and set it back in its place on the shelf like it never left.

See? Easy, peasy lemon squeezy. Maybe. I wonder what happens if dye gets into eyes? Will it dye his junk green, too, if he's lazy and uses shampoo for all his body parts instead of switching from shampoo to soap or body wash like a normal person? Oh my hell, that would be hilarious. And honestly, for the view alone, I might break my ban on sleeping with the asshole just to see if it left a mark.

Or maybe it'll push him over the edge, and he'll call my employer, who will fire me, thus confirming Rory's reason for hesitating when it came to being my reference for the job in the first place.

Yeah, this was definitely a bad idea.

I reach for the shampoo bottle again, when the *tap tap* against the door makes me flinch in surprise. The dye bottle slips from my fingers and tumbles to the black marble like a prop in a horror film. I'm so screwed. Biting back my shriek, I pick it up as the door squeaks open, and my heart jackhammers out of my chest.

"What are you doing?" Paxton asks.

I twist to face him, hiding the bottle behind my back. "Cleaning."

"There are shit stains in the shower?" he challenges.

"Depends. Do you shit in the shower?"

"Excuse me?"

"That's not a no," I point out.

"I'm offended you think I'd shit in the shower, let alone leave stains on the toilet." He crosses his arms, his biceps bulging. "Why are you being sneaky?"

"I think it's offensive that you think I'm being sneaky."

"Tatum," he warns.

"I'm trying to clean, and you're distracting me." I wave him off. "Go away."

"I would, but I figured I should probably shower *before* you clean. Don't you think?"

Oh. The man makes a good point.

"That's not a bad idea," I concede.

With a grin that could melt the panties off a nun, Pax asks, "Did you just agree that I'm right about something?"

"Even a broken clock is right twice a day," I return before wrinkling my nose. "No offense, but you kind of stink from your workout."

Refusing to move from the doorway, he points out, "You know, saying no offense before saying something offensive doesn't make it less offensive."

I bat my lashes back at him. "Would you prefer I say, 'Definitely take offense to this: you stink?'"

He doesn't. He actually smells amazing, which makes zero sense since the guy's still sweaty from his workout or…whatever. I part my lips and breathe through my mouth instead, determined to get out of here before I cave and fall to my knees to see if he tastes as good as I remember.

"Sure you don't like your men dirty?" he asks. He's closer now. Or maybe the bathroom's shrinking. Considering the lack of oxygen thanks to the bastard's pheromones tainting all logic, a shrinking bathroom is a real possibility. Hell, his broad shoulders practically take up every inch of the shower door.

*What are we talking about again?*

"Well, I'll…leave you to it." I start to move past him, pat his chest on instinct, then freeze.

Hello, pectorals.

And hello, deja vu. We've danced this tango before. It was at the concert. I shouldn't have touched him then, and I sure as hell shouldn't be touching him now. I shouldn't notice the muscles beneath his skin and the effort he's clearly been putting in at the gym since the last time I touched him like this, either. Seeing it is one thing. Touching him? Feeling his heat, let alone being up close and personal with the fresh bruises I noticed earlier? This is bad. Very bad. I need to get out of here.

"Sure you don't want to shower with me?" he questions.

I square my shoulders and drop my hand, propping it on my hip. "Sure you don't want to be kneed in the balls?"

His soft chuckle fans across my cheeks as he moves aside, giving me more space to move past him. Then, I get the hell out of Dodge.

I t's been ten minutes, and despite our little stare-down in the bathroom before I barged out, Pax didn't follow me. Instead, he did as I suggested and hopped in the shower. Or at least, I assume, since I heard the shower turn on ten minutes ago. This means there's no going back, and the bomb is ticking closer and closer to zero with every passing second.

I should leave. I'd be smart to. Especially when I know he's going to scream like a girl in five minutes or less when he realizes his precious sandy-blonde locks that go perfectly with his espresso-colored eyes are a very bright, very permanent green color by the time he finishes showering. Okay, maybe I'm being optimistic. It'll probably only be a minty color, and it'll wash out in a couple weeks because it's not like he'll leave it on for long, but a girl can dream, can't she? And maybe, if I'm lucky, it'll be the color of dog poop, and I won't be so attracted to him anymore. Oh, what am I saying? I'm optimistic, not delusional. The guy would look gorgeous in any color. It honestly isn't fair. Regardless, the desire to stay and watch the entire shitstorm unfold is too tantalizing for my own good, and even though I know I should get out of here, I kind of want to stick around to watch everything unfold. Hell, maybe I should make popcorn.

Probably a bad idea.

Seems it's one of many.

The water in the pipes cuts off a few minutes later, and I lift my head, staring at the ceiling from the first floor. I said I was staying, not delusional enough to be within arm's reach. Maybe I should've put the dye in the gel so it could sit longer. I have no idea if it even works fast enough to have an effect if it's washed away almost instantly. Although, his hair is pretty light, so…

A deep, throaty laugh filters from the second floor. The sound makes my lower belly constrict with something I'm not stupid enough to identify or label. My ears perk, and my spine straightens, my hands as still as a statue's as I fight the urge to book it out of the house.

Okay, so…something happened. But this isn't the reaction I anticipated, so what does it mean? I have no idea. He doesn't sound…mad. Or maybe he hasn't noticed yet, and he was busy looking at a funny text or something? Not likely. But hey, it's possible.

"Oh, Birthday Girl," he calls.

Yeah, no. I changed my mind. I'm not gonna stick around for this one. I check my pocket for my keys, then freeze.

Shit.

Where are my keys?

Patting my jeans, my panic swells as heavy footsteps sound from the foyer.

"Oh, Birthday Girl," he repeats.

He's getting closer.

He's going to kill me.

On instinct, I move around the kitchen island, leaving the cleaning supplies where they are, and duck into the pantry.

This is bad. This is very bad.

I cover my mouth, trying to steady my breathing in an attempt to make myself as quiet as possible, but I swear I can hear my own heartbeat. Or maybe it's Paxton's footsteps. The casual brush of bare feet against tile. Like he has all the time in the world.

"Are you hiding from me?" he calls.

I can hear the amusement in his voice, but I don't make a sound.

"You are, aren't you?" he decides. "Are you over….here?" He pauses. "No. Not by the table. How 'bout over…here?" His voice is further away, and I let out a quiet breath I didn't know I was holding. Maybe I'll survive this after all. "Tate?" he questions.

I shift my weight forward in hopes of sneaking a peek at his whereabouts through the cracked pantry door when the floor creaks beneath my feet.

*Shit.*

"Oh, Tate," he sing-songs. "What am I gonna do with you when I find you?"

He moves closer, the same casual lilt of his footsteps driving me more and more insane with every slow pass. "Should I spank you? Pin you up against the wall and whisper in your ear how you're a naughty girl?" He chuckles softly. "Not gonna lie. That sounds pretty fucking sweet, if you ask me." The jingle of keys slips through the door. "Might as well come out, Birthday Girl. Pretty sure you'll need these if you want to get out of here." Another soft chuckle follows his statement. "Actually, after last weekend, I guess you proved that isn't entirely true. But I'm not gonna let you borrow my car this time." A shadow moves across the crack in the door before his espresso eyes meet mine through the slit. "Found you."

My breath hitches.

A quiet creak cuts through the charged silence as he pushes the door open, and I step back, letting the pantry shelves press along my spine. The natural light kisses his tan skin, casting shadows along his strong shoulders as he moves closer, reaching behind him and grabbing the edge of the door. A towel is wrapped around his tapered waist, and his chest is on full display.

I don't know how he does it. How he manages to steal my breath every time I see him. I've been around hot guys before. Plenty. But none have done this to me. Caused such a…visceral reaction that it leaves my head spinning. I'd say it's my fear of facing the repercussions from the dye, but it isn't. No. This is all Pax, and I don't know how I feel about it.

The click of the door closing behind us makes me jump when we're blanketed in darkness. His steady breathing is a stark comparison to mine, and so is the heat of his body as he cages me in, stealing all the space in the large pantry until all I can see, smell, and hear is him and only him.

Holding my breath, I whisper, "What are you—"

"You got a thing for green?" he rasps. A warm hand hits my hip and tugs me against him.

Holy shit, batman. I have a thing for calluses, and the gentle tickle of his hand against my bare skin? Yup. It's a problem. A big problem, if the, uh, outline of a certain appendage is anything to go by. The terry cloth and my jeans are the only barriers separating us. It only turns me on more, which is wrong on so many levels.

"You stain my bra, I stain your hair," I whisper.

"You were the one who chose to wear your bra in the hot tub," he reminds me.

"Would you have preferred I was naked in front of your friend?"

"Touché." His hot breath hits my cheek. "So, what is this? An eye for an eye?"

My chin dips in a gentle nod, causing the top of my head to brush against his jaw. He's close. Really close. And thanks to the lack of light, it only amplifies my other senses.

It's official. Hiding in the pantry was a very...very bad idea.

"Then I guess that means I owe you, right?"

"What?" I whisper.

"For the beach. You got on your knees. Guess it's time to get on mine."

He drops down in front of me, his breath slipping through the fabric of my T-shirt and warming my belly as his hand trails along my outer thighs.

Ooookay, there.

Am I really doing this? Is he really doing this? I could tell him to stop. I could walk away. And I probably should. But the darkness is too much of a cover. It quiets the tiny voice inside my head. The one reminding me how much of a bad idea this really is.

The heat from his hands tickles my skin as he undoes the top button on my jeans before stopping. It's a request. A check in. A confirmation that we might be playing cat and mouse, but he won't go further if I don't invite him to. And I kind of hate it. The unspoken request. The convenient out he's giving me.

I should take it.

I won't, but I should. Lifting my hand, I run my fingers through his damp hair, smiling as I imagine what it must look like. Slowly, I roll my hips toward him, urging his mouth to my bare skin above my pubic bone without a word.

He reads me loud and clear.

Dragging my jeans down my thighs, he places another kiss beneath my belly button. It's enough to burn me up on the spot. I shift my weight to my right leg and he grabs the denim at my left ankle, tugging it off me entirely before moving to my right. We repeat the movements, his mouth never leaving my skin as he helps me shed my pants, while my pulse thunders in my ears.

"What color?" he whispers against my cotton boyshorts.

Giving the shelves more of my weight, I lie, "Green."

A huff of amusement escapes him. "No shit?"

My mouth lifts. "It's black."

"Mmm," he grunts, gripping my ass and tugging me toward him.

With a squeak, I grab the shelves behind me to keep from falling, and he kisses my slit through the scrap of fabric.

"So fucking wet," he rasps.

My eyes roll back in my head as his fingers find the edge of my underwear. He pushes them to the side, finally exposing me. I'm grateful for the darkness. The way it swallows us whole, creating a world of our own. Slowly, he kisses my center, dipping his tongue inside of me before using his lips to tease my clit. I fist his hair as my head drops back, my breathing as stilted as it was earlier. Adding a finger, he curls it inside of me, massaging my inner walls while circling the little bundle of nerves with his tongue. It feels...it feels illegal. This man's mouth. Honestly, it isn't fair. I bite my bottom lip to keep from begging him to let me come, my legs growing weaker and weaker with every sweep of his tongue and drag of his fingers. But it's too strong. The build. The ride. The euphoria just out of reach. And every time I think it's close, Paxton moves his mouth, torturing me. Dragging this out and pushing me higher and higher without ever letting me reach oblivion.

It's...pissing me off.

Twisting my fingers in his hair, I tug, hoping the slight twinge of his scalp will convince him to stop messing around. It's a warning. A plea. And he better believe it's the only one he'll get in this pantry. He smiles against my core, proving me right. He's playing with me.

*Sonofabitch.*

I don't like being on this side. The other end of the yo-yo, if you will. Nope. I'm the one who teases. Who edges. Who drives the other person crazy. Honestly, I'm not sure how he reversed the roles in the first place, but I don't like it. Not one bit. Grinding my molars, I consider my options and how few there really are if I have any hope of walking out of here with the orgasm I most definitely need. Then, it hits me.

"You know," I murmur. "It's totally okay. You can stop." I pat his head, giving him a gentle *tap tap* I've used in the past when the moment was gone.

When he pulls away, he lifts his head up, and even though I can't see him, I know he's looking at me.

"What?" he asks.

"I said you can stop. Not every guy is good at oral. My birthday was a fluke. Don't even worry about it. I'll just—"

His low chuckle cuts me off and rolls over me as he drops his chin to his chest, letting the top of his hair brush against my pubic bone. "You know, you almost had me worried—"

"Hey, there's nothing to be ashamed of. You did your part. Now, if you can just…give me two minutes to myself, I'll get this taken care of, then be on my way."

He kisses my inner thigh. "You gonna take care of yourself, Birthday Girl?"

"Seems I have to with a partner like you."

"Is that a dare?"

"You tell me."

Breathing in deep, he drags his teeth against the sensitive skin he just kissed, and my hips shift toward him, betraying me.

He smiles against my skin. "Count down from thirty."

"What?"

"Thirty," he repeats. "You stop counting, I stop eating. Go." He grabs my leg and forces it over his shoulder, leaving my pussy bared in front of him.

"Thirty," I say, my tone laced with boredom, though I've never been more on edge in my entire life. He seriously thinks all he needs is thirty seconds to make me come? I mean, he's good, but there's no way he's that—

He blows against my clit, and my hips jerk toward him. "Twenty-nine," he says.

"Twenty-nine," I repeat.

His finger dips into me again.

Hooooly Hannah Montana.

"Twenty…twenty-eight," I whisper. He adds a second finger, crooking them inside of me like before.

Shit, that feels good.

"Twenty…" I bite my bottom lip, my fingers digging into the shelves behind me as he draws a lazy kiss along my clit. "T-twenty-seven."

Shit. Shit, I'm already close. How am I already close?

"God, keep doing that," I beg, my hips lifting to meet his mouth and fingers in the inky blackness.

It's been…it's been I don't know? Ten fucking seconds, and like a spark, my body ignites. I fall apart, stars hitting behind my eyelids, my muscles tightening, my lungs seizing, and my jaw dropping as I come undone.

"Shhhhit," I seethe.

His hands find my ass, taking my weight until I'm a fucking puddle in his grasp. I don't know how long he holds me, how long I black out, or how long my body feels like mush. All I know is I'll never turn him down again. Not from an experience like that. Want me to crawl, rockstar? You got it. Want me to do your fucking laundry? If you'll eat me out after, I'll do your fucking laundry.

Ho—ly. Shit.

Slowly, Pax's lips trail kisses along my stomach and up my body, bringing me back to our reality and what just happened next to the boxed mac and cheese.

Making sure my Bambi legs can hold me, he lets me go and stands. But his mouth? It stays on me.

He skates his lips across my ribs, collar bone, and throat, then finally meets the tip of my nose. "Don't forget to do the dishes."

I blink past the post-orgasmic haze still clouding my nervous system. "What?"

"The dishes," he repeats, smoothing out my T-shirt as I stand bare from the waist down. "You forgot them last time."

Then, he turns on his heel and walks away, leaving my jaw on the fucking floor.

*Asshole!*

25

# PAXTON

With a sigh, I shift on the cold plastic seat and wait for them to bring Rafe in.

I've been putting this off. I shouldn't. But I couldn't help myself. Seeing your best friend incarcerated has a way of messing with your head, and time has a way of dulling memories and relationships, especially ones like this. He was my brother in every sense of the term except blood. Now, he's barely more than a stranger.

I wasn't lying when I told Roman I've written Rafe a lot over the years. I have. He's written to me, too. But seeing him face-to-face? It's been years, and I'm more anxious than I'd like to admit. I could really go for a cigarette right now, but I ignore the craving the same way I have since the night I met Tatum, chewing on the inside of my cheek instead.

When Rafe appears through the door on the right, an officer points in my direction, and my adrenaline spikes. A grin spreads across his face as he moves closer, sitting down on the empty chair across from mine leaving nothing but glass separating us as I bounce my knee up and down.

Reaching for the telephone, I pick it up, and Rafe does the same.

"What's with the hair?" he laughs.

Surprised, I scrub my hand over the dull, yellow-green color and shake my head. "It's a long story."

"I got time," he returns. "Obviously."

*Obviously.*

The weight in my chest lifts just like that. Memories of our late nights in his basement. Smoking weed, sharing a bottle of Jack. Talking shit about anything and everything because...we got time. Hell, it's all we had. And in a way, it's all we have now, too.

Dropping my hand, I lean closer to the glass and dive right in, catching him up on everything going on with Tatum Taylor, the bane of my existence and the woman I can't stop thinking about.

Once he's all filled in, Rafe laughs even more. "Glad she's giving you a run for your money while I'm locked up."

"Yeah, she's something else," I mutter. "How've you been?"

He shrugs. "Not bad. Roman said he ran into you."

"Yeah." I glance at the officer standing a few feet away and drop my voice an octave lower. "Seems he's following in your footsteps."

With a low laugh, Rafe argues, "Nah. They're not doing anything we wouldn't have at their age. Let him have some fun. He had to grow up way too soon, you know?"

I nod slowly. "Yeah, man. I know."

"I appreciate you keepin' an eye on him, though." He pauses. "How's the band?"

"Taking a hiatus for now."

"That's good."

"Is it?" I ask, cocking my head.

"Yeah. Maybe you'll still be around when I get out of here."

"You got an update?" We don't usually talk about it. When Rafe's getting out. There are too many politics behind weighted questions like timelines in prison to broach the subject very often, but now that Rafe brought it up? Yeah, I'm all ears.

"It's still early, but they're talking about next year."

"Seriously?" My mouth lifts. "Fuck, man. That's amazing."

"Yeah, I hope so." He hesitates. "Which is dangerous. Hope. But, uh, you know, I'm keeping my head down, doing my own thing, trying not to cause trouble, and the warden says he's been noticing my effort, so…"

"Well, damn." My grin stretches. "I'd hug you, but—" I tap my knuckle against the glass, pulling another laugh from Rafe.

"Thanks for the reminder."

"Glad I can be of service."

And just like that, I'm brought back to before. Before Rafe was arrested. Before my life went to shit. Before I got my head out of my ass and cleaned up my life.

When it was just me and my neighbor, Rafe. Playing outside from sunup to sundown. With no expectations. No chips on our shoulders. Just me and him.

The good ol' days.

I'm not sure how much time passes as we continue catching up before the officer walks up and taps his hand on his watch. Rafe looks up and nods. "Looks like my time's up."

"All right." I clear my throat, unsurprised by the lump forming in it or how hard it is to choke down. "I'll, uh, I'll see you later, okay?"

"Yeah, for sure." He taps his knuckles against the small counter. "And thanks for visiting, Pax. I know it's kind of a bitch seeing me like this, but I've missed talking face-to-face, you know?"

"Yeah," I breathe out. "Yeah, I agree."

"All right, I'll see you later." Hanging up the phone, Rafe stands, wipes his palms on his gray scrubs, and lifts his hands. The officer snaps the cuffs into place, leading him back through the door he originally stepped through, leaving me as hollow as before.

This sucks.

## 26

## TATUM

I shouldn't feel like I'm sitting on pins and needles, but I do. Hell, pins and needles is an understatement. It's more like spikes and daggers and one wrong move will wind up impaling me. Okay, yeah, it's a little dramatic, but also…is it? I dyed his hair, then hid in his pantry where he proceeded to find me, pin me to the shelves, and lick me until I came against his mouth before asking me to do the dishes, which I broke out of principle.

*Oops.*

Okay, maybe I'm not being dramatic.

I haven't seen Pax since the last time I was here. I'm still shocked he didn't call my boss about the whole thing. Or maybe he did and she's letting Pax fire me in person. It wouldn't surprise me despite our little rendezvous in the pantry.

Wiping my sweaty palms against my T-shirt, I reach for the door handle when my phone buzzes in my pocket. It's a text from Rory, so I open it.

RORY

Thought you might appreciate this.

A link to a news article shines back at me, making my brows pinch before I click on the tiny, granulated image. It only takes a second to load, and when it does, I cover my mouth to keep from cackling. Front and center is a photo of Paxton walking into a salon, the tips of his yellowish green hair on full display beneath a worn baseball hat.

Oh my hell, this is even better than I expected. Scrolling up, I read the title of the article. The Infamous Paxton Six is Known for His Laid-back Style, But Even His Rugged Good Looks Can't Save Him From the Green Monstrosity Hidden Beneath his Sexy Baseball Hat.

Unable to help myself, I scroll back to the photo and take a screenshot for safekeeping. Tucking my phone back into my pocket, I open the front door. In the foyer, there's a table and sitting on top of it is a box. Curious, I inch closer, ignoring my erratic heart rate. Like, seriously. Pick a speed, dammit. This slow and fast thing is making me dizzy. Or maybe it's the envelope attached to the box glaring at me. My name is scrawled across the top in big, blocky handwriting. Who knew handwriting could be sexy? I drag my finger along the bold letters, slip my nail beneath the edge, and pull the note out.

*Hey, Birthday Girl –*
*I'll be a few minutes late. Had to run to my*
*hairdresser after a strange mishap. Still not sure*
*how green dye got into my shampoo, but it seems one*
*of my employees has a vendetta against me. Because*
*of this, I've decided it's best if I run a tighter ship*
*around here. Inside is your new uniform. And before*

*you ask...yes. If Roman decides he ever wants to work for me, he'll be required to wear the same attire.*

    *Start in the bathrooms, yeah?*

*-Pax*

*AKA your boss.*

*Now, be a good girl and do as you're told.*

I tuck the note back inside the envelope, then set it beside the box, my curiosity getting the best of me. I should know better by now than to let it happen, but I can't help myself. Pax should've fired me after the stunt I pulled. Yet, here I am, opening a box from the devil himself.

When I lift the top off, I bite the inside of my cheek to keep from laughing. It's a black and white, frilly French maid outfit, complete with thigh-high stockings, a tiny white apron, and kitten heels.

*Wow.*

I pull the outfit from the box, examining the lacy fringe and low-cut top. Part of me wants to kill him. The other wants to slip it on just to drive the asshole crazy because I have no doubt I'll look incredible in this.

I weigh my options, and my mouth lifts into a grin.

All right, Pax. You want to play? Well, buckle up, buddy.

He won't know what hit him.

～

OKAY, SO MAYBE THIS WAS A BAD IDEA. I UNPLUG THE VACUUM in time to hear the stairs creak.

"Honey, I'm home," Pax calls. "And it seems you forgot your—"

He freezes on the top stair, his eyes flaring with heat. "What are you doing?"

"The outfit didn't fit," I lie. "Figured this was the next best thing."

His eyes stay glued to my chest. "You're topless."

I look down at my boobs. "Am I?"

Scratching his jaw, the man doesn't even bother trying to hide his interest as he moves closer. "Is this you getting back at me for the dishes thing?"

"No, breaking your dishes was getting back at you for the dishes thing." I beam down at him. "This is me making my own rules."

"Birthday Girl, if this is how you look making your own rules, I'll play whatever game you want."

It shouldn't be so enticing. The way he knows when to cave and when to stand his ground. When to push and when to give in. Hell, it makes me feel like a freaking yo-yo—again —but this time, I kind of like it. Honestly, I like it more than I care to admit.

"If you'll excuse me." I move past him, fisting the rag in my hand as I head into the music room. When he joins me, I keep my surprise locked down and head toward the guitars, wiping each of them and removing any fingerprints or dust that might've accumulated since last week.

Once I'm finished, I peek over my shoulder to find Pax reading *The Count of Monte Cristo* next to the window. The green dye from his hair is gone, covered with a sandy-blonde looking so damn natural, it's not even fair. I wonder how much he had to pay to get the appointment so quickly. It's not like he got the color from a walk-in salon. Nope, despite the man's best intentions to wear his rockstar title proudly, he's far from flashy. Honestly, I've rarely seen him in anything but a T-shirt and jeans, and not the expensive kind, either. The fact he likely had to pay a premium to a stylist because of me is the exact thing I need to get through today.

"Am I paying you to stare?" he asks without bothering to look up at me.

My annoyance flares, and I move closer. "Excuse me. I need to clean the window."

"Clean away," he encourages, his stupid eyes glued to the pages like I'm the least interesting thing in the world.

Aaaand there's the yo-yo effect again.

Fine.

I lean closer, rising onto my tiptoes and squirting the glass with the cleaner before lifting my arm and wiping it away. When his breath hits my nipple, my lungs refuse to deflate, and I suck my lips between my teeth.

*Focus, Tatum.*

I continue cleaning, ignoring the heat of his breath against me and how close he is to my boobs until another gentle breeze hits my bare skin and my nipples peak.

Unable to help myself, I look down. Paxton's sole focus is on my face. Not my chest. Not the unsteady rise and fall from my labored breathing. Nope. He's looking at me. Analyzing me. Watching me to see if he affects me the same way I've clearly affected him.

"Is there…" I gulp. "Is there a problem, boss?"

"What size are you?"

"What?"

"Size," he repeats. "Since apparently, I need to buy you a new uniform."

A breath of amusement slips out of me, but I don't back away. "What? You don't like my solution?"

"I like it plenty, but on the off-chance my neighbors look in the window, or Roman decides to stop by, or the paparazzi decides to invest in a new lens, I'd like to keep this view to myself."

His movements are slow and deliberate as he reaches up, brushing his finger against the tip of my nipple, and pulling another gasp from my lips. It doesn't matter that he had his mouth on me the last time I was here. This is different. I can't hide in the darkness. I can't brush it aside or act like he doesn't affect me the way I'm able to with every other guy I've been with. Actually, it's not even a comparison because none of the others have pushed me the way Paxton does. It's...annoying.

Stepping back, I put some much-needed distance between us. "This room's clean. I'll vacuum it at the end."

I give him my back and make my way toward the hall, desperate to fucking breathe.

"I'm throwing a party next weekend," he calls.

My heels dig into the ground, and I face him again. "What?"

"I said, I'm throwing a party next weekend."

I shake my head, confused. "So?"

"I want you to come."

The idea alone is laughable. I'm his maid. He's my boss *and* a rockstar with more groupies than I've had orgasms, which is saying something. Okay, yeah, we've hooked up a few times, but it means nothing. Absolutely nothing.

*Keep telling yourself that, sweetheart.*

"No thank you," I reply.

"Tatum,"—his gaze flicks over me as he walks toward me, covering what little distance I'd gained from seconds before—"I like this game as much as you do, all right? Walking into my house and seeing you like this?" He bites his bottom lip. "Fuck. You're like a wet dream, but...I want you to come."

"You've already made me come."

"You know what I mean, Birthday Girl."

My stupid heart flutters in my chest, and I breathe in

deep, tasting his breath. Cinnamon, maybe? My mouth lifts for the briefest of seconds.

"What?" He frowns.

Snapping back to our conversation instead of the reminder of home, I say, "Nothing."

"Pretty little liar," he muses. "Tell me what made you smile."

"Who said I smiled?"

"Not blind, Birthday Girl."

No, he definitely isn't. Honestly, I feel like his eyesight is a little too good, considering how much he picks up from my body language despite how well I try to hide it.

"Fine. Your breath smells like cinnamon." I lift a shoulder. "My mom loves cinnamon."

Understanding sparks in his gaze. "And you?"

Pretty sure he could taste like broccoli and I'd still crave him. But that's the problem, isn't it?

"Did you just vape or something?" I ask, trying to appear unaffected. "Is that where the smell comes from?"

He shakes his head. "I don't vape."

"Ah." I nod. "I remember. You prefer the real thing, right?"

"Don't smoke anymore, either," he admits.

My brows pull. "What?"

"Promised a pretty girl on her birthday I'd quit," he explains. "Haven't had a cigarette since."

Something twists in my chest, and for some reason I literally cannot explain, it almost makes me want to cry. Maybe it's the time of year. Maybe I'm close to my period. But the idea of this...untouchable rockstar quitting something for a girl he never planned on seeing ever again threatens to make me want to melt. I used to justify it. My attraction to him. The way I couldn't get him out of my head. Realizing the feeling was mutual during our years apart is...a hell of a lot more terrifying than I'd like to admit.

I need to get out of here.

As if he can taste my fight or flight instincts taking over, he pushes, "Come to the party."

"Can't. Sorry."

"Why? Because you'll be with your cowboy?"

My eyes fall to his lips, and I hate how fucking appealing they look. How tempting they are. "I think we both know this has nothing to do with Cowboy who went back to Georgia—"

"Texas," he corrects me.

"Texas," I mutter, "so you can stop pretending you're jealous."

"Who says I'm pretending?"

I scoff. "You're jealous?"

"Of Cowboy? No. Roman?" He hesitates, bringing his hand to touch my cheek, and for some insane reason, I let him. Liquid heat brands the side of my face as he runs his thumb back and forth across my cheekbone. "I wanted to strangle him, and he didn't even touch you."

"Plenty of men have touched me."

"Come to the party," he repeats.

So stubborn.

"Your stylist did a good job." I lift my hand and brush his hair away from his face. "Although, I think I miss the green."

He grabs my wrist, keeping my touch hostage as he pins me with his stare. "Come to the party."

"Why? So I can clean up after everyone?"

"If it'll get you here—"

With a laugh, I gently tug out his grasp. "I'm good, thanks. But, uh, speaking of cleaning, I should probably get back to work."

"Tate—"

"I'm a size six," I add. "And a 34D. You know, for the maid outfit since you insist I put the ladies away."

I give him my back and head down the stairs to the kitchen.

# 27

# PAXTON

"What's wrong?" Dodger demands.

I asked him to meet me at The Pelican after Tatum left for the day, and he agreed. Not gonna lie. I was hoping it would help me get my head on straight, although it seems like it hasn't done shit.

Glancing at the clock on the wall, I clear my throat and answer, "What?"

"I said, what's wrong?" he repeats, eyeing me carefully. "You're quiet."

I hesitate, thumbing the label on my bottle as I replay my conversation with Tate before she disappeared to the kitchen. "Remember Tate?"

"Huh?"

"Tatum," I clarify. "Your family friend's...cousin or whatever."

Recognition flashes in his eyes. "Tater Tot. Yeah. Why?"

I pause, knowing Tate will kill me for sharing anything about her with anyone, let alone the guy in front of me, but I don't know where else to turn. If she won't let me go to the source and answer my questions herself, I have to go to the next best thing.

"She's here," I say.

Dodger looks around the dim bar. "Here?"

"Not *here*," I tell him. "I mean in town."

Settling back into his seat, he shakes his head. "How? When?"

"Ran into her at a bonfire a little while ago, then she showed up at my place, and—"

"What do you mean, she showed up at your place?" he demands.

"It's a long story," I grumble. "Turns out she works for me, though. Cleans my house," I add. "Do you know if she was ever engaged?"

"Nah, not that I know of. Her family is more of a…friend of a friend kind of thing, though, so I'm not sure. Rory's the one my family's close with."

I nod slowly.

"Whatever happened with you and her, anyway?" Dodger prods.

"We hooked up, then she told me she was engaged and not to contact her."

"No shit?" He laughs. "Fuck, I didn't know she got married."

"She didn't," I mutter.

His forehead wrinkles. "She called it off?"

"That's the part I'm not sure about," I lie, finding the need to cover for her, though I have no idea why. It's not like she'd do the same for me if the roles were reversed. But I can't help it. I like her. And I want us to have a chance even if I'm still on the fence as to whether or not she actually deserves another one with me. Scratching my jaw, I tell him, "Tatum is a, uh…"

"Pain in the ass?" he offers dryly.

"Guess you could say that," I grunt, though he definitely hit the nail on the head. She's the biggest pain in the ass I've ever met, but even so, I can't get my mind off her. Seeing her in my home every week? Talking to her? Touching her? The push and pull is enough to drive any man insane, but what a way to go. "I'm throwing a party next weekend to help keep the media's attention, and I invited her to come."

Bringing the drink to his mouth, Dodger asks, "What'd Tatum say?"

My teeth grit at the memory. "She turned me down."

"No shit?" He laughs again. "Maybe you really do need the band to get laid."

"Fucking isn't our problem," I admit. "It's the commitment part she shies away from."

His shoulders lift in a shrug as he shifts on the barstool, getting comfortable. "Makes sense, all things considered."

Surprised, I cock my head. "What do you mean?"

His silence speaks volumes as he lets his drink hover an inch from his mouth before he runs his tongue along the top of his teeth and takes a drink. Setting it back on the bartop, he mumbles, "Nah. Nothing."

"Tell me," I push.

"Not my story, man."

"Kinda sick of being left in the dark, Dodge."

A divot forms between his brows, and I know I have him. Because yeah, sometimes I'm not privy to shit, and I get it, but again? After the last few months of fucking crickets when it comes to all things IndieCent Vows despite our recent agreement? The bastard owes me, and he knows it.

"Remember the guy who died a while back?" he asks warily. "One of my buddies, from the car accident?"

I nod.

"Yeah, well, she knew him, too. He was Squeak's older

brother." He sobers even more and takes another swig of his drink. "I think his death fucked with all of us."

"Including Tatum," I conclude.

Damn. The memory is foggy. It's been years. But even so, I remember Dodger's face when he found out. The way he was gutted. The drinks afterward. The weed. We did everything we could to help him forget, even if it was only for a little while. But the worst part? It was that he didn't even go to the funeral. Couldn't swing it, thanks to the band's packed tour. Pretty sure it haunted him for months. Hell, maybe it's still haunting him. Maybe it's why he hates Lockwood Heights almost as much as Tatum does. In all honesty, I get it. It's why I didn't want to come home, either.

"Seems ghosts have a way of haunting all of us, don't they?" he adds, referring to my mom.

Ignoring the dull but familiar hit of shame, I mutter, "Yeah, I get it."

And I do. I spent years ignoring my mom. Hating her for giving my dad's decision so much power that she couldn't even get out of bed most mornings. I was only a kid. A little fucking shit who lost his dad, but instead of grieving the way I should've been able to, I lost both my parents in every way. That's when the fighting started. When the need to be numb or drowning in adrenaline took over.

"You really like her?" Dodger prods.

"Yeah, man. I really do."

He hesitates, running his tongue along the inside of his cheek as he stares at the half-empty beer in front of him. "Look, I know you don't like talking about your past mistakes, and I get it. We've all screwed up more times than I can count, but..." He sighs. "I need you to promise me you won't screw up again. Not like you did with Raine."

Fuck, if the memory doesn't burn. Dodger's bike wasn't working, so he asked me to pick up his little sister, Raine, for one of our concerts while we were visiting his hometown. Instead of being there, I was having my cock sucked by a groupie in the back room while doped up on coke. It's one of the reasons I quit. One of the reasons I'm pickier with my one-night stands. One of the reasons I've worked on mindset and self-control and clean habits.

"You know I'm not that guy anymore."

He gives me a slow nod. "Still gonna need to hear you say it."

He's right. He does. And I can't even blame him for questioning me on this. For making me promise him I won't screw up again. Because if Raine's boyfriend hadn't shown up, she would've been hurt, used, and possibly killed. And it would've been all my fault.

"I won't screw up again," I promise.

"Good." Dodger takes in a deep breath and settles back in his chair. "So, she said she won't come to the party, huh?"

I nod, grateful for the subject change.

"But you want her there?"

My head bobs again. "I like her, Dodge. Even when she drives me insane."

Scrutinizing me over the rim of his drink, he asks, "You know if you hurt her, I'll kill you, right?"

"I know."

"Good." He downs the rest of his drink, then sets the empty bottle on the counter. "You said she's your maid?"

"Yeah?" I answer.

"And you use a maid service."

I frown. "Yeah?"

"So, you don't contact her directly when you need shit done, right?"

"No, I contact her boss," I reply.

"Reach out to her boss and say you want to hire Tatum for the party. Make her boss put the pressure on Tatum directly. When she shows up, you give her the night off. It's what I would do."

It's not a bad idea. If I can make the stakes high enough.

"Thanks, man. I'll give it a try."

"It's the least I can do after all the shit we're putting you through."

"At least you own up to it," I joke.

"I know. Let's just say, Judge isn't the most trusting guy you've ever met, and after everything that happened with Rudy…"

The dead guitarist's name hangs in the air, another ghost who loves fucking with my life despite never meeting the guy.

Forcing a wry smile, I mutter, "Yeah, no shit."

"I'm working on him, though," Dodge promises. "I am."

"I believe you."

And for some reason I can't explain, I really do. Dodger's a good guy. A grumpy motherfucker, but a good one most days.

"And, uh, speaking of Judge." I tug at the collar of my shirt, hoping his decent mood lasts long enough to fill him in on everything else that's been happening, lately. "Roman asked me to do him a favor."

Dodger's eyes narrow. "What kind of favor?"

"They want me to participate in a fight night."

Dodger's head falls forward. "Tell me you said no."

"Dodge—"

"Tell me"—he looks over at me—"you said no."

I hold his cold stare, refusing to cower or let him push me around despite it being his MO with everyone else. "I said I'd do one fight."

"Seriously?" Dodge groans. Surrendering his ice cold gaze, he pinches the bridge of his nose. "Judge is gonna kill you."

"He won't kill me 'cause you won't let him," I point out.

With a low laugh, he shakes his head in defeat, knowing I'm not wrong. "Only 'cause I'll kill you myself, dumbass."

"It's one fight," I argue. "And look at it this way, at least I can keep an eye on things and make sure they don't do anything too stupid. Right?"

He scoffs into his beer bottle before remembering he's already finished it. "Sure you can." The bottle clinks against the counter as he shakes his head again, considering my admission and what it might mean in the big picture. "Dumbass."

2 8

TATUM

My blood boils as I reread the message again.

I still haven't responded. I should. But I can't convince myself to cave and play Paxton's game. Not when I already put my foot down and said I couldn't attend.

"Hey, you good?" Rory asks from her side of the room. She's been holed up all day, her laptop and books scattered around her, and her hair piled on top of her head. Or at least, it's how she looked ten minutes ago. I'm too busy staring at the stupid message to acknowledge her.

I glare at the message again.

They're sending an outfit so you can dress accordingly.

I'm gonna kill him.

"Tate?" Rory prods. "You good?"

"Could be better," I grumble.

"What's wrong?"

"I have to work tonight." The screen goes black, and I tap the edge of my cell against my chin, considering my options. "Or maybe I don't. Depends on if I feel like getting fired or not."

Plopping down next to me on the couch, Rory says, "Uh, you most definitely do not want to get fired."

"You sure?"

"Yup. Especially because you promised me you'd give this job a real shot, remember?"

Boy, do I. It's the only reason I haven't told my boss to take the "client's" offer and shove it up his ass.

"That was before Pax decided to piss me off," I mutter.

"What does this have to do with Pax?"

I drop my phone in my lap and fold my arms. "He may or may not be one of my clients."

Her jaw drops. "Are you serious?"

"Maybe."

"Okay, catch me up. What's going on?"

*Where to start?*

Puffing out my cheeks, I say, "Okay, so…Pax is the music guy. The one with the music room."

"You mean, the house you said you're moving into before getting caught sleeping in said music room?"

"That's the one," I confirm with a mock thumbs up.

Her eyes bulge, making her look like she just saw a cocka-mouse—a half-mouse, half-cockroach—scurry across my comforter. "You're joking."

My mouth bunches on one side as I shake my head slowly. "Not joking."

"So, what does that have to do with you working tonight?"

"A few nights ago, Pax asked me to go to a party at his place, but I turned him down. Apparently, he found a loophole and reached out to my boss, requesting my presence so I can make sure the house stays relatively clean while it's filled with hundreds of guests for the night. Because that doesn't sound like a bullshit excuse at all."

Biting the inside of her cheek to keep her amusement in check, she muses, "Sneaky."

"Something like that." I face her fully. "And don't sound so impressed."

"What? Is there something wrong with being impressed with a guy who might just be your perfect match?"

"Why? Because he's manipulative and can't take no for an answer?"

She grins. "Exactly."

Reaching for her hand, I beg, "Come with me." My grip tightens with a needy squeeze. "Please?"

"You want me to come to the party?"

"If you don't want me to get fired for bailing or potentially stabbing the client, then yes. And it isn't a want. It's a need. Please?"

"Seriously?"

"Do I look like I'm joking?" I toss back at her. "You can clean, or cling to my arm, or…whatever you want. I'll even give you half the money I make from the job."

Taking in the look of desperation painted on my face, she caves almost instantly. "Fiiiine, but you don't need to pay me."

"If you're cleaning, I'm paying."

"I think we both know cleaning isn't exactly a chore for me," she points out.

She's not wrong.

"Still paying you," I argue.

"Fiiiine," she repeats. "But only because we both know you're more stubborn than me, and I'll love the front-row seat to see how this is going to turn out."

"Gee, thanks."

With a grin, she says, "You're welcome."

Satisfied, I slump back into the pillows on my bed, reach for the remote, and resume the show, typing a response to my boss.

ME

I'll be there.

BOSS

Thank you!

My phone vibrates again. My sister's name flashes across the screen.

Not today, Satan.

I silence the call, and set it face down.

Not today.

# TATUM

Two hundred people, my ass. The place is packed. Bodies gyrate in the middle of the room, and the wired speakers blare music so loud I can practically see the notes strung together. My lips curve up when I recognize the song. It's Doomsday. Rory must recognize it, too, because I catch her smirk as she bumps her shoulder into mine.

"Coincidence?" she asks.

My brows pull. "What else would it be?"

"He knows they're your favorite band," she reminds me.

She's right. He does.

Refusing to acknowledge the potential thoughtfulness behind the party's playlist, I wrinkle my nose and lift my chin toward the edge of the room. "Come on. Let's start cleaning." I reach for a flute on the windowsill, but a man balancing a tray of food intercepts me.

"I can take that, miss," he says.

"It's fine. I was hired to clean up—"

"Tatum, I presume?"

Rory and I exchange glances but don't answer him.

Deciding he's correct, the man explains, "My staff has been ordered to make sure you don't lift a finger." He snaps his fingers and lifts his arm high into the air, pointing to me while making eye contact with another server across the room. "Tatum," he mouths. His arm moves over Rory. "Rory."

The server nods their understanding, and Rory lets out a surprised laugh. "I'm sorry, what is happening right now?"

"I'm confirming the rest of the staff are aware of your presence this evening," the man explains, giving me his full attention. "Tatum, I was told you like Jack and Diets and chocolate shakes. Do you have any other preferences?"

*He knows my order?*

I shake off the spark of flattery, dousing it with sheer stubbornness.

*Focus, Tatum.*

"Pretty sure drinking on the job is frowned upon, but thanks." Glancing at Rory, I add, "Let's split up. I'll take the top floor, you take the bottom. I have my phone if you need me."

She opens her mouth to argue, and so does the waiter beside her, but I ignore them both, slipping through the crowd like water through a crack in a dam. Seriously. It is so. Freaking. Packed. When I reach the second floor, I press my ear to the secondary bedroom's closed door in hopes of confirming it's empty. With my luck, there are two people getting busy on the other side, and if it's Pax, I might literally stab something. Not because I'm jealous, mind you, but because... Nope. Not going down that road.

By some miracle, only silence greets me, and I push the door open. A few beer bottles sit on the windowsill, but otherwise, the room is untouched. Striding toward the small mess, I pick them up, then move to the next room. The soft strum of a guitar makes my ears perk and my heart race, though I refuse to acknowledge why. It's not like I want Pax to see how cute I look in the dress he had delivered to my house or anything. Because that would be ludicrous. I also refuse to acknowledge the fact that whether I want to admit it or not, I've been scanning every room for a glimpse of the familiar rockstar despite my best attempts to appear unfazed by this entire ordeal.

*Just open the damn door, Tatum,* I remind myself.

Grasping the handle, I push the music room door open. A few people stand inside. Some are messing with Paxton's guitars. Others flip through his music collection like they own it. I wonder if Pax knows they're in here. Knows they're touching his things. Knows they're making themselves at home in his sanctuary. *My* sanctuary. Did they find *The Count of Monte Cristo?* Did they flip through the worn pages the same way I did not so long ago? My mama bear instinct threatens to take hold, but I bite my tongue and close the door again, refusing to cause a scene over something that is absolutely none of my business.

Beer bottles in hand, I turn around, smashing into someone. Like a couple of bowling pins, we crash to the ground, the half empty beer bottles spilling over me and staining the slinky black dress Pax sent me.

*Shit.*

"What the hell?" the stranger squeals. She stares at the dark stain on her red satin dress, and my head falls forward.

*Well, isn't this fantastic?*

At least I didn't fall down the stairs, or push this woman down them.

*Right?*

With a deep breath, I push to my feet, ignoring the scattered beer bottles, and offer the stranger my hand. "I'm so sorry."

"You're going to be," the woman spits. Her face twists in

disgust as she shakes her index finger at me. "By the time I'm finished with—"

The words are lost on her tongue as she looks up at someone behind me.

"Careful," Paxton warns. His tone is low and growly and laced with way more sex appeal than is even fair at this point.

The stranger's lips part on a gasp and she pushes herself up before taking a step back. "Y-you're Pax—"

"The one and only," he confirms. "I'm also the owner of this house, and this beautiful woman is my guest of honor." His hand runs along the curve of my hip before dropping back to his side. "Now, you were saying?"

"S-she spilled—"

"Yes, yes I did," I interrupt. "And for that, I am super sorry. Would you like to trade?" I motion to the dress Paxton gifted me while the man's amusement seeps from his chest and into my back.

"She's kidding," he says.

"I'm not kidding," I volley.

"And what would *you* wear?" he challenges me.

Twisting to face him, I prop my hand on my hip and raise my chin. "I'm sure the maid outfit is still here somewhere..."

His brow lifts. "I mean, if it's on the menu."

I fight back my smile, refusing to take the bait no matter how much I want to. "I can fight my own battles."

"Of that, I have no doubt, but you'll have to cut me some slack for—"

My phone buzzes between us, interrupting Pax as we stand in the middle of the hallway, chest to chest. Annoyed, I pull it out of my purse. It's Lia. Again. She's called at least a dozen times over the last few days. She's also sent that many cryptic text messages, asking—no begging—me to call her. The cherry on top was when she even sicced my parents on me, which was the final nail in the coffin. Can she seriously not take a hint? I don't want to talk to her. I never want to talk to her. Not since—

"Who is it?" Pax murmurs.

"No one of importance." I look up at him again. "Now, if you'll excuse me."

His hand wraps around my bicep, preventing my escape. "You're late."

I cock my head. "Late?"

"You were supposed to be here an hour ago."

"Dock it from my pay," I dare him.

"With this attitude, I might." His attention falls to the beer bottles in my hands. "You're working?"

"You paid me to be here."

"I paid to get you here," he clarifies. "I told the rest of the staff to make sure you don't lift a finger."

Clicking my tongue against the roof of my mouth, I say, "Too bad I'm a terrible listener."

"Truest thing you've said since we first met." He tugs me a little closer to the side so we don't block the stairs. "You still being stubborn?"

"It's what I do best."

"Would you look at that? We've agreed on two things in one night." His attention slides down my body. "I like the dress."

I glance down at the garment in question, hating how well it fits. Silky. Black. With a long slit up the side and just enough support to make my boobs look incredible. Seriously. It's like it was made for me. My gaze flicks up to Pax. "You're lucky it isn't red."

"Are you saying there was a chance of you getting in the hot tub again?"

My phone buzzes in my hand, and I drop my head back. "God, I'm seriously going to kill her."

"Kill who?" Paxton prods.

"No one."

"You sure?"

My phone buzzes again with another call, and I silence it, peeking back at Paxton. "Now, if you'll excuse me."

Before he has a chance to follow, I dash down the stairs as another call blows up my phone. I start to tuck it back in its place, but a message appears.

OPHELIA

Tatum, will you please stop being a brat?

A brat? *I'm* the brat? Screw that. I open the message and subsequently, the last dozen she's sent, too. The first is from a few days ago.

OPHELIA

Hey, Tate! I know you're busy, but if you could give me a call, I'd love to chat for a minute. No pressure, though.

Hey, Tate! Just checking in to see if you can chat?

Look, I know I'm not your favorite person, but I have news, and I really want to share it with my little sister.

My teeth dig into the inside of my cheek as I stare at the title, little sister, unsurprised by the familiar guilt and resentment it brings with it. And sadness. There's sadness there, too, though I'm familiar with that particular feeling as well. Forcing my jaw muscles to relax, I continue scanning the onslaught of messages.

OPHELIA

Tate, please stop ignoring me. Please?

It would be nice if my little sister would answer her calls OR her text messages.

> Listen, Tatum, I'm tired of keeping this from
> everyone in hopes that you hear it from me.
> Will you please call me? I have news.

*News.*

I scoff. What? Did you save another orphan? Cure cancer? Learn a seventh language? What could my perfect, high-and-mighty sister want to share with little ol' me? I scoff again, unable to help myself. Like I want to know. Mom and Dad are probably forcing her to reach out or something. It's not like she'd be texting or calling out of her own volition or anything.

OPHELIA

> You're pissing me off, Tate. Call me. Please.

Aaaand, we're back to the beginning.

OPHELIA

> Tatum, stop being a brat.

A brat? Now we're name calling? Real mature, Lia. Another message buzzes.

OPHELIA

> You don't get to ignore my calls and
> messages, then get butthurt for being the
> last in the know, Tate.

*Ouch.*

OPHELIA

> Fine. Here it is. Mav proposed. We're getting
> married. I'd love to give you the details, if
> you're interested. Give me a call.

The sucker punch hits its mark, leaving me breathless.
*What the fuck, Lia?*

Legs weak, I lean against the wall and reread the message.

Mav proposed.

We're getting married.

Married.

Anger surges through my veins, and I squeeze my cell, my vision blurring.

They're getting married.

Racing the rest of the way down the stairs, I steal a bottle of Jack from the bar before flicking the lid off. It rolls on the ground, disappearing into the sea of dancing people in the middle of the room while I bring the bottle to my mouth. Liquid heat burns my throat as I swallow.

They're getting married.

My eyes ache with unshed tears, but I tell myself it's the liquor. That it has nothing to do with my sister and the happily-ever-after she's living without a single fuck to give for the rest of the world, let alone the man she buried. The man *we* buried.

I wipe my mouth with the back of my hand, then go in for another glug. The quicker the alcohol sets in, the quicker I can black out and forget this ever happened. At least, for a little while. It's funny. When you're used to surviving a day at a time, a little while is all you can ask for, isn't it? Squeezing my eyes shut, I open my throat and pour the liquor down, letting it wash over me as I welcome the numbness, praying it'll take over soon and I won't have to hurt so much. I won't have to hurt so deeply. Then again, I should know better than this. To believe the pain will go away.

I can't believe they're finally doing it. They're getting married. They're fulfilling the fucked-up circle of life or whatever. It shouldn't be a surprise, and in a way, I guess it isn't, but seriously? They're really just…moving on like that? Like he never existed? Like they didn't steal his happily-ever-after? And even though I knew they'd get married and ride off into the sunset, it still…hurts. Knowing he never will.

"Tate, are you—" Rory's eyes pop as I turn toward her. Staring at the bottle of Jack pressed against my lips, her eyes glaze with trepidation. "Whoa." She peeks up at me again. "Are you okay?"

Keeping a firm grasp on the neck of my liquid gold, I drop my arm to my side. "Fan-fucking-tastic. Haven't you heard the news?"

She frowns. "What news?"

"There's a wedding to be had," I announce, using my best hoity-toity British accent while batting my lashes.

Her frown deepens. "What are you talking about?"

"Your brother proposed." I swallow the bile coating my throat, well-aware it'll only be replaced with more.

"Mav proposed?" she asks, dumbfounded.

"Yup." I take another swig of alcohol. "How much do you wanna bet Jax will be at the wedding?"

The blood drains from her face.

"Exactly," I quip. "Which is why I led with fan-fucking-tastic. Who doesn't love a good ol' family reunion, am I right?"

Steeling her shoulders, Rory orders, "Tatum, put the drink down."

She reaches for the bottle, but I tug it away from her. "And why would I do that? Aren't we supposed to eat, drink, and be merry? A wedding's a celebration, isn't it?" I scoff. "And who doesn't want to commemorate your big brother's death by pretending he never existed, am I right?"

She jerks away as if I've slapped her. "What the fuck, Tate? Did you really just say that?"

My body floods with regret. "Shit. I didn't…"

"Didn't mean to throw my brother's death in my face like that?" Her eyes flood with crocodile tears, and her bottom lip wobbles. "I know you hate Mav for surviving when Archer didn't, but they're both my brothers, Tatum. *Both* of them."

I shake my head, but the cotton in my mouth is too thick to push past. Besides, even if it wasn't, what's there to say? That it isn't true? That I don't hate Mav for surviving when he's always been the lesser brother? Instead, I simply stand there, watching my best friend take a brutal blow straight to the chin while knowing I'm the one who dealt it.

"I know how much you wish your favorite Buchanan would've survived, but I can't play that game, Tate. Honestly, I refuse to." A tear rolls down her cheek, and she angrily wipes it away. "Now, if you'll excuse me, I'm going home. You can call an Uber." Then, she bolts toward the front door. I shake my head, willing the ground to swallow me whole and put me out of my misery once and for all.

I'm such a bitch. And to the person who deserves it least.

Bringing the bottle to my lips once more, I pour the burning liquid down my throat, savoring the trail of blazing heat. After all, I deserve it, don't I?

Fan. Fucking. Tastic.

# PAXTON

You'd think with all the money I have, I'd be able to enjoy my own party without putting out fires. Literally. Someone tried to light a firework in the kitchen. They probably thought this was a Harden party. Hell, maybe Hawke or Ford bribed them to do it, just to be dicks.

I wouldn't put it past them.

As I stride into the main room, I find a group of guys huddled around something. What the hell? Straightening my spine, I peer over their heads. A half-naked Tatum is standing on a coffee table in the center of the room. With her back arched, she twerks an inch from some asshole's face, and he reaches up, palming her backside. Rage sparks at the image, and my long legs close the distance before I stop short, recognizing Roman at the edge of the show.

"What's she doing?" I growl.

Roman barely casts me a glance, choosing to stare at a half-naked Tatum dancing on the coffee table instead as he strokes his chin. "Dancing? I guess?" he offers dryly. "Apparently, she's done with the body shots."

"Body shots?" I repeat. My blood boils as the words roll off my tongue.

He gives me the side-eye, warning, "You might want to stay away from tonight's video footage."

"Fucking hell." Shoving my way through the throng of lust-thirsty men surrounding the coffee table, I order, "Tatum, get your ass down here."

Her eyes are glassy and unfocused as she looks down at me and grins, biting her bottom lip. "You're sexy when you're bossy, Pax."

"Get down here," I repeat, my tone as sharp as before.

With a slow shake of her head, she runs her hands along her curves and sways her hips from side to side, looking like a fucking porn star in the dress I gave her.

I'm gonna kill her.

My glare deepens. "Everyone out!" I yell. "Now!"

"Aw, come on," Tatum pouts. "You wanted me to party, remember?" She tilts her head back, her long, dark hair falling over her face as her red lips part. "Now I'm partying."

No, now, she's spiraling.

"Roman!" I bellow.

My friend calls to someone else before the music cuts off like a scene in an old chick flick. One by one, Roman ushers people from the house as Tatum glares down at me from the coffee table. "I wasn't finished—"

"Get off the table, Tatum."

"Or what? What you gonna do? Tell my boss? You. Don't. Own. Me."

She loses her balance, tumbling to the side. I wrap my arms around her waist and tug her into me while losing my own balance in the process. With a thump, she lands on top of me as my ass hits the ground.

Fuck, that hurt.

Ignoring the twinge in my tailbone, I grumble, "Shit, you okay?"

Her head rolls to the side, and her eyelids flutter closed. "I think…I think I'm going to puke."

Grabbing the back of her neck, I pull her to the side and slide out from under her, wrapping her hair into a loose knot around my fingers in case she vomits. By some miracle, she holds it in, though I doubt she'll be able to keep it down for long. How much did this girl have to drink? I recount everything I did since she raced down the stairs, disappearing from my line of sight. Despite taking Tatum's side in the drink spill event, the woman Tatum ran into is a friend of a friend with some pretty strong connections in the music industry and pissing her off wasn't on my to-do list for the evening. After tracking her down and apologizing, I ran into Roman and we talked before a shady guy in a dark suit asked to chat with him. Yeah, that didn't set off any warning bells at all. Now, here I am, holding a drunk off her ass Tatum. It's been what? An hour? She got this shit-faced in one fucking hour?

Gently, I cradle her to my chest and carry her to the nearest bathroom. She lowers her head to me, burrowing into the crook of my neck, and reminding me of a little kid. When she lets out a few slow, controlled breaths, the scent of alcohol punches me in the face, confirming what I already assumed.

She's definitely gonna puke.

"Come on, beautiful." I lower her to her feet and touch both sides of her face in an attempt to get an actual read on her. Her skin is hot and clammy and her eyes are unfocused and glazed. Fuck, do I take her to the hospital to get her stomach pumped? Seriously, how much has she had to drink?

"Look at me, Tate," I order.

She shakes her head.

"Tatum, look at me."

"I think I'm gonna—" Like a bag of bricks, she collapses onto the tile floor and hunches over the bowl, vomiting her guts out. I pull her hair back just in time as she expels so much fucking liquid, I'm surprised the toilet doesn't overflow. My nose wrinkles at the putrid scent, but I rub her back with my opposite hand, making sure her hair stays as far away from the toilet as possible. "That's it, Birthday Girl. Get it all out."

Another heave wracks her body as she clutches the porcelain seat. Once she's finished, a sob breaks past her lips. Then another, and another, fucking obliterating the organ in my chest in the process.

*What the hell happened?*

My mind races, trying to put the pieces together, to sort out what might have triggered her to have this reaction, but I'm lost. Mascara streaks down her face as she squeezes her eyes shut, her hair falling in her face and hiding her twisted expression.

"Hey," I coo. The cold tile seeps through my jeans as I shift onto my ass and touch her shoulders. "Hey, come here."

Without protest, she burrows into my chest. Clinging to me like I'm a lifeline, her fingers twist in the black fabric of my T-shirt while she shatters into a million pieces. It makes me want to kill someone. Kill whoever hurt her. Whoever made her break like this.

"It's okay," I murmur. "It's gonna be okay."

"It'll never be okay," she cries. "None of this will be. Not ever."

*What the hell?*

"Sh…," I coo, unsure what else I can say as my mind reels. "Sh… I got you. I got you, baby."

Another sob wracks through her, and my grip constricts around her tiny frame. I need to calm down, but all I see is red, and it takes everything inside of me to keep from grabbing her face and forcing her to tell me who hurt her before promising retribution. Because I can't. Not right now. Not when it isn't what she needs.

Forcing my muscles to relax, I drop a kiss to the top of her head and stay on the ground, rocking us both on the cold tile. Back and forth. Back and forth. Until slowly, her sobs fade into cries, and her cries fade to whimpers and tiny hiccups of grief. I don't know how long it takes. Whether it's seconds or minutes or hours. My butt is numb, though. And my arms ache from holding her limp body against me. Even then, I wouldn't move for the world. Not until she's ready.

Pulling away from me, Tatum wipes her eyes with the heel of her hand, refusing to look at me as she lunges toward the bowl again, puking like before.

I climb to my knees and hold her hair away from her face. Vomit splatters along the back of the toilet and on the seat, making my stomach squirm on instinct, but I ignore it, focusing on the silky tendrils of hair in my hands and the flowery scent of shampoo clinging to it. Once she's finished, she slurs, "S-sorry."

*Oh, Birthday Girl.*

I'm the one who's sorry. We've all been here, and I don't envy her next twenty-four hours, that's for sure. The question is, why? She was fine in the hallway. A little prickly, maybe, but fine.

Who was calling her?

The question sits on the tip of my tongue, but I don't voice it aloud. Instead, I reach for the hand towel and bring it to Tatum's face. After wiping her mouth, I carefully urge her to look at me. My grasp on her hair stays firmly in place while I take in every micro expression and minute detail of her pretty face. Maybe I should have her stomach pumped. Or maybe she got everything out of her system? She puked a lot. Fuck, I don't know. I've been to parties before. Saw people shit themselves. Wake up in their own urine and vomit. I've witnessed the repercussions that come with substance abuse. But none of them were Tatum Taylor. And none of them scared the shit out of me like Tatum is right now.

Concern weaves itself through me as a crease forms between my brows. Mascara runs down her face, making her look like a broken Barbie, but just as beautiful. "You sure you're okay?" I ask.

"S-so sorry," she repeats, her words as jumbled as before.

"Don't apologize," I murmur.

"How can I not?" She laughs. "I'm supposed to be working—"

"We both know I didn't hire you to work tonight."

She sobers and leans against my touch. "Still sorry. I'm a…I'm a mess."

"You're not a—"

"Thanks for staying. I know I…I know I just puked every-where, and…most guys wouldn't stay, so."

I chuckle softly, unwrap her hair from my hand, and push it away from her face. "Not going anywhere, Tate."

With a slow shake of her head, she argues, "Arch wasn't going anywhere, either."

My body goes rigid, and I tilt my head. "Arch?"

"Archer Buchanan," she explains. "My sister's ex, her boyfriend's twin, and also his, uh, his s-savior." Her chest caves, and her chin falls to her chest.

This is the third time I've heard his name. Once in the hotel when she called him her fiance. Once at the bonfire when she warned me not to utter it ever again. And once at the bar with Dodger. But even then, no one called him a savior.

Well aware I'm walking in a minefield, I murmur, "Savior? What do you mean?"

"Car accident. Brain dead on impact, or so they say." She wipes at her eyes, smearing her smoky mascara even more, though I doubt she gives a shit.

At least it confirms Dodger's story.

"Fuck, Tate," I mutter. "I'm sorry."

"He was a donor," she continues, as if now that the dam is broken, there's nothing holding her back from spilling each and every deep, dark secret she's been holding in for as long as I've known her. "And who was at the top of the transplant list? His Mother. Fucking. Twin." She bites her lip and shakes her head, riding the line between looking like someone who might break down and sob again and someone who might commit murder. "Do you know how tired I am of feeling pissed about it? That I can't even be in the same room with them, let alone look them in the eye and con-congratulate them?" Her nose scrunches into a sneer. Like there's a putrid scent clinging to the room, and she's the only one who can smell it.

"Congratulate them?" I prod.

"They're getting married," she mutters. "Fucking. Married."

Married? Who's getting married? I have a thousand questions. The girl's talking in broken riddles, but the idea of overwhelming her feels about as productive as handing the girl another shot.

"Who?" I ask, carefully.

"My sister and Mav." She drags her knees to her chest and leans her back against the bathroom wall. "It's despicable."

"Marriage in general, or theirs?" I ask in an attempt to lighten the mood or some shit. I don't know? I don't know what I'm doing or why she's telling me this, but I'm grateful. Grateful she has someone when she's clearly spiraling.

"Theirs," she clarifies. "I hate them for it. For being happy. For moving on." A laugh escapes her. "God, that makes me sound like such a bitch. She's my sister. I should be happy for her, but…God, I hate her for it," she repeats. Her tone is so thick with resentment, I swear she might choke on it.

And that's what guts me.

The resentment. The way I can feel it eating her alive. She hides it well. Clearly. She's been hiding it for years. But it's still there. Hidden beneath the confidence and I-don't-give-two-fucks persona she wears like armor. Because she does care. So much so, it's killing her. The realization hits too close to home, bringing memories of my mom with it. The alcohol. The pain meds. The jumbled, nonsensical ramblings of a bitter woman in pain.

I shouldn't have left her.

I shouldn't have been forced to stay and take care of her.

They were her actions. I know this. But seeing the pain in Tatum's? I don't want to walk away. I don't want to leave. And what the hell does that say about me?

"I'm such a bitch," she breathes out.

"You're not a bitch." I move toward her and press my back to the wall beside her, resting my forearm on my bent knee. "Just a sad, beautiful, lonely girl."

She drops her head back and stares at the ceiling. "You're nothing like him, you know," she slurs. Her eyes are half-hooded as she rolls her skull toward me. "Or maybe you are." Another laugh escapes her. "Maybe you're exactly like him, and that's why I couldn't say no. Why I couldn't stop thinking about you." Her laughter quiets as she peers at me, taking me in the same way I am her. Moisture from her earlier tears still clings to her lashes, making her the most beautiful—and broken—woman I've ever seen. "Or maybe you're nothing like him," she decides. "Maybe no one will ever be like him." A divot forms between her brows. "Honestly, I'm not sure what's worse."

Neither am I. She clearly loves him. Has always loved him, if I had to guess. And competing with a dead guy? Call me a selfish prick, but I want to. I want to compete. I want to erase the pain in her eyes. The tremor in her voice. I want to erase all of it, if only to stop her from hurting like she clearly is right now.

"What was he…" I swallow. "What was he like?"

"Kind." She rests her head on my shoulder. "Like you. Sweet, too." I catch her eyelids fluttering in the mirror's reflection across from us. "He always saw what others didn't, you know? Even noticed a wallflower like me." Her mouth lifts, but her eyes stay closed. "I used to be a wallflower, you know."

"A wallflower, huh?"

"Mm-hmm."

"I can't picture it," I admit wryly.

"Of course you can't." Her laugh is as broken as she is. "Want to know why?"

"Why?"

She sniffs. "Because after he died, I learned it was easier to be a bitch and force people to look at you instead of blending in and disappearing altogether. Because the one thing worse than being hated?" Her voice cracks, and I can feel her getting worked up again. The tightness in her body. The uneven breaths. The dampness seeping into my shirt. But it's strange. Because even though I'd give anything to dry her tears, part of me wonders if she's been holding them in so long, they've turned to poison, and if she doesn't let them out, if she doesn't let this go, it'll kill her. I should know. I've seen it firsthand.

"What's worse than being hated, Birthday Girl?" I whisper.

"It's being forgotten." Her bottom lip quivers. "Everyone's forgetting him, Pax. They might not admit it, but they are. And that's the worst part of it all. Ophelia's marrying Maverick. She doesn't care that he's dead. That without him, Maverick would be gone." She crumbles even more. "I hate her, Pax. I hate Ophelia for what she did. It isn't fair how she gets her happily ever after and Arch gets...gets nothing. Not one fucking thing but an early grave." Looking up at me, her eyes red and raw, she whispers, "I don't want an early grave."

"Sh..." I shake my head as my own fear clogs my throat. "Don't say shit like that. I'm begging you."

She snuggles into me, her body sagging. "Thank you for keeping your promise."

My brows tug as I try to keep up with Tatum's spiraling thoughts. "What promise, Birthday Girl?"

"For quitting smoking." She licks her lips. "I'm not...I'm not sure I could survive another death."

The organ in my chest cracks. Lifting my arm, I wrap it around Tatum's shoulders. "That won't happen."

"Fate hates me, so I wouldn't sound so sure."

"No one could hate you," I murmur. "Even fate." I tug her closer. "Maybe it just has...a different plan."

"Fuck plans." She sniffs again. "Fuck plans and fuck fate and fuck Archer and fuck...fuck this stupid feeling." She claws at her chest. "I keep waiting for it to go away. For it to get better." She sucks in a shallow breath. "Why isn't it getting better? It isn't...it isn't fair."

I close my eyes, desperate to fix this. To find the words to take her pain away. But the truth is...there aren't any.

"You're right," I rasp. "It isn't fair. None of it is."

"You don't get it—"

"Maybe, I don't," I lie. "Not exactly. But I might have a pretty good idea, Birthday Girl." I rub my hand along her back, deciding, "But that's a story for a different day. I read your favorite book. *The Count of Monte Cristo.*" Her quiet sniffle guts me, proving she's still awake, but her sobs are slowing, so I keep talking. "I liked it. I liked it a lot. And you're right. It's better than the movie."

"Told you," she whispers.

I smile before sobering. "Gotta say, though. I can't imagine carrying such a big weight around, you know? The hate. The need for revenge over anything and everything else in his life. Isn't it exhausting?" I rub my hand up and down her bare arm. "I bet it's exhausting, Birthday Girl."

"It is," she breathes out. The words are so quiet, I'm not convinced I hear them. Maybe it was my imagination. Maybe it was Archer's ghost. But I'm not sure it matters, either. Because even if she's too stubborn to admit the truth, I know I'm right. Carrying around her frustration and pain and hurt is exhausting, and it's slowly killing the girl beside me, even if she refuses to admit it.

"You know what I wonder, Birthday Girl?" I continue. "I wonder if maybe...maybe the point of the count's journey was to let go of his resentment so he could finally...I don't know. Maybe he could move on and be happy with Mercedes."

Her head does the tiniest of bobs, but it's enough. Enough to give me hope that she's hearing me. That she agrees. That maybe, just maybe, she can learn a thing or two from the count's mistakes.

"Where's Rory?" she whispers.

"I dunno. I think she went home."

Her head bobs softly. "I was a bitch. I mean, I'm always a bitch, but I was an even bigger bitch than usual, and..."

"She'll be okay, Tate."

Tatum licks her lips. "What if she leaves me?"

"Rory's not gonna leave you."

The sheen in her eyes makes them brighter, somehow,

and the sight cuts straight through my chest. "And what about you?" she whispers. "You gonna leave, too?"

Her words are lazy, but just as slurred, though I have a feeling it has more to do with exhaustion than the alcohol left in her system. I hesitate, taking in our reflection as silence envelops the bathroom. She looks…so much younger like this. Her makeup is stripped from her. Her guard is down. It gives me a glimpse of the Tatum she keeps locked away. She looks more vulnerable, too. And broken. So fucking broken. I want to give her the world. Want to tell her she has nothing to be scared of. Nothing to fear.

*You gonna leave me, too?*

Her quiet snores reverberate through my chest as she falls asleep against me, and I drop a kiss to the crown of her head. "Not a chance, Tatum."

# TATUM

My eyes feel like they're glued shut, but I pry them open anyway. Well, for about a millisecond. Grimacing, I toss my forearm over my face and let out a groan.

Noooo. My head is killing me. I can feel it pulsating behind my eye sockets and between my brows. Smacking my tongue against the roof of my mouth, my nose wrinkles. Yup. My breath tastes like ass and my mouth feels like it spent last night traipsing around the Sahara Desert. I roll onto my side and open my eyes again, this time squinting in hopes of blocking out the morning light filtering in through the window.

Okay, *morning* might be a bit of a stretch. It appears the sun is high in the sky, refusing to wait for anyone, including a very hung-over Tatum Taylor, AKA me. Or at least, I think I'm hung over. That, or I got hit by a truck and don't remember. Actually, I don't really remember much at all.

*Where am I?*

White walls. A four-poster bed. Silk sheets. A guitar in its stand. Wait. Am I at…Paxton's? Shit, why am I at Paxton's?

And not just *at* Paxton's, but in his room. In his bed. Blindly, I reach for my boobs, confirming I'm not naked, and let out a, "Thank you, Jesus," under my breath. I didn't sleep with him. I didn't break my rule. That's something, isn't it? I sit up slowly in an attempt to keep the walls from spinning—it doesn't work—and press my palm to my temple. The party. What happened at the party? It's all a blur. A really foggy, blur.

Perfect.

Stairs creak outside the bedroom, and I tug the sheets tighter around me, my head still throbbing. When Pax appears in the doorway, my spine straightens, but I don't say a word.

Balancing a tray of...something, he enters the room. "Drink this." He offers me a glass of water. "And take these," he adds. In his hand are two white pills.

I quirk my brow at him.

"Aspirin," he clarifies. "For the headache."

"Oh."

He sets the tray on the nightstand. "I also brought some toast, crackers, and a Gatorade, if you're up to it. But first,"—he drops the pills in my palm—"aspirin."

Grateful, I pop them into my mouth and reach for the glass of water. I'm so parched, my tongue still feels like sandpaper, so I take a big gulp, hoping to erase the feeling.

"Don't chug it," Pax orders. "Pretty sure you puked up a lung last night. No need to do it again."

I lower the glass and lick the moisture from my lips as I study the man in front of me. He looks good. Freshly showered in a T-shirt and jeans. His blond hair is still damp and pushed away from his face, giving me the perfect view of his toasty, espresso gaze. "Why are you being so nice to me?" I ask.

Reaching up, he dabs at the corner of my mouth with his

thumb before dropping his hand back to his side. "Because I'm pretty sure you're mean enough to yourself for the both of us."

The cold, dead organ in my chest heats a couple degrees thanks to the warmth in his gaze before it sparks a memory from last night. I'm on my knees in front of the toilet. Pax is holding my hair back. I was so pissed. I... My shoulders fall, the night flashing in incoherent and undecipherable pieces, leaving me even more lost.

Okay, this isn't great. I've been black out drunk a time or two, and even then, I felt like I could sweep the evening under the rug. Now, though? With Paxton two feet in front of me while sporting a sweet, caring personality I'm pretty sure I don't deserve? It's confusing and off-putting and...not great.

"What happened, Pax?" I ask.

"You drank too much."

"Really? I had no idea." My mouth twitches. "Anything else?"

"You puked."

"You mentioned that already."

"You gave everyone a show," he continues.

My eyes thin. "What kind of show?"

"One on a coffee table."

I rub at my tired eyes, still feeling lost. "Sounds promising."

"Trust me, you had quite the audience." He leans closer, his cologne somehow managing to distract me from my throbbing headache. "And if they weren't there, I would've let you continue."

My attention drops to his mouth for a moment. Then, I look him in the eye again. "I'm sure you would've. I've heard I'm the queen of putting on a good show after a few drinks."

With a smirk, he scratches his jaw. "You have no idea."

"Anything else?" I prod.

"Roman kicked everyone out."

"Including Rory?"

He sobers slightly and nods. "Yeah."

Niggling hits the back of my mind, but I stick a pin in the feeling. "Go on."

"You fell on top of me, and I carried you to the bathroom."

"Which is when the puking happened," I assume.

"Exactly."

"That's good, I guess," I mutter. "At least I made it to the toilet. What happened after?"

"We talked and…" He hesitates. "I carried you here." He motions to the bedroom, and I drag my hands along the silky black sheets.

All right, he most definitely breezed over something, but I can't quite put my finger on what.

Unsure if I even want to know the answer, I ask, "And where did you sleep?"

"In the spare room."

"You didn't think to put me in the spare room?"

"I could've."

"But?" I prod.

"But the idea of you sleeping anywhere other than my bed felt wrong."

*Felt wrong?*

I pull my lips between my teeth and bite down on the plump flesh, fighting the urge to blush because…what the hell? And why is that kind of hot? We aren't together. Or at least, we weren't. Actually, we were kind of enemies, so… why am I in his bed, and why is he looking at me like this? There's a softness in his gaze that wasn't there before.

"So, we didn't like, hook up, right?" I ask.

He shakes his head. "Not even a kiss goodnight."

I nod slowly. Somehow, I'm grateful and disappointed at

the same time, which makes zero sense. I stick a pin in that, too. "Let's back up," I decide, searching for light on all the blind spots from last night. "What did we talk about?"

He squeezes the back of his neck but stays quiet.

"Tell me," I push.

"You sure you want to know?"

I grimace. "Is it bad?"

"Not to me," he offers with a shrug.

*Well, that sounds promising.*

Forcing myself to not cower, I sit up a little straighter on the bed and keep my head held high. "Okay, tell me."

"For starters, you mentioned your sister."

Aaaand, just like that, I deflate like an overblown balloon. My sister. The engagement. They're getting married. The conversation is splotchy at best, but I can still see Ophelia's text and how much it hurt. Dread and regret tug in my chest. I fist the sheets, fighting the urge to rub at the aching spot. "And Mav," I offer. "We talked about Mav."

His head dips.

Fighting past the fresh knot in my throat, I whisper, "And Arch."

Pax lowers his head again. "Yeah. And Arch."

"That's why Rory left," I realize. The stone in my stomach triples in size. "Not because Roman kicked her out, but because I was a bitch."

He grimaces. "I'm sure you weren't—"

"I was." I press my forefinger to my tear duct, and stare down at the black residue from last night's makeup. I can't even look Paxton in the eye, let alone my best friend, but the fact is, I screwed up. Big time. "It's hard sometimes," I murmur. "Remembering that she might've lost one brother, but without that loss, she wouldn't have her other one."

Paxton's sigh somehow breathes a bit of life into me,

grounding me in the moment when I could so easily get lost in my shitty history and regret.

"When did it happen?" he asks.

Fiddling with my ring, I answer, "A lifetime ago."

And it's funny. Because Pax probably thinks I'm fudging the numbers on purpose or keeping shit vague to keep him in the dark, but in all reality? It's the truest statement I've ever made. I'm not that girl anymore. But I don't know who this one is, either. It's like my life has been split in two. With Archer and without. And damn, if it doesn't hurt.

"You loved him?" Pax rasps.

"I did." I let out a sad laugh. "I did love him. I loved him so much." Another pathetic laugh escapes me. "Which is so weird because I knew he didn't love me. I knew he'd never love me. Not only was I younger than him, but he was too infatuated with my older sister to even consider opening that door, you know?" My forehead wrinkles. "And I hated it. That she had what I wanted, completely took it for granted," I clarify, "and found a way to throw those feelings, the feelings I desperately wanted to be directed at me, right back in his face by falling for his twin brother instead."

I don't know why I say it. Why I word vomit some of my deepest, darkest secrets to a guy I've been determined to keep at arms' length, but I do. Pax nods slowly, and part of me wonders if I've already told him all of this. If I already aired out all my dirty laundry to a guy I'm not even sure I like at this point. Okay, that's a lie. I do like him. I like him a lot, actually. And that's the scary part. Regardless, the idea of letting drunk Tatum steal this conversation from me feels wrong, and if I can steal back those memories by replicating them when I'm mostly sober and will actually remember what we talk about, then I need to do it. Even if it doesn't make sense. Even if it's uncomfortable. Even if it makes me want to break out in hives.

"Do you still love him?" Pax asks. It isn't accusatory. It isn't laced with pity. It's genuine and open and maybe even a little hesitant or guarded. Like he knows that whatever my answer is, it's real. It means something. It isn't delusional or irrational or proof I've been stuck in la-la land for years with no escape.

And honestly, that validation? It's the only thing making me want to give him an answer.

I press my lips together, hating how easily a simple question can threaten to knock me on my ass. Do I still love him? Did I ever love him? Do I even know what love is? I'm not even twenty-six, and all I've ever done is sleep around, ward off intimate emotional connections like they're the Plague, and screw up like I did last night.

Sensing my discomfort, Pax sits on the edge of the bed, leaving an inch of space between us. "You don't have to answer."

"I love the idea of him," I whisper. "And maybe that's all it ever was because, like I said, he never returned any of those feelings, but…I guess I'm a sucker for an underdog story, and knowing Archer will never get his…moment in the spotlight or whatever, it sucks. And it isn't fair. And I guess, for a girl who grew up reading and absorbing as many happily-ever-afters as she could, it's a hard pill to swallow."

"What is?"

"The realization of how few happily-ever-afters actually unfold in real life." I shove my hair away from my face and press my finger into the corner of my eye again. "God, maybe I'm still drunk. I have no idea why I'm telling you this."

Pax shifts closer to me on his bed, and for some reason I can't explain, I don't pull away. If anything, I fight the urge to move closer.

"Have you ever heard of the composer John Cage?" he asks.

"What?"

"John Cage," he clarifies. "He's from the 1930s or something like that."

I shake my head. "Yeah, no. I've never heard of him."

"His most famous piece is probably 4'33"."

"Haven't heard of that one, either," I note.

He smiles. "It's a song where the performer is supposed to sit in silence for four minutes and 33 seconds while the audience listens to whatever sounds are going on in the room. Things like the air conditioner humming, or other people shifting around in their seats, or the traffic passing by outside. Shit like that."

I quirk my brow. "Sounds like a nutjob."

"Maybe a little." He pauses, his smile softening. "He had this other song, though. 'As Slow As Possible.' People who would perform it were instructed to play the song as slow as possible. And I mean aaaas sloooow aaaas pooooosssssiiiiiblllle." He drags out the words, emphasizing them.

My brows lift. "Like literally?"

"Yeah. Literally. Then he died," Pax says with a shrug. "And all of these people tried to figure out a way to…memorialize the guy. This board gets together, calculates the length of the song and how long each note should play so the piece stays accurate to Cage's composition. They decide to pick a location in some small town in Germany and use a church to play the song the way it was meant to be played. As. Slow. As. Possible. Wanna take a guess how long the performance is?"

"I don't know? A few hours, maybe?"

The mattress dips as he leans closer, stealing all my attention. "Six hundred and thirty-nine years."

My eyes bulge. "Are you serious?"

"Yeah." He chuckles. "Crazy, right?"

"How is that even possible?"

"They use an organ, since the pipes are able to hold a note

or chord for an extended period of time. A piano string will stop vibrating at some point," he clarifies, "but an organ? It goes and goes as long as there's air passing through it."

"You're joking."

"Not joking. Six hundred and thirty-nine years, Birthday Girl."

With wide eyes, I rest my back against the headboard. "That's insane."

"Yeah, it's playing as we speak."

"The same note," I say, shaking my head in disbelief.

"Yeah. The same note. Then, based on the mathematical calculation, when it's time for a new note to play, someone from the church is tasked with changing the chord. It's a huge event. People travel from across the world when it happens."

"Just to hear the chord change."

"Yeah."

"That's insane," I repeat.

"It is, but it's kind of cool, too. Don't you think?"

My mouth lifts as I absorb Paxton's fascination. He's so… animated. It makes him look younger. Cuter. Not hot. Cute. There's a difference, and I'm pretty sure I've never wanted to kiss him more.

Ignoring the urge, I point out, "Sounds nerdy."

"But cool," he pushes.

"Sure, it is." I give him the side-eye, keeping my thoughts on lockdown because okay, yeah. It is kind of cool. That one person can affect people so much, a group of people sign up multiple generations to honor him.

*Crazy.*

"So what's your point, Pax?" I ask.

"Points," he clarifies. "I have multiple."

I chuckle softly. "And they are?"

"One, it's okay for someone to make a lasting impression."

My teeth dig into the inside of my cheek. "And two?"

"Two, there's nothing wrong with taking your time to appreciate something, even if it's a single note played over years. Honestly, there's beauty in it. With celebrating something to the fullest. With accepting the beauty that something is, even if it's as small as a single note or chord. And you can take your time, Birthday Girl. You can take your time and appreciate it for what it is and how it makes you feel. *You.* Not anyone else."

The words hit hard. Harder than I expect. Maybe they shouldn't. Maybe they should. Honestly, I'm not sure. And I'm not sure if it matters, either. Not in the long run.

"And when the composer decides it's time for a new note?" I whisper.

"Then, I think that's worth celebrating, too. But the cool thing is, you're the composer for this song, Tate. You and *only* you. You get to decide when you're ready to move on, to let go, to choose when a new chord is played and what that chord is. Your sister, and her fiance, and Rory? They're composing their own songs, but even if they're at a different pace or in different keys, it doesn't take away from yours."

Well, shit. I shift on the bed, unsure what to say or how to react. Because it's strange. How…fitting his analogy is. Nerdy, but fitting. Whether it's my life or my grief or… anything at all, I've been so busy focusing on—and criticizing —other people's journeys, I haven't been able to accept my own.

"Thank you," I finally whisper.

"Anytime." He grabs my knee and squeezes. "And who knows? Maybe you'll learn to appreciate the new note, too. Whenever you're ready to play it."

I look down at his hand, the familiar lump lodging like a cork in my throat before I swallow it back.

"And on that note—pun intended," he murmurs as he stands, "I'm gonna give you some space."

"Wait."

He stops his retreat. "Yeah?"

"How do you…how do you know so much about this? I'm pretty sure I got more from this conversation than I did years of therapy, so…"

A grimace etches into his handsome features, and he sighs. "It's, uh, it's a long story."

It is. I can tell by the look on his face. The sadness in his eyes. The curve of his shoulders. And even though I have no good reason to pry—and would slap him if the roles were reversed—I remind him weakly, "I told you mine."

"You did, didn't you." Giving in, he says, "My dad left when I was twelve. My mom lost her shit, turning into a shell of a human being. And instead of being there for her. Instead of helping her and being patient with her, I hated her for it. I'd already lost one parent, and she decided to take another one from me? It wasn't fair." He shakes his head. "So, I left as much as I could. I roamed the streets. I got into trouble. I stole. I fought. I did whatever I could to get back at her and bring the spotlight back to me. My pain. My loss. *Me.*" He exhales. "Want to know how she responded?"

"How?"

"By spiraling into a deeper and deeper depression before killing herself a few years later." He sighs again. "Morbid, right? IndieCent Vows was finally going somewhere and she called, asking for money. I told her she didn't deserve a cent, then hung up the phone. Got a call from the coroner a week later."

Like a punch to the gut, I try and steady my breathing, but also, "Shit," I breathe out.

He chuckles softly. "Yeah. If you wanna shower, you can borrow my clothes. I don't mind."

"You want me to wear your clothes?"

Mirth dances in his brown eyes as a smile tugs at the corner of his mouth, and this time, it's more genuine. Hell, it even reaches his eyes. "As long as you don't dye them green."

Grabbing hold of the lightness in his words, I reply, "I make no promises."

"Then I'll let you walk home naked."

I laugh. "Don't tempt me."

With a slow shake of his head, he studies me. "You'd do it, too."

"One hundred percent." I hold his gaze, refusing to back down, though there's no need. He's already caved.

"All right, fine." He tosses his hands in the air, then disappears into the closet, returning with a worn, white T-shirt and gray sweats. "You can dye my clothes whatever color you want as long as you let me give you a ride home when the time comes."

I take the offered clothes and bring them to my chest, feeling lighter than I have in a long time. "When the time comes? What does that mean?"

"Nothing, unless you want it to." He rocks back on his heels, looking sexier than any man has the right to. "I was just thinking, what if we give Rory some breathing room for a few hours—give her a chance to calm down and maybe cut you some slack—before I drop you off?"

"And what would we do in the meantime?"

He shrugs. "I dunno? You hungry?"

My stomach grumbles, but I ignore it, tossing my legs over the side of the bed until the plush white rug tickles my bare toes. "Depends."

"On?"

"On if eating food together categorizes this"—I wiggle my finger between us—"as a date or not."

He steps forward, stealing the space between us. "And if it does?"

Staying quiet, I will my heart to slow the eff down.

"Tatum, I like you," he murmurs. "I like your spunk. I like your face"—he nudges my head up, forcing me to look at him—"and your hair." His hand trails down my length. "I like your smile and your tenacity." He lets the ends of my hair go. "I like you drunk. I like you sober." Squatting down, he kneels in front of me, wedging himself between my thighs as I sit on the edge of the bed. "I like you, and I think you might like me, too." A shy smile plays at the edge of his mouth, and I swear it's directly connected to the stupid organ in my chest. "Hang out with me today. Or this evening or tomorrow or… whenever. I'll take whatever time you're willing to give."

He would, too. I can see it. Taste it. Feel it. His desire. And not only on a physical level, but an emotional one.

"Sounds needy," I tease, hoping to lighten the mood.

"Only for you." He brushes his lips against mine in the softest of kisses, surprising the hell out of me. But I don't pull away. I don't smack him or call him a horn dog. I simply sit there. Feeling his lips move against mine before lifting my head a bit more and returning it. The kiss. Still soft. Still gentle. Hell, it's fragile, almost. But I'm pretty sure I've never felt anything like it, and I can't help but crave it more until he pulls away, stands to his full height, and steps back.

"You can think about it while you shower, yeah?" he offers.

We've never talked like this. We've never said what we feel or broached subjects that make me squirm. Okay, that's a lie. Paxton has. A few times. And I've always shied away from it. Hell, shied away from it is putting my response lightly. More like shoved it away and ran in the opposite direction until my lungs gave out. But I don't want to anymore. Or at least, not right now. Not after I told him about Arch and he opened up about his mom. And the kiss? I can still feel it.

Lost in the ghost of his touch still lingering on my mouth, I force myself to nod. "Yeah. Yeah, okay."

I swallow the bite of bagel in my mouth as the cool water laps at our bare feet. I'm still surprised Tatum said yes when she met me in the kitchen after her shower. That she agreed to let me buy her breakfast at the little bakery down the street from my place. That she didn't demand to be taken straight home after spilling her life story and the real reason behind every shady action since we first met. To be fair, she said she'd let me buy her breakfast because Rory hadn't responded to her message yet, and she didn't want to get stabbed by entering her apartment before her best friend was ready to see her, but I'm not complaining.

"This is good." Tatum lifts her bagel into the air and takes another bite.

"I know it's no lobster roll, but I'm glad it'll suffice."

She smiles around her bite before wiping some excess schmear from the corner of her mouth. "I'm impressed you remember that little tidbit." Her gaze flickers to the calm water. "You got the ocean part right, though."

"Glad you approve," I return.

"I do." She pauses to squish her bare toes in the sand. As

soon as we got here, she left her shoes by a random log, so I did the same. It's been nice. Going slow. Enjoying our morning. Walking lazily down the coast. It's been really nice, and I wonder if she's liked it, too.

"So," she continues, "after my little mental breakdown last night, I think you owe me."

"Oh, I do?"

"Yup."

"I did buy you a bagel," I point out.

"I meant you owe me information," she clarifies.

"Such as?"

"Let's see…" She clicks her tongue against the roof of her mouth. "For starters, what brought you here?"

"Here?" I look around the empty beach, grateful there isn't another soul in sight, thanks to owning most of it.

"I mean to Harden Heights," she clarifies. "If you're not close with your band, why'd you decide to settle here while you wait for the band's hiatus to end?"

With a shrug, I take another bite of bagel and draw a smiley face in the sand with my big toe. "I'm from here."

Her jaw drops in surprise. "Seriously?"

"About thirty minutes south," I explain. "I grew up in The Drift."

"What's The Drift?"

My head snaps up. "Fuck, you're really not from around here, are you?"

"Not even close."

"The Drift is a strip of land where all the poor people live. It isn't close to the water or the country clubs or the university. It's where the lackeys and blue-collar folk stay. It's also where the drugs are, and the gangs are, and every other… potentially unsavory class of individuals likes to congregate."

"Congregate, huh?" She smiles, kicking a bit of sand toward me. "You sound like a textbook."

"You're the one needing a geography lesson," I return dryly.

She smirks. "Okay, so if you're from here, what's the rest of the band's excuse?"

"Where Judge goes, Dodger goes, and Judge is from here, too."

Surprised, she asks, "He's from The Drift?"

"Nah, he's from the rich side of town. His family founded the university and basically owns the entire place."

"Really?" She takes the last bite of bagel, then licks the excess cream cheese from her thumb. "Don't get me wrong. I don't really know the guy, but he kind of puts off more of a Drift vibe."

I chuckle softly, knowing she's not wrong. "That's 'cause he hates his family."

"Aw, noted." She taps her forefinger against her temple. "So why did you all come back?"

It's a difficult question, and I hesitate before answering. Not because I don't trust her, but because I know the guys like to keep things close to the chest, and whatever's going on with Judge's family is making him even more guarded than usual.

"It's complicated," I finally admit.

Reading between the lines, Tatum says, "You don't have to tell me if you don't want to."

I break the last of my bagel into small pieces, tossing them one by one into the water. "Judge's family is close, even if they do hate each other. When his nephews started stirring up shit, Judge's brother, Titas, called him home to keep the boys in line."

Her brows pull. "Aren't the boys adults?"

"In age, yeah," I reply. "But they're also loose cannons, and since they're expected to take over the family business once they graduate, their personas matter."

"And they aren't meeting their father's expectations," she concludes.

"Exactly. They're too busy fucking shit up, which is why Judge is here." I hesitate. "It's why I'm here, too."

Like the little detective she is, she tilts her head, collecting more pieces than I'm putting down, despite my intentional ambiguity. "And what do you have to do with Judge's nephews?"

"Judge's family is hoping the extra publicity from the band will be enough to keep the boys' sideline shit where it belongs—on the sidelines and out of the public eye."

She bites back her scoff. "They really think that'll work?"

I shrug. "It's Judge's family, not mine, although it doesn't hurt that we're killing two birds with one stone, either."

"What do you mean?"

"If we're able to stay relevant in the gossip magazines, it'll help our fans not forget about us. Or so I'm told."

"That's a thing?"

"You have no idea." I shake my head. "Mindy, the band's publicist, insists all publicity is good publicity."

"Oh, then I'm sure you're her favorite," she teases.

I scratch my temple. "I dunno. Dodge and Tuke put up a pretty good fight for first place."

"Not Judge?" she assumes.

"Not even close," I admit with a laugh.

"Well, I still think you win first place on that front," she replies. "Don't think I haven't noticed the paparazzi outside your gate, anxious to catch a glimpse of the infamous Paxton Six." She pauses. "Which I assume is not your real last name, right?"

"Turner," I tell her.

"Turner. Got it." She hesitates again, as if making a mental note, then clears her throat. "Although, Paxton Turner, the photos of you walking into the salon with green hair are probably my favorite leaked photos to date."

My eyes widen. "You saw those, huh?"

"Yup." She brings her fingertips to her mouth and kisses them. "They were chef's kiss, let me tell ya."

"Gee, thanks."

"You're welcome," she returns shamelessly. "But my point stands. Seems you're good at creating buzz just by being here."

"I'm trying." I shrug. "But I've been a little preoccupied pursuing my maid, so…"

She beams at the thought before it turns sassy, and she counters, "Sounds very boring."

A bark of laughter escapes me. "Hardly."

She joins in, the lightness of her laugh acting like a cool glass of water on a hot day. To be honest, after last night's spiral, I wasn't sure I'd see this side of her again. The glimpse is refreshing. And more addictive than I want to admit.

"So, what does the great and powerful Pax do when he isn't playing rockstar, or trying to keep the public eye on him instead of his bandmate's nephews?" she prods as we make our way down the coastline.

"Lately?" I pause. "Stalking my maid is pretty fun."

"And reading *The Count of Monte Cristo*," she adds.

"And playing the guitar."

"And working out," she continues. "Excellent work, by the way. Although, the random bruises are an interesting addition."

"You noticed, huh?"

Looking unimpressed, she shoves me playfully. "I mean, they're kind of hard to miss, Pax."

"Oh, really?"

"Yeah." She quirks her brow, shamelessly checking me out. "They clash with your pretty face."

I laugh even harder. "You think I'm pretty, huh?"

"I think you're looking for me to stroke your ego, which —as we've previously discussed—is already big enough as it is, thank you very much." Pulling her hair over her shoulder, she adds, "But seriously. What's with the bruises?"

It's a good question, and honestly, I'm flattered she's noticed. After meeting Jagger a couple weeks ago, we exchanged numbers and meet up a few times a week to train. He said it was so I wouldn't embarrass the family for giving me a slot. Even though I'm pretty sure he's going easy on me, I've appreciated the extra help. But the bruises? Not so much.

"I've, uh," I scratch my temple, "I've been sparring with a few buddies lately."

"Sparring?" She digs her heels into the sand. "As in, fighting?"

I nod.

"Well, damn." Biting her bottom lip, she scans me up and down with newfound appreciation. "That's hot."

A rumble of amusement escapes me. "Glad I have your approval."

"Any other hobbies?" she asks, surprising me with her interest.

"I like to travel," I offer.

"Yeah? Me, too. What's your favorite place you've ever been to?"

"Croatia, probably, but Thailand was pretty sweet, too."

"I've been to Thailand!" Tatum gushes. She shoves me playfully. "Did you do the fish pedicure thing? Where you stick your feet in the water and the baby fish eat all the dead skin off?"

My stomach rolls at the thought. "Gross."

"Yeah, but it left my skin so smooth, you wouldn't even believe it."

"Your skin is already pretty damn smooth, Birthday Girl."

A soft pink tinges her cheeks, and her attention drops to the sand beneath her feet. "I think you're being too kind."

"And I think— Fuck! Shit!" I jump up and down, my foot burning with a vengeance.

Joining my meltdown, Tatum drops the last of her bagel in the sand and jolts back, staring as I lose my ever-loving shit.

"What's wrong?" she screeches. "What happened?"

Balancing on one leg I lift my foot into the air, finding the skin on the bottom of it hot, red, and angry. "Jellyfish. I stepped on a—"

"Jellyfish!" She flaps her hand behind us toward a translucent blob on the sand. "There's a jellyfish!"

"No shit," I say, caught between barks of laughter and groans of excruciating pain.

Moving closer, Tatum suggests, "Here. Use me for balance. Let's take a look."

"I'm fine."

"Don't be a tough guy." She pats her shoulder, urging me to lean into her. "I got you."

Giving in, I grab her shoulder to keep from falling on my ass and lift my foot a little higher into the air. A tiny divot forms between her brows as she assesses the damage, gently dragging her fingers along the raised flesh before grimacing. "Ouch."

"Stings like a bitch." I try not to flinch away from her soft touch, but fuck, it throbs. I feel like my foot was dipped in a vat of acid or is sitting in a barrel of hot coal, and it isn't getting better. No, it's getting worse. A lot worse. "Fuuuuck," I seethe.

"Do you want me to…" Her eyes lift to meet mine, and her nose wrinkles. "You know."

"What?" My forehead pinches as the angry sting hits a new level. Fuck, this hurts. It really hurts. Seriously. Do they do amputations for shit like this? Because I haven't been in this much pain, since…shit, I don't even know when.

Tucking her hair behind her ear, Tatum explains, "I heard that if you…you know, it makes the sting go away."

Distracted by the blinding pain crawling up my ankle, I grit out, "Gonna have to spell it out for me, Birthday Girl."

"Pee on it. Do you need me to pee on it?"

My eyes bulge, and I tear my attention from the bottom of my foot to the girl who just confirmed I'm hallucinating because there's no chance in hell she said what I think she did. "What did you say?"

"I said, I heard peeing on a jellyfish sting helps the pain go away," she blurts out.

"You'd pee on my foot for me?"

Shimmying away from me, she bounces on the balls of her feet like I'm the one who suggested it when we both know it was her.

"Don't make it weird," she starts.

Despite the pain, I throw my head back and laugh even harder, caught off guard by the ludicrousness of the situation. But fuuuuck, this hurts like a bitch!

"Okay, seriously. Come on, big boy." Wrapping her arm around my waist, she helps me hobble to the side of the beach and away from the water.

"Fuck," I grit out, trying not to black out from the blinding pain. "No, I'm fine."

With a gentle shove, she tips me over, and I collapse onto my ass, barely catching myself with my hands at the last second. My foot hovers a few inches from the ground as I grind my teeth to keep from crying like a baby.

"Okay, so here's the deal," she announces. Glancing left and right, she reaches for the drawstring on the gray sweats I let her borrow before turning her attention back to me. "What happens at the beach, stays at the beach. We clear?"

I glance up at her. "You talking about when you sucked me off or—"

"All of the above. Now, lay back and close your eyes because this is not allowed to be used for your spank bank on the off chance you have a kink I don't know about."

I burst out laughing again and lay back on the sand, tossing my forearm over my eyes to cover them. "Not into that kink, Tate. Sorry, if it's disappointing."

"Well, at least we agree on one thing. Now stop moving your leg."

I force my muscles to stay in place and fight the urge to writhe on the ground, but fuck, it feels impossible. "Fuck, fuck, fuck."

"Don't. Move."

The buzzing in my ears is almost enough to drown out the rustle of fabric, but I stand my ground—er, sit my ground—refusing to move as I try to control my breathing.

"Man, this is so embarrassing," Tatum mumbles.

Warm liquid hits my foot, and I fight the urge to pull away when the blazing fire starts to ebb, being replaced with a softer, more manageable discomfort I can handle.

"Keep 'em closed," Tatum warns.

My muscles relax as I rest the back of my head against the sand. Okay, I'm gonna be okay. It's getting better. I can breathe.

A few seconds later, Tatum announces, "Okay, you can open."

Uncovering my eyes, I lift my head again, finding a fully-clothed Tatum a good five feet away.

Arms crossed, she stares down at the sand, refusing to look at me with a blush on her cheeks making her look fucking gorgeous. I've never seen Tatum shy before. Even when she was puking in front of me and drunk off her ass, she wasn't shy. But this? This is something for the books, and

I clench my fists to keep from reaching out and tugging her into a bear hug.

Shifting her attention to the blue sky above us, she mumbles, "How's it, uh, how's it feel? Better?"

With another low laugh, I roll to my knees and push myself to my feet before cautiously approaching her. "I'm good. Are *you*?"

"Yup. Happy as a clam." She motions to the water, still refusing to look at me. "Now, go…wash off or whatever, and never—I mean *never*—mention this to anyone ever again. We clear?"

I splash in the water, letting it reach my knees and thoroughly cleaning off every possible droplet of…nope. Not gonna think about it. "Thanks again, Tate, I—"

"I said don't mention it," she snaps.

She covers her eyes like a little kid during a scary movie. It's adorable and strangely…vulnerable, proving she wouldn't pee on just anyone. The reminder I was the lucky one she helped is enough to wash away whatever lingering embarrassment is still clinging to the moment because yeah, writhing on the ground like a baby is not the impression I wanted to leave this girl with.

Jogging toward a still motionless Tatum, I grab her hands from her face and lower them, forcing her to look at me. "I owe you."

"You don't--"

"Not gonna pee on you," I clarify.

"Pax," she groans, shying away from my touch, but I hold firm. When she realizes I'm not letting her get away, she sags a little more and grumbles, "I told you not to—"

"Thank you." I kiss her forehead. "Thank you for taking one for the team." I bend closer and kiss her pretty little scowl. "Thank you, thank you, thank you."

Swatting my kisses away, she peeks up at me with the cutest fucking scowl I've ever seen. "You're welcome."

Fuck, she's pretty like this. She's pretty all the time, but like this? Peeking up at me through her lashes, the tinge of pink still resting on her cheeks? A glint of curiosity in her pretty gaze? It's enough to make me kiss her again. And without the teasing. Because I want to. Because I'm stupid enough to hope I can get away with it.

I close some of the distance between us, my fingers itching to wrap around her waist so I can seal the deal when Tatum's phone buzzes. She takes it out of her pocket, dousing what's left of our chemistry just as quickly. I can't help but wonder if it's her sister again. If she's going to say something to cause Tatum to spiral again. If all the work I've put into making her smile today will be erased with a single message. Fuck, I hope not.

Helpless, I watch as she checks her phone. Her brows are pulled low and her mouth moves as she reads whatever she's looking at, but I'm still left in the dark, and I don't like it.

"Everything okay?" I ask.

"Rory responded." Her fingers fly across the screen. "Said she could meet me at Grinds in thirty minutes."

Disappointment flares in my chest, but I ignore it. "Want me to drop you off?"

Looking up from her screen, she gives me a glimpse of her indecision before she nods softly. "Yes, please."

I guess that's that.

33

# TATUM

I shouldn't be nervous, but I am. Bouncing on the balls of my feet, I give myself a quick pep talk and open the door to Grinds. After Rory texted, Pax stopped by my apartment so I could change before dropping me off at the coffee shop, yet again proving he's way sweeter than his rockstar persona leads people to think he is. Paxton's been different this morning, but I don't hate it. And I don't feel like I'm being pitied, either. That's the weird part. Whenever people find out I'm damaged goods, they think treating me with kid gloves is the safest route. It only pisses me off more. But, Pax? He's been himself, only the…softer, less guarded version. Then again, so have I. Maybe it's because we're more similar than I realized. I mean, talk about some heavy baggage. His mom committed suicide after he refused to give her money? That's…rough. Really rough. It only impresses me more. I had fun with him this morning. More fun than I want to admit, if I'm being honest with myself, but I refuse to taint the experience by overthinking shit. Not after my night from hell.

Speaking of which, where is my best friend?

The nutty scent of coffee wraps around me like a hug as I search the small shop for Rory. After begging her to meet with me, she said she'd be at Grinds for the next hour or so, and if I felt like stopping by, she'd allow it. It's pretty much the only invitation I would've expected after the things I said to her yesterday.

When I spot Rory sitting at a small booth near the back, I stride closer and slide into the seat across from her, practically choking on my apology in hopes of getting it over with as quickly as possible. "I'm a bitch," I announce. "I'm sorry—"

"I forgive you."

Jerking back, my brows hitch. "That's it? That's all it took?"

She tucks her hair behind her ear while avoiding my gaze. "I think I know you better than to expect any other kind of response than the one you gave me after finding out about the wedding. And if I can cut you some slack, then you can cut me some, too."

And there it is. Her reason for being so forgiving. Because she needs me to do the same.

*Sneaky, Rory. Very sneaky.*

"Why would I need to cut you slack?" I question.

Her lips press into a thin line before she looks down at her hands, clicking her short nails together.

"Squeaks," I push.

"I called my mom."

My stomach lurches as all the potential repercussions of a single phone call rush to the surface. Shit. That isn't what I was expecting. Don't get me wrong. It's not like she never talks to her mom. Her relationship with her parents is as strong as mine. But calling her after a big, fat wedding announcement? That's a different story. Add in the guilt wafting off Rory in waves, and I know I'm about to have my world rocked.

"Squeaks," I repeat, though it's more of a plea than a warning like before.

"Apparently, Lia didn't want you to find out about the wedding through the grapevine, but after one too many ignored calls, she finally just texted you the announcement then called everyone else."

"Yeah, I assumed as much."

"I talked to Mav, too," she adds carefully. "Anyway, my mom asked if we're planning to come to the engagement party as well as the wedding, and I said..." Her gaze finally meets mine, already welling with tears as if her panic might swallow her whole.

"What did you say, Rore?"

"Don't kill me."

"Rore..."

"I said yes."

Hunching into my seat, my head lolls forward in defeat. It's not like I actually thought I could get away with missing the wedding or the engagement party, but surrendering this quickly feels like a low blow. I don't want to go back. Not only because of Lia, but because I spent my teenage years torching every bridge and olive branch in existence. Facing everyone again? It feels about as comfortable as a punch to the boob.

Pinching the bridge of my nose, I mumble, "Guess it makes sense, since he's your brother and all."

"And Lia's your sister," Rory adds, as if she has to remind me.

"And that," I mutter. I feel like I've been tossed into the deep end of a pool with my hands tied behind my back, and I hate it. I shouldn't be surprised. I know I shouldn't. Not by the engagement or the looming travel dates ahead of me thanks to said engagement. But it doesn't make me feel any better.

Mav and Ophelia have been together for years. Honestly, it's a shock they weren't hitched before Archer's body was in the ground, they were so obsessed with each other. Of course, they'd decide to tie the knot at some point. So why does it have to piss me off so much? It doesn't matter. They don't matter. Not when it comes to my grief. It's like Pax said. I'm composing my own song. I'm living my own journey. And just because their song is a little different, it shouldn't detract from my own.

Right?

*Man, why is this so hard?*

"Rory?" the barista calls from the front. My best friend stands and heads to the pick up counter before returning with two iced lattes.

As she hands me one of them, I ask, "What do I owe you?"

"You know I've got it." She slips back into the booth across from me. "Anyway, if it helps, I'm not too happy about going back to Lockwood Heights, either."

*Duh.*

"We'll get through it," I promise, though I'm not exactly convinced. Picking up my latte, I take a sip, hoping the creamy cup of deliciousness will find a way to calm me down.

*Great, Tate. Let's turn to substance abuse to fix our problems, shall we?*

Blah. I can still hear my old therapist's voice warning me about substance abuse after I came home sloshed at seventeen and my parents had to hold my hair back as I puked my guts out.

Like Pax did last night.

I repeat, *blah.*

With a sigh, I decide to focus on someone else's trauma for once. "You sure you're ready to face Jax again?" I ask.

Rory scowls back at me. "Not in the slightest—"

"Squeaks?" a low voice interrupts.

*Squeaks?*

No one calls Rory Squeaks unless they're from Lockwood Heights.

My body tenses, and I stare at my coffee, willing the universe to stop hating me for one day. One. Freaking. Day. If only I was so lucky.

Eyes bulging, Rory pastes on a smile and stares up at someone behind me. "Dodge!" When she stands, the infamous Dodger Anders pulls her into a hug. He towers over the girl, making her look like a little kid as he squeezes her tight before releasing her and turning his attention to me. "Tatum, right?"

"That's me," I confirm. "It's been awhile."

"Yeah, a few years, right?"

I nod. "Crazy how time flies."

"Like the wind," he agrees.

"You should sit with us," Rory offers. "Like Tatum said, it's been forever, and I'd love to catch up. How are you? How's the band and everything?"

"On hiatus at the moment." He leans closer. "Apparently, family drama can be found outside of Lockwood Heights, too. Shocker, am I right?" He plops down into the booth and spreads his legs wide beneath the table.

"Well, at least we're not alone," Rory muses, tossing me a knowing look.

Reading Rory's expression, Dodge asks, "Wait, is there family drama I don't know about? New or old?"

"A mix," Rory confirms, grimacing. "I'm not sure if the cat is officially out of the bag, but, uh, Mav proposed, so…yay."

"No shit?" He laughs. "That's amazing. Congrats to them."

"Yeah." Rory smiles. "It'll be…great."

"Great," he repeats. "You don't sound very optimistic."

"It's just…Lockwood Heights, am I right?"

He chuckles. "Right."

*Right?* What's his problem with Lockwood Heights? I study the side of his face while searching my memory for any kind of hint or clue Rory might've dropped in the last handful of years as to why Dodger might be running from Lockwood Heights, but I come up empty. If I'm being honest, I usually avoid all things Dodger—and everything family related—so it's not like it's Rory's fault I'm left in the dark. But still. Something doesn't add up.

Feeling my stare, Dodger's attention slides to me. "What? You're surprised?"

"Maybe a little," I admit. "I thought Rory's and my Lockwood Heights baggage was for a party of two."

"I wish. You're not the only one who prefers to keep their hometown where it belongs." He dips closer. "Fucking behind them."

My eyes thin. "And what are you running from?"

"The past," he answers cryptically. "Just like you two."

"Who says we're running?" Rory interrupts.

Dodger smirks. "You know our families, Squeaks. You really think they don't talk?"

Her body slumps forward. "Of course, they do." She groans and scrubs her hand over her face. "What am I going to do? I don't want to go. I don't want to face him."

"Him," Dodger repeats. It isn't a question. It's a dare. He wants to hear her say it. Jaxon's name. The man who's been haunting her for years. The man who she refuses to let go of, despite the bastard being married *and* with a kid. Yeah, it was a dark day in high school when she got the call about his engagement. She should've gone to the wedding. If she wanted to save face, she would've. Instead, we both hunkered down in our dorm and binged *Gilmore Girls* the entire weekend. I don't regret a second of it, and neither does Rory. But maybe it would've been good for her. To see him sign his life away. To hear him say the words, "I do," to someone else. Someone who isn't her.

Steeling her shoulders, Rory announces, "Jaxon Thorne," with more bravado than I've ever seen.

"Right," Dodger murmurs. "The asshole."

Her bottom lip wobbles, and she squeezes her eyes shut, letting out a slow breath. "Ignore me for a second. I just need to cry."

*Aaaand there's the baby deer I know and love.*

"Don't cry," Dodge replies. "What do you have to be afraid of?"

"I don't know? Embarrassing myself? Again? Looking like an idiot? Again? Showing up with no date and no prospects while drooling over a guy who's married with a kid?" She wipes at her cheeks angrily. "Yeah, that sounds like an amazing way to spend my time celebrating my brother's wedding, don't you think?"

Scratching the scruff along his jaw, Dodger offers, "I'll go."

Like a record scratching, Rory's mouth snaps shut, and her head swings toward him. "I'm sorry, what?"

"I said, I'll go." He shrugs. "As your plus-one."

"You'll go as my date?"

"Yeah, why not? It's not like I wouldn't have gone anyway."

"I thought you hate Lockwood Heights," I remind him.

"They're family," he answers without even casting me a glance. "And so are you, Rore. So what do you say? Want to be my date?"

"I mean, you're…" She scans him up and down, taking in his weathered face, charismatic lift of his lips, and tattoos peeking out beneath the collar and sleeves of his T-shirt. "Sure," she squeaks. "Sure, I'd love to."

I groan. "Then, who will I go with?"

"I mean, you and Pax looked pretty…"—my best friend doesn't even bother hiding her amusement—"something last night."

"Pretty something?" I repeat with a laugh.

"You know what I mean," she argues.

"Yeah, but I don't," Dodger rests his elbows on the table. "What's going on with you and Pax?"

"Nothing," I tell him.

"You sure about that?"

"Yes," I say, doubling down while silencing the tiny voice inside my head from shouting otherwise.

He frowns. "Shame."

"What makes you say that?" I ask.

"This job can be…isolating, especially with assholes for bandmates." He stands and raps his knuckles against the table. "It was good catching up. Rore, you have my number. Use it, yeah?"

"Yeah, of course," she replies.

Then he turns to me. "Good seeing you again, Tatum."

I nod slowly. "You, too."

# 34

# TATUM

"You know, we needed this," I announce while perusing the depressingly empty freezer. Seriously. Where are the Eggos? The ice cream? The popsicles? And it wouldn't kill us to stock up on some of those frozen cream puffs or premade taquitos, either. I lift a frozen pound of ground beef a few inches off the shelf in hopes of finding something delicious and processed and relatively premade but come up empty. "Although, it would've been smart if we'd planned ahead a little better."

"You're the one who forgot to go to the grocery store this week, not me," Rory says from her perfectly made twin bed.

"Hey, I was a little busy cleaning," I argue.

"And dreading Paxton's party," she argues. "Which, by the way, I still haven't gotten the details on yet."

Ignoring her, I suggest, "There's also UberEats?"

"And risk someone touching my food?" She shivers. "No, thank you."

"Fiiiine." I push the freezer door closed and pad back to my bed, plopping on the messy sheets. "What do you want to watch?"

"I mean, we're only on season three of *Gilmore Girls*…"

"You just like the fact that you're named after one of the main characters," I tease.

"Technically, both of the main characters, but—"

My phone buzzes in my lap, and I look at the screen, finding an unknown number.

UNKNOWN NUMBER

Hey, Birthday Girl.

Birthday Girl.

Butterflies swell in my stomach as I fight to keep from swooning. I haven't seen Pax since the beach, and even though I'd never admit it out loud, and have kept myself busy cleaning other houses, I've kind of missed him since he dropped me off at Grinds. And how did he get my number? Normally, I'd be creeped out, but all I can think about is how he went through the effort to track it down.

*Swoon.*

Attempting to keep the butterflies in check, I add Paxton's contact information to my phone, then type my response.

ME

I'm sorry, who is this?

PAX

I'm sorry, do other gentlemen call you
Birthday Girl?

"Who has you smiling?" Rory asks.

Feeling like I just got caught with my hand in the proverbial cookie jar, I flip my phone facedown in my lap and jerk my head toward my best friend. "Hmm?"

She grins. "I asked who has you smiling."

I wave her off. "I'm not smiling."

"You're most definitely smiling. Which is adorable by the way. Is it Pax?"

My teeth dig into my bottom lip before I give in and nod. "Maybe."

"Good for you," she decides. "You know, you could always invite him over."

"And have your beast bite off his testicles?" I grimace. "No, thank you."

She lifts a brow. "One. Rude. Hades would never do that—"

My pointed look cuts her off.

"Okay, he'd never do it without my permission," she clarifies. "But seriously, you should invite Pax. I'll even put Hades in his kennel so Paxton's testicles are safe."

I stay quiet, considering my options. I could say no. I should say no. Besides, he's probably busy, and it's been only forty-eight hours since we talked. He's probably come to his senses and is over the whole "I like you" bit. Right? Then again, our little walk on the beach is probably one of the most memorable encounters I've ever had with the opposite sex. I mean, pretty sure peeing on someone all because of a jellyfish sting would make the list for anyone, but adding it to every other experience I've shared with Pax? I don't know. It feels like the list is getting longer and longer, and… I probably should've played this better because it's clear Rory knows me way too well, and now, I'm on her radar.

"Cat got your tongue, Tater Tot?" she prods.

"He's probably busy," I reply while trying not to squirm from my best friend's scrutiny. But seriously. When did she get so good at calling me out on my bullshit?

"You won't know unless you ask."

"And it's a girls' night," I point out.

"Only because we don't have any other friends."

Touche.

And also…*ouch.*

I open my mouth to argue that we're cooler than

everyone else we know anyway, but my phone buzzes again, distracting me. Unlocking my screen, I read Paxton's message.

PAX

Your silence isn't very reassuring.

What were we talking about? Oh. Right. Other gentlemen calling me Birthday Girl. Biting the edge of my lip, I write my reply.

ME

You're not used to being on this side of a relationship, are you?

PAX

Are you saying we're in a relationship?

ME

I meant the general term, not the romantic one.

PAX

Shame.

My mouth lifts again before I can stop it, and my phone buzzes with another message.

PAX

Any chance you're free tonight?

ME

Depends. How'd you get my number?

PAX

I may have bribed Roman to do some digging.

Of course, Roman's to blame. I shouldn't even be surprised at this point. He's probably the one who gave Pax a ride to pick his car up when I borrowed it after the hot tub incident, too. When I walked outside the next morning to find his car gone, I almost had a heart attack but was too stubborn to reach out to Pax directly to tell him his car was stolen while under my watch, and I had no way of paying him back for it. Yeah, talk about an awkward conversation. Thankfully, when I pulled into Pax's house for work a few days later and found it parked inside the garage like it never left, I was able to breathe a massive sigh of relief. Regardless, Roman's a slippery fellow, that much I know.

ME

Seems Roman's a man of many talents.

PAX

You have no idea. So what do you say? Are you free?

I peek up at Rory and catch her staring at me as she scratches Hades behind his ear.

"What'd Pax say?" she asks.

"He, uh, he wants to know if we're free."

"*We*." She snorts. "Yeah, okay. And you better say yes."

My nose wrinkles as I look down at my phone. Typing out a dozen different responses, I finally land on two words.

ME

Maybe. Why?

PAX

I figured you might be interested in a do-over.

ME

Gonna need more details.

PAX

Come on, Birthday Girl. Let me surprise you.

I peek up at Rory again. The idea of ditching her is more than I can stomach, especially after my drunken bitchery from a couple nights ago. And so, even though it kind of kills me, I pull on my big girl panties and respond.

ME

Can't. I have plans.

PAX

Should I be jealous?

ME

Nah, I see Rory like a little sister, so you're safe.

PAX

You had me worried for a minute there. Why don't you bring her along?

Ignoring my best friend's stare, I type my response.

ME

Color me intrigued.

PAX

Figured you might be.

ME

Is this because you owe me after the beach?

PAX

I believe you said, "What happens at the beach, stays at the beach," remember?

By the way, my foot feels much better, thank you for asking. And might I add, your pee is magical.

My eyes bug out of my head, and I look over my shoulder, confirming Rory hasn't managed to read minds or texts from across the tiny room, and this conversation is between me and Pax and *only* me and Pax.

*Hallelujah.*

ME

Tell me, did you even read your previous text before sending it?

PAX

Maybe. But the idea of you losing your shit over a completely normal circumstance like peeing on a friend to help the guy out was worth looking like I have a urine kink during a texting conversation.

I bite the inside of my cheek to keep from grinning like a lunatic.

ME

Well, would you look at that. Seems like my plans can't be changed. But good luck on your do-over.

PAX

Aw, come on, Birthday Girl. You know you're curious.

He's right. I am.

ME

I'm gonna need details.

PAX

You'll have to wait and see, but I promise you won't regret it.

"What's he saying?" Rory interrupts.

I peek up at her, unsure how to answer her. "He, uh, he wants to know if we can go to his place so he can have a do-over."

Confusion and intrigue gleam in her eyes as she tilts her head. "A do-over, huh?"

"Yeah, but I told him I already have plans with you."

"So?" she challenges. "Don't you want to see what his do-over entails?"

"Well, yeah, but…" I peek at my cell, indecision gnawing at me. "You really think we should go?"

She flinches back, and Hades lifts his head, sensing her discomfort. Ignoring her protective pup, Rory demands, "I'm sorry, who said I had to go?"

Preparing myself for a battle, I sit up a little straighter, pointing to my chest. "Uh, me?"

"No, thank you." She gives me a syrupy sweet grin and reaches for the controller.

"Squeaks…"

"Seriously, I think I'll pass," she interrupts. "I'll stay here, and you can catch me up on all the gory details tomorrow morning after you do the walk of shame."

"Hey!" Grabbing my pillow, I toss it at her. "Rude."

"Or accurate," she quips.

"Come on. If I'm going, you have to come."

"Seriously?"

With my hands pressed in front of me in a prayer gesture, I plead, "Please. You know I can't do this without you."

The look she gives me is bland at best, but I already know she'll give in. Why? Because she's the bestest friend a girl could ever ask for, and she knows I won't go unless she's by my side.

"You really want me to come?" she whines.

"Yes, I really, *really* do."

"Fiiiine." She waves her hand toward her phone. "Tell him we're on our way. I'll go change, then you can get ready." She points to her beast. "You. Stay." Then, she rushes into the bathroom.

Scrunching my face, I type my response before I can talk myself out of it.

ME

Rory and I will be there in thirty.

PAX

See you soon.

35

# TATUM

"I still can't believe you dragged me along for your date," Rory grumbles. "Actually, scratch that. I can't believe I *let* you drag me along for your date. What was I thinking?"

"That you love me?" I offer. "Besides, it's a good thing you're here. This way, the night will stay relatively…safe."

"Safe," she repeats. Her brow lifts in a perfect arch as we park outside Paxton's perfect house.

"Yeah." I shrug. "Safe."

"Mm-hmm," she hums, clearly unconvinced. "Whatever you say, Tater Tot. Lead the way."

As I push the passenger door open, a warm breeze carries the scent of the ocean with it. I pause, breathing it in.

Safe.

I'm grateful Rory didn't push me on it. Make me question my sanity for being here when it's clear Paxton's holding it captive. Yup. He probably has a jar with a label on it and everything. Tatum's Sanity. It's tucked right between Tatum's Curiosity and Tatum's Libido, because he sure as hell owns those, too, after all our steamy encounters over the years.

Honestly, it isn't even fair at this point. How he's managed to consume so much of my time, my thoughts, my everything since the moment we first met. It doesn't make this less scary, though. If anything, it makes me more anxious.

The last time I was at Paxton's, I woke up in his bed with my makeup a mess and the taste of vomit in my mouth. Yeah, not so great. My fight or flight instinct rears its ugly head at the memory, and Rory grabs onto my arm, reading me way too easily.

"Come on, scaredy cat. I'm sure Pax doesn't bite," she says. I open my mouth to argue, but she cuts me off. "Nope. I don't wanna know." Once we reach Paxton's porch, Rory lifts her free hand to knock when the front door opens, revealing Dodger.

"Hey, Squeaks." His attention shifts to me. "Tatum."

"Hi?" I reply.

*What's he doing here?*

"Don't worry. I'm not here to ruin your fun," he jokes. "I actually only stopped by to say hi to some friends, but I'm about to head out. Perfect timing, though. They're about to start playing."

"They?"

"You'll see," he replies. "And before you yell at Pax for inviting anyone else, it wasn't his idea. It's just the way things worked out. Now, if you'll excuse me, I have some nephews to strangle." He gives us a mock salute, slips out the door, and jogs down the short set of stairs, reaching a parked motorcycle.

Funny. I thought it was Pax's.

"Well, on that note." Rory tilts her head toward the still open doorway to Paxton's home. "Should we…walk in?"

With a shrug, I tug Rory with me as we make our way inside. The place is cleaner than the last time I was here.

Like, a lot cleaner. And since I'm his cleaning lady, I can't decide if I'm offended or impressed that he found someone on such short notice. Am I finally out of a job? That kind of sucks. But also, the state of this house after being jam-packed with a shit-ton of drunk people was disgusting, and I'm kind of glad I didn't have to deal with it.

As we make our way toward the back of the home and down the stairs leading to the walkout basement, I notice a soft melody in the distance.

"What is that?" I whisper.

Rory's shoulders lift, and we follow the sound past the theater room to the large glass doors.

They're left open, creating a large, open space from the hardwood floors to the open beach. The song is louder now. It's an acoustic version of one of my favorite songs.

"Come on," Rory urges, her curiosity matching my own.

My hair blows in the gentle sea breeze as we step over the threshold onto the back patio. The jacuzzi is open but empty, its steam swirling in the air. We move around it, the familiar melody spurring us on.

*Seriously, where is everyone?*

Lanterns hang on black poles, creating a path for us to follow. Reaching down, Rory takes her shoes off, so I do the same, letting the warm sand slip between my toes. When the bonfire comes into view, my forehead wrinkles as I stand on my tiptoes, trying to catch a better glimpse of the shadows surrounding it.

The fire casts a glow on Paxton sitting to one side with a guitar in his lap. Next to him is a man with a small drum, and on his opposite side is—

"No freaking way," Rory mutters under her breath. Turning to me, she adds, "Did you know about this?"

"How would I have known?"

"I don't know? But this?" She smiles. "Damn, Tate. Pax

wants you bad." She tugs my arm again, and I force my legs to move as Cooper, the lead singer of Doomsday, begins the chorus of one of their biggest hits.

It's…insane. And over the top. And probably the sweetest thing anyone has ever done for me. I'm not sure whether to sneak around the side to listen from afar so I don't interrupt the coolest thing I've experienced or traipse right up to the small group of spectators and pop a squat right next to the freaking singer of Doomsday.

*Like, holy shit, Batman.*

"So, are we going or what?" Rory whispers.

I can feel her looking at me, but I can't stop staring at Paxton playing the guitar. The easy way he holds it. The way his mouth moves as he joins in on the chorus. It's sexy as hell. He's sexy as hell. As if he can feel my gaze, his attention cuts across the beach, and his mouth lifts into the most seductive smile I've ever seen. I'm too stunned to speak. Or move. Or do anything, really. I haven't seen Pax in his element since my twenty-first birthday. And maybe it's because I didn't know him back then, or maybe he's only gotten more attractive with age, or maybe he's simply a better guitarist than he was before, but I don't even need to know the reason behind it. All I know is I've never been nervous around a guy. Never felt giddy and swoony and speechless, and a little nauseated, if I'm being totally honest. But right now? Right now, I do. I really, really do.

Still holding my gaze, he leans a little closer to the drummer, says something to him, then sets his guitar down before pushing to his feet. Without missing a beat, the rest of the band keeps playing. Cooper's voice is like a freaking angel as he continues singing the song while Pax jogs toward us.

"You made it," he says.

"We did," Rory returns. "And also, bravo, Paxton." She

motions toward the bonfire, then gives him a slow clap. "Seriously."

He smiles at my best friend. "They were supposed to be at the party the other night but got held up. Figured a little show on the beach by the fire was a solid Plan B." Squeezing the back of his neck, he turns his attention on me. "What do you think?"

My heart thrums faster and faster as I take him in, unsure what to say.

And it's funny. Seeing how careful he's acting. It's as if he knows exactly how easily I could be scared away if he doesn't play his cards right.

Joke's on him.

After a surprise like this, he's holding a royal flush. The question is, does he know it?

"Well, I think you hit it out of the park," Rory announces. "Shall we?"

With a slow nod, Paxton steps aside and places his hand on the small of my back. I swear it scalds me to the bone, but I don't pull away. I don't want to pull away. The realization is staggering, and I fold my arms as he leads us to the bonfire.

Blankets lie scattered along the sand, along with a few beach chairs, a cooler full of drinks, and all the supplies needed for s'mores.

Other than the members of Doomsday, a few groupies and superfans are peppered throughout the circle, each of them singing along with Cooper. Noticing there's only one spot beside Paxton, I move toward a blanket on the opposite side, reaching for Rory and tugging her with me so she doesn't have to sit alone.

Pax doesn't question it as he moves back to his empty spot, picking up his guitar and strumming right where he left off.

By the time the next song starts, I'm singing the lyrics,

soaking up every single note. Seriously. Talk about a dream concert. The man I grew up idolizing is so close I can see his perfectly straight smile while he gives me the performance of a lifetime. Song after song, the band plays until my vocal chords ache. It's perfect. Absolutely perfect. When the final notes ring out across the sand, cheering ensues, and Cooper turns to Pax.

"You wanna take the next one?"

Paxton's eyes meet mine across the fire before he raises a shoulder. "I guess I should probably represent IndieCent Vows, huh?" He hesitates. "Uh, let's see…"

His sandy-blonde hair falls forward on his guitar as he begins plucking at the strings, and I'm not going to lie. It's hot as hell. The way his straight white teeth dig into his bottom lip. The slight furrow of his brow. The way he leans forward slightly, his spine curving, as he plays the intro to a familiar song.

Oh, and did I mention the stubble along his jaw, or the natural curl of his lashes, or the veins along his forearms? Yeah, I'm a goner. A big, fat, wet-pantied goner. And then he opens his mouth, surprising the shit out of me.

Cooper might have the voice of a fucking angel, but Pax? Pax has the voice of a natural. It's a little grittier. Less trained. More raw. It's less raspy than Dodger's, but just as unique. Tilting my head, I watch him, refusing to blink in case I miss a single second. A single note. A single word.

It takes me a second to place it, thanks to the slower, lulling rhythm. I think it's in a different key, too, making the lighter theme of the song feel…sexier, almost. Forbidden, even.

*Calls to Me* by IndieCent Vows. It's about a girl he can't get out of his head. A girl who drives him insane. A girl who isn't his, but one he can't let go of, even though he's tried.

Before tonight, it was one of my favorites. This version,

though? It's something else, entirely, and I'm so enthralled, I can hardly breathe.

Feeling Rory's stare, I glance at her, confirming what I already knew. Yup. She's watching me. When she knows she's been caught, she squeezes my hand. It's a silent promise. That she's here. That she knows how conflicted I am, despite both of us knowing I have no reason to be. And it's true. I have no reason to feel conflicted. No obligations to anyone.

So why do I feel...guilty? For falling for the man in front of me. Being interested in him. And not just his body, which is pretty much carved from stone. But his soul, too.

Yeah. I always knew Pax was dangerous. Always knew he could make me feel this way if I gave him the chance. I just didn't know he'd manage to slip past my defenses even if I didn't open the door.

By the time he finishes the song, I'm officially soaked and need a minute to regroup, because this? This isn't safe. But it is tempting. More so than I'm willing to admit, and if I have any hope of surviving the rest of the night, I need to get my head on straight. And soon.

"I'm going to the restroom. I'll be back in a second," I whisper to Rory.

She gives me a thumbs up, then leans back on her hands as Doomsday takes over for another song.

## 36
## TATUM

After going to the bathroom, I wash my hands, then head back outside, finding Paxton leaning against the edge of the open doors leading outside. My breath catches in my lungs as the moonlight shines around him, making him look even more like a Greek god than he normally does.

Forcing my feet to move, I walk toward him. "Hey, is the concert over?"

He nods. "Yeah. We're just chillin'."

"Awesome."

"So, what'd you think?" he prods, reminding me of a shy little boy in need of approval. It only makes me fall for him more.

"What did I think?" I fold my arms to try to focus on the concert part and not his thoughtfulness behind it. "I can't believe you convinced Doomsday to come play."

"I owed you an introduction, remember?"

I nod. "Well, yeah. But still, that was insane."

"Just wait 'til you meet him." Pax offers me his hand, and I stare at it, surprised by the memory it sparks and how hard it hits out of nowhere.

*"I hate ice skating," I mutter.*

*"Aw, but you're so good at it," my mom gushes.*

*"No, I'm not. Ophelia's—"*

*"Don't compare yourself." She reaches down and adjusts the fluffy pink hat on my head. "You are you, and Lia is Lia, remember?"*

*I look down at Lia's hand-me-down skates covering my feet. "Yeah, yeah. I know."*

*"Good girl. Do you want my help or would you rather—"*

*"I got it."*

*With a nod, she stands. "Stay close to the wall, okay?"*

*My head dips as I take a deep breath, peeking up to find my mom skating toward my dad and their friends at the center of the rink. Sometimes, after the hockey games, the arena opens to the public for ice skating. Everyone loves it. Everyone but me.*

*Clinging to the side barrier, my fingers dig into the tiny lip beneath the glass as I shuffle along the ice. I wish I could just sit on the bench with my book, but noooo. Stupid ice skating. Someone zooms past, and my body stifffens, preparing to be tackled or knocked on my bum, when another person stops beside me.*

*"Hey, Tater Tot."*

*I glance up at Archer, giving him a weak smile. "Hey."*

*"You doin' okay?"*

*My attention shifts to the skating maniac who almost made me fall. It's Maverick. Of course, it's Maverick. He's chasing after Ophelia, and she's screaming at him to go away. My parents aren't even bothering to intervene. Why would they? Mav driving Ophelia nuts is more common than the two playing nicely most days.*

*Would've been nice if he didn't almost knock me over in the process, though.*

*"Sorry about Mav," Archer adds, following my line of sight.*

*"It's fine."*

*"He didn't bump you, did he?"*

*I shake my head.*

*"Good." Offering his hand, he adds, "Want me to help?"*

*I stare at his outstretched hand, my tongue growing to three times its normal size. Do I want his help? I mean, if anyone else had asked, I'd for sure say no, but Arch? Arch is different. He's always been so...nice, and when I'm with him, my palms sweat, and my head gets dizzy, and... I gulp, shaking my head again.*

*"You sure?" he asks.*

*My vocal cords refuse to work, so I nod instead, watching as he raises his offered hand and squeezes the back of his neck. "All right. Well, if you need me to beat up my brother for you, let me know, okay?"*

*Like a stupid bobble head, I nod again, and off he goes, catching up with his brother who's pulling Lia's pigtails.*

The memory vanishes, dissipating as quickly as it hit, and I suck my lips into my mouth. Would things have been different if I'd taken Archer's hand that day? We were kids, and I know it didn't mean anything on his end, but still. What if...what if—

"Hey, you good?" Pax murmurs.

Forcing myself to breathe, I peek up at him. The softness in his gaze. The reassurance shining in his eyes. The easy stance. Like we have all the time in the world to stand on the beach while I debate whether or not I want to hold his hand. And the truth is, I've never held a guy's hand before. I've kissed countless guys, slept with plenty, but hand-holding? He's my first, and part of me wonders if he knows it, too.

My lungs deflate on a slow, controlled breath before I give in, praying he can't feel the slight tremble in my fingers. If he can, he doesn't say anything. He simply gives me a soft squeeze. His hand is warm and rough and way more comforting than any touch has a right to be. I like it, though. I like it a lot.

Lacing our fingers, he murmurs, "Come on," and guides me through the small throng of people. Each of them takes a turn telling him how freaking amazing his performance was, and Pax smiles at each of them, running his free hand over his shaggy head, squeezing the back of his neck, accepting their compliments with humility and grace and a confidence I can't help but find hella attractive.

When we finally reach the bonfire, Pax takes a deep breath and looks down at me, his forehead wrinkling with concern.

"Is there a problem?" I ask.

"I'm second-guessing this decision."

"What decision?"

"The whole…introduction part."

I laugh, surprised by his sudden change of tune. "Hey, no take backs. I thought you wanted a do-over."

"I do want a do-over," he says with a huff. "Just not at the expense of…"

"Of?" I prod.

He stays quiet, eyeing me warily.

"Oh, come on," I push. "You were doing so well. Besides, you've already come this far. Might as well hold up your end of the deal and introduce me, right?"

"Yeah, there's only one problem."

"What's the problem?" I ask.

"Coop's a flirt."

I smirk. "So?"

"So, he's a flirt, and I'm willingly introducing him to a girl who isn't mine. Does that sound like a bright idea to you?"

I don't bother answering because he said *mine.* The four letter word makes my breath catch, and I replay his statement one more time. *Mine.* Before, I would've run the opposite direction from a trigger like that. Now, though? Now, it only feeds my interest. Don't get me wrong. It's not like I'm ready to give myself to the guy or whatever, but...is that what he really wants? Me? In all my messy glory and with all my fucked-up baggage?

I've had guys want me before, but none of them knew... everything. None of them knew anything. The difference is staggering, and I'm not sure how I feel about it.

When I realize he's staring at me, a question shining in his pretty espresso eyes, I push aside my inner spiral and try to focus on our conversation. What did he say again?

*I'm willingly introducing him to a girl who isn't mine.*

Right.

"So?" I repeat.

"So, I know I'm known for being the dumbass of my band, but this feels like a low point, even for me."

I laugh. "Whatever, Pax. Now, you're being ridiculous."

I go to smack his chest, but he grabs my wrist and tugs me into him, pinning me with his penetrating gaze. "Tell me this isn't a stupid idea."

"Is this you not being jealous again?"

"Nah, I'm very jealous, and I have no problem admitting it."

Pulling back slightly, I take in the heat in his eyes and the tightness in his jaw. It's a major turn-on. Seeing him like this. Honestly, I'm jealous. How sure he is of himself, including when it comes to showing his insecurities. Without shame or fear of judgment. He said it himself. He's very jealous and has no problem admitting it. Like, *damn.*

"Good," I decide. "Girls like it when guys are jealous."

His brows lift. "Oh, they do, do they?"

"Not toxically," I clarify. "But it's nice knowing you're wanted."

"Agreed. So, do you want me?"

Rolling my eyes, I tug my hand from his grasp, ignoring the stupid pitter-patter in my chest. "About this introduction…"

He grumbles something under his breath, but I don't hear anything specific as he lifts his chin at someone over my head. "Hey, man. What's up?"

"Not much." I turn around to find the infamous Cooper Johnson staring down at me. "This your girl?"

*Don't swoon. Don't swoon. Don't swoon.*

"Not yet," Pax jokes. "But I'm working on it."

I smirk up at him, then offer my hand to the infamous Doomsday lead singer. "Hi, I'm Tatum."

"Nice to meet you, Tatum. How'd you like the performance?"

How'd I like the performance? Is this man serious?

"You guys killed it," I gush, trying to keep my enthusiasm in check, but seriously. It's Cooper freaking Johnson. Clearing my throat, I add, "If I'd known I'd be meeting you, I would've brought a poster for you to sign or something."

With a grin, he glances at Pax behind me, then tucks his hands into his pockets, offering, "I mean, I have a sharpie. I could always sign where I usually do—"

"Not a chance," Pax interrupts. His fingers brush against my hip as if he wants to pull me into him, but he stops at the last second, dropping his hand back to his side.

I bite the inside of my cheek to keep from laughing. Yeah, I've heard the rumors. I know exactly where the infamous Coop likes to sign. "Aw, come on, Pax. It's just my boobs. I'm sure Coop wouldn't mind."

Pax glares down at me. "The only name that'll be on your skin is mine."

"Uh-huh, keep dreaming, buddy." I lift my forearm to Cooper. "Here would be great."

Retrieving a Sharpie from his back pocket, he bites the

lid with his teeth and pulls the cap off, scribbling his name across the inside of my arm. Arms crossed, Pax watches, not even bothering to hide his frustration, and I can't decide what I like more. The look on his face, or the fact that my favorite artist of all time is writing his name on me.

Actually, I take it back. Sure, both things are pretty freaking epic, but only one of them is making my pulse vibrate and my knees weak, and that's terrifying on a whole new level.

Yeah, Pax.

I'm pretty sure you don't have anything to worry about, which gives *me* something to worry about.

Nibbling my bottom lip, I stare at the thick, bold signature etched onto my arm as Cooper adds "XOXO" above it.

"Coop, you promised me a tour of your tattoos!" a girl calls from my left.

Capping the marker, Cooper gives me one more smirk. "Guess that's my cue. Nice to meet you, Tatum."

"You, too." I smile back at him, surprised by the lack of butterflies assaulting my stomach. I mean, it's Cooper freaking Johnson, and I'm not falling all over myself? Who have I become? Oh, I know. A girl who's infatuated with a different rockstar. The one still glued to my side. "And thanks again for the concert!"

"Anytime, Tatum."

As he leaves, Pax turns to me when someone calls his name. It's another girl. She's blonde. Her boobs are falling out of her tight red top. It matches her lipstick. The top, not her boobs. That would be weird.

Then again, standing here feels weird, too, when a girl is clearly fawning over the guy beside me. And why wouldn't she? He's Paxton Six. Not Pax Turner. Not the guy who held my hair back while I puked my guts out or pinned me to the cupboards in the pantry before shattering my world. He's Paxton Six.

So, why do I feel so off-balance?

"I'm, uh, I'm gonna track Rory down," I announce.

Ignoring the girl, Pax drags his hand down my arm, tracing Cooper's signature. "You sure?"

"Yeah, totally. I don't want her to feel like the third wheel or anything. You should go," I urge. "Bask in your rockstar awesomeness."

"I thought you said I already have a big enough head?"

"You do," I agree, "But you're only a rockstar once, right? Go. Have fun. I'll be…around."

I know he wants to push back. I can see it in his gaze. Feel it in his fingertips against my bare forearm. Instead, he gives in, surprising me, though I can't say I'm not disappointed.

"Come find me before you leave," he tells me.

"Who says I'm going anywhere?"

His gaze flicks from my bare arm to my eyes. "Please, Birthday Girl?"

*Damn you and your pleases, Paxton Six.*

Tucking my hair behind my ear, I murmur, "I'll, uh, I'll come find you."

"Promise?"

I gulp, forcing my head to bob. "Yes."

"Thank you."

# TATUM

"Well, if that isn't the hottest thing on the planet, I don't know what is," Rory muses. The stairs probably aren't the most comfortable place to sit, but they give the best view of the front door, and watching the small audience—most of which are groupies—slowly stumble their way out has been pretty solid entertainment for the past two hours. It's late, and I'm exhausted. But I promised Pax I wouldn't leave without saying goodbye, and for some reason I genuinely can't fathom, the idea of going back on said promise feels…wrong. But so does tracking the guy down because that feels desperate, and I am many things, but I refuse to let desperate be one of them. So, where does it leave me? With my ass on the stairs with my best friend beside me.

Resting my chin in my hand and my elbow on my knee, I twist toward Rory. "What was the hottest thing on the planet?"

"Pax singing to you."

"Pax wasn't—"

"He totally was," she argues. "And the song choice?" A quiet whistle slips out of her. "Damn."

Damn is right. The thought alone is enough to leave me hot and bothered, which is a huge problem if I have any hope of keeping my one rule by not sleeping with the guy again. The question is…do I need to? Keep the rule, not sleep with him.

I've had it for so long I'm starting to wonder why, and it's a scary thought.

With my elbows on my knees, I rest my chin in my hands, announcing, "I'm choosing not to overthink it."

"Probably wise, since I'm overthinking it enough for the both of us." She bumps her shoulder against mine.

"We should get going," I decide.

"Sounds good. I'll just…hang out here until you're ready."

"What? You're not going to say goodbye, too?" I ask.

"Already texted him."

"I'm sorry, I didn't know that was an option. And since when do you have his number?"

"Since your twenty-first birthday," she quips.

My jaw drops. "Are you serious?"

"Yup. Dodger gave it to me in case I had any issues getting ahold of you."

What are the freaking odds? Although, it's probably for the best. If I'd known she'd had it all these years, I have a feeling I would've caved and reached out to him during one of my low points.

*And if I had, maybe there wouldn't have been so many of them.*

The voice is quiet as it tickles the back of my brain, catching me off guard. What would it have been like? If I hadn't lied all those years ago? Would we have dated? Would we still be dating? Would we be—

I shut the thought down before it has a chance to take hold.

Unlocking my cell, I announce, "You know, I think you make a good point. I'm going to—"

She smacks my phone out of my hands, and it falls into my lap. "Nope. No deal. Messaging him goodbye is an option for me because I'm just the cherry on top of the sundae. You, my dear friend, are the main course. Go. I'll stick around for ten more minutes. If you're back by then, we can leave together, but in case you decide to let things get freaky—"

"Rory!" I scold.

"No use lying, Tater Tot," she says. "You forget how well I know you, and after a declaration of interest like the one he put out tonight? Well, let's just say I'd be dropping my virgin panties in a heartbeat if someone did something as thoughtful as what Pax did for you this evening. Although, I do have a paper to finish tomorrow morning for my English class, so the ten minutes starts now. Go."

After a gentle push from my best friend, I stride down the stairs. The place is a mess, but I don't bother touching any of it as I make my way to the beach. He can have his *other* cleaning service do it for him, for all I care. Everyone's gone. And it's strange. Feeling the shift in the air. The charged energy from when the little concert first started to the subtle high after it finished, to this. A soft, comfortable ambiance I want to wrap myself up in. The bonfire is settling, but it still crackles as Pax cradles his guitar to his chest with a beer by his side.

"Well, would you look at that," he says. The firelight dances in his gaze as he watches me approach. "I owe Coop a hundred bucks."

Planting my ass on the sand next to him, I stretch my legs out. "A hundred bucks? Why?"

"He bet you'd stay."

"And you bet I'd leave?" I challenge, though I can't decide

if I'm offended or impressed with how well he knows me. "I promised, didn't I?"

"Pretty little liar," he murmurs. "Remember?"

I do. He called me that the first night we met. When we were playing an unofficial game of Twenty Questions. I lied about my favorite food. My favorite color. Everything.

"Well," I draw a tiny heart in the sand, "it seems I'm capable of turning over a new leaf after all. For tonight, anyway," I add dryly.

He smiles against the rim of his beer. "I guess I'll take what I can get." Setting it back in the sand, he continues strumming whatever melody's inside his head. "Thanks for coming."

"Thanks for having me. This was...this was incredible, Pax."

With a slow nod, he sighs. "Ready to give me a chance yet, Birthday Girl?"

I wish I knew the answer. Wish I knew if I was even capable of giving him a chance. A real one. A chance he deserves and has earned time and time again. He's a good guy. Thoughtful. Patient as a saint. He's done everything right. Has listened to my every request. So why can't I let go?

*Why won't you let me go, Arch?*

Observing Paxton's profile in the flickering orange light, I take in the fullness of his lips. The strength in his jaw. The tiny pinch of his brows as he strums a particularly hard combination of notes. He's nothing like him. At least, not on the surface. But beneath the cocky rockstar persona, I can't help but notice the way their souls match. Not entirely. But little things. Tiny, seemingly insignificant similarities. Or maybe I'm reaching. Maybe I'm desperate to replace Archer. Maybe I'm desperate to justify my connection with Pax.

Without looking up from his guitar, Paxton notes, "You're staring at me awfully hard, Birthday Girl."

He's right. I am. And even though I've been called out, I can't stop. "I know what you want from me, Pax."

"I mean, I kind of spelled it out for you."

I ignore his thinly-veiled sarcasm, and push, "You know what I mean, Pax."

The strumming quiets, amplifying the tension between us. But he doesn't say a word. Doesn't push me or question me or challenge me or…anything. He simply stares, waiting for me to take the lead. To make a decision. To do…something. And I want to. I want to do something, but if I do, what then? What happens next? What happens when one night turns into two? I've never gotten this far. Not with anyone.

"Pax," I whisper. "I'm not…I'm not the girl you think I am, and the thought of ruining whatever perception you have of me, only to leave you disappointed, it's…it's more than I can take."

"Not gonna disappoint me, Tatum."

"You don't know that."

"I do. It isn't possible to disappoint someone with no expectations. Only a chance. That's all I'm asking for."

"And what if I can't even give you that, Pax? What if the only thing I have is…" I lift a shoulder, then motion to my boobs. "A great rack."

His full lips tilt up in satisfaction. "It *is* a great rack."

I bite back my amusement, grateful for his sense of humor and how contagious it is. "Glad you agree."

"You think I'm dumb enough to argue with you, Tatum Taylor?" He shakes his head and sets the guitar aside. "I'm not asking for anything. Not really. Only a chance."

A chance. He makes it sound so simple. He has no idea.

The moonlight shines above us while the crackle of the fire and familiar rhythm of the ocean drowns out the charged silence, bringing with it the promise of peace. And it isn't fair because I haven't felt peace in…in who knows how long? I shift forward on the blanket, unsure what to do or where to go or what to say. He's close. So close, yet so far. And suddenly, I hate how small the blanket feels. How I wish it would shrink even more, so I could justify shifting closer to him to see if he smells like cinnamon again.

"Give me a chance, Tatum," he whispers.

"And if I'm not enough?"

His movements are slow, calculated, as he closes the distance between us, inch by torturous inch, before letting his gaze drop to my mouth, and I swear I can hear my own heartbeat in my ears. "Then give me this." He brushes his lips against mine, stealing a kiss, making my toes curl into the sand at the edge of the blanket as his mouth moves over mine.

*Give me this.*

So, I do.

And instead of fighting it, fighting him, I give in, letting go for the first time in…ever. And it feels strange. And scary. And warm. And almost…right. Because I can give him this. I can give him my body. I can give him my time. I can give him anything he wants. Anything but my heart. Because the stupid organ in my chest? It doesn't belong to me. Hasn't belonged to me since I was a little girl, and even though I'd do anything to get it back so I could give it to someone else, I don't think I can. The realization stings, but I push it away, praying my body and my time and everything else I have to offer is enough.

*Please be enough.*

My fingers find the edge of his shirt, and I tug him closer, pressing my front to his. He drags his tongue along the seam of my mouth, and I open for him, craving him desperately. When his tongue dips into my mouth, I suck softly. He groans, shifting closer.

*Yes. Give me this.*

I lean back, and he follows, climbing onto my body until every inch of him pushes me into the sand. It's going to be a bitch to get out of my hair, but I don't care. I only want to feel him. Weaving my fingers along the hair at the nape of his neck, I spread my legs, cradling his waist and the hard line of his erection.

He smiles against my mouth. "I think you like me."

"I like your house."

His smile grows, and he steals another kiss, grinding into me.

"And your musical ability," I add.

Trailing his mouth along the underside of my jaw, he murmurs, "Anything else?"

"Your face isn't half bad, either."

He nips at my throat. "And?"

"Your cock is top tier, too."

Sucking my skin into his mouth, he drags his tongue along the small patch of flesh. Teasing. Tasting. Warning.

"And my shining personality?" he prods.

I lift a shoulder. "Meh."

With a low laugh, he cages me in on both sides, staring down at me as the moon and softening firelight outline him. "Meh?"

"Meh," I repeat.

When he starts to pull away, I cling to his shoulders. "Okay! Okay! Your personality is a solid B+."

He rolls to one side, smacking my ass, surprising the shit out of me.

With a yelp, I squeal, "Hey!"

Another bruising kiss silences me as Paxton slides his hands beneath the hem of my shirt, massaging my breast as his tongue teases the seam of my lips. I've missed this. This feeling. Being cared for. Appreciated. Worshipped. And not by just anyone. Let's be real. No one's ever cared about me. Not like this. Fucked, sure. But appreciated? Worshipped? It's different. He's different. Even the first night we met, he was different, and even though a not-so-small part of me could feel it, I was too petrified to label him as anything but a rockstar, and it might be one of the biggest mistakes of my life.

Cupping my breast, Paxton kneads me softly until my nipple pebbles against his palm. The feeling shoots straight to my core, and he rips his mouth from mine, trailing kisses along my throat. His head disappears beneath my shirt, and he sucks my nipple into his mouth.

*Ooookay, yes. Yes, that will do just fine.*

I writhe beneath him, the heat of his tongue too much, yet not enough. Not even close. My back arches, and I hold him to me, lifting my hips in search of friction.

"We're wearing too many clothes," I announce.

"Is that an invitation?"

"Lose the pants or watch me play with myself," I dare him. My hands start their descent before he even has a chance to make a decision. The sound of my zipper mingles with the crackle of the fire as he drags my jeans down my legs, exposing every inch of me. His eyes glow with interest, and his lips part with need. It's a heady combination. I force myself to stay still when I feel like I'm burning up from the outside in. The same familiar zip follows, and he pulls his erection out, pumping it slowly in his fist as I lay beneath him. And boy, is it a sight to behold. I zero in on the veins along the back of his hand, and the sight turns me on even more. Shit, I could watch him all day. Tugging and rubbing and turning me into a wet mess. Unable to stand it, I let my knees fall apart and spread my folds, slowly circling my clit while biting my bottom lip. I could come like this. Just like this. With his eyes on me and his cock in his hand.

"Fuck, you have no idea how sexy you look like this," he growls, staring as I play with myself.

My lips curve up. "I think I have an idea."

His attention flicks from my fingers to my eyes. "So cocky."

"I believe you're the one who's cocky," I point out. "Pun intended." He chuckles. "And I'm the one who's empty," I continue. "So, what are you going to do about it?"

A low rumble claws its way up his throat as he reaches for his jeans, retrieving a condom from the back pocket. Placing the thin foil between his teeth, he rips the package open and slides it on before grabbing my thigh and dragging me closer to him as he stays on his knees. Tugging me into him, my lower back and ass completely off the ground, he lines himself up with my entrance, the head teasing my opening as he holds me in place.

This is it. The last moment I could say no. The last chance I have to shove him back in the box with all my other one-night-stands. But I don't want to. I want more than one night. I want a chance. A chance to prove I can do this. I can connect with someone without feeling guilty or like I'm cheating on a ghost. I can enjoy this. This moment, this connection, this feeling.

With his fingers digging into my thighs, Pax waits, a question in his espresso gaze. I lower my head in the smallest of nods. Satisfied, his hold tightens, and his attention drops to where our bodies connect as he thrusts into me.

Watching the need in his eyes. The obsession. It's the hottest thing I've ever seen.

He pulls out, leaving me with just the head before pushing in again, his movements torturously slow and deliberate.

"Touch your clit," he orders.

I slip my hand between my thighs, feeling him enter me as I circle my clit. It feels incredible. I feel incredible. He feels incredible. Every inch of him. My body stretches around him, accommodating his size as he picks up his pace, hitting the little bundle of nerves inside of me, making me feel like I'm seconds from exploding. Sweat clings to my skin, leaving me hot and tingly.

"Fuck, Birthday Girl," he growls. "You have no idea how pretty you look taking me like this. Spread out beneath me. Your tits bouncing. Your hair in the sand. The fire dancing off your skin."

His words are like gasoline, making me burn from the inside out. "Don't stop," I beg. "Don't you dare fucking stop."

He bends forward, and I hook my ankles around his waist, holding on for dear life as he cages me in and pushes into me over and over again. I can see it. Feel it. Taste it. My orgasm. I'm so fucking close, I can't breathe. My lungs cease to work, my fingers dig into his lower back, and my jaw falls as it rips through me, tearing me apart and leaving me float-ing. The familiar twitch of his erection and freeze of his muscles follow, a low curse slipping past his lips as he comes inside me. It's stupid. Reckless. So fucking reckless. Giving my body to him again. But I don't care. Not in this moment. Because it's like he said, if this is all I can give him, he can have it. He can have all that's left. Every piece of me.

"Fuck," he grunts.

I smile. "Yes, Captain Obvious. We did just fuck."

"Well." He lifts his head, giving me a glimpse of his boyish grin. "It's been great. Really great. But, uh, I guess I'll see you around, or…?" His face tilts to one side, his eyes dancing with mirth.

I quirk my brow. "Seriously?"

"I mean, it's what we do after actual sex, isn't it?"

"It's what *I* do," I clarify.

Moving closer, he runs his nose along the tip of mine. "And what do *I* get to do?"

"Daydream about all the things you should've said to convince me to stay."

"Like hire your favorite band?" he quips.

I fight my grin. "Something like that."

He starts to climb off, but I tug him into me, letting his weight settle into my bones as he gives in immediately. I love it. The feel of him pressed against me. His soft cock still nestled inside. The mint on his breath. The scent of sex and campfire and ocean and…Pax. I want to bottle it up and keep it forever.

"You gonna run this time, Birthday Girl?" he murmurs.

It's a good question. One I kind of hate. Because with Pax? It isn't easy. To run. To leave. To write off our interactions as meaningless when it doesn't *feel* meaningless. But the idea of promising him more? Promising something real and tangible and lasting? I don't…I don't know if I'm capable of something like that, even if he makes me want to be.

"Not gonna answer me, huh?" he prods.

His earlier words echo through my mind as he stares down at me, brushing the hair from my forehead.

*You gonna run this time, Birthday Girl?*

"It's what I do," I admit.

"Then I guess I'll have to invest in some running shoes, 'cause I'm sure as shit not gonna let you get away again." He drops a kiss to my forehead, then rolls onto his back, tucking me into his side. I feel him slip out of me. And it leaves me weirdly…empty. I don't know how I feel about it. But what I do know is that I like this.

And that much is terrifying, but I'm too weak to walk away, let alone run.

Not this time.

After my little rendezvous with Pax on the beach, we put the dwindling fire out, and he led me to his bathroom where he proceeded to wash my hair. Wash. My freaking. Hair. I asked if I should be worried that he had any intention of dying it as payback for what I did to him, but he assured me his motives were innocent…until he fell to his knees and worshipped me with his mouth. But I digress. Once my hair was sand free and we'd both gotten off —one for him and two for me because, and I quote, he's, "generous like that,"—we spent the night in Paxton's bed.

Yup. I slept over. Voluntarily this time, and not because I was drunk off my ass, thank you very much. It doesn't mean I'm in love with him or anything. It doesn't even mean we're official or whatever. It means we had a sleepover. Simple as that. Or at least, it's what I keep telling myself to keep from losing my shit. We slept together. And we didn't just have sex twice, which is most definitely one of my biggest rules, but we actually *slept*. Midnight snuggles included. I blame it on the post orgasmic haze, but if I'm being honest, I think there's more to it.

And *that* realization? It's a hard pill to swallow. But I'm trying.

Stretching in Paxton's bed, I realize the sheets on his side are cold to the touch. Where did he go? And how long has he been gone? I turn my head toward the open door and breathe in deep. *Coffee.* The smell brings a smile to my lips as I roll onto my side, reaching for my phone on the nightstand.

A text from Rory shines back at me.

RORY

Hey! Just wanted to let you know I made it home safe. Have fun! Text me when you wake up.

She must've sent it last night, but I was too distracted to notice. With a yawn, I type my response.

ME

Hey, just woke up. Glad you made it home safe.

The three little dots appear almost instantly before her reply delivers to my phone.

RORY

No worries. Figured you were a little preoccupied last night. Did you have fun?

ME

If you count three orgasms and a few sore muscles, then yes.

RORY

Three?! Damn. I'll be sure to give Pax a high-five the next time I see him.

ME

I'm sure he'd love that. Are you still at home?

RORY

Nope. I'm at the library with Hades finishing
my English paper.

ME

I still have no idea how that terror passed
service dog school.

RORY

Whatever. He's nothing but a big ol'
sweetheart.

ME

Who hates anyone and everyone around him.

RORY

Anyone and everyone but me, which is all
that matters. ;) Are you spending the day
with Pax?

ME

Not sure yet, but I'll figure something out.
Good luck on your paper. I'll see you at
home.

RORY

Mmmkay. See you!

The stairs creak as I read her message. Looking up, I find
Pax balancing the same tray as the last time I was here. And
it's strange. Replaying both events. Their similarities. Their
differences. I definitely don't miss the headache this time
around, though.

"Morning, sleepyhead," Pax greets me.

"Morning."

He sets the tray on the nightstand, then grabs one of the
coffee cups, offering it to me. The sheets pool at my waist as I
sit up and take the dark blue mug from him, breathing in the
mouth-watering, nutty aroma before taking a small sip.
"Mmm."

With a soft smile, he adds, "Glad you like it." Holding the second cup to his chest, he sits beside my hip on the edge of the mattress. "How'd you sleep?" he asks.

"Good. You?"

He smiles. "Really good."

"Thanks for the coffee." I glance at the tray. "And breakfast."

"Anytime."

Sucking my top lip between my teeth, I go in for another sip of coffee, unsure what to say or do. I've never been in this position. I've always been up and out of there before the other person has had a chance to wake up, and that's *if* I passed out in the bed after sex in the first place. This? Coffee and talking and post orgasmic glow-esque vibes? It's...I don't even know. Do I ask what he's doing today? If he can give me a ride home? Do I assume he wants me to stay and hang out? I don't know!

"Hey." He taps my outer thigh with the back of his hand. "You good?"

"Yup."

He smirks. "You sure? 'Cause you look like you're two seconds away from having a panic attack."

Forcing my muscles to relax, I drag my thumbs across the side of the faded logo on the coffee mug. "I'm good. Only... trying to figure out what happens next now that I've slept over and...everything."

"Me, too," he admits.

My eyes widen. "You're saying you're not a seasoned pro at this?"

His low chuckle makes my stomach flip as he shakes his head. "Don't get me wrong. I know I'm good at faking like I know what I'm doing. But this is my first time, too. Liking someone." He drops his voice low and leans closer like it's our little secret. The fact that he likes me. That this is his first time wading through the waters of a fresh relationship. And even though I'm flattered, I'm surprised, too.

My brows tug down in the center as I peek up at him over the rim of my cup. "You're telling me you've never had a girlfriend or anything?"

"Are you insinuating you're my girlfriend?" he volleys.

Panic swells inside of me, and I rush out, "No, no, no, that's not—"

"Kidding," he laughs. "And, no. No girlfriends. A few casual, consistent hookups, but it was all physical."

Physical.

I bite the inside of my cheek to keep from asking what this is then. If it's different. If it's more than physical for him, too, even though I have a feeling I already know the answer.

"Do you..." I steal a piece of toast with jam from the nightstand and take a bite, chewing slowly as he watches me.

"Do I...?"

Swallowing, I force out, "Do you have any plans today?"

He nods. "Sparring session with one of Judge's nephews."

"Oh." I take another bite, trying to imagine it. Pax going toe-to-toe with another human being under the guise of a good workout and a solid way to let off steam. Weird. But I guess I can't I give him crap about his coping mechanisms when mine have always been less than stellar. "That sounds... *fun?*" I question.

With a laugh, he returns, "It is fun, actually. Do you wanna come?"

I stay quiet, unsure what to say.

Sensing my hesitancy, he explains, "Last time I mentioned it, you said the idea of me fighting is kind of hot. I'm happy to give you a front-row seat if you're interested."

I take another sip of coffee, considering the invitation. Part of me wants to say yes, but I also don't want to look needy or clingy or...I don't even know.

With a frown, he starts, "You don't have to—"

"I want to," I rush out. "I just have a few houses scheduled to clean today, and…"

Understanding sparks in Paxton's eyes. "No pressure, Birthday Girl."

That's the problem, though. Isn't it? Because he's right. There is no pressure. Not from him. He's been nothing but patient and kind and thoughtful, but I'm so caught up in my own head that I can barely hold a conversation right now, let alone an entire day with the man. What if I screw it up? Are we taking things too fast or too slow or…dammit, I don't know?

"Seriously, Tate," he murmurs, as if he can see the wheels in my head turning. "We're good."

"Rain check?" I ask.

"Yeah, anytime."

The soft smile at the edge of his mouth eases my nerves and somehow quiets the carousel of thoughts plaguing me, proving exactly how awesome Paxton Turner really is.

Shifting closer, I brush my lips against his cheek. "And I do mean it. I want a rain check."

"Yeah?"

"Mm-hmm," I hum. "A hot and sweaty Pax beating the shit out of one of Judge's nephews sounds like a pretty awesome way to spend my day. I just…I guess I feel like some time to breathe and let my brain catch up on everything that's happening is probably…," I lick my lips, "a smart thing to do. You know?"

"Yeah. Yeah, I get it. This is a lot."

"Yeah, but it's a good lot," I tell him.

"It is a good lot," he agrees, leaning in and kissing me. My toes curl in his sheets as I tilt my head, savoring the feel of his lips on mine. When he pulls away, he adds, "So you're not running?"

I shake my head, ignoring the tension in my fingers as I cling to the coffee mug. "Not planning on it."

"All right, Birthday Girl. I'm gonna believe you, but don't think I won't pull out the running shoes if I need to. You hear me?"

With a smile, I nod. "I hear you."

39

TATUM

I really wish Rory wrote papers faster. Or at the least, that she would've left Hades to help fill the quiet of the apartment. Instead, I have nothing but my thoughts to keep me company.

It makes me feel like I'm insane.

But this is what I wanted, wasn't it? For Pax to drop me off so I could have some time to wrap my head around last night and all it could mean if I let it?

Before I can talk myself out of it, I grab a pen and the worn black notebook from my laptop case, needing the release it brings more than my next breath. The tip of my pen hovers above the page as I search for something to say. Something to flesh out my feelings instead of letting them fester inside of me like I usually do until it becomes too much.

And after last night? It's a bit too much.

*Hey, Arch.*

*It's been awhile. I'd ask how you are, but you're dead, so...*

I sniff and force myself to continue.

*Things are weird here. I moved in with Rory. She's doing really well. Better than me, actually. Not that it's a surprise. Mav and Lia are getting married. Strangely, I think you'd be happy for them.*

I suck my lips between my teeth.

*I want to be happy for them, too.*

"Keep going," I whisper to the empty room, no matter how petrifying it feels. "Keep. Going."

*There's this guy... It feels weird telling you about him. But it also feels weird admitting that it feels weird telling you about him, so...I'm not sure what it says about me, but it is what it is.*

Just write it, Tatum!

*Last night we hooked up.*

I stare at the five simple words, watching as they blur together before forcing myself to continue.

*We've hooked up before last night, but last night felt different. More intimate, I guess. Less like fucking and more like, real, or whatever.*

I hesitate, and blow out a slow breath.

*I like him, Arch. And it's weird liking someone who isn't you, even after all these years. But it doesn't feel wrong, either. That's the strangest part about it. And then I start to wonder if I'm wasting way too much time analyzing my feelings over a potential relationship with someone that is still so new in the big scheme of things.*

I pause again, tapping my pen against the edge of the page until a little bundle of dots appears as my anxiety claws at me. I want to close the journal. I want to close it and hide it and never open it again, but the pull to keep going, to keep writing and to keep feeling is too strong. Too consuming.

*He did something really thoughtful last night. Honestly, it had you written all over it. You were always thoughtful. You were always good at paying attention to the little details no one else would notice.*
*He does it, too.*
*Pays attention. Takes note. Cares.*

*He cares, Arch.*

*He cares about me. And for the life of me, I can't figure out why. But what's scary is how I'm starting to care about him, too. Scratch that, I think I've cared about him for a while now, and I haven't known how to handle it. How to wrap my head around it. How to protect myself and my feelings while putting my heart out there after everything that's happened.*

*It's scary, Arch. It's really scary.*

I lick my lips and stare at the last paragraph.

*Anyway, I guess that's it. I'm scared. And I care about him. And I wish you were here.*

*Miss you.*

*-Tatum*

~

As I rinse the glass under the faucet, the front door opens, revealing an exhausted Rory. It's been a long day. The sun is already setting, and I've been contemplating cutting bangs just to pass the time.

"Hey," I call.

She sets her laptop on the kitchen counter, unclips Hades' leash from his collar, and hangs it on the hook by the front door. "Look at you doing the dishes."

"Hey, I know how to clean," I argue.

Unconvinced, she folds her arms. "You know I'll only do them again once you're finished."

With a soft snort, I rinse the bubbles from my hands and grab the dish towel. "And here I am trying to be helpful."

"Nah, you're trying to stay busy so you don't overthink shit," she argues.

*Man, she knows me too well.*

"Not enough houses to clean?"

"Already finished the ones I had scheduled," I mumble, dipping the sponge into the warm water before scrubbing an especially stubborn stain.

Rounding the edge of the kitchen, she approaches the sink and hipchecks me out of the way so she can get to work cleaning the last few glasses and bowls hidden in the soapy water.

"Soooo…" She drags the word out and starts scrubbing my cereal bowl with a new sponge from beneath the sink. "How was last night?"

I rest my hip on the edge of the counter, my gaze narrowing. "Fiiiine," I mimic, stealing her inflection.

"And?" she prods.

"And what?" I laugh. "I already told you about everything this morning, remember?"

"There's no way a two minute texting conversation held all the details of an entire night."

"I hate to disappoint you, but I'm not sure there's much more to catch you up on," I lie.

"Mm-hmm. Sure. Does this mean Pax found your weak spot?"

"He found my G-spot," I quip.

Flicking some bubbles at me, she groans. "Gross."

"I believe the word you're searching for is jealous."

She smirks and starts cleaning again. "That, too. But seriously, are you guys good?"

"I think so."

"You thinking about running again?" she prods, giving me the side-eye.

I throw my hands in the air and groan, "Why does everyone think I'm going to run again?"

"That's not a no," she points out. "And what do you mean everyone?"

Pinching the bridge of my nose, I grumble, "Let's just say, you're not the only person to ask me that question in the last twenty-four hours."

Her eyes bulge. "He asked if you're planning to run?"

I avoid her gaze, choosing to pick at my cuticles instead. "Yup."

"And what did you say?"

"Well, the first time he asked, I said, I don't know, and the second time, I pretty much said, I wouldn't, so…"

"And what did *he* say?" she pushes.

I drop my hand and look up at her. "He said, he might have to invest in some good running shoes because he isn't letting me get away again."

Her jaw drops. "Okay, swoon."

*My thoughts exactly.*

Anxious for a subject change, I ask, "So, did you finish your paper?"

"Subtle," she notes with a knowing glint in her eyes while rinsing the bowl in the trickling water and setting it on the drying rack. "And yes, by some miracle, I did finish my paper. Can I tell you how excited I am to actually graduate and be done with school?"

"Yeah, I can imagine," I answer. "What do you say we celebrate? Maybe have a girls' night?"

"What about Pax?" she asks.

"What about him?"

"You don't have plans?"

He hasn't texted. I mean, I knew he wouldn't. He told me he was meeting one of Judge's nephews to work out and hit each other, so it's not like he'd have access to his phone or whatever. Then again, it's been a few hours. How long does a sparring session usually last? And does it even matter? I'm the one who said I needed a little space. Me. Not Pax. So why does his lack of reaching out make me feel like I kind of want to vomit? I paste on a fake smile and prop my hand on my hip. "I do have plans."

"Oh, really?"

"Yup. You, me, and Ben and Jerry are in for an epic night."

It's one of the few traditions we've fully embraced from our families. Our addiction to ice cream and movie nights. Honestly, it makes me miss them. My parents. My aunts and uncles. Even Ophelia. We grew up spending every Friday evening going to the grocery store with our mom and dad to pick out our very own pint of ice cream. After, we'd pile onto the couch, pints and spoons in hand, then vote on what movie to watch. The memory is melancholy at best. I need to call her. And soon.

"Have you called and congratulated Lia yet?" Rory prods, as if the mention of Ben & Jerry's took her down the same memory lane it did with me.

I shake my head. "Not yet. How 'bout you and Mav?"

"Yeah, actually. That man is so in love with your sister it's not even funny."

I sober even more. "I know he is."

"It'll be weird, though." She hesitates, her gaze glued to the drying dishes on the counter, though I know she's mentally far away. "Not having Arch as the best man."

She's right. It will be.

Willing the pressure behind my eyes to go away, I dig my fingernails into my palms. "Who'd he ask instead?"

"Reeves," Rory answers. "Not surprising, though he did confirm all the guys will be there, so…"

"I assume that includes Jax?"

"Yup."

She looks like she's about to puke, and it makes me want to hug her.

"Did you ever tell Mav what happened?" I ask.

She shivers. "Nope, but all the girls know, and there's no way Lia didn't pass the info along at some point over the years, so I doubt he's completely in the dark."

True. And I can't even fault him for it. Not this time.

"Good point," I concede.

"Yeah." She sighs. "Mav also asked me to pass a message along to you."

My nose wrinkles. "What kind of message?"

Lifting her hands in air quotes, she drops her voice low, mimicking her older brother. "Tell Tate to call Opie. She misses her."

Puffing out my cheeks, I give in and nod slowly. "I'll see what I can do."

"I know you will. And on that note, I'm going to clean up, then we can go to the store and pick up ice cream."

"Deal."

AN EMPTY PINT OF MINT CHOCOLATE CHIP ICE CREAM SITS next to my phone on the nightstand as Rory and I watch a dating show instead of *Gilmore Girls*. It's super stupid and way over-dramatized, but after a few episodes, we can't help but cheer and boo every couple on the island. When my phone rings, I push the empty pint aside and grab it from the table. It's my dad.

Confused, I answer it.

"Is it Sunday?" I ask.

"Figured this was worth breaking our rule," my dad mutters. "Since when is my daughter famous?"

"Famous?" I laugh. "What are you talking about?"

"Blake," my dad calls to my mom.

"I'll send it right now," my mom answers through the cell.

"Send what?" I ask.

Reaching for the remote, Rory pauses our show before giving me her full attention. I lift a shoulder, then push the speaker button, so we can both hear the conversation. "Rory's here, too," I announce.

"Hey, Squeaks!" my dad calls. "Tell me about this guy, Pax."

"Pax?" she squeaks. Her eyes bulge, and she gives me a look that screams, *what do you want me to say?*

"How do you know about Pax?" I interrupt, because, uh, what the hell?

"Check your text, babe," my mom interjects.

Opening the app, I click on the link, barely scanning the headline before gasping. "Are you kidding me?"

**Paxton Six Has Been a Dirty, Dirty boy. Luckily, His Maid Seems More Than Willing to Offer Her Services—In Public! Oh, My!**

*IndieCent Vows guitarist, Paxton Six, seems to be enjoying his time off in small town, Harden Heights and was recently seen heating things up on the beach with his latest fling. Sources say the woman in the photo is his maid, though she'll be leaving the beach dirtier than she left it if the photo is anything to go by. The question is, is this true love or is the penniless maid only spending her time with Paxton Six for his money and connections to the rock band, IndieCent Vows? Seems only time will tell.*

Curious, Rory darts to my bed and collapses onto it. As she reads the article over my shoulder, a gasp slips out of her. "No freaking way."

"So?" my mom prods. "You okay?"

It's a good question, but I'm so blindsided by the whole thing, I don't even know what to say. "I mean…yes?" I laugh, inspecting the article all over again. "What the hell is this?"

"This is what happens when the paparazzi sniff out a famous person's new relationship," she answers. "Aunt Mia went through the same thing when she started dating your Uncle Henry."

"Yeah, but I'm not even officially dating Pax, yet." With a scoff, I scan a few more lines of the article. "Just offering my services, apparently."

Rory's elbow connects with my ribs, and I jerk away from her, mouthing, "What the hell?"

"Tatum's downplaying her feelings," Rory announces to my family. "You should've seen what he did for your daughter last night. Pax is the sweetest guy ever and treats Tate like gold."

With wide eyes, I scold, "Rore!"

"What? You don't want to fill your parents in on what isn't in the article? Or should we let them focus on how good he is in bed, er, *beach*?"

Fighting the urge to smack my best friend, I examine the photograph attached to the article again, and damn. Not going to lie. This probably isn't a photo any parent should have to see, let alone the world. The lens on the camera is something else, and even though the image blurs out the intimate bits, it doesn't take a genius to see I'm clearly enjoying being railed on the beach last night. My head is thrown back. My mouth is open wide. And my legs are wrapped around Paxton's waist while his pants are wrapped around his ankles.

Yup. If that isn't the definition of scandalous, I don't know what is.

"Rory's right. Pretty sure we didn't need to see that," my dad grunts, and I swear I can hear the embarrassment in his voice.

Biting back my amusement, I point out, "Honestly, it's kind of a miracle this is the only article written about me so far."

My mom chuckles in the background, and it makes me love her even more.

"You're not helping, Blake," my dad grumbles.

"I mean, it's kind of funny," she argues, standing up for me in a way that makes me want to crawl through my cell and hug her.

"Right?" I interject. "How did you even find this article?"

"Your sister sent it to us," my mom answers. "Asked us to check in with you to see if you're okay."

Squeezing my eyes shut, my humor dissipates.

*Of course, she did.*

"How...kind of her," I mumble, unsure what else I'm supposed to say.

"She loves you," my dad returns as if I need the reminder. "So, do I at least get to meet him?"

Him. As in Pax. Right.

Forehead wrinkling, I mutter, "I don't, uh—"

Another call coming through cuts me off, and I peek at the screen, surprised to find Paxton's name flashing back at me. "Hey, someone's calling," I announce. "I have to go, but I'll call you later."

Before I have a chance to end the call, my dad adds, "If you need us to do anything or if you need money or—"

"Seriously?" I screech. "I'm not dating Pax for his money!"

"We know, baby," my mom rushes out. "Your dad just meant that if you want to quit your job so you're not dating your boss anymore, we can help until you find something else."

I roll my eyes. "That's very sweet—and not subtle at all, by the way—but I appreciate the offer. I'll talk to you guys later."

"Tell Pax we can't wait to meet him," my mom adds.

I end the call and answer Paxton's. "Hello?"

"So, you're dating me for my money, huh?" Pax's silky voice greets me.

Rory fans herself, falling back onto my bed, shamelessly swooning over the guy as I take my phone off speaker in hopes of achieving an ounce of privacy now that my conversation with my parents is over.

Bringing the phone to my ear, I say, "I'm sorry, who is this?"

"This is the guy you're boning for his money."

My mouth lifts. "Which one?"

"Very funny, Birthday Girl. Did you see the article?"

"Maybe."

"You pissed?"

I shift on the bed, pressing my back to the headboard as I pull my knees to my chest. "Why would I be pissed? Because I look like a gold digger?"

"Yeah."

My lips bunch on one side while I ignore Rory's penetrating gaze. Am I pissed? Not really. But I'm used to dealing with shitty people. Dying your blonde hair black, painting your nails black, and doing your makeup darker than your soul in high school is a pretty solid way to star in the rumor mill. Add in a handful of one-night stands, picking up random jobs while traveling to pay for said travel, and quitting at the drop of a hat because of a flight change or a spur of the moment decision is a great way to get on a few people's shit lists. But being accused of sleeping with someone for their money? That's new. I don't know how I feel about it. "Do you think I'm a gold digger?" I ask.

"I think you could get a lot more from me than my money."

My heart skips a beat, and I look down at my lap, trying to hide my smile. "Does that scare you? Knowing I hold all the cards?"

"Nah, I didn't say that. Although…"

A knock hits my door, and Hades lifts his head from Rory's bed. Unfolding herself from mine, Rory walks toward the door and peeks through the peephole as Hades jumps down, letting out a booming bark that shakes the pictures on the walls.

"Wait, you have a dog?" Paxton asks through my cell.

"It's Rory's," I return as Rory pauses to address the monster in the room.

"Hades, no bark," she scolds. "Everything's fine." Reaching down, she scratches his ear, and the fight seeps from his rigid posture with the simple touch before his furry butt hits the ground at her feet. Satisfied he won't attack whoever's on the opposite side, Rory reaches for the door handle, revealing a devilishly attractive Paxton on the opposite side.

Hades growls up at him, and Paxton's eyes bulge. "You have a *big* dog."

"He's nothing but a big ol' sweetheart," Rory tells him.

"Don't listen to her," I call. "He hates everyone but Rory, including me, and I've known him since he was a puppy." Realizing I'm still pressing my phone to my ear, I hang up our call so we can talk face-to-face. "Also, what are you doing here?"

Pax opens his mouth to answer when a low growl cuts him off.

"Aaaand, we're gonna go hide so Paxton keeps his nether regions," Rory announces.

Not bothering to hide his amusement, Pax counters, "I thought you said he's a big ol' sweetheart?"

"Best not to test it." She forces a smile, then loops her fingers beneath Hades' collar. "Come on, big boy." Hades follows as she darts down the short hall to the bathroom before locking the door behind them.

Which means I'm all alone. With Pax. In my safe space. After I had intimate photos leaked on the internet all because of him.

Clearing my throat, I repeat, "Seriously, what are you doing here?"

He lifts his hand, showcasing a simple black card between his two fingers. "Giving you all the cards."

Confused, I stand from my bed and stride closer to him. "Pax, I was kidding."

"Yeah?" He raises a shoulder. "Well, I'm not."

I could tell him to leave. I could yell at him for being the cause of said photos being leaked, then slam the door in his face. There's only one problem. I really don't want to. Not after the party. Not after waking up in his bed after he took care of me. Not after the beach and the borrowed clothes and the ride to Grinds and the concert and this morning. So much is changing, it's hard to keep up, but the scary part? I want to try.

I like Pax. I like him a lot. And even though it's terrifying, I can't convince myself to keep fighting it. Honestly, it's exhausting, and I'm tired. Tired of causing friction with every single thing in my life.

"I thought you were sparring?" I murmur.

"I was." His shoulder hits the doorjamb with a quiet thump as he leans against it. "And now, I'm here to apologize."

"For what?"

"For the paparazzi being a bitch."

I glance at the card still pinned between his fingers while attempting to catch up to the one-eighty my night just took. But seriously. Is he offering me his credit card? Why? And so, what? We got caught hooking up on the beach, someone decided to snap a few photos of it, and basically called me a money-hungry slut. Okay, that part wasn't so great, but still. It doesn't explain why Pax is on my doorstep or why he's offering me his money when I've never asked for it.

"Talk to me, Birthday Girl," he prods.

I tear my attention from the card pinched between his fingers, only to find Paxton observing me. Is he…nervous? And if he is, is it because of the article, or is it because he's afraid I can be bought off? Honestly, the latter makes me feel…dirty. Dirtier than the article ever could. Especially after last night and this morning. I thought…I thought he liked me. Saw me. Understood who I am beneath all the bitchiness and the snark. The possibility I was wrong? It kind of hurts.

Keeping the realization on lockdown, I announce, "I'm aware the paparazzi are a bitch."

"They are," he agrees.

"Yeah, but it doesn't mean you owe me anything." My fingers dig into the edge of the door as I fight the urge to slam it in his face. "Honestly, I'm trying really hard not to be offended that you think buying me off will make me forgive you for something not in your control."

The corners of his eyes crinkle with amusement as he slowly shakes his head. "That's not why I'm offering you the card."

"So, why *are* you offering it?" I demand.

His stupid smile threatens to cut through my bravado, but I hold strong.

"I'm being serious," I push.

"I know you are."

"So why are you smiling?" I snap.

"Because you're cute when your feathers are ruffled." His smile stretches wider. "And I'm offering you the card because I know how much you like to piss people off."

My forehead wrinkles as I grip the edge of the door, trying to piece together what he's throwing down, but I'm coming up empty. How much I like to piss people off? What does that have to do with anything? They wrote an article making me look bad. That's that.

*Isn't it?*

"What are you saying?" I ask.

"I'm saying you should take the power back. Go fucking wild. Give them something to talk about." He dips forward, his lips hovering over mine. "I dare you."

# 40

# TATUM

I feel like I might throw up. I shouldn't be surprised. It's not like this call will be a walk in the park, but the physical response to the whole thing? It makes me hate it even more. Forcing myself to push the call button, I wipe my hands against my thighs one at a time, then shift my phone to my opposite ear.

"Hello?" my sister answers.

"Hey," I murmur.

"Tatum?" Ophelia asks.

"Yeah, it's me."

Silence greets me, so I check the screen, confirming the call is still connected. It is. Which means I've rendered my sister speechless. I'd give her crap for it if I wasn't as surprised as she is. Don't get me wrong. I've known I'd have to rip this Band-Aid off at one point or another, but actually going through with it? It's kind of a modern day miracle, and she knows it as well as I do.

"Uh, hey," Lia finally says. "Hi. How are you?"

"I'm good, how are you?"

"Good, just…hanging out with the girls."

"Oh." I gulp. "You can call me later or whatever."

"No, I'm good," she rushes out. "I can chat."

"Okay? Uh."

*Why is this so hard?*

"Hoooow's the wedding planning going?" I press my hand to my forehead, willing the conversation to move forward.

*God, I sound so stupid.*

At least I waited until Rory was in the shower to call so there isn't a witness to this stilted conversation.

"It's good," Lia answers. "Overwhelming, but good."

"Awesome. I, uh, I've been meaning to call to congratulate you."

"Yeah?"

I don't miss the surprise in her voice. It isn't bitchy or snooty. It's genuine, only tacking on more guilt for the time I spent avoiding her.

"Yeah." I chew on the edge of my thumb, then drop it to my lap. "Sorry I didn't…respond to your texts."

She doesn't answer, but the background noise goes quiet. She probably went to another room or something. I'm grateful for it, though. The privacy. It's not like her friends don't know about the drama we've had as sisters. Nope. I've made my feelings crystal clear from the very beginning, and even now, I don't regret it. Not because my sister deserved my asshole behavior, but I spent years shoving aside my feelings, pretending like they didn't exist, and where did it get me? Absolutely nowhere. At least Lia knew where I stood when it came to her and Mav, even if it did paint me as the bitch.

"I get it," Lia finally murmurs. "Why you didn't respond to any of my texts."

Part of me wonders if she does get it. If she understands why I'm so hot and cold. So unpredictable. Why I've spent years distancing myself from her and Mav and…everyone, even if it isn't fair to them.

"I want you to know I'm excited for you," I add. "I think you and Mav are…are really great together."

"Thanks, Tate." The sadness in her voice tugs at my heart. "That means a lot."

"You're welcome."

"Listen, I've been meaning to ask you something." She hesitates. "And you can say no, okay? Like, genuinely, I totally understand if you want to say no, but—"

"Spit it out, Ophelia."

Silence greets me, and I squeeze the edge of my cell, praying for patience.

"Would you…would you be my maid of honor?" she asks.

*What?*

I pull my phone away from my ear, convinced I've heard her wrong. Did she really just ask me this? After all the bullshit we've been through? After my lack of support for years, not to mention the way I totally threw her under the bus with Archer before *and* after he passed?

"Y-you want me to be your maid of honor?" I ask.

"Is that weird for you?" She hesitates again. "If it is, I totally get it, I just…"

Twisting the blanket in my lap, I admit, "I kind of figured you would've already asked Fin or Dylan or Raine or…" *Anyone else but me,* I silently finish.

"You're my little sister, Tate," she returns. "You mean more to me than almost anyone else in the world."

My mouth ticks up, catching me by surprise. "Almost?"

She laughs. "You know what I mean, smartass."

And I do. I know what it's like to love someone. To put them above everyone else. Even my big sister. Shame and regret twist inside of me at the reminder of how much time has passed since we really spoke. Since I refused to hear her out or let my hate go. Too long.

Cotton fills my mouth, but I force out, "I'd be honored, Lia."

It's only half a lie. Honored? Yes. Absolutely losing my shit about all the situations that are guaranteed to be a mind fuck throughout the process? Also, yes. And sometimes it sucks how two opposing feelings can be on the same coin like this one. Even so, Paxton's right. Carrying the hate I've carried for someone I'm supposed to love—my own flesh and blood—is exhausting. And I'm tired of lugging it around day in and day out, knowing it doesn't do me, or anyone else, for that matter, a single fucking speck of good.

"You're the best, Tatum," Ophelia breathes out. "You really are. Thank you."

"Don't mention it." I pause, caught between ending the call on a good note and opening the puss-filled sore refusing to heal, no matter how much time I've given it. "Can I...can I ask you something?"

"Yeah, of course."

*Just say it, Tatum.*

"Do you ever..." A lump clogs my throat, and I force it back, well aware if I don't say it now, I never will. "Do you ever think about him anymore?"

Him.

I don't need to say his name. Ophelia already knows.

"I think about Archer every day," she whispers. "Every. Fucking. Day."

*Me, too.* The words are on the tip of my tongue, but I swallow them, replacing the admission with another question. "Do you miss him?" My voice cracks, and I rub at the corner of my eye, willing the pressure behind them to go away. But it's too much. All of it. Ophelia. Archer. His absence. My pulling away. It's killing me.

"I miss Archer more than I will ever be able to describe," Ophelia promises.

"Yeah?"

"Yeah." She sniffs. "And I know there is nothing in this world I can say to convince you otherwise, but I wasn't happy when I found out, Tate. I promise you I wasn't. I was heartbroken. I didn't look at Archer's death as a solution to a problem, and neither did Mav. It wasn't fair. It'll never be fair. *Ever.*"

"And that's it?" I bite the edge of my thumb as a tear slides down my cheek. "Learning to accept that life isn't fair, and it is what it is?"

"Honestly?" Her pause settles into my bones, siphoning the last of my hope that one day, with enough time, I'll stop missing him, and it won't hurt so much. "Kind of, yeah." The defeat in her voice pulls at me, strumming an ounce of grace I've refused to give her before now. Before this moment. This conversation. This confession. "I know it isn't the answer you want to hear," she adds, "but...but there is no answer in the universe that'll bring him back. That'll make everything okay. That'll take away the sting of fate's twisted idea of balance. Mav and I have spent years working through it. Processing the guilt we carry every single day for Mav surviving when Archer didn't. It wasn't fair. It still isn't fair. And if we could go back and have a say in how things went down, I know Mav would change places with his brother in a heartbeat. But do you want to know something, Tate?"

My grief grows and grows until I swear I can't breathe, but I force out, "What?"

*I can't fucking breathe.*

"I think the real reason you've hated me for years is because we both know I can't say the same," she whispers. "I can't say I would go back and choose to bury Maverick instead of Archer, and that brings a whole other messed-up wave of guilt I have to carry." Her voice cracks, and my head falls forward, knowing this is the crux of my frustration and pain and feelings when it comes to my big sister. The person I've always looked up to. Always envied. Until the truth came out that proved she wasn't the person I thought she was, and I can't even blame her for it. "Now, if I could put myself in that casket so Mav and Arch could walk away together, I would, but that isn't an option either, you know?"

She sniffles again, and I want to tell her to stop talking. To stop saying things like this. But I don't. Instead, I sit silent, memorizing her words as if they have the power to heal everything we've been through, even when it feels impossible.

"But what I'm most sorry for?" she continues. "Is how I was too self-absorbed at the time to recognize the pain you were going through. I'm so sorry I wasn't there for you. That I didn't know…"

We've never talked about it. Even dancing around the subject made me want to bite Ophelia's head off over the years. The fact that I loved Archer and am now stuck with living in Ophelia's shadow for the rest of my existence. Or at least, it's what I thought until…until Pax showed me I don't have to live in the darkness of her shadow. That I can let go and move on. That I have more power than I've given myself credit. I should remember that.

"You're not the only one who screwed up," I murmur. "I was hurting, and I took it out on you. It isn't fair, and I'm sorry it took me so long to reach out and to…" *Breathe.* "To forgive you."

"Dammit, Tatum," she cries. "You couldn't let me fly out so we could finally have this talk in person and I could give you a hug?" A pathetic laugh filters from my speaker. "I'm a mess over here."

"Me, too," I admit with a laugh that's just as pathetic as hers. "I love you, Lia."

"Love you, too. More than you will ever know."

And for the first time in…forever, I honestly believe her.

"Thanks for calling," she whispers.

"I'm trying," I admit.

"I know you are." She sniffs again, and so do I.

*I'm trying.*

41

TATUM

I'm still not entirely sure how going on a shopping spree is taking the power back from the stupid paparazzi who think they have me pegged. But Pax is right about one thing. Okay, he's right about a lot of things, but he's also right about this. They're going to write whatever they want. Make up whatever lies they feel like creating. And it has nothing to do with me. Not really.

Thanks to my dad's time in the NHL, the drama behind my Uncle Colt's relationship with Jaxon's mom before he settled down with my Aunt Ash, and Uncle Henry "slumming" it with my Aunt Mia, I've heard all about the bullshit the paparazzi like to throw at the wall, hoping the drama will stick long enough for them to cash in on their photos or articles or…whatever they can sell while the story's hot.

It happened with Archer, too. After his death. Most of the memorials were pretty on point…if you didn't care about Archer. They focused on the positive. On Maverick's life-saving surgery. On his adorable relationship with his sweetheart, aka my sister, now that he had a heart again. They always managed to skim over the whole unexpected death of his twin brother, but hey. What can you do?

I push the thought aside and grab another dress from the rack. Paxton hired a private jet to fly us somewhere tonight, telling me it would be the perfect cherry on top of an updated article. Honestly, it's such a bold move, I'm impressed. Even though he's keeping me in the dark about where he's taking me, I know I need to be ready by seven with a new dress, shoes, purse, hair, the whole nine yards.

Not going to lie. It is a little hilarious. Playing right into the paparazzi's fake-ass story. Pretending like I'm the star in *Pretty Woman* or any other rom-com with a solid butterfly moment where she comes out a different person, complete with highlights, a new handbag, and main character energy.

Ridiculous.

But the really crazy part? It's that I have no idea if I have an audience for this little act. How can you tell if someone's following you when you got caught with your pants down, literally, two days ago? And if I didn't notice then, when I was alone with Pax on the beach, how am I supposed to notice now?

Glancing over my shoulder, I take in the other customers scattered around the boutique before attempting to focus on the clothing in front of me.

"What do you think of this one?" I ask.

Rory stops her perusal, taking in the dress I'm holding. It's silky and short and red, just like the dress that stained my bra not so long ago. Paxton will love it.

"It's gorgeous," she decides. "Kind of like one you already have, though, isn't it?"

"This one's a little shorter, and the top is cut differently," I add, showcasing the neckline.

Tilting her head, she decides, "I say go for it. Besides, the color's perfect."

"Right?" My mouth splits into a grin. Yeah, Paxton's gonna die when he sees me tonight.

"What do you think of this?" Rory holds up a creamy peach dress with spaghetti straps. Maverick informed her that Lia picked light peach, cream, and white as her wedding colors. I reach for Rory's dress and rub the fabric between my fingertips. It's like butter. Soft. Smooth. Breathable. Perfect.

"It's beautiful," I murmur.

"You think?"

"Yes. Jax won't know what hit him," I add with a wink.

She rolls her eyes. "I don't care about Jax or his opinion of my outfit, so…"

"Come on," I tease. "We both know there's no harm in rubbing a guy's nose in what they missed out on, even if the door was never really open in the first place."

She lifts the dress higher into the air, examining it. "True, but—"

"Sir, we don't allow cameras in this facility," a woman announces.

I turn to the front of the boutique, surprised to find a camera pointed directly at me. "What the hell?"

The familiar click-click of a photo being snapped makes my nose wrinkle.

Following my gaze, Rory sighs, then shifts to give the camera her back. "Seems you have an audience after all."

I'd find it funny if he didn't seem so forceful.

The woman's voice cuts through another round of photo snapping clicks. "Sir, I insist—"

"I'm a customer," he argues.

"Then I'm sure you don't mind leaving your camera at the front desk while you shop." The young woman reaches for the camera, but the paparazzi jerks away from her, making the girl's face flame with embarrassment. "Sir, this is my first day. Can you please—"

My legs move closer like they have a mind of their own as I call out, "Hi, is there a problem?"

"Tatum," Rory warns from behind me.

"It's fine," I tell her.

The flash of the camera blinds me, and I pull back, blinking in an attempt to regain my eyesight.

Damn, that thing's bright.

"Sir," the employee begs.

Still half blind, I step between them, refusing to let this poor woman fight my battle when the paparazzi reaches for my arm. My knee goes up on instinct, I swear, connecting with the man's balls before he even has a chance to realize what's happening. In a flash, he doubles over, cursing as Rory rushes toward me.

"I—we'll be—uh—" With wide eyes, she looks up at me, her shoulders practically touching her eyes in a massive shrug of discomfort.

*Well, this just got interesting.*

Helpless, I stand beside her, unsure what to do because no matter how many scenarios I could've dreamed of finding myself in today, this is one I never saw coming. So, what now? I could always drag Rory out of here and pray I don't get arrested for assault. Or I could stand my ground until the bastard decides I'm not one to mess with and leaves on his own. Hell, maybe if I'm lucky, the door will hit his ass on the way out. A girl can dream, can't she? Yup. Now that I think about it, the latter option feels like the way to go.

"We'll be taking these dresses," I announce. "Please put them on this card." I glare at the man on his knees. "It belongs to Paxton Six."

Stepping around him, I follow the girl to the front desk. As she rings me up, the paparazzi mutters something into his cell, but I don't pay attention to him. Instead, I keep my head held high and hand the girl Paxton's credit card.

"Would you like anything else?" she asks. The girl looks absolutely terrified. Hell, her hand's shaking, and she can barely hold my gaze without it darting to the man on the floor behind me. It'd be comical if I didn't feel so bad, considering this is kind of all my fault.

"Is this really your first day?" Rory whispers to her.

She nods, peeking at my best friend. "Uh, yeah. Great way to start, right?"

"Memorable," I offer, my tone thick with sarcasm. "And yes. I would like something else. Do you have any of the red heels in a size seven? I think they'd look great with the dress, don't you?"

As if seeing what we're purchasing for the first time, her head bobs up and down. "Uh, yes. Yes, I think they'd go great. I'll, uh, I'll be right back with those shoes."

"Thanks."

As we wait, the bell on the front door chimes as someone else enters the building. Or maybe the sniveling paparazzi decided to leave. That would be a pleasant surprise. I don't bother checking, determined not to give the asshole another second of my energy or attention, even if I'm more curious than I'd like to admit.

"You know, when Paxton told you to go wild, I'm pretty sure he didn't mean kneeing anyone in the balls," Rory quips beside me. She peeks over her shoulder and blanches. "Uh, hello, officer."

"Miss?" a low voice interrupts.

*Shit.*

With a fake smile, I turn around, trying not to cower. "Uh, hello?"

"Hello," the officer returns. "We received a complaint."

"Yup, and he's right there." I point to the asshole at the back of the store.

Without following my finger, the officer places his hands on his hips. "Yes, well, I'm sure there are two sides to every story—"

"Yeah, and I have the right one," I interrupt. "I'm sure there's a camera in here somewhere to prove it."

"And we'll be sure to look into that," he placates, though he doesn't back away or even give the asshole a second look.

Fighting my annoyance, I reply, "You do that." I turn back to the front of the shop, preparing to pay for my things and get the hell out of Dodge as quickly as possible because a confrontation with the fuzz was *not* on my bingo card for today.

"Miss, are you the, uh, the owner of this card?" The officer reaches for the black card on the counter and lifts it into the air, reading the owner's name out loud. "Paxton Turner?"

*Well, shit.*

Buzzing hits my ears while I stare at the officer's mouth, trying to read the words coming out of his lips since my hearing has apparently decided to exit the building.

*Don't panic, don't panic, don't panic.*

"I'm sorry, what?" I ask.

"This card," he repeats. "Does it belong to you?"

"It sure does," I lie.

"Then, I assume you won't mind showing me your ID with the same name on it."

*Well, double shit.*

"I, uh, I don't…"—I give Rory a panicked look, my calm facade cracking like an overcooked cookie—"have it with me at this time, but—"

"Is it stolen?" he demands.

My eyes bulge. "No, of course not!"

"Miss, I think it would be in your best interest to come down to the station with me."

Ignoring my racing heart, I ask, "For what?"

"For having a stolen credit card in your possession and for assaulting a civilian," he clarifies.

*Well, triple shit.*

"What?" Rory interrupts. In a flash, she transforms from my quiet, timid mouse of a friend to a damn-near mama bear, twisting around and facing the officer with her head held high. "She didn't assault anyone!"

"Did you or did you not hit that man?" The officer points to the exit, and I follow his line of sight, only to find the paparazzi's camera pointed directly at me. He's still in the building, documenting my little chat with Officer What's His Name.

Yup. This will make for a *great* story. But hey, let's look at the bright side, right? If Paxton's goal is to stay front and center in the gossip column, I'm doing him a huge favor, and he owes me big time.

Glaring at the paparazzi, I raise my hand and give him my middle finger.

*Document this, motherfucker.*

Rory reaches for my arm and tugs it back to my side, scolding, "Tatum! Will you just…play nice for once in your life?"

She's right, but still. This is bad. Very bad. I've never been arrested before, but this is a complete misunderstanding. Isn't it? I mean, I did kind of knee a stranger in the balls, but he also deserved it, so…

*Not the time, Tatum.*

Ignoring Rory's *what the fuck, keep it together expression*, I ask the officer, "Are you arresting me?"

"Not at this time, no." The bastard doesn't even look apologetic. "But I think your friend will agree that it's in your best interest to cooperate and let me take you to the station to see if we can figure out exactly what happened."

"Of course it is." I give him a smile, then add, "Hey, Rore?"

"Yeah?" she squeaks.

"Make sure you give Paxton his credit card back, okay?"

"I'll meet you at the station," she promises. "Don't say anything."

I give her a thumbs up. "Wouldn't dream of it." Tilting my head up at the officer, I add, "Lead the way, Officer."

"You know, when I said go wild, I didn't think you'd take it as a challenge," I tell Tatum. And I mean it, too. Getting a call from Rory, begging me to meet her at the police station so I could potentially bail out her best friend was a first for me. I bite back my amusement as I open the precinct door.

Thankfully, the guy who had his balls kneed-in cleared up his side of the story pretty quick after the store offered to drop their own suit against the asshole in exchange. And since I was able to show my ID at the precinct and corroborate Tatum's story, confirming I gave her the credit card to use and she hadn't stolen anything, we were good to go.

Tatum's hair dances in the light breeze as we make our way down the short set of stairs toward my bike parked at the curb.

"Thanks for picking me up," she says.

"Anytime, Harley Quinn."

"Falling for a villain," she muses, giving me the side-eye. "Sounds about right."

My pulse quickens, and my steps falter as I hang onto her

words. Did she just admit she's falling for me? If she did, I doubt she meant to let it slip, but my chest warms nonetheless.

*You're something else, Birthday Girl.*

"Seriously, though. Thank you," she adds. "That was a little…intense."

I catch her fiddling with her gold ring and reach for her hands, pulling us to a stop on the sidewalk. Is she nervous? Shaken, maybe? I guess I don't blame her. Sometimes I forget that being invited to a police station for questioning isn't a common activity for most people.

Bringing her fingers to my lips, I kiss them softly, and ask, "Was this your first run-in with law enforcement?"

Her laugh eases the tightness in my chest. "Yes, but I'm okay," she answers.

"You sure?"

"Yes," she repeats. Her gaze bounces around my face as I press another kiss to her fingertips, causing what's left of her worry wrinkles to soften. "Although I kind of like having all your attention like this."

"You always have all of my attention."

Her eyes crinkle with amusement, but she doesn't argue. Instead, she asks, "Is this your first time picking up a friend from the cops?"

"Not even close," I reply.

"Oh, really? Do tell."

I throw my head back and laugh. "You want the light version or the heavy version?"

"There's a heavy version?"

She has no idea.

"My best friend growing up, Roman's older brother, actually, he's in prison for pushing drugs," I explain. "Although, after saying it out loud, I guess it doesn't count since I didn't technically bail him out, but you get the gist."

Her brows furrow. "What?"

I let her hands go and scratch my temple. "Probably should've started with the light version, huh?"

"Pax, that's…" She bites her bottom lip. "That *is* heavy. How is he? How are you? Do you still see him? How much time is he doing? Does Roman hate you for it? Did you know what he was up to behind your back? Were you in on it and just didn't get caught or—"

"Whoa, there," I interrupt. "At least give me a second to answer your twenty questions, yeah?"

She closes her mouth and drags her fingers across them, pretending to zip her lips and throw away the key.

With a soft chuckle, I lead her closer to my bike, diving right in to the nitty gritty of my fucked-up childhood. "Let me give you the CliffsNotes version. Yes, I knew what he was doing, and no I wasn't around when he was arrested, but yes, I still talk to him and see him whenever I'm in town." I pause, replaying her onslaught of questions in an attempt to address all of them. "All things considered, he's doing good. Took his sentence on the chin and should be out in the next year or so, and no, Roman doesn't hate me, even though it does make me kind of feel like shit about the whole thing. Uh, I think that's it?" I glance at Tatum again. "Any other questions?"

"What's his name?" she prods.

"Rafe."

She gives me a slow nod. "And how are you?"

My brows dip. "Me?"

"Yeah. It can't be easy. Seeing your friend locked up."

Scratching my jaw, I consider her question. No one's ever asked me this. No one's ever thought to. I'm not the one behind bars, so why does it matter? Why would anyone care? Add in the whole rockstar bit, and I'm pretty sure most people would say I don't have shit to complain about. And maybe I don't. Even so, the fact she's thinking of me, of how I feel, how I'm handling shit, it means more than she knows.

Gripping her hand, I continue guiding her toward my parked bike a few feet away, answering, "I'm all right."

She tugs me to a halt. "Pax."

"Seriously," I return. "I mean, yeah. It fucked with my head, and I wish I would've pushed him harder to drop all the illegal shit, but he was young and stupid, and I was young and stupid, and we can't change the past, so why dwell on it?"

Her lips bunch before her head dips in a slow nod, but she doesn't say anything else. And the quiet? It messes with my head, especially after giving her a glimpse of my past.

"So…you wanna hear about a few of my lighter run-ins with the cops?" I ask, attempting to change the subject and lighten the fucking black cloud hovering over us after my little walk down memory lane.

She grabs hold, instantly. "I'm sorry, did you say *your* run-ins?"

With a shrug, I tell her, "We've all had our run-ins, haven't we?"

She scans me up and down, clearly impressed. "Damn. Didn't think it would be such a turn-on, but…"

My grin widens. "Oh, really?"

"Yup. And now, I'm going to need all the gory details, so I can save them for later." Pulling her hands from mine, she taps her temple and tacks on a wink that douses my imagination with gasoline.

I like it when she's like this. When she's open and playful. I like it a lot. And the idea of her touching herself when I'm away? My cock hardens just thinking about it. Might as well add fuel to the fire, right?

"Let's see, which time? Uh," I search my memories for a few of my lighter interactions with the law. "Breaking and entering…"

Her jaw drops. "Are you serious?"

"It was Dodger's house, but the security system went off, and thanks to my priors…well, you get the gist."

"Uh, I don't, but we'll circle back. What priors?" she demands, her brow arching.

"Possession of weed when crossing state lines." My tongue clicks against the roof of my mouth as I sort through the shadier side of my past. Giving her the side-eye, I add, "And another misdemeanor you might be familiar with. Trespassing."

She clutches at her chest like a girl from the fifties. "A man after my own heart."

"Glad you approve," I laugh.

Bumping her shoulder with mine, she murmurs, "And here I thought you were an upstanding citizen."

"Hardly."

"It's okay. Neither am I, even if I don't have the record to prove it." She shrugs and laces our fingers together again as we stand beside my bike. "Anything else?"

*Yes.*

Well aware it doesn't paint me in the best light, I answer, "Assault charges and underage drinking." My expression constricts, but I push through the shame growing inside me. "I got into a fight at a bar when I was seventeen."

"Damn."

"Yeah."

"That one kind of makes sense, though," she decides. "Because of the sparring sessions and everything."

And everything.

If only she knew how loaded those words are.

"Right," I mutter.

Sensing I'm keeping something from her, she murmurs, "It is only the sparring, right? That's the only habit you've kept from your shady background?" My lips press together, and her jaw drops again. "Are you still into shady shit, Pax?"

Glancing over my shoulder at the precinct we barely left, I shush, "Wanna keep your voice down, Birthday Girl?"

Catching on, Tatum hooks her arm through mine, guides me past my parked bike, and walks us further down the road. Once we're a safe distance from any potential eavesdroppers, she asks, "So, what's up? I want to know."

I stay quiet, pressing my tongue against my cheek as I weigh my options. I want to tell her. I also want to *not* fuck anything up.

Sensing my hesitancy, she sobers slightly, adding, "I want to say it's okay, and you don't have to tell me, but considering my lack of emotional connections with the majority of people, and the fact I've really been trying to let you in lately, I kind of feel like you owe me." She pulls her hand from mine and crosses her arms. "So? What are you hiding? What's the big secret?"

Reaching up, I tuck her hair behind her ear, considering my options. I want to tell her. I do. But will it put her in the crosshairs of anything? I don't think so, but Judge hasn't exactly been very forthright, either, and I sure as shit don't know everything. That being said, she's right. She's risked being vulnerable with me, shouldn't I do the same?

When she catches me staring at her despite my silence, she squirms. "What?"

"Just thinking."

"About what?"

"About my secrets." I move closer, my need to pull her into me is almost more than I can bear. So, I do. My fingers dig into her hips as I tug her toward me, savoring the feel of her curves pressed against my chest on the side of the road. "I like you."

Her eyes soften, and her hands find the belt loops above

my ass as she bats her lashes up at me. "I'm pretty sure you've mentioned that already."

"Glad you remember," I quip. "And even though you haven't said it back, you did mention you're falling for a villain, so I'm gonna go out on a limb and say I think you like me, too."

Her attention falls to my mouth. "No comment."

"Uh-uh." I burrow closer, dragging the tip of my nose along hers in an eskimo kiss. "Secret for a secret, Birthday Girl. I wanna hear you say it."

"And if I do, you'll tell me about the shady side of your extracurricular activities?"

"Cross my heart," I promise.

"Fine. I, uh…" She takes a deep breath, toying with the hem of my T-shirt. "I think I might like you, too, Pax."

The same warmth in my chest spreads, and I tighten my hold around her waist. If I could record this moment, the tiny inflection in her voice, the shift of her gaze, the lift of her mouth, I'd record it all to keep for rainy days. But I also know if I ask her to repeat it, if I push her more than I already have, she might clam up. So instead, I give her another tight squeeze of appreciation. "Now was that so hard, Birthday Girl?"

Her lips purse. "I believe it's your turn, Mr. Security."

"All right," I concede. "Here's the thing. I'm trying to figure out what to tell you without…"

"Without what?"

"Without incriminating you."

Her breath hitches. "You're really serious? Pax…"

"Do you remember when I told you Judge's nephews are into some shady shit?" I ask.

"Yes?"

"Well, running an underground fighting ring is one of them."

"Is that where the bruises are coming from?" She doesn't look pissed. She looks…confused.

"Yes and no," I mutter.

"Gonna need more than that, Pax."

"Technically, I haven't brawled yet. The bruises are from the sparring sessions, like I told you."

Her gaze narrows, and she pulls out of my grasp, folding her arms again as if the physical barrier is strong enough to fortify the emotional ones I've spent so much time eradicating. "I feel like there's a but coming on," she murmurs.

"But," I say, confirming her suspicion. "I'm kind of…in training."

"Training," she repeats, her expression on lockdown.

"Yes."

Unfolding her arms, she tucks her hair behind her ear as she studies me, carefully. "Doesn't it defeat the purpose of you being here to draw the public's attention *away* from their shindigs if you're participating in them?"

"Maybe."

"Hmm." A pebble skitters across the sidewalk as her gaze falls to the ground and the toe of her shoe scrapes against the asphalt. "Can I ask you something?"

"You've asked me a lot of somethings."

She rolls her eyes. "Why do you do it? Why fight? And why stop after becoming a rockstar? Or did you never stop at all and—"

I lift my hand to quiet her. "Man, you're full of questions today."

"That isn't an answer," she quips. But the walls? They're lower than a few seconds ago, proving she cares more about my honesty than whether or not I'm somewhat involved in something less than legal.

Giving in, I explain, "Growing up, I needed an outlet."

"An outlet," she repeats. A tiny furrow forms between her brows.

"Yeah."

"And?"

"And fighting was my outlet of choice until Rafe was arrested."

"And then?" she pushes.

"Then, I turned back to music and had my first taste of performing in front of people, which turned into my next outlet."

"Which is why you started going stir crazy as soon as you got home," she realizes.

"Exactly."

She moves closer, dragging her fingers down my forearms before linking our fingers together. "And it's why you agreed to participate in the underground fight."

"Partially," I concede. "Roman asked me to do him a favor. I figured it was the least I could do after everything that happened with Rafe."

Her head tilts as she stares up at me before a small smile toys at the edge of her lips. "Well, at least it's not drugs."

Now that we're toe to toe, nearly chest to chest, I laugh and reach for her waist again, tugging her into me. When she lets me, the last of my reservations vanishes, and I let out a sigh of relief. "Depends on how you look at it."

"Oh, really?"

"We all have our vices." My touch is gentle as I drag my hands along her bare arms, push her hair away from her face, and tuck it behind her ear. It's still strange. Having thought about this girl for years. And yet, here she is. Within reach. And without her armor. My heart pounds harder as I take in the vulnerability in her gaze and the slight part of her lips. Damn, she's beautiful. "Thankfully, I've found a new vice recently."

"And what's that?"

"Being with you." I nudge her chin up and kiss her, tasting her smile as she leans into me, giving me her weight. And I like it. The trust that I'll catch her. That I won't let her fall. Hell, I'm not sure if she even realizes it. The trust she's slowly giving me. Bit by bit. Or maybe she does. Maybe it's why she pushed me on this, demanding I let her in and tell her what I've been up to.

When I pull away, she grins up at me, her brow quirking. "I'm your new vice, huh?"

"Yeah, Birthday Girl. I think you are."

"Hmm." Her eyes thin, but I don't miss the curve of her mouth. "Nah, you just wanna see me naked again."

Another laugh rumbles from my chest. "You have no idea, do you?"

"That I'm irresistible?"

"That you're mine." Unable to help myself, I kiss her again, savoring her sweet taste before resting my forehead against hers.

"So cocky," she notes, lifting her chin. It's a silent request. A tiny olive branch. A modicum of proof that she wants more, and I'd be a fool to do anything but give in. Pretty sure I'd give her anything, if she only asked for it.

Bending down, I kiss her a third time. "So, about our date tonight…"

"Mmm, yes," she sighs against my mouth. "About that."

"Did you find a dress?"

Her head bobs. "Maybe."

"And shoes?"

She grins.

"Good girl."

43

# TATUM

fter a short ride on Paxton's bike, he drops me off at my apartment, telling me he'll be back in an hour for our date. I was so excited until after I hopped out of my shower. I blame the hot water and the quiet. Regardless, now that I'm home, the idea of going on some adventurous date after my run-in with Officer Butthead feels a little...exhausting. All I really want to do is mentally recharge and compartmentalize everything that's happened over the last few days. As I fix my hair and touch up my makeup in the bathroom, a soft knock echoes from the front door, and I give myself one last second in front of the mirror before rushing to answer it.

On the other side is a handsome as ever Paxton in a dark gray suit, holding a dozen red roses.

"Why, hello."

"Hey." His genuine smile turns devilish as he scans me up and down. "You look..."

I smooth down the silky fabric. "Do you like it?"

"Fucking love it."

"Why, thank you."

"Here." He offers me the roses, and I step aside, inviting him in before heading to the kitchen in search of a vase.

Glancing around the empty apartment, he asks, "Where's Rory?"

"Taking Hades on a walk."

"Ah, of course."

I can feel his gaze on me as I fill a vase with some water and set the roses inside.

"They match your dress," he murmurs.

"Seems you have good taste," I reply.

"Seems we both do. So," he rounds the counter, grabs my hips, and sways us back and forth in the empty kitchen. "I want you to know I had some pretty epic plans for tonight."

"Had?" I challenge.

"I figured after the police run-in, you already had enough excitement for one day."

My chest swells at his thoughtfulness and how well he seems to know me. My wants and needs. Hell, sometimes it feels like he knows me better than I do, and even though I should find it a little off-putting, it isn't. Not in the slightest.

"That's quite the assumption," I note. Linking my fingers at the nape of his neck, I toy with the semi-short strands of sandy-blond silk. "You know, you could've told me there was a change of plans before I spent the last hour getting ready."

"It was a spur of the moment decision. Besides, I had to make sure my plan B would still knock your socks off."

"And what's plan B?" I ask.

"You'll see. Although, it does still require clothing—for now—so I don't feel too bad about leaving you in the dark. Besides, this view?" His attention falls to my boobs, and he whistles. "Damn, Tatum."

"Told you I have a good rack," I quip.

His low laugh brings a blush to my cheeks before he plants a kiss on the tip of my nose that makes me want to melt. Then, he lets me go, causing a swell of disappointment beneath my sternum.

Seriously. When did I get so needy?

"Shall we?" he asks.

Offering his hand, he waits for me to take it, and when I do, my heart flutters even more. After our conversation on the side of the road today, I'm pretty sure I've never felt more connected to someone. He's letting me in. Even when it's scary. And it's enough to convince me to do the same.

He brings the back of my hand to his lips, kissing me softly, then guides me toward the hallway. Once my door is locked behind us, we mosey down to The Pelican and find a booth.

It isn't a flight to a random state or anything like he initially promised, but the comfort pick is oddly thoughtful, and I fight the urge to keep from swooning.

As he slides off his dress coat and lays it carefully on the opposite side of the booth, I ask, "Aren't we a little over-dressed for The Pelican?"

"Nothing wrong with dressing to impress, Birthday Girl."

I check him out, realizing the man makes a good point. He's definitely impressive in a button-up. And when he undoes the buttons around his wrists and rolls the sleeves to his elbows? My mouth waters.

Yup. He makes a *very* good point.

A curve forms at the edge of Paxton's lips, proving I've most definitely been caught drooling over the guy as he picks up his menu, thumbing through it. "So, what's your stance on drinking games?"

"Are you hoping to get me drunk?" I tease.

"Figured you could use a good excuse to loosen up a bit." He shifts closer. "And this way, I can make out with you in the back of the Uber when I take you to my house for the rest of plan B."

"The rest of plan B?" I challenge.

"Don't order food," he adds cryptically.

"Fine, but only because you've piqued my curiosity." My mouth lifts. "So, what are the rules for your drinking game?"

"Answer a question or take a shot."

"Simple." I lace my fingers on the menu in front of me. "Straightforward. I like it."

"Thought you might. I'll get the shots. What do you want?"

"Whiskey, please," I tell him.

Within minutes, he comes back with six shots, setting three in front of me and lining up his own on the opposite side of the table.

After sliding into his seat, he says, "You go first."

"Okay." Drawing a circle along the top of the closest shot glass, I ask, "What did you think of me when you first saw me?"

"I thought, *please be legal, please be legal.*"

I cover my snort with my hand. "Okay, your turn."

"What did you think of me when you first saw me?" he prods.

"I thought, *if Rory wasn't here, I'd totally bang this guy in the alley.*"

Throwing his head back, he laughs.

"My turn," I announce. "How pissed were you when you thought I was engaged?"

Tongue in cheek, he stares at me from across the booth and shakes his head back and forth. "Livid." He brings one of the shot glasses to his lips and tosses it back.

I nudge him with my foot beneath the table. "And?"

"Already took a shot."

"Tell me!" I beg.

Licking his lips, he asks, "You really wanna know?"

I nod.

"I finally realized why some people cheat. Because with you? I was so desperate for another taste, I would've come running. And that scared the shit out of me." He pauses, surprising me with his honesty. "Why'd you tell me you were engaged?"

Digging my teeth into the inside of my bottom lip, I fight the urge to deflect. To shy away from the truth. To take the shot and keep the game moving. Instead, I murmur, "I think we both know the answer to that."

He reaches across the table but stops himself from touching my hand. "I wanna hear you say it."

I could. It's a question I've mulled over more times than I can count over the years. Why did I tell Pax I was engaged? And why did Archer's name slip past my lips when Pax pushed me on it? Was I really so pathetic? So damn delusional? Even after all these years, it's confusing and irrational and immature. I should've told him the truth. Should've been strong enough to express my feelings, no matter how terrifying they were. I lift the shot glass to my lips, but instead of pouring it back, I stop myself and set it back on the table. "I knew that if I didn't stop you from chasing me, there's no way I would've gotten away."

His brows dip. "And that's a bad thing?"

"At the time? Yes."

"And now?"

I pick up the glass and swallow the Jack Daniels, ignoring the burn as it glides down my throat.

"Fair enough," he murmurs.

"So, what happened with you and the band?" I ask.

He tilts his head. "What do you mean?"

"I ran into Dodge a little while ago, and he said something…kind of strange, honestly," I admit. "I wanted to ask you about it."

"What'd he say?"

"Just that your job can be isolating, especially with assholes for bandmates." I hesitate. "Pretty sure he was referring to himself."

"At least he owns up to it," Pax mutters dryly.

"What happened?"

"Nothing, really. That's the fucked up part." Pax's frown deepens as he stares at the shot glass in front of him. "You know I was the stand-in, right?"

"You were?"

"Yeah." He shrugs. "The original guitarist, Rudy, he grew up with Judge. They were best friends. Talked about starting a band and brought Dodger along after running into him at some dive bar. Rudy was running his mouth, Judge stepped in. They were outnumbered, and Dodger had their back. After that, they considered themselves brothers, and Dodger joined the band."

"And Tuke?"

"The record label set them up."

I nod, too curious about the turn in conversation to continue playing our little drinking game. "And you?"

"After Rudy died from a drug overdose the night before a show, I wound up stepping in and landing the gig."

My eyes widen. I've never heard this story. He must've felt like such an outcast. That had to have been hard. I can't even imagine. Thumbing the edge of the empty shot glass in my grasp, I muse, "They must've been impressed with your performance."

"They were desperate, and I did the job." He smiles, but it doesn't reach his eyes. "Even now, I'm not an official member, as fucked as it sounds." His chuckle falls flat, making me want to hug him. "I get paid to play. *Got* paid to play," he clarifies. "Not to contribute creatively, and I sure as shit am not on any of the copyrights for the music or anything like that. Just show up and play the songs they want me to play."

"Does it bother you?"

"Not at first, especially 'cause Tuke has the same deal. But…"

"You started caring?" I assume.

He sighs. "Judge is a hard man to read, and to get close to, thanks to Rudy's death."

"I guess Judge and I have that in common," I murmur.

His eyes soften. "Guess you do."

"And so do you," I add carefully. "Don't think I haven't forgotten that little tidbit about your parents."

"Gotta love when a solid origin story kicks you in the ass, am I right?"

"Mm-hmm. The real question is, how do you make it look so easy?" I ask. "You've had as much hardship as the rest of us, if not more. And here you are, a well-adjusted, sexy, musician with a side-hustle that gives you very lickable muscles."

He chuckles. "Glad you find my side-hustle worthy of your appreciation, but I'm not sure well-adjusted is quite as fitting as you might think."

"Well, would you look at that?" I quip. "You *are* capable of being humble."

His laugh lightens. "I'll drink to that."

He picks up another glass, and I do the same. Clinking them together across the table, we each take a shot before I ask, "So, I already know your history with fighting, what got you into music?"

"Isn't it my turn?" he challenges.

"Humor me."

"Only if you dance with me afterward."

I glance at the crowded dance floor and nod. "Deal."

"All right. What got me into music," he says, repeating my

question. "Let's see. My dad got me a guitar for Christmas when I was seven. He taught me basic chords and shit, then online tutorials took over until he left. I refused to touch it afterward until I walked in on my mom trying to trade it for some pain meds from a neighbor the same night Rafe was arrested. That's all it took. Seeing where my life could end up if I didn't pull my head outta my ass and the lifeline that was six feet in front of me if I could just let go of my resentment toward my dad and play again. So, I did. I stole it straight out of her hands and refused to go anywhere without it after that."

"So in a way, if it wasn't for Rafe, you might not've ever chased your dreams and become a rockstar," I realize.

"Yeah." He nods. "I guess you're right."

"I kind of love that," I admit, bumping the toe of my shoe against his calf beneath the table in hopes of turning his frown upside down, even if I get it. The guilt he must carry for being the one to turn his life around before it was too late. But he can't change the past any more than I can, and trust me, if anyone's tried to figure out how to change the past, it's me. "Talk about turning lemons into lemonade, right?" I add.

"Guess so." He picks up the last shot and throws it back. "Now, what do you say?" Slipping out from his side of the booth, he offers me his hand. "Shall we?"

Moving to the center of the room, we dance, swaying our hips to the beat. The song is slow and sultry, and I blame the two shots of alcohol swimming through my veins as I arch my back and grind my ass against Pax, though it doesn't feel like he's complaining, if the bulge in his slacks is anything to go by. Yup. Talk about the perfect way to end an evening. I could dance like this all night. Lifting my arms, I wrap them around Paxton's neck as he pulls my ass against him and dips his head, pressing his mouth to the curve of my neck. The heat of his lips makes my thighs press together. I arch my hips even more, craving him more than I should, considering the not-so-private ambiance we're basking in. When the back of my strap catches on something, my dress loosens, and I clutch at the fabric, realizing my top is most definitely broken.

*What the hell?*

My body stiffens, and I try not to lose my shit as I look down, taking in the broken strap. Considering the price of this bad boy and the fact that I'm seconds away from potentially flashing someone, I'm kind of pissed. Just when the dancing was getting good, this happens? What do I do now?

Moving closer, Pax murmurs, "Hey, you good?"

"My dress." I keep my hand on my boob, then with my opposite hand, fiddle with the strap, trying to figure out how to fix the damn thing.

When he realizes what I'm doing, Pax turns me to face him and messes with the frayed fabric for a solid two seconds until his fingers find the top button of his dress shirt, and he slowly undoes it.

"What are you doing?" I ask.

"Here." Sliding his shirt off, he places it on my shoulders, leaving himself in nothing but a white undershirt showcasing his strong arms.

Aaaand, am I drooling again?

Seriously. Since when are shoulders a turn-on? Since the first time I saw Paxton shirtless. But I digress.

Oblivious to my dirty thoughts, Pax pulls me close, grabs the front of his shirt I'm shrouded in, and uses it to cover me so I can slide my arms into place.

Not gonna lie. It makes my ovaries want to burst.

Once my arms are through the holes, he keeps me close, buttoning it from the top to the bottom, one by one until I'm covered. Satisfied, he rolls the sleeves to my elbows and grabs my hand, giving me a quick spin. "There. Much better. And on that note, are you hungry?"

"Yes?"

"Perfect." His spine curves as he cuts through the distance between us and kisses my forehead. "Because dinner just arrived."

"How do you know?"

"Roman texted." His hand meets my lower back. "Come on."

HE WAS SMART TO HIRE AN UBER BECAUSE I'M DEFINITELY buzzed, and it isn't only from the shots. Personally, I blame the cologne clinging to his dress shirt and smothering me in all things Pax. Or maybe it's the slight scratch of his palm on my thigh as he opens the gate through an app on his phone with his opposite hand, refusing to stop touching me for even the briefest of seconds. Once the Uber driver parks out front, Paxton opens the door and guides me outside. Instead of leading me to the front door, he tilts his head and guides me around the side until a candlelit dinner comes into view.

"What do you think?" he asks.

"I think you really want to get laid tonight," I tease.

He pulls one of the chairs out for me, and once I'm seated, reaches for two of the silver covers hiding tonight's meal. Lifting them, he reveals a tray of cold lobster rolls and another of hot ones. "I didn't know if you preferred the buttered or mayo version, so I had both flown in."

My gaze flicks up to him, caught between wanting to hug him or kiss him or just break down and cry. "What did you say?"

"I said, I didn't know if you preferred the buttered or mayo version, so I had both flown in."

"Pax," I whisper.

"I was going to fly us to Maine, so you could order for yourself, but…"

"But because you kind of had to bail me out of jail, you figured this was a solid backup?" I finish for him.

Setting the cover on the edge of the table, he squeezes the back of his neck, looking shy. "If we're being technical, I didn't actually bail you out 'cause you were never arrested, but—"

I grab the collar of his undershirt and tug him toward me, kissing the shit out of him. Thankfully, he doesn't put up a fight and joins in immediately, swallowing my thanks without missing a beat. When I finally let him go, he stands to his full height, and I give him a watery smile.

"You, Paxton Turner, are something else."

His gaze falls to my lips before he meets my eyes. "Only for you," he murmurs. "Let's eat."

# PAXTON

I't's been two weeks. Two weeks since *I love you* first crossed my mind. Two weeks since I looked down at Tatum in my shirt, the ocean rolling in behind her, the smell of warm, buttery lobster rolls filtering through the air, and I knew she was it for me. Two weeks since Tatum kissed me, pouring every unspoken feeling into it until I nearly fell on my ass and proposed right then and there.

Two weeks of knowing she isn't ready for that step—or the dozen before it—and if I'm not careful, she'll run away. But I wouldn't change these two weeks for the world, even if I'm forcing myself to take things slow. To let her set the pace.

I've always chosen the hard route. Maybe it's because my dad left. Maybe it's because of Rafe or my mom. But I've never shied away from the heavy shit, and even though Tatum's yet to even fully commit to what she knows I want, she's letting me in. Slowly. And I refuse to take any minute baby step for granted.

Tonight, we're at her place, despite her reminding me that my place is bigger and more private. I told her I don't care. I want to be in her space, too. I figure the more time I spend infiltrating her life, the less likely she is to want to push me out of it.

As Tatum invites me inside, I rock back on my heels, taking it all in. I've only been here once or twice, but the studio apartment is nice. Small, but nice. It kind of reminds me of my childhood home. If there was more trash on the counters and it smelled like my mom's cigarette smoke.

It feels more like Rory than Tatum, though. I glance at Rory's perfectly made bed and the mess of sheets covering Tatum's. The comparison makes me smile.

"Make yourself at home," she announces. "I need to go to the bathroom, but I'll be right back, then we can pick a show or whatever."

"Sounds good. I'll be here," I return when my phone rings. As I pull it out of my pocket, Tatum disappears into the bathroom, and I answer the call. "Hello?"

"You know, when we mentioned entertaining the paparazzi, having nude photos leaked and an arrest connected to you wasn't exactly what we had in mind," Dodger mutters.

With a low laugh, I walk around the room, perusing the photos hanging on the wall. "Isn't this old news at this point?"

"Maybe for you, but they just posted the article, and Mindy's pissed," he adds, mentioning the head of our PR firm.

"Sorry."

"Yeah, whatever." The amusement in his voice fades, replaced with concern. "She okay?"

"Yeah, man. Tatum's good. Like I said, this is old news."

"Good. Mindy asked if you'd give her a call, though. Just to make sure she's in the loop."

As I collapse onto Tatum's bed, something hits the ground

with a quiet thump. I look over the edge, finding a worn notebook. "Sure thing. I, uh, I gotta go. I'll talk to you later."

"See ya, man."

I hang up the call and reach for the open notebook so I can put it back on the bed. When my attention catches on the name Archer written in swirly, girlish handwriting, my adrenaline spikes.

*What the...?*

Before I can stop myself, I begin scanning the words on the page. It's a letter. A letter to Archer. How old is this? It must be new, considering it was opened to this page. Unless Tatum was rereading it, but why would she? Shoving my questions aside, I focus on the words, my heart thumping faster and faster with every line.

*Hey, Archer.*
*I miss you.*

*Shit.*

*I miss you a lot, just like always. But a little less today. And more. Which is strange, you know? How can someone miss someone more and less than usual? It's almost like...I miss you more because I catch myself not thinking about you and that feels...wrong. But also kind of good, which makes me feel guilty. Surprise, surprise. And round and round I go. It's confusing and annoying and distracting.*
*I don't know.*

*I kind of met someone.*

My breath catches, and I reread the sentence. She met someone. *Me.* She's writing about me? Talking about me with him? The realization hits harder than a blow with a baseball bat, and my fingers dig into the worn pages.

*And I kind of like him, too. I also kind of hate him because I think he's the culprit behind my whole missing you conundrum.*

Fuck, Birthday Girl. I would hate me, too.

*Is that weird? It feels weird. Lots of things feel weird. Kissing him doesn't, though. Feeling guilty afterward does. I know I don't owe you anything. But choosing to forget you? Choosing to be happy and to focus on my...whatever...with someone who isn't you? It's like a sore tooth. You know what I mean? Like, I can't help but pick at it. Add pressure to see if it still hurts or if the initial pain is going away. Maybe it's why I'm writing you. To see if it still hurts. Spoiler alert: it does.*

"What are you doing?" a soft voice whispers.

I snap the journal closed, my neck practically spraining as I look up to find Tatum staring at me.

She looks...she looks fucking perfect. A pair of boyshorts

play peekaboo beneath an IndieCent Vows hoodie. It's the same one I caught her in when I showed up after the naked photo leak. Her long legs look like they go on for miles. But her eyes? They're guarded and unsure, which I'm not sure is any better than the daggers I expected.

*Fuck. What the hell was I doing?*

Guilt stabs between my ribcage. I set the journal on the edge of her bed, standing slowly. "Tate—"

She raises her hand. "Stop."

"Tatum—"

"I said, stop," she repeats.

My stomach clenches, and I fight the urge to rush toward her. To pull her close and to apologize and to do anything I can to erase the haunted look in her eyes and the hurt I know is there. But I don't. Instead I stand there. Helpless.

"Tatum," I murmur. My tone is softer now as I clench my hands at my sides to keep from reaching for her.

"Answer my question." She looks...numb. Her throat constricts on a swallow before she repeats, "What are you doing?"

My attention falls to the worn black notebook. "Invading your privacy," I answer. "And betraying your trust."

I'm not sure what else she was expecting me to say, but her brows raise. "Well, at least you're honest." She folds her arms. Not angrily. More in an attempt to keep her from falling apart. It only kills me more. "Want to tell me why?" she asks.

"It was an accident." I scrub my hand over my face. "I know you don't believe me, but it's the truth."

"We've already established you're not a liar." She sucks her lip into her mouth, but I don't miss the way it trembles before her attention falls on the journal. "What did you..." Her fingernails dig into the fabric of the hoodie covering her arms as she shifts back on her heels. "What did you read?"

*Fuck.*

She looks petrified. Like she's seen a ghost. I wipe my hands along my jeans, caught between a rock and a hard place. I want to fix this. I need to fix this. But how? What do I say? How do I tell her that I impulsively, and a hundred percent accidentally, stole a piece of her. A piece she may or may not have been willing to give. Scratch that. A piece she *wasn't* willing to give. If she was, she would've told me herself. Instead, I took the opportunity from her, and she'll never get it back.

*How do I fix this?!*

"I, uh," I take a slow step toward her, anxious to fix this. To erase the tension in her body. The fear and unease radiating from her. "I read about a girl in love."

Something flashes in her eyes, but she doesn't look at me, choosing to stare at the notebook instead. "I told you I was taken."

"I know," I rasp. "I'm sorry."

Her eyes snap to mine. "For getting caught?"

"For invading your privacy and betraying your trust despite it being an accident."

A sheen hits her pretty gaze as she forces a smile, holding my stare and breaking my heart in the process. "You're, uh, don't mention it." She lifts a shoulder, her sad, broken smile never moving, while looking more guarded than I've ever seen. "And I mean that literally," she adds.

Forcing my movements to stay slow and controlled, I move toward her, one step at a time. I want to run. I want to tug her into me and never let go. But the same fear as before —the fear I've been carrying since the moment she broke down in my bathroom all those nights ago—holds me back, so I keep my pace in check. When I reach her, I lift my hands, leaving an inch of space between her and my touch as I inspect her expression, searching for any clue or hint telling me she wants me to stop. Surprisingly, I don't find it. The realization hits harder than I expect, and I cup her face. Carefully. Slowly. Hell, it's barely a touch, but it's enough. Enough to give me hope. That I didn't fuck this up beyond repair. That she's still here. Still willing to talk this out. To let me fix this.

"Tatum, I'm sorry," I rasp.

She doesn't look at me, choosing to focus on the logo printed across my T-shirt instead. "You already mentioned that."

"About Archer," I clarify. "I can be sorry for more than one thing."

"You already mentioned being sorry about Archer, too, remember?"

"The night you stayed over." I nod. "I'm sorry."

Her shoulders sag. "What for this time?"

"For making you feel guilty."

She rolls her watery eyes, choosing to stare at my chin instead of meeting my eyes, but it's closer to the target, so I count it as a win. For now. Even though it kills me.

"Who says I was writing about you?" she whispers.

A low, sad laugh escapes me, and I pull her into a hug, gently caressing her back as I rest my cheek against the top of her head. "You're right. No need to make my head any bigger."

With a quiet sniffle, she reaches for the hem of my shirt at the base of my spine. "Exactly."

"Do you forgive me?" I murmur. As the words slip out of me, I swear my heart fucking stalls, and so do my lungs. Because if she says no. If she holds this against me. I don't know what I'll do.

*Please don't hold this against me, Birthday Girl.*

"Forgive you for having a big head or for reading my journal?" she whispers.

"Both."

Letting out a quiet, shuddered sigh, she pulls away and peeks up at me. "Yeah. Yeah, I think I do."

My spine curves as I kiss her softly, careful not to push her if she isn't ready for physical intimacy after our first... whatever this is. "You look beautiful," I tell her.

"I know." She smiles, and even though it's forced, it's enough of a glimpse of the girl I've fallen for that the vice around my chest eases, letting me breathe easier. "But it's nice hearing you agree with me."

I chuckle and shake my head, dragging my hands along the hoodie once more before tangling our fingers together. "And you say I'm the one with the big head. Come on, Birthday Girl. Let's watch a show."

It's been a week since Pax found my journal. I never thought it would see the light of day. Having it see the light of day by the guy you're talking about in said journal? That was an entirely new mindfuck, but I survived it.

He didn't mention it afterward, and I'm grateful. Even so, there's something comforting about…about not being alone anymore. That journal contains my deepest, darkest secrets. And even though I know he didn't have enough time to dive into every page, knowing he had time to dive into at least one and still stick around is cathartic, almost. Like maybe I'm enough, broken pieces and all.

Or maybe I'm simply feeling particularly sentimental since I haven't seen him recently. Pax has been missing since Tuesday. And even though I've been elbow deep in cleaning houses—Pax's included—to stay busy, it's been strange. Not having him around. I've missed it—missed him—more than I've even wanted to acknowledge, if I'm being completely honest. Add in the reason for his absence, and I'm a mess.

Who volunteers for the Make-A-Wish Foundation, anyway? Paxton Six, that's who.

Shoving the reminder of all things Pax aside, I watch Rory in the kitchen as she finishes zipping her backpack. "You sure you have to go to the library?" I ask.

Rory nods and slides it over her shoulder. "Yeah, sorry. Pretty sure this semester is going to kill me, but you can come with me if you want."

"And be bored out of my mind?" I shake my head. "You know I love you, but no one can make me do that."

She laughs. "Well, all right, then. You good hanging out here by yourself? I can always leave Hades if you—"

"I'm good," I reply, trying not to look desperate. "Besides, Hades likes to throw off my groove anyway. I'll just stay here, sneak into your ice cream, maybe watch a movie or two, it'll be—"

My phone buzzes, and I look at the screen, finding a message from Pax. My stupid heart skips a beat. I roll my eyes out of principle. Seriously? Come on, heart. You know better than this even if he is kind of perfect.

Sliding my thumb across the screen, I open his message and melt a little more into the cushions on my bed.

PAX

Hey, Birthday Girl.

ME

Why hello, Mr. Security.

PAX

Missing you.

"There's that smile again," Rory notes.

Feeling like I got caught with my hand in the proverbial cookie jar, I flip my phone facedown in my lap, jerking my head toward my best friend. "What smile?"

She grins. "That one. I like to call it the Paxton effect."

I shake my head. "Nerd."

"You know you love it." She snaps Hades' leash onto his collar. "By the way, can you thank him for me?"

"For what?"

"For making me feel less guilty about ditching you tonight. Make sure you lock up when you leave."

"Who says I'm leaving?" I counter as she heads toward the door.

"Aw, you're cute." Grasping the handle, she twists it and opens the front door. "Love you!"

I bite my lip to keep from arguing with her when we both know she might be onto something. Instead, I reply, "Love you!" as the front door closes behind her.

Satisfied I'm alone, I unlock my phone again, finding another text from Pax.

PAX

This is the part where you say you miss me, too.

ME

Do I?

PAX

Shit, I hope so.

My mouth lifts.

ME

Miss you, too.

PAX

Good or else this would be really awkward.

*Knock, knock.*

My head snaps toward the front door.

Is he really here?

Unfolding myself from my bed, I pad toward the entrance and rise onto my tiptoes to peek through the peephole.

There he is. Chocolate shakes in hand.

Unlocking the door, I lean against the doorjamb, saying, "What are you doing here? I thought you weren't getting in until tomorrow."

"Changed my flight." His gaze slides down my body, dancing with mirth. "I like your outfit."

After a quick glance at my body, I grimace. "It's a coincidence."

"Sure, it is."

I tug on the hem of the IndieCent Vows hoodie I purchased online a few years ago and clear my throat. "So?"

"So…" He moves forward, and my nostrils fill with the familiar scent of his cologne, making my mouth water.

I don't know how he does it. How he can make me want him like this. Physically. Emotionally. I wasn't kidding when I said I missed him. I missed him a lot. And being near him again? It's like a drug. One I'm too weak to stay away from.

Maybe it's time for a new note.

The thought flutters through me before I have a chance to stop it, leaving me a little anxious, but also at peace because if I know anything about the man in front of me? He's worth it all.

"So, am I allowed to come in or are you going to keep eye fucking me in the hallway?" he asks.

With a smile, I open the door the rest of the way and reach for one of the shakes. As he steps over the threshold, I scoop a giant bite of icy, creamy, heaven-sent deliciousness into my mouth, then walk toward my bed. He follows, closing the door behind him and leaning against it, his gaze never leaving me.

"So I take it you're happy to see me?"

"I mean, you did bring me a chocolate shake, so…"

His smirk widens. "Glad I'm good for some—" His phone rings, cutting him off, and he takes it out of his pocket.

"Who is it?" I ask.

Without looking up at me, he mutters, "Roman."

"Are you going to answer it?"

His head bobs slowly, and he lifts his cell to his ear. "Hello?"

*Pause.*

"Hey, man. What's up?" Pax asks.

*Pause.*

"What do you mean, change of plans?"

I wait, more curious than I'd like to admit.

He sighs. "Yeah, I know the place."

*Pause.*

"Tonight?" Pax asks.

*Pause.*

Pax's gaze connects with mine, and he sighs again. "Yeah, I know you told me these things move quick, but I didn't think—"

Roman must cut him off because his molars grind, and he shifts his cell to his opposite ear. "Yeah. Yeah, I'll be there. See you then."

The call goes dead, and Pax looks down at me again, finding my attention solely on him. He doesn't seem too frustrated, only caught off-guard, maybe? Honestly, I'm not sure.

Licking some of the excess shake from my spoon, I ask, "Everything okay?"

"Yeah." He continues his stare and clicks his tongue against the roof of his mouth. "It seems there's a…change of plans."

"I heard." I shovel another bite into my mouth. "Does this mean you're leaving?"

"Yeah, the, uh, the fight's tonight."

"Like the underground, shady AF fight?" I ask. "*That* fight?"

His mouth lifts. "That's the one."

"Oh." I pause, attempting to hide my disappointment. "Okay. Well, good luck, I guess? Will you at least let me know how it goes or whatever?"

"You could always come with me," he suggests.

"Come with you?"

"Yeah. Although, if you want me to be able to focus tonight, you might want to change." He takes in my bare legs and bites his knuckle like he can hardly keep his hands to himself.

My lower belly heats with the simple look, but I ignore it, challenging, "And why would I need you to focus?"

"So I don't get my ass kicked?"

My spoon hovers an inch from my mouth. "You're serious?"

"You mentioned a raincheck, remember?"

Giving in, I unfold myself from my bed. "Here." I hand him my barely touched shake. "Hold this. I'll be out in ten."

I TAKE MY TIME WITH MY MAKEUP, MAKING SURE IT'S ON POINT before I exit the bathroom. When Pax sees me, his lips part and his eyes trail down my body, taking in my black crop top, low-slung jeans, leather jacket, and cherry-red heels—the same ones he purchased for me.

When his gaze meets mine, a muttered, "Fuck," slips past his lips, and I smile.

"You like?"

"I like a lot." He stands from the edge of my bed and strides toward me. When he reaches me, his hands slide along my waist, pulling me into him. "Maybe a little too much."

"So, it works?" I prod. "For wherever you're taking me? You didn't give me much to go off—"

"Trust me, it works." His attention dips to my cherry-red lips. "It works perfectly."

"Good." My teeth dig into my bottom lip as I fight back a smile. Reaching for his hands around my waist, I unwrap them from me and step back. "Now, where's my shake?"

"Freezer," he answers.

"Perfect. I'll eat the rest later. Let's go."

When we reach his bike parked outside, he slips one of the helmets onto my head, bringing with it a strong shot of deja vu. The memory of all those nights ago at the concert where we first met. Maybe it's the darkness enveloping us. Maybe it's the smell. Or maybe it's me and how much I've changed since we first met. Since I first climbed onto the back of his bike.

I had so many walls back then. So many barriers. So many fears. And now? Now, all I feel is peace, and it's because of the man in front of me.

"Fuck, you look hot," Pax rasps. Gripping the bottom of the helmet, he drags me into him and steals a kiss through the gap from the open visor. And even though it's quick, my toes curl in my heels, and my knees go weak before he pulls away and snaps the screen closed.

I'm not sure how long we drive, but by the time we pull off the main road, my butt feels like it's being poked with pins and needles, and any glimpse of the ocean is long behind us. Is this The Drift? Is this where Pax grew up? He's told me things here and there, but we've never visited. I've never asked him to take me here. Not unless he was ready. And even though I know one of the main reasons we're making this visit is because Roman set up a fight, Paxton didn't have to invite me to tag along. He didn't have to open that door. The reminder makes me feel like I'm being wrapped in my favorite blanket, and I squeeze his waist a little tighter in silent thanks. That he trusts me. That he wants me here. In his life.

A few minutes later, we pull off the road into a large parking lot filled to the brim. Half the spots are lined with expensive cars. The other half is brimming with motorcycles like the one I'm on. Interesting. Paxton made it sound like there wasn't a lot of money in The Drift. This parking lot proves otherwise. Bright muscle cars, exotic black luxury vehicles, suped-up bikes. They're peppered around the lot, making me feel like I stepped into a James Bond movie.

Seriously. What is this place?

Pax pulls into an empty spot, then cuts the engine as I stare up at the old industrial building. After he climbs off the motorcycle, Pax lifts my helmet, undoing the strap beneath my chin. I kind of like how he takes care of me like this. Without a request. Without a suggestion. Like he's so aware of my needs, he can anticipate them before I even recognize them myself.

Oof. That's a little scary, isn't it? Or at least, it should be. If I'm being honest, a lot of scary things have seemed less terrifying with Pax around, and I can't decide if I'm getting braver or if Pax is the culprit behind the change.

I stick a pin in the realization and turn to the cinderblock building. A heavy beat filters from the dimly-lit windows. It also reminds me of the first time we met, when I snuck into Paxton's performance, though this time it's a completely different event, and I'm not sure I'm ready for it.

"You nervous?" I murmur.

"About the fight? Nah, it'll be fine." He tacks on a rueful smile. "Besides, even if I lose, you can take care of me after."

I roll my eyes, attempting to keep my rising—and

completely misplaced—anxiety at bay. "Well, isn't that comforting."

"Don't worry, Birthday Girl. I'll be fine." His hand finds mine. Lifting it into the air, he kisses my knuckles. "Where's your phone?"

I pull it out of my pocket, and he takes it, sliding it into one of the side bags on his bike. As I watch it disappear, I ask, "Why do you need my phone?"

"Phones aren't allowed in the building."

"Why?"

He locks the side bag, offering his hand. "So it can't be used against anyone inside."

"That sounds promising."

"Welcome to The Drift," he quips. "Come on. I don't want to be late."

4 6

# TATUM

P ax's hold is tight as leads me inside, keeping me behind him. The *thump-thump* of my heart quickens with every step as we move toward the heavy metal doors separating us from whatever's inside the building. Well, heavy metal doors and a tall, black man with a shaved head and arms the size of my legs crossed over his burly chest.

"Can I help you?" he asks.

Pretty sure the guy stole Barry White's voice, but there's an intimidating edge hidden beneath the low, smooth timber that is scary as fuck. Feeling out of place, I lean into Pax's side, and he squeezes my hand.

"Tacos," Paxton answers.

The guy nods. "Phones?"

"Left them at my bike."

"I'm sure you did," he replies. "Mind if I pat you down just in case?"

Pat him down? Okay, so they take this stuff seriously. Good to know. The security guard searches Pax for a phone, then crooks his finger at me, motioning for me to step toward him. When I do, he runs the backs of his hands along my torso, then feels my waist and down my legs, confirming I'm not hiding a cell phone anywhere. With an apologetic look, he checks beneath my boobs too, and I quirk my brow. "Is this really necessary?"

"Considering the people inside, yes," he grunts. He drops his hands and bobs his head. Stepping aside, he gives us room to pass, adding, "You're good to go. Have fun."

Once we're out of earshot, I turn to Pax. "Tacos?"

"Ford is obsessed with Mexican food," Paxton answers.

"Who's Ford?"

"One of Judge's nephews," he explains. "Whenever he gets to pick the password, he chooses a Mexican dish."

I chuckle softly. "Okay, but why is that kind of adorable?"

Paxton smirks. "Bet he'd love to hear you call him adorable. Come on."

As we move a little further into the building, I try to keep my jaw from unhinging, but it's kind of hard, considering the atmosphere. Dim lights hang overhead, highlighting the lack of color in the entire establishment. Everyone is dressed in different shades of gray and black, and for once, I'm grateful to have chosen the same so I wouldn't stand out. Not in this crowd. They blend into the cinderblock walls and concrete flooring while the musky smell of weed clings to the air. My nose wrinkles as Paxton tugs me around the crowd circling a round platform in the middle of the large space. Someone's getting their ass kicked in the middle of it. Two shirtless men, their strong bodies on full display, go head-to-head. Or at least, it's what I assume they're supposed to be doing. Instead, the bigger guy is bent at the waist, covering the back of his head with his arms as his opponent wails on the dude like there's no tomorrow. I squint, realizing I've seen the smaller guy before. Well, small is relative. Every inch of his body is corded muscle, but compared to the man who's getting his ass kicked, he's like a tiger compared to a bear. Not that it matters. He's clearly the better fighter, and it shows.

"I've seen that guy before," I tell Pax. "At the bonfire, maybe?"

"Jagger Harden. Another of Judge's nephews."

The ones Rory told me to stay away from. Guess she was onto something.

I nod. "Oh."

"What do you think?"

Nibbling my bottom lip, I watch the fight unfold. Jab. Kick. Knee. Twist. Block. They're both so fast. It's like a blur. The half-naked torsos aren't bad to look at, though. Peeking at Pax, I admit, "I guess I can see the appeal."

"Glad you approve," Pax says with a laugh. He continues tugging me through the crowd as a ref steps between Jagger and the unconscious opponent lying at Jagger's feet. The ref grabs Jagger's hand and lifts it into the air, making the audience's cheers reach a fever pitch that leaves my ears ringing.

"Took you long enough!" someone yells behind us.

I turn to find Roman staring at me.

"You sure you want her here?" he asks.

"She won't be a problem," Paxton promises.

Roman hesitates, analyzing me before giving Pax his attention. "Well, hurry up. You're late."

My brows tug at the center as Paxton lets me go, grabs the collar of his shirt, then tugs it over his head, exposing his back and torso for the crowd to see.

Ooooh, okay. So we're diving right in, I guess. Cool, cool, cool. Yup. That's…that's totally normal. To strip down in the middle of a crowded room with a solid hundred people scattered around. What isn't normal is the way my heart can't decide if it wants to give out or battle a hummingbird's wings.

*You're just anxious. It'll be fine*, I remind myself.

But seriously, why am I freaking out right now? I just saw Jagger beat the shit out of someone and didn't even bat an eye, so what the hell is wrong with me?

"Hey, wanna hold this for me?" he asks, offering me his T-shirt.

Fingertips tingling with panic, I take it, murmuring, "Do you have like a…a warm up period or whatever?"

Paxton rolls his shoulders, swinging his arms back and forth like he's stretching out his muscles and glances at me. "We're a little late, so there isn't time, but it'll be fine."

"Fine. Yeah." I gulp. "Sure."

He frowns. "You okay?"

"Yeah," I lie. "Yeah, totally. I'm…just a little nervous. This is all new."

His brows dip. "You sure?"

"Yeah, yeah I'm sure," I rush out. "Good luck."

He nudges my chin up with his knuckle and kisses me. "I'll be fine."

Fine. Right. I stare at the man in front of me, praying he couldn't feel my quivering bottom lip during our kiss as a strange, almost unrecognizable feeling ignites inside of me.

It's fear.

Okay, I'm familiar with fear. All too familiar with it, if I'm being honest, but not when it comes to something like this. It's a fight. A silly, five-minute fight. The realization makes zero sense. I've done stupid shit most of my life. I've jumped out of airplanes. Slept on park benches. Left with strange men for reckless one-night-stands. And none of them, none of the situations, ever left me with this feeling. This over-whelming sense of dread.

Attempting to keep my emotions in check, I paste on a fake smile as he starts toward the small stage, biting my tongue 'til I taste blood as I fight the urge to call for him. To tell him to stop. To get out of here. To leave with me.

A smile plays at the edge of his mouth before his coffee colored eyes drift to Roman. "Keep an eye on her."

*No, no, no, you don't understand,* I mentally scream, but I can't convince my tongue to work. To form words, let alone an actual sentence.

Instead, I watch as he saunters into the ring like he owns it. And maybe he does. Maybe he'll be fine. I'm sure he'll be fine. This isn't his first rodeo, right? So why do I feel like I'm going to vomit? I'm just nervous for him, that's all. It's completely normal. *I'm* completely normal. There's nothing wrong.

Nothing. Is. Wrong.

The muscles along his back bunch and flex as the referee motions for him to come closer.

He's fine.

*He's fine, he's fine, he's fine.*

"Paaaaxton Six," the referee booms. "Lead guitarist for the billboard-smashing band, IndieCent Voooows!"

Sweat clings to my hairline, and the world starts to spin, my bottom lip quivering like a freaking leaf. It hits out of nowhere. The panic. The fear. The full-blown fucking meltdown threatening to swallow me whole.

*Breathe,* I remind myself. He's fine. He's right…he's right there. And he's fine.

What the fuck is wrong with me?

I don't care what happens to others. It's what I promised myself all those years ago, and it hasn't been an issue with the exception of a select few, including Rory who's more averse to risk than I was to committed relationships before I met Pax. So why do I care? Why is my body being thrust into fight or flight mode when it's only a fight? A simple, stupid fight? My brain gets it, but my other senses? Yup, I'm pretty sure I'm about to have a panic attack. Or puke. Or both. Or—

"Trust me, your boy's gonna be fine," Roman interrupts. His words cut through my inner spiral like a cold knife through butter. It isn't much, but it's enough to keep me from crumbling to the ground. "Stand here," he adds.

His touch is nothing but mechanical as his hand falls to my shoulder and he tugs me closer to him a bit away from the stage.

Stand here. Stand. Here. I can stand here.

I hold on to the order, willing my legs not to give out, no matter how much they feel like Jell-O.

Satisfied, Roman lets me go and folds his arms again, looking as menacing as before when another man takes the stage. Who is this guy? Tiger stripes ink the skin along his back, reaching around his ribs and fading along his front. I'd laugh at the ridiculousness if he didn't look like he could kill me with a single swat of his meaty hand.

But wait. Why would he be joining Pax on the stage unless—

"He's fighting Pax?" I choke out.

"Goes by Killian," Roman informs me. "Don't worry. Pax can take him."

My head shakes back and forth. "You don't know that! He's huge and—"

"He'll be fine, Tate," Roman says, barely casting me a glance. "Your boy might look like he was spoon fed all his life, but he knows how to fight. He's got this." He hesitates. "He better, anyway."

I pale even more. "Why?"

"Because I have two grand on him."

"Two grand?" I squeak. "Are you serious?"

"That's pocket change compared to some of the numbers

we've been dealing with lately. Now, pay attention. Once the ref blows the whistle, the fight starts."

Just like that, the whistle blows, the sound ringing in my ears, and Killian explodes forward, throwing a quick jab-cross-hook. Paxton narrowly dodges and counters with a sharp leg kick that echoes in the run-down warehouse. When it connects with Killian's outer thigh, I flinch back, covering my mouth. Holy shit. Okay, so maybe this isn't so bad. I'm fine. Pax is fine. And I have no reason to freak out.

Everything. Is. Fine.

And also, like, damn. That was kind of hot.

Or at least it would be if I could convince my body to stop freaking out for two seconds so I could appreciate Paxton in all his half-naked glory. How is it that my brain and body can feel so…out of sync like this? Is this normal? It sure as hell doesn't feel like it. Focus. Focus on Pax. On the way he looks. Confident and shirtless and…see? Still hot. Now, if only I wasn't so distracted by the possibility of Pax being on the other end of Killian's fury so I could actually enjoy the view, that'd be great.

"How does it end?" I ask Roman, forcing my feet to stay planted where they are when all I want to do is climb on the stage and drag Paxton off of it. "How do they declare a winner or…whatever?"

"First to surrender loses."

My eyes bulge. "I'm sorry, did you say first to *surrender*?"

"Yeah. Now, pay attention." His meaty hand falls on top of my head, and he turns my face toward the stage like I'm his own personal doll, but I'm not ready to drop the conversation quite yet. Not when Paxton's in the center of the ring, fighting for his life.

I push, "And when you say surrender…"

Roman shrugs. "Tap out or pass out. Those are house rules."

"Tap out or pass out," I repeat. I turn back to the fight, my pulse thumping faster and faster with every passing second. Stay. Calm. "Perfect."

Killian winces from another of Paxton's solid hits but pushes forward, unleashing a flurry of strikes until Paxton is backed up against the edge of the mat. Using his forearms to protect his face, Paxton blocks Killian's fury, then slips under a right hook and lands an underhook, following up with a flying knee attempt that grazes Killian's temple.

"Holy shit," I murmur.

Paxton's fast. And Roman's right. This clearly isn't his first rodeo. Maybe all those bruises were worth earning after all.

The crowd's roar is deafening, but I swear I can still hear Killian's curse as he swings out his leg, sweeping Paxton to the ground.

"Holy shit," I repeat, my stomach plummeting. "This is bad. This is bad. This is bad."

"He'll be fine," Roman promises.

I bounce on the balls of my feet, my own anxiety ratcheting higher with every passing second while the crowd chants around us. The fighters roll on the ground, each fighting for the upper hand, until Killian lands a jab to Paxton's face. His head snaps back, and I cover my mouth, fighting the urge to vomit.

*Fuck. Fuck, fuck, fuck.*

Using raw strength, Paxton rolls out from beneath Killian's grasp and stands up, giving me a perfect view of the welt forming above his left eye. Blood trickles from his eyebrow, but no one even bats an eye. Why is no one batting an eye? Oh, that's right. Because no one's crazy like I am. Chest heaving, Pax winds up for another hit, striking Killian's nose. The crowd gasps, and so do I before Killian counters with a brutal elbow, and Paxton's knees buckle, but he manages to stay up. It isn't enough, though. It isn't enough because in one swift move, Killian flips Paxton into a choke-hold, and my legs buckle.

*No, no, no, no, no.*

Paxton's face turns red, his eyes bulging as he scrambles in Killian's grasp, making my stomach flip in on itself.

"Roman," I seethe, choosing to show him my fury over my crippling fear. Heaven forbid I give someone a glimpse into my mental breakdown or how close I am to losing my shit. "If you don't get in there—"

"Fucking watch," Roman scolds. "Your boy has him right where he wants him."

"Bullshit—"

The rest of my words get lost on my tongue as Paxton lifts Killian and slams him onto the ground, breaking free. Twisting around, Paxton charges forward with a final combination—jab, cross, uppercut. And it's strange. Watching the lights go out. The way Killian's face goes slack and his legs fold beneath him. Paxton's opponent collapses onto the mat, buckling like a soda can as the crowd loses their fucking minds.

Everyone but me. Instead, I simply stand there, my hands at my sides, my vision blurring, my stomach swirling. I feel like I just stepped off the most vomit-inducing rollercoaster. Like I just walked through a serial killer's house. Like I just escaped death. Now, I'm numb. *Empty.* And numb.

Stepping forward, the referee raises Paxton's battered fist into the air, declaring him the winner while I stand on the sideline, reeling.

Pax waves at the crowd, taking a quick bow like he just finished playing a show in Amsterdam before striding toward me like he's on top of the world.

Part of me wants to hit him. To yell and scream at him for making me feel this way. The other part wants to kiss him and pull him close and take away every ounce of pain he must be feeling after a fight like this. It's strange and confusing and I have no idea how to respond or react or… anything at all. I wonder if I would've had this response with someone else. I wonder if I would've had this response if Archer had never died in the first place.

I wonder if I'll be normal—or sane—ever again.

But there's one thing I do know, and it's that I need to get my shit together…now.

"Hey, Birthday Girl," Pax murmurs. His bloody knuckles brush against my chin as he nudges my head up. "What'd you think?"

*Don't freak out.*

I paste on a smile. "I think you owe me another chocolate shake for scaring the shit out of me like that."

"Is that right?"

I smack his chest, forcing my lungs to dispel any pent-up oxygen.

With a laugh, he grabs his discarded T-shirt from me, tucking it into the back of his pants before he hooks his sweaty arm over my shoulder and tugs me into his side. "I believe this is the part where you tell me I did good."

"You scared the crap out of me," I repeat.

"And?"

"And…" *He's okay,* a tiny voice inside my whispers. I hold onto it. The voice. The reminder. The evidence standing in front of me. *He's okay.* "Good job kicking his ass," I add grudgingly.

His smile widens, and he leans down for a kiss, but I'm too overstimulated to reciprocate. No. Now, all I feel is numb. Tingling spreads from my parted lips, down my body, and out to my limbs. He pulls away, a slight furrow in his brow, and a questioning look shining in his gaze before understanding replaces it.

"Fuck, Tate. I'm—"

Rising onto my tiptoes, I hook my arms around his neck and tug him into me, kissing him with every ounce of fear and panic and…relief that he's okay. And he takes it. He takes it all, wrapping his arms around my waist, forcing me against him. His hold is so tight, my ribs scream in protest, but I don't care. I don't care at all. Because this man? This man is okay, and he knows that all I need right now is proof that's true. That he's in front of me. That he's still breathing. That he isn't going anywhere, and fuck if that isn't the scariest thought of all. Because I've never cared if the men I sleep with go anywhere. I've never cared if they vanish into thin air. I've never cared about their well-being or their safety. Not since Arch. And that's the scariest thought of all. Because if something can happen to Arch, then something can happen to Pax, and the idea of something happening to Pax is…it's not okay. It's not okay at all.

*Please don't go anywhere.*

"Pax," someone interrupts.

Pressing his forehead to mine, Pax sighs. "Yeah, Rome?"

"If you're gonna fuck, do it in the back room. We have another fight in five."

Pax nods slowly, his forehead brushing against mine, before he drags his fingers along my arm and takes my hand, refusing to let me go as he tugs me through the throng of people and into a back room.

The warehouse has been abandoned since I was a kid, but I remember it like the back of my hand. Same four walls. Same dusty floor. Same broken windows. It's crowded tonight. More than I thought it would be. I guess Roman did his job and spread the word. Or maybe every fight night is like this. And the shit parked out front? Hell, I can practically smell the money wafting through the air. It mixes with the expensive colognes and perfumes like a rich person's potpourri. Refusing to look for any familiar faces from my previous life or current one, I drag Tatum through the throng of people in search of privacy. A few of them reach out, trying to congratulate me on the win, but I barely look at them. Hell, I can't see anything right now. Not one fucking thing except the fear in Tatum's eyes when I stepped out of the ring and pieced together what the hell was going on.

Choosing one of the rooms a little further away in hopes of it being empty, I twist the handle and push the door open. The hinges creak in protest as I pull Tate with me, closing the door behind us with another squeak from its hinges.

"I'm sorry," Tatum blurts out.

Finding the light switch, I flick it on, then turn on my heel and cock my head. "What?"

"I said, I'm sorry."

"You have no reason to be sorry."

"I lost my shit over something so stupid—"

"It's not stupid," I interrupt. Cupping her face, I drag my thumbs along her cheek bones, committing the feel of her silky skin to memory while fighting my own inner loathing. I can't believe I brought her here. I should've known. Fuck, of course I should've known. That she'd react like this. I mean, I told her. I told her I was gonna fight. That I'd been sparring for weeks. That I used to fight as a teen. And she never cared. Hell, if anything, she told me the idea of it all was hot. I thought she'd like it. She'd like the adrenaline and the ambiance and the people and the energy. But it doesn't matter. Because tonight she wasn't using her head, she was using her heart, and I fucking stomped all over it despite knowing everything she's been through. Running my thumbs along her cheeks, I beg, "Tatum, look at me."

Her eyelids close as the fight seeps out of her. "I feel so stupid."

"Not." I lean in and kiss the tip of her nose, careful to keep my split lip away from her. "Stupid."

"It was only a fight."

"Not." My lips skate across hers in the barest of touches. "Stupid."

Her bottom lip trembling, she breathes out, "I don't know if I can do this."

My body flinches back as I register the weight of her words. The determination. The sheer stubbornness, but more so, the fear. Her fear is driving her, and if anyone knows what it feels like, it's me. "Tatum, don't say that."

"Pax, I'm serious—"

"I fucked up," I growl. "Okay? I fucked up. *Me.*" The word lodges in my throat, making it hard for me to breathe, let alone say something to ease the fear emanating from the girl in front of me. I need to fix this. To apologize. To unload the crippling pain she's suffocating from. The problem is, I don't know *how.* "I know your past, and I still brought you here." I keep holding her face, willing her to look at me. "This is on me. Okay, Birthday Girl? It's all on me."

"Don't you get it?" she whispers. Reaching up, she grabs my wrists and slowly forces me to lower my hands from cradling her cheeks. "It *was* me. I'm the problem. The one who's fucked up." A pathetic whimper slips out of her. "You were fighting, which I knew you were going to do, by the way, and honestly, it was hot as hell. I know that." She forces a smile, but it's wobbly at best. "Shit, Pax. You looked really hot up there. All rippling muscles, and…" She pulls her lip into her mouth, biting on the plump flesh as her hands roam my pecs and abdomen. "And I'm extremely attracted to you, but…instead of enjoying it like any normal red-blooded woman would, I freaked." She sniffs. "I completely freaked, Pax, and what is wrong with me, you know?"

"Come here." I grab her face again, desperate to feel her, to take away her pain, to fix this. When her back hits the door with a tiny thump, I order, "Tell this pretty little brain to shut the hell up, okay?" I kiss her forehead, hoping it'll soften my demand. "I'm the one who messed up. I'm the one who should've known this would trigger you. It's on me, not you."

"Don't you get it?" her voice cracks as she peeks up at me, tears clinging to her long, thick lashes. "You shouldn't have to worry about triggering me. No one should have to worry about triggering anyone. It's juvenile and stupid—"

"Not. Stupid," I seethe. "Stop belittling yourself or your feelings. Do you understand me?"

Her head dips in the smallest of nods. But her eyes? They're like steel, gleaming with a familiar dose of stubbornness I both love and hate. Especially in this moment.

"Pretty little liar," I muse, tucking her hair behind her ear. "You don't believe me."

"Just stating the facts, Pax."

Facts.

It's a load of bullshit, but how do I convince her of it? How do I make her see how much she means to me and that her feelings? They don't have to be a bad thing. They don't have to hold her back or keep her from me. Hell, nothing can keep her from me. Not a single fucking thing.

"Close your eyes," I order.

"Pax…"

"Close them."

Her eyelids flutter closed, shocking the hell out of me, while also proving how desperate she is to let go, even if she won't admit it to herself. Untucking the T-shirt from the waistband of my pants, I grip the cotton between my teeth and rip a strip of fabric from it. What's left of my shirt falls at our feet as I slowly tie the makeshift blindfold around Tatum's head, careful not to catch any of her hair in the knot.

She's trembling. Her breathing is shallow. Her lips are parted. The combination proves her fear is still driving her. Still keeping her from me. And even though I know it's only a physical response made to keep her safe, I need it to stop. Now.

"Pax," she whispers, "what are you—"

"Careful or I'll gag you, too." Bending forward, I kiss her softly, savoring the sting from my busted lip. "And I'd really hate losing access to this pretty mouth, Birthday Girl."

Her throat tightens on a swallow, but she stays quiet, believing my threat isn't empty. Then again, I guess it isn't. I do love having access to this pretty mouth, but right now, this isn't about me. This is about her. Her fear. Her past. Her future. And fuck, I want her future to include me. Gently, I reach for her hands, keeping my movements slow as I guide them to my face. "Do you feel this?"

Her hands tremble as she runs her fingers along my jaw and finds the edge of my mouth. "Yes," she whispers.

Nibbling on the edge of her finger, I murmur, "This mouth is yours." I smile. "This mouth gave up smoking for you."

She sucks her bottom lip between her teeth and bites down, but she doesn't utter a single word.

Guiding her hands lower, I let her linger on my biceps. "These muscles? They're here to protect you."

She continues her path down my body, finding the edge of my pants before moving to my semi-hard dick. When her palm brushes against it, my hips shift forward, and I bite back my groan. "This cock?" She smiles. "This is to give you pleasure. To make you scream my name. And to give you babies, if you ever ask for them." I grasp her wrist and bring it up, over my abs and along my bruised side to my pounding chest. "And do you feel this, Tatum?"

She shies away, but I force her to stay where she is, letting the steady *thump-thump* seep into her palm as I cover her hand with mine. "This heart is yours."

"Pax," she breathes.

"Listen to me," I order. "This heart is yours, and even though I'd give anything to protect it from being hurt or compromised, all because I know how it would affect you, that isn't in my power." I grasp her fingers and bring them to my mouth. "But it isn't in yours, either."

Her lips quiver, a shaky breath slipping past them and hitting my face harder than any punch my opponent could've thrown tonight. This girl. This fucking girl. She holds all the cards. Owns every piece of me. If only she'd take them.

"I know it's scary, Birthday Girl," I rasp. "I know opening yourself up again after losing someone you love is scary. But the past few weeks have been the best in my life. And I'm really hoping you'll let me give this heart to you despite knowing you can't control the future." A low chuckle rumbles through my chest. "Let's be honest, if you could, there's no way you would've let me run into you again after all these years. But isn't that the beauty of fate? That sometimes it delivers exactly what we need when we least expect it?"

"Pax," she breathes out with the same weak bravado as before I dragged her in here. Before I pushed her against the door and blindfolded her in hopes of swaying her stubborn resolve. "I want you, okay? I want you so much, but I can't do it again. I can't."

I curl in closer to her, anxious to carry the weight of her pain, while knowing I can't. I can't do anything but love her and be by her side and promise I'll do everything in my power—for the rest of my life—to take care of her and be the man she needs me to be, if only she'll accept it. "I fucking love you, Birthday Girl."

Her head rolls forward with her shoulders, making her look small and fragile. "Don't say that."

"I love you, Tatum Taylor. I love every fucking inch of you. I love your soul. Your body. Your sweet side. Your bitchy side." My mouth lifts. "I love when you're tired. When you're drunk. When you're snippy and happy and everything in between."

"Pax," she whispers.

Letting go of her hands, I touch beneath her chin, and with the lightest of pressure, lift her head before leaning down and kissing her. It's soft. Gentle. But so fucking charged, I can feel it in my bones. It's a promise. A prayer. She raises her hands and grabs my wrists as I cup her cheeks again, holding her exactly where I want her. My mouth moves over hers, and I drag my tongue along the seam of her lips, tasting her tears. The slight tang of salt wrecks me, and I squeeze my eyes shut as she opens her mouth wider, letting me in.

My cock strains between us as she sucks on my tongue, well-aware of how close I am to stripping her down and marking every inch of her if it'll convince her to stay. To admit she loves me, too, even if it's scary. Slowly, my hands trail down her cheeks, then lower. I grab her throat to keep her in place, refusing to let her walk away when I know there's a tiny voice inside her head begging her to do exactly that. When my other hand grazes the outside of her breast, I palm her fully, savoring the feel of her pebbled nipple against my palm. She gasps as I take my feel, massaging her through the thin fabric of her top. My knuckles are bloodied and bruised, and the kiss makes my busted lip throb in discomfort, but I can't find it in me to care. Not about anything but the girl in front of me.

"Please," she whispers. "Please. I need you."

I kiss her harder, swallowing her plea while undoing the top button of her jeans and shoving them down her body and onto the floor. When she realizes I have every intention of giving her exactly what she wants, she blindly reaches for my pants and tugs them off me. The head of my erection bobs against her stomach, pulling a soft smile from Tatum's lips. And I like it. That she knows what she does to me. That she likes what she does to me. The reminder proves exactly how many cards she holds when it comes to our relationship, and I wouldn't trade it for the world. Slowly, she strokes my length from base to tip, and my balls tighten with need.

"Fuck, Birthday Girl," I growl.

Gathering my precum against her palm, she squeezes me, well-aware of exactly what she's doing and how close I am to the edge, despite not even being inside her. Grabbing her wrist, I shove her hand above her head, adding her second until she's helpless and squirming. Without a word, I reach for her thigh, and she jumps, trusting I'll catch her. Once her legs are wrapped around my waist, I press her spine to the door again.

"Keep your hands up," I order.

She nods, the blindfold still in place.

With both hands on her hips, I pull back slightly until the tip of my cock finds her wet slit. Then, I push inside her tight little body, one inch at a time, as her mouth opens on a moan. Once I'm fully seated, I press my forehead to hers, sharing her air while giving her a minute to adjust to the intrusion.

"I love you, Birthday Girl," I growl. "I love your tenacity. Your grit. I love your body. Your soul."

"If you're trying to make me come with your words alone, you're pretty good at it," she whispers. "Now, if I could just convince you to keep moving, that'd be great."

I smile and nip at her mouth. "I love your sass, too. Even when you're a pain in the ass. And I don't want you to say it back. Not until you're ready. But I need you to know I love you. I'll always love you. From now to forever." Burrowing my head in the crook of her neck, I pull out, then push in again, desperate to feel her let me in physically after the mind-fuck we just endured. Her wet heat surrounds me and my eyes roll back in my head. She feels so good. Too fucking good. "Tatum, a condom," I groan. "Shit—"

"I have an IUD." Her hands find my shoulders. "Don't you dare stop." I thrust into her again, this time even harder, and she whimpers. "Keep going. Please keep going."

So, I do. As her nipples rub against my chest, my hips piston back and forth, driving us both toward oblivion. Her fingernails claw against my bare shoulders and her body shakes with every ounce of friction until I'm convinced I could do this forever. Maybe not last, she feels too fucking good, but being buried inside her like this? Feel her like this? Taste her like this? Touch her like this? It makes all the shit I've been through worth it. Everything. Every single thing. Because it led me to her.

Sweat breaks out along my skin as I suck on her neck, my balls aching with need. "Tell me you're close," I order.

"I'm close. I'm really close. I'm—shit." The word breaks into a whimper as her body squeezes around me, and I spill inside of her, determined to fall over the edge right along with her. Muscles tightening, tingles spreading, cock jerking. I fall apart and ride the high, already craving the next time I can be inside her so we can do this all over again. As she drops her head back toward the ceiling, I trail kisses along her exposed throat, paying special attention to the tiny bruise I gifted her with. But fuck, if it isn't hot.

"Can I take off my blindfold now?" she whispers.

With a smirk, I reach up and tug the scrap of cloth off, dropping it to the ground. She blinks in an attempt to let her eyes adjust as I cup her cheek and force her to look at me.

When our gazes connect, I repeat, "I love you. Just so we're clear."

Her mouth lifts into the smallest of smiles. "I believe you." When it falls, she adds, "And that's why this is so scary."

## 48

## PAXTON

The wind is cool against my bare chest as I drive Tatum home. Call me a sucker, but I didn't think to pack a second shirt on the off-chance I ripped my first one apart. Even so, I'm grateful for it. The contrast of cool air to my heated skin and my heavy thoughts as Tatum clings to me on the back of my bike. The feel of her pressed against me is the only thing keeping me from spiraling. From tossing her over my shoulder and dragging her back to my place without giving a shit about her boundaries or her needs.

Maybe that's the problem. Because I do care. Even if it kills me. Even if my boundaries and needs don't align with hers. Like right now. She'll always come first. Always.

We take the long way home, but even then, there's only so much procrastinating I can do before I reach Tatum's street. After we pull up to the curb, I cut the engine, climbing off my bike and slipping off my helmet. Reaching for Tate, I undo the strap beneath her chin, then set her helmet on the grass as she sits motionless. Numb. Staring into the distance. A shell of a person. Seems her afterglow has worn off since we left, and now she's so lost in her head, she can't even look at me. I hate that I'm the one to do this to her. To push her into this state, even if it's irrational on her part and accidental on mine. It doesn't matter, and sure as shit doesn't dissipate the fog she's lost in.

"Hey," I murmur.

Her eyes cut to mine and she forces a smile. "Hey."

I want to ask if she's all right, but I'm not stupid. Of course, she isn't all right. She's still shaken. Scared. Of her feelings for me and what they could mean if she decides to accept them instead of pushing me away.

*Please don't push me away.*

Threading my fingers through her hair, I kiss her forehead and breathe in her scent, letting the sharp citrus smell ground me. "We're gonna be okay."

Her head bobs in a jerky, mechanical nod. "I should go inside."

"Let me walk you up." Offering my hand, I help her off my bike, and we take the stairs to the second floor without a word. When we reach her welcome mat, I ask, "Is Rory home?"

Forehead wrinkling, she glances at front door. "I don't, uh, I don't know."

"I'm not gonna leave you here alone."

"I'll be okay, Pax." But instead of reaching for the handle like I expect, she moves closer, pressing her cold fingertips to my bare stomach. My abs clench on reflex, and her lips curve up before she brushes her hand along a bruised rib and a hiss of pain slips past my gritted teeth.

Her smile falls, and she starts to pull her hands away. "Shit, I'm sorry—"

I snatch her wrist, preventing her from pulling away entirely. "You're good, Birthday Girl."

"I don't wanna hurt you," she whispers.

*Then invite me inside*, I want to push, but I bite my tongue, forcing the words to stay locked up tight even if it kills me.

"Not gonna hurt me," I murmur. Bringing her hand to my mouth, I kiss her knuckles and let her go. "I love you."

Something flashes in her eyes before she looks down at my bare chest, unable to hold my gaze. "Thanks for inviting me tonight."

I scoff. "Don't mention it. And I mean that literally," I add, tossing her own words back at her from when I found her letters to Archer not so long ago. I wonder if she'll write about tonight. If she'll tell him what she's too scared to tell me. The thought leaves me hollow.

Balancing on her tiptoes, Tatum skates her lips across my cheek. "Goodnight, Pax."

As she moves to step away, I grab her wrist again, keeping her close. "We're not done," I warn. "I'm letting you walk in this apartment without me because I know you need a minute to get your head on straight, but this is *not* me letting you go, and this sure as shit isn't me giving you up. We clear?"

Her eyes turn glassy as she nods again. "Yeah." She swallows. "Yeah, I just need a minute."

"Tate."

Weakly, she tugs out of my grasp and unlocks her front door, killing me more and more with every passing second.

"Tate," I beg.

"We'll be okay," she promises, then disappears inside, closing the door behind her with a quiet click.

Scrubbing my hand over my face, I stare at Tatum's front door for a solid minute before forcing myself to walk away. She'll be okay. We'll be okay. She said it herself, and even if she hadn't, I'd still fucking know it, despite tonight being a bitch. Why? Because Tatum's it for me. I know it, and deep down, I think she knows it, too. That's why she's scared.

As I make my way back to my bike, my phone rings. My heart pounds faster, and I pull it out, hoping to see Tatum's name, but only Dodger's shines back at me.

*Why's he calling me?*

I could send it to voicemail. I probably should, considering where my head is. Instead, I answer it. "Hey, what do you need?"

"Hello to you, too," Dodger returns. "I'm calling to check in. How'd the fight go?"

I dig my fingers into my sore neck as I replay the night, unsure what to say. "I won," I admit.

"Congrats. I knew you would."

"Yeah, thanks."

"So, if you won, why do you sound like shit?" he pushes.

I pinch the bridge of my nose and exhale. "I took Tate to the fight, and—"

"You what?" he shouts.

Pulling my cell away from my ear, I look at the screen, then slowly bring it back to my ear. "I said, I took Tate to the fight, and—"

"Why the fuck would you do that?"

"Dodge, calm down," I order.

"I thought you said you were trying to take care of her, not feed her to the fucking sharks."

"What's your problem?" I snap. "I'm not in the mood to be yelled at, all right?"

"Why'd you bring Tatum to the fight?" he demands.

"Because she wanted to come?" I offer, well-aware the invitation was my first mistake of the evening, though I'm too bitter to rehash it with Dodge, considering he clearly feels like being an asshole tonight.

"I don't give a shit if she wanted to come," he argues, proving my assessment is on point. "These events are dangerous. You know that. How could you be so fucking careless?"

I grind my teeth, bend down, pick Tatum's helmet up, and place it in the saddlebag, so I can get out of here as soon as I'm finished with this conversation. "What's going on?" I push. "What aren't you saying?"

*Silence.*

I shift my cell to my opposite ear, trying to read between the lines no matter how little information he's giving me right now. "Dodge, it was one fight with a bunch of college students and locals."

"Yeah, locals from The Drift," he reminds me.

This again? Pretty sure if I had the power to crawl through the phone and shove him, I'd do it. "You forget I'm one of them," I growl.

"Nah. If I'd forgotten, I wouldn't have let you fight at all."

"Let me?" I scoff.

"You know what I mean." His silence blares through the phone, leaving me uneasy. "Listen, it isn't only the locals I'm worried about."

"What are you saying?"

"If it was only locals, do you really think Judge would be here?" Dodge demands. "That I would be here?"

"What are you saying?" I repeat. "Stop talking in riddles, and tell me what the fuck is going on."

"You really wanna know how Rudy died?" Dodger seethes. "He died because Judge messed with the wrong people at one of these fucked-up gatherings. They lost a shit-ton of money, thought Judge played them, and killed his best friend for it, all right? That's why Judge pulled the plug on these events. It's why they should've stayed dead in the first place. You understand?"

I don't. I don't understand at all. What the hell is Dodger

talking about? Leaning against my bike, I point out, "Rudy died from a drug overdose."

"Did he?" Dodger challenges.

And fuck me, I don't know. I don't know how he died. I don't know anything. Not anymore. Not after the inflection in Dodger's voice, hinting otherwise. Why would they lie?

Dropping my head toward the night sky, I ask, "Why are you telling me this now?"

"Because I need you to understand. And I need you and Tatum to be safe."

I look up at Tatum's building, catching her silhouette in the window. "We're safe."

"Good." He pauses. "'Cause I'm pretty sure you don't wanna get caught up in this."

He's right. I don't. Not before I answered this call, and sure as hell not after. "I gotta go."

"Me, too. We'll talk later, yeah?"

"Yeah." My hands shake as I hang up the phone, dialing Roman.

He answers on the third ring.

"Hey, man," Roman greets me. "I was gonna call you in the morning."

"Oh?"

"Yeah, you did good tonight."

I did good tonight? That's what he wants to talk about? Considering the bombshell Dodger threw at me on top of Tatum's meltdown, my fight is the last thing on my mind. Hell, if it wasn't for the stitch in my side and my swollen lip, I'd say it happened a week ago. Funny. How time moves so slowly yet so fuckin' fast sometimes.

"Any chance you want in on another one?" Roman continues. "Ford wants to set up a drag race, then Hawke has a few ideas we're gonna feel out, but I'm thinking a couple months from now, we'll do the same thing as tonight. You in?"

"I, uh," I hesitate. "Nah, man. Tate didn't take it so well."

"Yeah, I noticed. She was losing her shit while you were in the ring. She okay?"

I glance at her building again, unsure how to answer. "Just dropped her off so she can get some rest."

"I get it," Roman mutters. "No worries, man. Seriously. Gotta keep your woman happy, right?"

"Yeah," I murmur. "Happy and safe." I pause, replaying my conversation with Dodger. I want to ask if Roman knows the shit he's really meddling in, but I also know the guy. If I don't play my cards right, he'll hang up and stonewall me until he winds up in a casket or next to his brother in a jail cell. "Listen, I need to ask you something."

"Yeah, for sure. What's up?"

"Have you talked with Judge to hear him out?" I question. "What he has to say? Why he thinks this shit is a bad idea?"

"Are you asking if we know about Rudy?" Roman challenges.

My lungs stall as I realize how easily Roman connected the dots, though it doesn't make me any less uneasy. "You know about Rudy?"

"We all know about Rudy," Roman replies. "And Judge is a good guy, all right? But he should stick with what he knows best, which is music, and let us continue doing what we do best, which is making money and giving the people what they want. And what they wanted tonight was you. Fuck, man. You delivered. Congrats again. If Tate ever decides she has the stomach for this, give me a call. I'll get you set up. If not, no worries. You fucking killed it, which means we all fucking killed it. Stay safe, all right?"

The call goes dead, and I tap the edge of my cell against

my chin, knowing I just took ten steps backward with the guy, though I have no idea what to do about it.

*Fucking perfect.*

# TATUM

It's been two days. Only two days. Yet, it feels like a lifetime. When Pax walked me to my door, I knew he wanted me to ask him inside, but I couldn't. I couldn't invite him inside. And I hate myself for it.

I hate myself for a lot of things, but I especially hate myself for that.

Tugging my pillow to my chest, I stare at the blank television, too exhausted to do anything else other than crave chocolate shakes and lobster rolls, the first of which I devoured as soon as I made it home after the fight. I shouldn't have called in sick. Maybe if I'd found the discipline to get out of bed this morning, I wouldn't be hurting so much. Or maybe not.

Who the hell knows?

The familiar clink of keys against the counter greets me, but I don't turn toward it.

Rory's home again. She took Hades for a walk. She also invited me to join her, but I turned her down. Add another tally to the *Tatum's a failure* column. Perfect.

"Okay, what's going on?" Rory demands. "I've given you

forty-eight hours, and you're still at ground zero, which means ignoring you has given us no results. Talk to me."

My attention snaps from the blank television to my best friend. "There's nothing to talk about."

Arms folded, she quirks her brow. "Liar. What's going on?"

"Nothing."

"Tate…"

"Seriously, I'm fine," I lie.

Striding toward me, she climbs onto my mattress and mirrors my position, pressing her back against the headboard and bringing her knees to her chest as Hades moseys after her. With his nose in the air, he gives a quick sniff, confirming I'm not a threat, then grunts, takes a slow circle, and plops on the ground at the foot of my bed. Rory bumps her knee against mine. "Okay, spit it out. What happened with Pax? Was he mean to you? Do I need to beat him up?"

The idea alone is enough to make my mouth twitch while also making me want to cry, simultaneously proving how off my rocker I really am.

"What?" she challenges. "You really don't think I could beat him up?"

I give her the side-eye but don't comment.

If only she knew the beating he gave Killian two nights ago.

"I mean, I could probably convince Dodger to," she offers. "Or I can always sic Hades on him. Isn't that right, Hades?" Hades lifts his head and rests his chin on the mattress, giving me puppy dog eyes for the first time…ever.

Tears slip down my cheeks, and I wipe them away. "Stop looking at me like that, Hades."

"Holy shit, Tate." She shifts onto her knees, facing me fully. "Okay, now I know something is wrong. Don't cry."

"I'm fine."

"No, you're not. We all know I'm the crier and you're the vault, so what's going on? I know I've been a little busy, but I thought you were enjoying your time in lover's paradise. I had no idea—"

"Like I said, nothing's wrong." I lick my lips. "Not really. And that's the messed up part."

"Tate," Rory pleads. "Please talk to me."

"I would, I just…" my voice cracks. "I don't know what to say."

"Why are you sad?"

I fight the urge to curl away from her and throw a pillow over my head no matter how overwhelming the feeling is. Why am I sad? It's such a simple question. One that could be used on a toddler, and they'd be able to give you an answer. But me? The only conclusion I have is pathetic at best.

"Come on, Tater Tot," Rory pushes.

Digging the heel of my hand into my eye socket, I murmur, "I'm sad because I'm in love with him."

Her silence only confirms I'm actually on crazy pills, and my shoulders heave on a broken sigh. "I know. I know it doesn't make sense, okay? That's why I'm freaking out."

"Then help me understand," she begs. "Why is being in love with Pax a sad thing?"

"Because the last time I was in love, I had my heart crushed into a billion pieces." The pressure in my chest grows until it's hard for me to breathe. Lifting my hand, I chew on the edge of the IndieCent Vows hoodie sleeve, my anxiety ratcheting as scenario after scenario flash through me. "What if…what if it happens again?"

Her frown deepens, and she stares at me without a word.

When the silence is too heavy, I joke, "Gee, thanks for the vote of confidence."

"It's not that, it's just…" She hesitates. "I'm not sure I know the answer to this one."

"Yeah, well, neither do I," I grumble. "Which is why I've been hiding in bed for the last two days."

"What if…what if you call Lia?"

Nibbling on the edge of my thumb, I admit, "I don't know if I've earned the little sister right to pick Lia's brain and ask for advice quite yet."

With a sigh, Rory squeezes my knee. "Earned the right? Don't you get it, Tate? It isn't something you have to earn. You two are family. She loves you. And if she knew you were hurting or stressing about something she had the power to help with, she'd be here in a heartbeat. I guarantee it." She squeezes my knee again, then lets me go. "And in the meantime, I'm getting ice cream for us. It's clear you need it, and once I'm back, we can binge watch a show of your choice as a consolation prize. Deal?"

"Rory…"

She gives me a look that would make my mother proud. "Deal?" she pushes.

I nod, albeit grudgingly. "Deal."

"Perfect. And I'm leaving Hades for moral support."

"Gee, thanks," I mutter.

With a quiet click, she exits the apartment, and I toy with my phone, my indecision gnawing at me. "Come on, Tate. Just call her," I mumble under my breath. Giving in, I dial Lia's phone number, and it rings.

"Hello?"

"Uh, hey," I murmur.

"Hey, Tate. What's up?"

I don't answer right away, unsure if I have the stamina to survive a few minutes of small talk when we both know that if I'm calling, there's a reason behind it. Holding onto the reminder, I dive right in. "Can I ask you something?"

"This feels like deja vu, but yes," she returns.

I press the edge of my sleeve against the corner of my eye,

too tired to appreciate my sister's dry wit, let alone comment on it. "How do you do it?"

"Do what?"

"How do you love someone when you know how much it hurts to lose them?"

Silence ensues, proving I probably should've been a little more up front about the topic instead of knocking her on her ass with one question.

"Sorry," I mumble. "You don't have to answer or whatever. I just figured with everything that happened, you might have some words of wisdom or something, and I could kind of use them right now."

"Oh, Tate." She sighs. "You really want to know the secret sauce to opening up again?"

My vision blurs with tears, and I wipe them away. "Yeah."

"There isn't one," she offers weakly. "I'm still scared most days. When Mav is a minute later than he told me he'd be, I'm on the tracking app or I'm calling him or I'm texting him or I'm scouring the internet for any potential articles about a freak accident or a collision or…something."

Defeat settles beneath my sternum as another tear slides down my cheek. "So it doesn't get better? It doesn't go away?"

"The fear of losing someone?" she asks. "Honestly, no. I don't think it does, especially when you've already experienced it."

My head falls forward. "That isn't the answer I was hoping for."

"I know," she whispers. "But life isn't all rainbows and butterflies, Tate. You know it as well as I do."

"So, what's the point?" I ask. "I'm in love with him, Lia. I'm in love with Paxton, and even though I'm able to admit I love him, the idea of losing him is absolutely…" I wipe beneath my nose with the sleeve of my hoodie. "It's absolutely terrifying."

"Well, yeah," she concedes, "but, so is missing a moment that you could've had with him all because you let fear hold you back from being with him in the first place."

She's right. It's the reason I can't roll out of bed. The reason I'm struggling to do anything at all. Because I miss him. I miss him so damn much, it hurts to breathe. But he's right there. Open and willing to give me a chance. To let him love me. So, why is it so hard to accept, let alone embrace fully?

"And if he's as amazing as he has to be in order for a girl like you to fall for him, then he'll be understanding of that," Ophelia continues. "He'll reassure you and hold you and kiss you when the moments get rough. When the fear is overwhelming and you're having a hard time keeping it in check. And slowly, those moments when it's too much will start to lessen over time, even if they never go away completely. To be honest, I don't think they ever will," she adds, carefully. "But here's the thing, Tate. It's okay. It's okay to accept it. To acknowledge it. But to let it control you? Control your future or who you love or how you spend the rest of your life? That's where you draw the line. That's where you give it two middle fingers. Which, now that I take into account who I'm talking to, feels like you're the perfect woman for the job."

With a pathetic laugh, I dry the moisture from my cheeks, exhaling slowly. She's right again. If anyone knows how to give two middle fingers to someone or something—including my own fear—it's me.

"Thank you," I whisper.

"You're welcome," she returns. "So, is he coming? To the wedding and/or engagement party?"

"Pax?" I ask.

"Yeah." I can hear the smile in her voice. "We're starting to put together the guest list for both, and I'd love to meet him."

The idea alone is enough to make me break out in hives. But that's what a normal couple does, isn't it? They meet each other's families. They travel together. They rely on each other.

I could really use him right now.

"Tate?" Lia prods.

"I, uh, I haven't asked him yet," I admit.

"Well, you should," she pushes. "Although you might want to give him a heads up that our family's a bit overwhelming and will have no problem kicking him to the curb if he ever hurts you."

My mouth lifts, well-aware she's not wrong.

"I'll be sure to pass the info along," I murmur.

"That's my baby sister," she returns. "I love you."

"Love you, too."

hecking my phone for the hundredth time since I dropped Tatum off two days ago, I send another text.

ME

Missing you.

I don't wait to see her response, knowing she won't reply until she's ready. But I can't help myself. It's taken everything inside of me to keep from barging to her place and beating down the door until she talks to me. Lets me in.

I hold onto the words she spoke before she left, "We'll be okay," as I tuck my phone into my saddle bag on my bike and head inside the gate.

You'd think I'd be used to it by now. The barbed wire. The chain link. The buzzing of doors and tedious forms. Once I've jumped through the prison's hoops, a guard leads me to the same room, the same seat, the same phone, and I rest my elbows on the counter, waiting for Rafe to appear.

I've debated on whether or not it's a good idea to come here and air out Roman's dirty laundry, but after Dodger's words of caution and Roman's flippant response to Rudy's death, I couldn't stay away.

Rafe appears a few minutes later, saying something to the guard before he collapses in the seat across from mine like this is just another day in the life of an inmate. Now that I think about it, I guess it is.

I pick up the phone, and Rafe does the same.

"Hey, man," he says.

"Hey."

His brows crease. "What's wrong?"

I should've known he'd call me out as soon as he saw me. Might as well get it over with. "Did you ever hear about Rudy?" I ask. "The guy I replaced in IndieCent Vows?"

"The guitarist?" His forehead wrinkles. "Yeah? What about him?"

"Did you know he was Judge's friend?" I prod.

Recognition hits his gaze, and he gives me a slow nod. "Yeah, man. I heard. Tough break."

My eyes cut to the guard as I confirm our conversation is still relatively private. Somewhat satisfied, I dip closer to the glass, dropping my voice low. "You think it was an accident?"

"I think it's none of my business." Tilting his head, he shifts the phone to his other ear. "I think it's none of your business, either."

"And what about Roman?" I ask. "You think it's any of his business?"

Tongue in cheek, Rafe stares at me but doesn't answer, proving he's more in the loop with whatever Roman's involved in than I initially assumed. The thought doesn't make me feel any better.

"You're not worried?" I push.

"About Rudy?" Rafe shakes his head. "Pax, it was years ago."

"So?"

"So, it was *years* ago," he repeats, emphasizing the timeline as if it makes any of this better. "Besides, the same players aren't around anymore, Roman's a big boy, *and* he isn't stupid. So, no. I'm not worried."

"Rafe, he's your brother," I grit out.

Rafe's jaw tics the same way it did when we were kids and I pushed him too far. Apparently, I'm doing the same thing now, but I don't know how to stop. How to drop it. How to let this go.

"No offense, Pax, but it's been a while since you've been to town," he reminds me. "There's more at play than you know, and like I already said, Roman isn't stupid. He's got this."

"So, you're okay with it?" I push.

"As much as I can be, yeah." He rests his elbows on the table, watching me. "You can breathe, man. I'm keeping an eye on things."

Keeping an eye on things? The bastard can't be serious.

"How?" I demand. "Maybe you've forgotten, but you're behind bars."

"And maybe you've forgotten how well I make friends," he argues. "You really think I'd let Rome do something stupid?" A soft chuckle echoes from the phone. "Come on, man. Have a little faith. He's good. I promise."

I want to believe him. I do. It's not like I haven't been to my fair share of fight nights, and they've never been a problem. Not once. But I know Dodge, and he's never had an issue crossing the line into illegal territory. If he's spooked, he has a good reason to be. Doesn't he?

"You sure you're good?" I ask.

Rafe pauses, drawing his lips into his mouth before sobering even more. "Listen, I appreciate you and your bandmates lookin' out for Rome and the rest of the guys, but you can't come in at half-time and expect to know the plays, let alone participate in the game or understand shit. They have it under control."

"Maybe they do, but I can't just sit back—"

"Yes, you can."

"Rafe—"

"Seriously, Pax." With a smile, he scratches his jaw. "Fuck, man. Do you know how happy I am for you? Whatever guilt you hold for me being here. For your mom or your dad or Roman. Fuck that shit. We're good, and we're happy for you. But you gotta be happy for us, too, and let us do our own thing, even if you don't agree with it."

Count on Rafe to say it like it is. Maybe it's the real reason why I'm here. Because I feel guilty. Because I want to keep them safe. Want to keep everyone safe. But it isn't easy. Not when I don't know what they're up against.

"You want me to let it go," I realize.

"Yeah. I do."

"At what cost?"

"At the cost of Roman's future," he says as if it's enough to justify his seemingly hands-off approach. "Rome's making money. Having fun. And building a fucking empire. Who are you to judge how he makes it?"

Blindsided, I shift back in the shitty-ass chair, considering his words.

*Who am I to judge how Roman builds his empire?*

I'm his older brother's best friend. But is it enough? It's easy to talk shit and criticize a person's decisions from the outside looking in, especially when you care about the person. And if anything happens to Roman, I'll be gutted. But Rafe is right. I don't know the full story, and if I'm being honest, I don't need to know the full story. It doesn't involve me, and the guys owe me nothing. But letting go? Giving in and taking a backseat so someone else can make their own decisions—good or bad—is scary as hell. The realization is a hard blow as I stare at my best friend across from me. He has more skin in the game than I'll ever have, and if he supports Roman, if he accepts his brother's decisions, then who am I to do any different?

"You promise he's being safe?" I push.

He holds my stare, never flinching. "Safe as he can be."

My knuckles crack as I squeeze the phone in my hand before forcing the tight muscles to loosen. "Fine," I grunt. "I'll let it go."

"Good man." Rafe grins. "Now, stop wasting time rehashing boring shit you have no control over. Tell me about your girl. How is she? Roman said she freaked the other night."

"Yeah." My shoulders slump in the uncomfortable chair. "She lost someone close to her a few years ago, and it messed with her."

"Been there, am I right?" he jokes before sobering. "How are you handling it?"

"Me?"

"Yeah. It's gotta be hard."

I nod, surprised by how on-point his assumption is. It is hard. Seeing her spiral. Being given a front-row seat to her greatest fears without any power to scare them away. Not really. Because I can't guarantee my safety anymore than I can guarantee the sun will rise in the morning.

All I know is, I miss her. I want her to be happy. I want to erase her fears and convince her it's okay to be vulnerable. That she doesn't need to waste time overthinking scary possibilities when we could be spending what time we have on this earth *together*.

But I can't force her to make this decision, no matter how much I wish I could. It's on her. All I can do is be patient and hope the pros of opening up and giving me a chance will be worth the potential cons of heartbreak.

So here I am. Twiddling my fucking thumbs and distracting myself with Roman's empire-building tactics. Or at least, I was.

*Now what?*

"She'll come around," Rafe promises.

"I hope so."

"She will," he reiterates. "You're a good guy, Pax. It's why she's scared. She doesn't wanna lose you."

My eyes narrow. "I know the feeling."

With a low chuckle, he volleys, "Then you know she has no reason to worry."

I scoff. "Whatever, asshole."

"I'm just sayin', man." He lifts one hand in defense before adding, "But maybe wait 'til I'm out so I can come to the wedding, yeah?"

I laugh a little harder. "Oh, so now we're getting married?"

"You tellin' me my little brother's intel is off?" he challenges.

"Are you saying Roman's spying on me for you?"

"Already told you, Pax," Rafe reminds me. "I'm good at making friends, and I know what's going on outside these bars. Maybe you should start trusting me."

I roll my eyes. "Yeah, man. Whatever you say."

"Glad you see it my way. Now about the wedding..." He cocks his brow and leans back in his chair, looking about as humble as Tom Brady during the Superbowl.

"Yeah, man," I grumble, scratching the edge of my nose as I try to keep my amusement in check. "I think I can make that work."

5 1

TATUM

**M**y hands shake as I stare up at Paxton's house. After my call with Lia, I took a much needed shower and asked Rory for her keys as soon as she got home with the ice cream. She handed them over without batting an eye, making me love her even more.

Now here I am. Trying not to overthink or overanalyze things so I can listen to my heart and tell Paxton what I never had the guts to tell Archer. Even if it's scary. Even if I want to run in the opposite direction and hide.

*Breathe.*

Raising my chin, I head up the short set of stairs to the porch, lift my hand, and knock on Paxton's door while trying to keep my panic under control.

It'll be fine.

*It'll be fine, it'll be fine, it'll be fine.*

Seconds later, the sliver of glass in the door gives the perfect view of a just-showered Pax walking toward me. My heart skips a beat, and a burn hits my eyes at the sight. I knew I missed him. I'm not completely inept at deciphering my emotions, but seeing him again? It's enough to make my knees buckle and confirm what I already knew.

I really do love him.

When Pax realizes I'm the one on his doorstep, his smile warms, and he opens the door. "Wondered who was here, since I didn't open the gate. Hey," he greets me.

"Hi," I whisper.

"Hey." His smile turns hesitant, and he squeezes the back of his neck. "I'm glad you're here."

"Me, too," I return, surprising myself with just how true the words are. "Mind if I come in?"

He steps aside. "I think you already know the answer to that."

And I do. I'm always welcome. Even when I'm his pretty little liar or the pain in his ass or his friend's potential one-night-stand. His door has always been open, come hell or high-water. The reminder of everything we've been through, everything I've put him through, flashes through my mind and leaves me on pins and needles.

So much so, I can barely make it into the foyer before I blurt out, "I love you." The three words tumble out of me, making me feel jittery and anxious, and a little excited, too. It's like I'm at the top of a hill on a rollercoaster, peering over the edge and preparing for the adrenaline rush I know is just around the corner. Even when it's scary. Even when I don't technically know the outcome. Not yet. I'm along for the ride, and as long as he's by my side, I think I'm okay with it. "I love you so much," I repeat, taking in his toasty espresso gaze as he watches me. "And that's a weird thing for me to say. But I do. I love you a lot, and I honestly didn't think I'd ever love anyone ever again. So, first, I want to apologize if loving you makes me act a little crazy."

His smile softens, and he tucks his hands into his pockets, rocking back on his heels. "You're not crazy, Birthday Girl."

"Well, that's debatable," I mutter, "but let me finish." I take another deep breath. "I love you, and sometimes, I *am* going to act crazy. I'm going to act crazy, and I'm going to push you away, and I'm going to freak out when you don't let me know you're running late, or that you ran into traffic, or that your flight was delayed. I'm going to act crazy when I can't get ahold of you, or when you don't text me goodnight. I'm going to act crazy and clingy, and I'd like to think there's a chance those quirks will go away with enough time, but I honestly don't know if they ever will, and if we're going to do this—"

"We're already doing this," he reminds me.

"Let me finish," I repeat, giving the guy a pointed look until his mouth snaps closed and he crosses his arms to keep from reaching for me. It only makes me want to skip to the part where we kiss and make up even more, but I hold strong, knowing that if I don't get everything off my chest, I'll regret it. "Thank you." I take another deep breath and step forward, meeting him in the center of the foyer. "As I was saying, if we're going to do this, if we're going to keep doing this," I clarify, "then I need you to be okay with it. With the good and the bad and the ugly. And I need you to be safe. And I need you to take your vitamins. And exercise every day so your heart stays healthy and strong. And I'm going to need you to not get into fights and not piss people off at your concerts or at the grocery store or…anything. I need you to be safe, and to put up with my crazy, and to accept that letting you in is the hardest thing I've ever done, but I know you're worth it. All I'm asking is for you to take a few seconds to decide whether or not my crazy is worth it, too, and—"

Rushing toward me, he grabs my face, silencing me with a kiss I feel in my soul. It burrows and it weaves and it twists, tying me to him until I don't know where I end and he begins. But I love it. His easy acceptance. His devotion and passion. I love him. I love him so much it hurts. But it's a good hurt. A hurt that reminds me I'm alive. He's alive. And we have the chance to make something great. Together.

Pulling away from me, he rasps, "Totally worth it, Birthday Girl."

I roll my eyes. "I mean—"

"I love you," he interrupts. "I love you crazy. I love you sane. I love you bitchy and sweet and sober and drunk."

Digging my teeth into the inside of my cheek to keep from beaming like a lunatic, I murmur, "You know, I feel like I've heard this speech before."

"Maybe so, but that was *like*." He kisses me again. "This is love. Pay attention, or I'll have no choice but to start over." His lips brush against the edge of my mouth another time, making me laugh. "I love that you're messy, despite cleaning for a living."

I gasp. "I'm not messy!"

"I love that you deny that you're messy, and—"

I smack his chest. "Watch it, mister."

"I love that I found you after all these years, and that you dyed my hair, and peed on me, and—"

"Pax!" I screech.

But he doesn't stop. He just cradles my face, turning me into a puddle.

"I love you, Birthday Girl, and there isn't anything you could do that would make me stop." His calloused thumbs run along my cheeks. "I love you."

"I love you, too," I whisper, surprised by how effortless it feels. To love him. To admit I love him. Despite the heartache and the fear. I love him. And it's enough. Because a single second with Pax is better than the last forty-eight hours without him. And even if I only get another second or minute or day, it'll be worth it. He's worth it.

Always.

5 2

PAXTON

A LITTLE WHILE LATER...

Ever since the fight, things have been calm. Quiet. And fucking bliss. Tuke flew in for a quick visit to sign a few papers today before heading to Los Angeles for a role he scored in a movie. It's only a cameo, but it's nice to see he's still alive and hasn't died from too much weed. Not that you can overdose, but if someone managed to pull it off, it'd be Tuke.

The band is still officially on hiatus, but I don't mind anymore. It seems settling down with someone you love has a way of quieting the other noises around you, and Tatum and me? We've never been happier.

That being said, I was surprised by a certain phone call from Judge and Dodger a couple weeks ago. Add in today's meeting making everything official, and I'm excited to share the news with Tatum.

Balancing the bottle of wine with two wine glasses, I open the door and step onto the back patio in my bathing suit. I would've invited Tatum over to tell her the good news if I didn't already know she'd be here, but it's almost better this way. She's in the dark, and I can surprise her any way I want.

She doesn't notice me right away. She's too busy soaking up the moonlight, looking gorgeous as ever. With her hair piled on her head, Tatum tilts her head up to the night sky, and my chest swells with gratitude. I still can't believe she chose me. I'm the luckiest bastard alive.

"Do you think Judge's family would be willing to sell it?" she asks.

"What?" I laugh.

"The house," she clarifies. "While you were grabbing the drinks, I decided this is officially my happy place."

Keeping a straight face, I clear my throat and ask, "You like it here, huh?"

A smile plays at the edge of her lips. She opens her eyes and turns to me, watching as I step into the jacuzzi. With the hot bubbles licking at my skin, I sit down, careful to keep the glasses and wine from submerging in the water before she takes one of them from me.

"Like it here?" She rolls her eyes. "Oh, my dear boyfriend, you have no idea. Want to know a secret?"

I nod.

"When I came to clean the house for the first time, I literally told Rory I was in love with the owner because this place was so perfect."

"No shit?"

She laughs. "Yup. Who knew I was actually onto something." She waves the glass through the air, motioning to the bottle in my grasp. "Now, gimme the goods, sir."

The red liquid spills into her cup, and I do the same to my own glass before setting the half-full bottle on the side table outside the water beside Tatum's phone.

As she takes a sip, Tatum melts a little further into the jacuzzi, letting the hot water reach her chin and soak the tendrils of hair that have fallen from her messy bun. "Mmm.

Seriously, this is the best way to spend a night after a long day cleaning."

"You could always quit, you know."

"We've already discussed this," she reminds me. "I like cleaning."

"Yeah, yeah. I know." Moving closer, I kiss her temple. "Just reiterating that the offer's still on the table."

"And I appreciate it," she returns. "Want to know what else I appreciate?"

"What?" I ask.

"When you spoil me with a glass of wine and a hot soak after I get home every night."

"Home, huh?" I kiss her again. "I like the sound of that."

"Right?" She peeks around me, taking in the house and beach in one long look. "Mmm, if only."

She has no idea. Despite Tatum never filling me in on what she told Rory when she first came to clean my house, I've always known she loves it. The jacuzzi. The view. The music room. The beach. She stays here every night despite neither of us ever officially talking about moving in together. And during today's meeting, I figured pulling a few strings was the least I could do.

"Speaking of *if only*…I have news," I announce.

"Hmm?"

"The band invited me to be an official member of Indie-Cent Vows."

Her lips part. "Are you serious?"

I nod.

"What does that mean?"

"It means I get royalties for IndieCent Vows' songs now and don't need to rely on touring or recording new songs to make money."

"What?" She shakes her head. "Pax, that's insane."

"Yeah." I nod, as blown away as she is. "I was surprised, too."

"Since when?"

"They called a week ago, asking if I was okay with it. Obviously, I said yes, and I signed the paperwork this morning."

"Pax, that's…" Beaming up at me, she lets out a laugh. "That's incredible. Why didn't you tell me?"

"I didn't want to jinx it."

"Okay, I get that," she concedes. "But still. A little heads-up would've been nice." She wraps her arms around me, and climbs into my lap, careful not to spill her drink in the bubbling water. "I am so happy for you, it's not even funny."

With a grin, I kiss her, taking advantage of our new position. "I had a feeling you might be."

"So, what do you think made Judge and Dodger change their minds after all these years?" she asks.

I hesitate, considering her question. Ever since the phone call, I've been wondering the same thing. And even though, I don't have an actual answer, I reply, "I think they felt bad that I was waiting around for shit with Judge's nephews to clear up, so they figured this was a good way to say thank you for my patience." I brush my nose against hers. "Wanna know the best part, though?"

She quirks her brow. "There's a part better than you being a full-blown member of the band?"

"Yeah." Dropping my free hand to her ass in the water, I tug her into me. "I bought something for us."

"Us?" She frowns. "Pax, you know you don't have to—"

"Ask me what I bought, Birthday Girl," I push, anxious to see the look of surprise on her face. Because if she thinks my status with the band changing is a big deal, she's gonna lose her shit.

Her eyes thin, and she leans back, slightly. "Okay, now I'm suspicious."

"Ask me."

"What did you buy?"

Holding her stare, I tilt my head toward the house, watching as a tiny crease forms between her brows.

"What do you…" Her voice trails off as understanding sparks in her hazel eyes, and her jaw drops. "You're joking."

"Not joking."

"Seriously?"

"Yeah." I laugh while trying to commit her expression to memory because shit. It's damn near priceless. "And when you're ready to move in *officially*," I emphasize, "the place is as much yours as it is mine."

Holding back her grin, she rests her forearms on my shoulders, careful not to spill any of her drink as she slowly shakes her head back and forth. "Pax."

"What do you think?" I ask.

"Pax, this is…it's too much."

"Hardly," I argue. "Besides, this wasn't a home until you stepped in it, Tatum Taylor." She presses her lips together, and I know she's debating on whether or not she wants to push the issue, so I add, "It also doesn't hurt that if you move in, I'd have fewer run-ins with Hades, and will keep my balls intact."

Mirth dances in her pretty gaze as she gives in, saying, "Now that might be your best argument, yet." Leaning in she kisses my cheek like she can't help herself.

Neither can I. Anytime she's around, I want my hands on her. And not in a possessive or sexual way. Simply put? I like the reminder. That she isn't a figment of my imagination like I spent years believing before we reunited. She's here. She's real. And she's all mine. For as long as she'll have me.

"Okay, yes," she decides. "Yes, I'd love to move in."

"Yeah?"

"Yup. On one condition."

"What's that?" I ask.

"Well…" She looks down into her glass, swirling the red liquid. "While you were grabbing the wine, my sister called."

Over the last few weeks, I've learned a little more about Tatum's family dynamic, and it's been interesting, to say the least. Even though the crux of her friction with Ophelia has revolved around Archer, Tatum's always been competitive with her sister, feeling lost in her shadow long before she developed feelings for Archer. But what's really fascinating? It's seeing Tatum mend the relationship. Letting go of her resentment in hopes of strengthening the sisterly-bond she's missed over the years. They've been talking more. Sending texts. Tatum even added me to the family's group chat, and it's been quite entertaining. Honestly, I'm jealous of how amazing her family is. They've been nothing but welcoming so far. It's a bittersweet reminder of everything I've lost over the years, though Tatum's had no issue sharing them with me, and I'm grateful for it.

"How's Lia doing?" I ask.

"She's good," Tatum returns. "They finally picked a date."

"No shit? That's awesome," I reply. "When is it?"

"Well, apparently, their wedding venue had a cancellation, so they decided to combine the engagement party with the actual wedding."

I cock my brow. "Isn't the engagement party in a few weeks?"

She grimaces. "Yes?"

"No shit?" I repeat. "That's fast."

"I know, but Lia said they've been ready to take this step for years, they just didn't know how. And now that they've decided to take the plunge and the wedding venue opened up, they decided, why wait? Why put their life on hold for another second, let alone another year, you know?"

"I can understand the sentiment," I agree, squeezing Tatum's ass still resting on my lap. "Although I don't envy your parents."

"Right?" She grimaces. "Bring on the Red Bull."

"I'd say so," I agree dryly.

Tatum takes another sip of her wine before tossing back the rest of it like it's water.

"You good?" I ask.

"Yeah." She clears her throat and sets the empty glass next to the bottle and her phone on the side table before giving me her full attention. "I was just wondering if you...you know, if you want to come with me?"

We haven't talked about it, but I guess I'd always assumed I'd be tagging along despite the lack of official invitation. Watching her squirm at the possibility is adorable as fuck. "You want me to come with you to the wedding?"

"If I say yes, will you run in the opposite direction?" she asks, barely holding my gaze as she steals my own glass and downs the rest of it in hopes of settling her nerves.

With a low laugh, I point out, "You're the runner, not me."

"That isn't an answer, smartass," she grumbles.

"Of course, I'd love to come. Although, now that you mention it, I do have a few of my own conditions."

"Like what?"

"For starters, how does your family feel about sharing a room?"

"With them?" Her nose wrinkles. "Probably not great—" I splash her and she laughs even harder. "Kidding. I'm pretty sure as long as they see how happy you make me, we'll be good to go."

"Good," I reply. Dipping my hands back beneath the water, I drag them along her spine, memorizing every curve.

"Because I'm pretty sure I'll go crazy if I don't get to spend every night with you by my side."

She bites her lip, fighting a grin. "So corny."

"You know you love it."

"I love you," she clarifies.

"I love you, too." I kiss her softly. "Oh, and I have one more condition."

"Someone's greedy tonight."

"You'll like this one, I think," I tell her.

She peeks up at me, those hazel eyes making my cock harden beneath the water. "What?"

Hooking my arm around her, I pull her into my side and drop my voice low as if delivering a secret. "You make sure to take notes so that when we finally tie the knot, our wedding will blow theirs out of the water."

Her face scrunches in the cutest smile I've ever seen. "Deal."


The End

# EPILOGUE

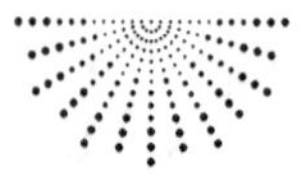

## TATUM

*A while later...*

"Where are you taking me?" I ask. I'm still not sure how he did it. How he managed to keep the location a secret for so long. I blame the noise-canceling headphones he gifted me for my birthday and the sleeping pill he placed in my hand as soon as we got to our seats.

*Clever, Paxton Turner. Very clever.*

With a yawn, I peek out the airplane window in hopes of piecing together where we are, but I'm as clueless as ever.

"Rise and shine, Birthday Girl." Pax kisses my cheek, then laughs. Reaching up, he runs his thumb along the side of my face, and my brows furrow.

"What is it?"

"Sleep lines." His smile softens. "Fuck, I love you."

My heart pitter-pattering like always whenever he says those three words, I lean into his hand, soaking up his affection. "Love you, too."

"Come on." He grabs our carry-ons from the overhead

bin, hooking his backpack over one shoulder while grasping the handle to my bright red bag and leads the way from our first class seats to the jetway.

As we pass an adorable couple talking to their toddler, my brows bunch. "Are they speaking…German?"

Tossing me another smirk over his shoulder, Pax reaches back and wiggles his free hand, urging me to take it. When I do, he tugs me toward him, pulling me to his side instead of letting me trail behind. "Surprised?" he murmurs.

"Uh, definitely. Germany?" My eyes widen as the word rolls off my tongue. "Are you serious?"

"Welcome to Berlin, Birthday Girl. But we should hurry so we don't miss the train."

"Train?"

"Come on, slow poke."

"But what about Berlin?" I motion to the windows lining the walls giving us a gorgeous view of a country I've never visited until now.

"We'll see the sights when we get back. Come on," he repeats. "If we miss the train, we're screwed."

"And where is the train taking us?" I ask.

"Halberstadt."

The name makes me pause. Halberstadt? Why does that sound so familiar? Before I have a chance to question him on it, Pax tugs my hand again, and I pick up my pace.

Halberstadt, it is.

It's a four hour train ride, but I soak up every second. Peering out the window, I take in the different shades of green covering the hills and the gray and sand-colored cobblestones lining the roads. By the time the diesel engine pulls up to the station, I'm like a full sponge, practically brimming with excitement and awe. We've traveled quite a bit over the last year, and it's been nothing short of incredible.

There are a lot of perks to loving a rockstar who's also obsessed with travel, and a surprise trip for my birthday is definitely one of them. After arriving, Pax arranges for a car to take us to an adorable bed-and-breakfast with a red door and poppies planted out front.

"This place is gorgeous," I gush as the driver opens the back door and the gentle breeze hits my cheeks.

Lacing our fingers together, Pax lifts my hand, bringing it to his lips. "Thought you might like it. Welcome to Halberstadt."

Halberstadt. There's that name again.

Then I hear it. The low hum of an organ. It's the same note, er, *notes*. Like a single chord being dragged out to infinity.

*It can't be.*

Tilting my head, I shift my attention from Pax to the cozy bed-and-breakfast, to the small church across the street. It isn't anything spectacular to look at, if I'm being honest. Hell, it blends in with the rest of the landscape. Sandy gray stone. Arched windows. Humble, almost. It only makes the avalanche of awe rush over me more.

"The song," I whisper. Turning back to Pax, my lips parting, I ask, "How did you…"

"They're changing the chord in a few hours. Figured we could check in to the bed-and-breakfast, maybe unpack, then head—"

I wrap my arms around his neck and kiss him as hard as I can, caught off guard by the building pressure behind my eyes. This man. How in the world is this man so freaking sweet?

When my heels touch the ground and he pulls away,

finding my eyes red, he says, "Seems Squeaks is rubbing off on you."

I sniff, pressing my finger against the corner of my eye in hopes of warding off a sobfest. "Apparently."

"So, how do you feel about it?"

With a mock glare, I wipe beneath my nose. "Not great, thank you very much."

He laughs. "I meant being here, not turning into Squeaks."

"Oh." I sniff again. "It's perfect, and you're perfect, and…" I exhale slowly. "And we should go inside."

"I like your thinking." Pax tosses his arm around my shoulders and guides me into the bed-and-breakfast. It's cozy and cool and homey and…absolutely perfect. Once we're settled into our room, Pax opens a bottle of wine, pours me a glass, and hands it to me as we sit on the terrace overlooking St. Burchardi Church. The same familiar hum of the organ plays as we sip our drinks until the bottle is empty and a timer on Paxton's phone rings from the bedroom.

"It's time," he murmurs. "Come on."

It's beautiful in its simplicity. The church. And busy. The stone archways almost give the place a castle-like feel straight out of a fairytale with warm stained wooden beams along the tall ceiling. It's the perfect church for a quaint, small town like this one. A simple organ of rich wood and tall pipes stands roped off near the back of the building. It's smaller than I expected. The realization intrigues even more, calling to me like a homing beacon. I move through the crowd, my fingers threaded with Paxton's until we reach a small open space near the front.

"Sorry, it's so busy," Pax mutters. "I debated on bringing you when they weren't changing the pipes, so it would be a little calmer, but—"

"It's perfect."

His brows dip in concern. "You sure?"

I nod. "Yeah, Pax. Absolutely perfect." Reaching onto my tiptoes, I kiss his cheek. "Honestly, I couldn't have asked for a better destination." I look around the church in awe. "It's crazy, you know? How a single person can make such a lasting impact on so many people's lives. Like seriously, look at all of these people. They're here to watch someone change a pipe on an organ so it can play a new chord in a song written by an experimental composer who was convinced that the experience of the song was more important than the actual song itself." I shake my head. "It's crazy, don't you think?"

"Inspiring," Pax decides.

Reverence spreads in my chest, and I squeeze his hand. "Yeah. Definitely."

"Do you think any of them are ready?" he asks. "The locals. They've experienced the same note for almost two years. Do you think they're ready to experience something new?"

I consider his question and the weight it holds. There's something comforting in the familiar. I should know. I was too stubborn to pull myself out of the destructive rut I was in for years until I met Pax. And it's crazy to think about it. How much time I spent drowning in sadness and resentment. I still miss Archer. I always will. But there's something healing in it, too. In letting go. In accepting change instead of fighting it. In learning to appreciate the new sound while accepting how much you'll miss the old one.

"I guess we'll see," I whisper when a woman appears at the edge of the audience.

Slowly, she walks through the crowd and removes the rope barrier separating everyone from the organ. Methodically, she slides gloves on as an older gentleman speaks to the attendees in German. I don't know what he's saying. I can't understand him. But even if I could, I'm not sure I'd be able to take my eyes off the woman as she carefully picks up a pipe resting on a white cloth on top of the organ. The man goes quiet, and the woman nods at him, approaching the organ once more. Sliding the pipe into place, the chord changes, and a wonder-filled hush blankets the church except for the beautiful new chord ringing throughout. Like a wave, it rolls over me, and I close my eyes, committing it to memory. The sound. The feeling. The acceptance of change and all it brings with it.

"How long have you been planning this?" I whisper.

"Since the moment I told you about the song." He glances at the organ again, then looks down at me and cups my face. "Listen, I know I've given you this speech a few times, but, uh, let me do it one more time, yeah?"

"What are you talking about?" I ask, trying to keep my voice low so I don't disturb any of the other attendees.

Instead of answering me, Pax reaches into his pocket and retrieves a little black box, making my heart stall in the process.

Holy shit. If that's what I think it might be, I'm going to pass out. Or vomit. Or vomit, then pass out. Honestly, anything's possible considering the circumstances.

"I love you, Birthday Girl," Pax murmurs. The slight rasp of his voice mingles with the low hum of the organ, making me weepy but in the best way possible. "I love your loyalty. I love your heart. I love your sass and your wit. But most of all, I love how deeply you love. How you let it consume you, even when it's scary or reckless." Keeping me tucked into his side, he opens the box and kisses my temple. "I love you so much, and I'm really hoping you'll do me the favor of giving me the rest of your life to keep loving you. To keep showing you how much you mean to me. How you're my everything." A sheen hits his eyes as he exhales slowly. "Will you marry me, Birthday Girl?"

I stare at the gorgeous diamond ring tucked inside the box and all it signifies. "You're doing this here?" I whisper.

"Not sure there's a better place to do it." He faces me and takes the ring out, reaching for my left hand as my stomach knots and my vision blurs with unshed tears. Rubbing his thumb along the back of my hand, he slips the diamond into place and brings it to his lips. "You're the only one for me, Tate. And I know Archer is some pretty steep competition, but I'm pretty sure I'm the only one for you, too. I want to make it official. Will you marry me?"

Marry me.

After Archer's passing, I was pretty positive I'd never want to hear those words. Not from anyone. But seeing Pax? The love and devotion and reverence in his pretty brown eyes? It blankets me in so much peace and assurance, I don't even have to question it. My feelings or my answer. Obviously, there's only one.

"Yes." With a watery smile, I lift my chin, and he kisses me again, making me the luckiest girl in the world.

~

THUMBING THE WORN PAGES, I OPEN THE SAME NOTEBOOK I've carried around for years. After the pipe change, we ate dinner at a restaurant down the street, drank another bottle of wine, then came home and made love before Paxton fell asleep. And even though I said yes, and meant it with every fiber of my being, there is still something I need to do.

The tip of my pen hovers over the page for a solid minute, my eyes welling with tears as I press it to the paper.

*Archer,*

Hi. It's been a minute. Not since I've thought about you. I still think about you every day. Still wonder if a piece of you is out there. Watching over us. In the beginning, when I started seeing Mav and Ophelia and...everyone really, moving on, I thought that because they didn't appear heartbroken, they didn't think about you anymore. Didn't miss you anymore. But now that I'm here, I see how wrong I was. How unfair I was. To them. And to myself. And to you. Like you're so easily forgettable, am I right? Not even close.

I want you to know I'm happy. It's taken me WAY too long to recognize that I can be happy while still missing you. I didn't understand it before, but I do now.

If you are out there somewhere watching over me, you've probably caught a glimpse of two—or a billion—of me with Pax. He's pretty great. Super patient and understanding. You'd love him. I know you would. You'd approve, too. Of how he treats me. I don't know if you sent Pax to me, but if you did, thank you. And if you didn't, well, still thank you. He won't replace you. No one can replace you, Archer. But he does make me happy.

When I was in the church today, I couldn't help but wonder if you were watching me. If you were there, hidden in the song. I can't wait for you to watch the rest of my life unfold and all of the note changes to go with it. And maybe, just maybe, we'll be able to listen to the completed piece together. As. Slow. As. Possible. But until then, I'll keep writing my own song, grateful for every note that comes my way and how it shapes who I am.

Love always,

-Tate

# HIJACKED EPILOGUE

## JAXON

*Let's back up a bit, shall we?*

I should probably be in a better mood. After all, one of my best friend's is getting married and has been head over heels for the girl for years. I think all of us have known they'd tie the knot at one point or another. Add in everything they've been through to get here, and I'm pretty sure they're soulmates.

Guess I'm a little jaded after my own experience. It doesn't help that I just dropped off my daughter, Poppy, to my ex. A shiver runs up my spine from the memory alone as I reach for Maverick's parents' front door and walk inside without waiting for an invitation. To be honest, his parents would be offended if I did anything else.

It's quiet for what feels like the first time in months as I take in the empty foyer before walking further into the house. Ever since Maverick announced his proposal to Ophelia, the hinges have been working double time to accommodate all the Sunday brunches as family and friends gather to plan their big day.

475

The question is, where is everyone? I mean, I know I'm a few minutes early, but still. I take in the empty kitchen and large family room. A veggie tray, bowl of fruit, and basket of bagels sit on the kitchen counter as Maverick's mom appears from the opposite hallway. Her hair is the color of honey at the moment, though I've seen it range from black to silvery blonde over the years. I'm pretty sure this color suits her best. When she smiles, her eyes crinkle in the corners, and it never ceases to amaze me. The way she carries herself. So inviting and genuine. It reminds me of her daughter, Rory, though Archer, Maverick's twin, was the same way.

"Jax." Opening her inked arms, she strides toward me and pulls me into a hug. "Hey, you're early."

I return her grasp with a smile, wrapping my arms around her willowy frame. "Hey, Aunt Mia." The name rolls off my tongue with ease, despite the lack of actual blood-relation. Even so, she's family, thanks to being one of my mom's best friends. Always has been, always will be. Letting her go, I explain, "Sorry I'm early, I dropped off Poppy and figured, why head home only to turn back around and—" My phone vibrates in my pocket, making my brows dip as I pull it out. "Shit, one sec." It's my ex, Iris. My stomach bottoms out at the six letters shining from my screen before I glance back at my Aunt Mia. "Sorry, I have to take this."

"No worries." She motions to the sliding glass doors off the kitchen. "People are going to be here in a few minutes, if you want to use the balcony for some privacy."

"Thanks."

Heading toward the glass doors, I answer my phone and bring it to my ear. "Hey, Iris—"

"You forgot her backup bottle."

My muscles seize as I register her words. Of course, that's why she's calling. It's not like she doesn't have a dozen bottles at her place already. And I know I put it in the diaper bag. I fucking know it. It was in the side pocket where it always is. I also made sure to pack at least four extra diapers, two binkies, and diaper rash cream, since the last time Iris watched her, she came back with a sore bum. So no. I didn't forget the bottle. I know it, and so does Iris. She's calling to pick a fight.

Squeezing the bridge of my nose, I mutter, "Are you sure? I thought I—"

"I'm not an idiot, Jax. It's not here."

I grind my teeth and drop my hand to my side. "Never said you're an idiot, Ris. I'm sorry if I forgot to pack—"

"If?" she snaps.

Breathing in deep through my nose, I pray for patience and step outside, hoping the fresh air will help ground me. It's warm and bright, making me squint as I offer, "I'm at Mav's right now, but I can swing by and drop off another bottle in a couple hours. Does that work?"

A quiet splash from the pool echoes over the wrought iron railing, distracting me. I walk toward the sound, confused. I thought I was early? Ophelia suggested a lazy pool party so all the ladies could get some sunshine and the kids could play in the water as everyone catches up. But if I'm early, who's in the pool now?

The warm wrought iron seeps into my forearms as I wait for Iris's answer and peek over the edge. The grass surrounding the pool is green, but free of the dozen bodies I have no doubt will be scattered across it within the next half-hour. Mav, Ev, Reeves, Griffin. They'll be here soon with their families. The chairs surrounding the pool are empty too, except for a stack of folded towels. Aunt Mia must've laid them out in preparation for the looming chaos.

Someone's in the pool, though I don't know who. Thanks

to the light reflecting off the surface, I'm half-blind up here. Squinting, I try to collect clues on who it might be. Baby blue bikini. Tan skin. No kids. No boyfriend or husband. She's alone. A divot forms between my brows and I bend closer, trying to place the stranger beneath the water's rippling surface. She kicks her legs, stretching her arms in front of her as she swims from one end of the pool to the next, her head never breaking the surface. My dick stirs at the imagery, her body rolling like a mermaid's, her long hair trailing behind her. Her baby blue swimsuit outlining her tight ass.

*Who the hell is this girl?*

"Are you even listening to me?" Iris snaps. The venom dripping through the speaker is almost enough to convince me to drag my attention from the woman beneath me, but not quite.

"Yeah, sorry," I mutter. "I'm here."

Except I'm not. I'm still lost in the water. The fluid movements. The sun-kissed skin. The subtle curves. Fuck, thanks to the fallout with Iris, I haven't wanted anything to do with the opposite sex until this very moment.

At least I know I'm not dead.

When the stranger reaches the opposite end of the pool, her head breaks the surface and she flips onto her back, not bothering to open her eyes as she lazily soaks up the sun above us.

Gorgeous.

Fucking gorgeous.

And almost familiar.

Cocking my head, I take her in again, from toe to head. The sun glistens off the water, painting her into a mirage. Long legs. Short torso. Oval-shaped face. Rosy cheeks. Why do I recognize her?

As if she can feel my stare—as if she can read my fucking thoughts—the woman lowers her legs into the water. Brushing her wet hair away from her face, she peeks up at me on the balcony, the view threatening to knock me on my ass. Recognition sparks in her pretty gaze and her pouty lips part as a stone falls in my gut, confirming what a small part of me already knew, but didn't want to acknowledge.

Well, if it isn't the baby of the family, Rory Buchanan.

She's definitely not the little girl I remember.

Not even close.

And here I am, blatantly checking her out like she's a piece of meat which is the last thing she needs, and the last thing I should ever do, especially after the last time we spoke.

"Fuck," I breathe out.

Iris gasps. "Excuse me?"

I hold Rory's gaze for another beat, my dick stiffening even more. Shit. She's...I thought she wasn't supposed to be here until tomorrow. Sure, I didn't blatantly ask Maverick when his little sister would be arriving for the wedding festivities. Considering our history, I had to beat around the bush, but I thought...it doesn't matter. Clearly, I was wrong. And clearly, she isn't the little girl she once was. Like an expensive bottle of wine, time has only made her sweeter, but just as unattainable.

*She's still a kid*, I remind myself despite my subconscious calculating how old she must be. Not that it matters.

It. Doesn't. Matter.

Holding my stare, she kicks her feet beneath the water's surface, keeping herself afloat, her small breasts bobbing in the glistening pool like a wet dream.

*Snap the hell out of it!*

This is Rory! Sweet, innocent, little Rory.

"Hello?" Iris snaps.

Giving Rory my back, I walk inside. "Sorry, there was a... bee. I'm here."

Find out what happens between Jaxon and Rory in
*A Little Crush* by Kelsie Rae

# ALSO BY KELSIE RAE

Kelsie Rae tries to keep her books formatted with an updated list of her releases, but every once in a while she falls behind.

If you'd like to check out a complete list of her up-to-date published books, visit her website at www.shopauthorkelsierae.com/

Or you can join her newsletter to hear about her latest releases, get exclusive content, and participate in fun giveaways.

*Interested in reading more by Kelsie Rae?*

**The Little Things Series**

(Steamy Don't Let Me Next Generation Series)

(Steamy Contemporary Romance Standalone Series)

A Little Complicated - Maverick and Ophelia's Story

A Little Tempting - Reeves and Dylan's Story

A Little Jaded - Everett and Raine's Story

A Little Secret - Griffin's and Finley's Story

A Little Broken - Tatum and Paxton's Story

A Little Crush - Jaxon and Rory's Story

**Harden Heights Series**

(Steamy Contemporary Romance Standalone Series)

Jagger's Story - Coming Fall 2025

Ford's Story

Hawke's Story

Roman's Story

**Don't Let Me Series**

(Steamy Contemporary Romance Standalone Series)

Don't Let Me Fall - Colt and Ashlyn's Story

Don't Let Me Go - Blakely and Theo's Story

Don't Let Me Break - Kate and Macklin's Story

Let Me Love You - A Don't Let Me Sequel

Don't Let Me Down - Mia and Henry's Story

**Wrecked Roommates Series**

(Steamy Contemporary Romance Standalone Series)

Model Behavior - River and Reese's Story

Forbidden Lyrics - Gibson and Dove's Story

Messy Strokes - Milo and Maddie's Story

Risky Business - Jake and Evie's Story

Broken Instrument - Fender and Hadley's Story

**Signature Sweethearts Series**

(Sweet Contemporary Romance Standalone Series)

Taking the Chance

Taking the Backseat (novella)

Taking the Job

Taking the Leap

**Get Baked Sweethearts Series**

(Sweet Contemporary Romance Standalone Series)

Off Limits

Stand Off

Hands Off

Hired Hottie (A *Steamy* Get Baked Sweethearts Spin-Off)

**Swenson Sweethearts Series**

(Sweet Contemporary Romance Standalone Series)

<u>Finding You</u>

<u>Fooling You</u>

<u>Hating You</u>

<u>Cruising with You</u> (A *Steamy* Swenson Sweethearts Novella)

<u>Crush</u> (A *Steamy* Swenson Sweethearts Spin-Off)

**Advantage Play Series**

(Steamy Romantic Suspense/Mafia Series)

<u>Wild Card</u>

<u>Little Bird</u>

<u>Bitter Queen</u>

<u>Black Jack</u>

<u>Royal Flush</u> (novella)

**Stand Alones**

<u>Fifty-Fifty</u>

Sign up for Kelsie's <u>newsletter</u> to receive exclusive content, including the first two chapters of every new book two weeks before its release date!

Dear Reader,

I want to thank you guys from the bottom of my heart for taking a chance on *A Little Broken*, and for giving me the opportunity to share this story with you. I couldn't do this without you!

I would also be very grateful if you could take the time to leave a review. It's amazing how such a little thing like a review can be such a huge help to an author!

Thank you so much!!!

-Kelsie

# ABOUT THE AUTHOR

Kelsie is a sucker for a love story with all the feels. When she's not chasing words for her next book, you will probably find her reading or, more likely, hanging out with her husband and playing with her three kiddos who love to drive her crazy.

She adores photography, baking, her two pups, and her cat who thinks she's a dog. Now that she's actively pursuing her writing dreams, she's set her sights on someday finding the self-discipline to not binge-watch an entire series on Netflix in one sitting.

**If you'd like to connect with Kelsie, subscribe to her Patreon. Patrons receive a wide range of goodies including:**

- Exclusive sneak peeks of works-in-progress
- ebook releases one week early
- Signed paperbacks on all new releases
- Exclusive special editions
- So much more

You can also sign up for her <u>newsletter</u>, or join <u>Kelsie Rae's Reader Group</u> to stay up to date on new releases and her crazy publishing journey.